Champeen

OTHER BOOKS BY HEATHER ROSS MILLER

FICTION

The Edge of the Woods
Tenants of the House
Gone a Hundred Miles
A Spiritual Divorce and Other Stories
In the Funny Papers: Stories
L'oree des bois
A l'autre bout du mond
La jupe espagnol

POETRY

The Wind Southerly
Horse Horse Tyger Tyger
Adam's First Wife
Hard Evidence
Friends and Assassins
Days of Love and Murder

Champeen

A Novel by

HEATHER ROSS MILLER

SOUTHERN METHODIST
UNIVERSITY PRESS

Dallas

This novel is a work of fiction. Names, characters, places, and incidents are either
the product of the author's imagination or are used fictitiously.

Requests for permission to reproduce material from this work should be sent to:
  Rights and Permissions
  Southern Methodist University Press
  PO Box 750415
  Dallas, Texas 75275-0415

Lyrics from "Paper Doll" by Johnny S. Black used by permission of
Edward B. Marks Music Company

Jacket photograph: Temple University Libraries, Urban Archives

Jacket and text design: Tom Dawson

Library of Congress Cataloging-in-Publication Data

Miller, Heather Ross, 1939–
    Champeen : a novel / by Heather Ross Miller. — 1st ed.
      p.   cm.
    ISBN 0-87074-446-1 (acid-free paper)
    I. Title.
  PS3563.I38C47   1999
  813'. 54—dc21   99-42722

Printed in the United States of America on acid-free paper

10   9   8   7   6   5   4   3   2   1

for
Ardis
who twirled fire,

for
Ann, Janice, Emily,
who did not

Some of this book, in quite different form, appeared in *The Phoenix*, literary magazine for Pfeiffer College, and also in a publication by the NC Review Press.

I thank Washington and Lee University and the Glenn Committee for the grant and the sabbatical that allowed me to revise and finish this book.

I thank Bill Harrison for his generous reading.

1

I went out to Wal-Mart tonight and I saw an old woman in a pale yellow VW driving around and around the parking lot. She peeled around the asphalt like some kind of hot-rodder. With tight kinky hair the color of my mother's prized Briar Rose sterling and a long cigarette in her mouth, she struck terror in me. I watched the VW bounce around Wal-Mart, yellow and smooth as an Easter egg, the old woman bouncing inside, her hands like shovels on the wheel, and it was a vision like those I used to have. Those highly personal and sensational moments that made me feel I was on the brink of something. Preadolescent and weird.

I was afraid to get out of my car. I sat there with my window rolled down and I watched her. She wasn't a fragile old thing. This woman was tough and meaty and she meant business. The cigarette bobbled as she muttered things to herself. The VW glistened in the security lights, not a smudge or a dent anywhere on it. She just kept peeling it around the asphalt.

Nobody else out at Wal-Mart seemed to notice. After a while she rocketed to the exit and disappeared, the yellow Easter egg back-firing once.

I sat there waiting for her to come back. I had a feeling she could have been looking for me. Had things to tell me. And I was embarrassed about it. She didn't come back. So I got out and slammed my door and hurried inside.

Wal-Mart always smells like toasted cheese sandwiches, caramel corn, and the sizing on new fabric. I thought first to get a fat little diary sort of a book, something with a paisley print binding and a brass lock and key. But the pages weren't broad enough for the things I wanted to write. The spines too flimsy. I got a big blue account ledger, a heavy sturdy thing with reinforced edges and a spine both stitched and glued. It would absorb anything I could think of to write.

And what I'd been thinking of was how to make up with my two daughters after the big fight we'd had. It's not the best thing, maybe, for three women to live in the same house. Sarah and Hannah are stubborn. I'm more stubborn, and I don't remember what we had the fight about. But after they'd both gone out, and I settled in for an evening of television, I saw something stuck on our best photograph. It's the one of us all together, I'm sitting with Hannah in my lap, and Sarah stands beside me, everybody smiling and healthy, our hair shining clean, our teeth like white precision. Hannah and Sarah are still little girls in the picture. And I'm still young enough to believe in those weird visions I once had.

They'd stuck a little pink Post-it note on my head: *A Born Loser.* Sarah and Hannah meant it for a joke, to get the last word. But I couldn't bear for them to think that, even for a joke. So I drove out to Wal-Mart to get a book to write this down in.

I want to get this straight for Sarah and Hannah. And for Kelby, too, even though he won't read it out there in California. He lives with Brenda, the blue-haired woman. And I'm forty-three years old.

I want to think it through. I will probably never write a word, but here it starts, at least, the thinking it through. I can make some lists, put down names, tabulate a few facts for Sarah and Hannah. But the thinking, the remembering, it spreads way out past the page, way past my hand.

I SPENT THIRTEEN YEARS in Badin being waked and wrapped in a crocheted afghan and then hauled around by Joan Gentry trying to catch Franklin in some infidelity.

"Look in there, Titania Anne Gentry," she pointed, "he's walking that hussy to the bathroom. See him? That's your daddy."

I looked at the cold night trees against the lighted apartment window where Joan pointed. I saw Franklin and the hussy walking to the bathroom.

"Yes," I affirmed, "that's him."

I wished myself back in our own apartment on Entwistle Street, safe and sweet and unconscious as a warm pie. I pulled the afghan over my face. Shut up, shut up, I wanted to tell Joan, I don't care about Franklin.

But it was a thing Joan Gentry did to me. A thing Franklin caused. And they made their daughter a part of the thing. Mother and daughter drove around Badin those nights in the black Ford that belonged to my Uncle Morton, who was off by then in the navy firing machine guns at the Japs and Hitler. He came back after the war and took the Ford away. Aunt Della was always mad he left that car with his spoiled baby sister, Joan Gentry. Aunt Della couldn't drive and every time she tried to learn, she hit something, scratched the black paint, knocked off a headlight.

"Don't you dare touch this car while I'm gone," Uncle Morton laid down the law before he left for Norfolk. "I don't care if I get killed, Della. You still don't dare touch this car until I get back."

Joan and I drove up with him and Della to Salisbury, where he had to catch the train for Norfolk. On the way out of Badin, Uncle

Morton said, "These damn little apartments out here, one just like another. Why don't you move to Albemarle and get a decent house?"

He spat out the window of his black Ford.

"They've got decent houses out here, too," said Joan. "You're just not used to the way it all looks, Morton."

"Damn," he said again, glaring at the rows of apartments crowding the hilly streets. The stubborn duplexes and quadruplexes confused him, the steeply pitched shed roofs, clapboard and batten and six-over-six sash windows.

"I can't ever find you in this place." Uncle Morton looked over his shoulder at me in the back, grinned. "Hey, girl, whatcha doing with that thing? Gonna hit somebody?"

He sized up my twirler's baton. I grinned right back. "I'm gonna hit you."

"Don't do that. Here." Uncle Morton tossed me a roll of Life Savers, all five flavors. I settled down to eat every last one, rolling them around my mouth, sucking thoughtfully until my tongue was sore and my inside cheek puckered.

I considered that Uncle Morton didn't know a lot of things. He didn't know exactly where the Narrows Dam held back Badin Lake and forced the big Yadkin River to pump power right through it back to Carolina Aluminum on Highway 740.

He didn't know about the air raid blackouts and other things we had to put up with in Badin because we smelted aluminum for airplanes. We were more important than Albemarle with its unexciting textile mills.

But Uncle Morton was right about the way it looked. Every apartment like every other apartment. And those French Colonial bungalows that Joan called decent houses were really no better, all of them with the same covered porches and gabled dormers and kudzu trailing the eaves.

"That damn mill never closes, does it?" Uncle Morton drove us past the smelter, the luminous ingots stacked high in the sunshine behind a chain fence topped off with barbed wire. "They work all the damn time."

"It's not a mill, Morton." Joan Gentry smoothed her blond hair. "It's a smelter, Morton. A plant. Don't call it a mill. It's not like Wiscassett or Cannon, Morton."

He slowed for the change of shift at the Dead Man, a zebra-striped pyramid in the center of the street. He watched the workers cross from the parking lot to the Olympia Cafe to the gatehouse in front of the smelter yard.

"Looks like a damn mill to me," he grunted.

"Well, it's not," insisted Joan.

Uncle Morton swung around the Dead Man. Its zebra stripes swirled by on the diagonal. I slid my sore tongue along my puckered inside cheek. The taste of cherry and lime glowed on my lips.

"My daddy works in there," I pointed. "My daddy works grave-yard."

"He does not," Joan Gentry frowned at me and pinched my knee. "He does not work in the potroom. He works in the payroll office. Why'd you say such a stupid thing?"

A line deepened between her eyes, her carefully plucked brows. Joan wanted to be superior, in everything. It meant a lot to her that Franklin Gentry didn't work in the potroom. I, however, wished he did. The smelter belched all night, threw red sparks in the dark air, and I listened in my sleep, stirred, trembled, and slept more soundly. I wished my father worked in the middle of those red sparks, naked to the waist, glistening with sweat and dirt, punching the big crucibles and swinging the cranes.

I admired that hot loud dangerous place. I wanted to claim it through Franklin. But, as Joan had said with her superior and self-righteous air, he worked in the payroll office, wearing an ordinary

5

shirt and smoking cigarettes and coming home to throw down an inch of bourbon at a time, declaring, "Goddammit, shit!" every evening and all weekend.

He was a failed big-league baseball player.

He was a failed chiropractor.

Joan Gentry was a failed movie star, a failed piano player. I carefully planned never to do those things, play baseball, play pianos, practice chiropractic, act in the movies, work in a payroll office. I'll twirl fire, I promised myself, and win prizes. I'll be a champeen. I'll do it right in front of Sebastian McSherry, too, the handsome man next door, before this is over with.

Back then I could only do two things really well. One was twirl a baton. I had big plans to twirl fire, the baton burning at both ends. The other thing I did really well was make up stories. I had even bigger plans there, such as the capture and seduction of Sebastian McSherry, a man I'd never seen in real life, just imagined to myself until he was more real and alive than a man had any right to be. He was a soldier, a paratrooper.

These were ambitious intentions for somebody living in a small North Carolina aluminum-smelting town in the 1940s and the stories often got the upper hand of me. My father, Franklin Gentry, managed to aid some of these stories, even though he didn't know about it and wouldn't have cared if he did. Like when he gave me some white shoe skates instead of ordinary roller skates with straps and toe clamps for my thirteenth birthday, swapping off God only knew how many leather coupons in his 1944 war ration book.

World War II raged overseas. Things were connected in peculiar and perilous ways. I didn't know it yet, but the connections would get me in the end. Things as simple and as complicated as those white shoe skates. As fire-baton twirling. As good-looking soldiers gone off to shoot and get shot. And then, too, the maddening way things got shoved around in my life to make room for other things to happen.

6

For example.

Because Joan Gentry wanted to make a piano player out of me, maybe put me in the movies, we borrowed our neighbor Jettie Barefoot's big black York piano that summer. And I banged on it until another neighbor, old Mr. McSherry, banged on the apartment wall with his stick to make me shut up. Joan blessed out Mr. McSherry and threatened to write to Sebastian to come back to Badin and do something about that old man, maybe put him away, she emphasized.

And that's how I found out about Sebastian McSherry, a man I began to dream up stories over and love, a man I'd never laid eyes on or even heard about before. He fanned up the stories in my eager mind until nobody in the town of Badin, North Carolina, could take him away from me.

Not even Erskine "Sonny" Kelly, who would have liked to, had he known, blond and tough, pinching my neck and twisting my arm because he could get away with it. Because I let him get away with it. My normal boyfriend.

Not even Carol Jean Spence, already thirteen but easily intimidated and pushed around, my best girlfriend, with a grown brother in the navy, so she ought to have known lots of stuff about men. But didn't.

Things were connected. The shoe skates started it.

I couldn't skate. I already imagined those skates as real marching boots with white tassels. I already imagined Sebastian McSherry applauding me, licking his lips while I skated big Figure 8's, twirling a fire baton and flashing my red-sequined body in his face.

The birthday itself, however, which embarrassed me, had to be gotten over first. It seemed to me back then there was always something to be gotten over first.

Franklin bragged, "If Badin Lake froze over, I'd get you some real ice skates, Ti Baby. You could be Sonja Henie and get in the movies."

"You could've gotten her some real shoes, Franklin," observed Joan Gentry. She lifted the white boot, spun the heavy hard wheels under a finger, her red nail shining.

"You could've gotten her some sheet music, or a record by José Iturbi, or something she's used to. Bubble bath."

"I want these skates." I claimed the boot from my mother and grinned at Franklin. "They're great."

"She can't even skate," added Joan. "She'll fall and break her neck."

Joan Gentry wasn't impressed by physical skills. Dancers, Olympic figure skaters, baton twirlers. If they got in the movies, she didn't admire them for their pirouettes or their double axels or their high aerial pitches. They impressed Joan only if they were pretty and could play eighty-eight piano keys without missing a note. If they, like José Iturbi, could finger out "Humoresque" or "Claire de Lune," smiling all the time, showing perfect teeth as well as perfect touch. And only if they kept it up year after year, winning all the time. Big-league champeens making plenty of money to pay for the lights and buy new furniture. Getting in the country club.

Years later, just this very night, when I saw that old lady barreling the yellow VW around that Wal-Mart lot and smoking a cigarette, though it scared me a little, I felt she meant business. I felt she knew how to make the best of it. Which was exactly like my mother, Joan Gentry. They had things to tell me. Why, then, did it embarrass me so?

If Joan had been with me at Wal-Mart, she'd have pointed a finger, "Look at that old fool in that yellow car. She can't make up her mind, can't find a place to park that silly car."

But here in the remembering, in the thinking it back up, I just feel the way I did on my November birthday, a cold raw wartime Carolina afternoon, when everybody made the best of it. Joan splurged her sugar rations and frosted a big two-layer cake in thick pink. Thirteen candles dripped over *Happy Birthday, Titania!*

Carol Jean Spence and Erskine "Sonny" Kelly both grinned because they were in on the surprise and had been told before to bring their skates. Then Franklin presented me the shoe skates, poked me in the side, and teased, "Thirteen years old, Ti Baby, a teenager. That means thirteen-going-on-eighteen."

"Thirteen-going-on-nothing," scoffed Joan from the sink, where she was filling glasses with ice.

I felt so silly sitting at the kitchen table, them looking at me with such unabashed approval and love. I also felt genuinely pleased and honored. I looked back at their faces through the glow of my candles and smelled the hot wax in the real sugar frosting, repeating Franklin, "I'm a teenager."

"I already am," said Carol Jean. "It's nothing."

Sonny shrugged. "I'll be fourteen in three months."

"So?" Franklin poured an inch of bourbon. "You want a drink, Mr. Sonny Fourteen?"

Sonny perked. "Yeah."

Franklin chased down the bourbon with tap water. "Maybe when you get to be Mr. Sonny Fifteen," he grinned. Then encouraged me, "Cut the cake. I got to get back to work."

I knifed my cake, admiring the way the blade slipped quickly through the soft yellow layers and the pink frosting.

"I want a lot of frosting," Sonny Kelly reminded me. "Pile it on. I don't like the cake, but I love the frosting."

"That's greedy," said Carol Jean Spence. She held her plate forward, a little smile crooking over her face. "You ought to eat everything. There's a war going on. My brother's in the middle of it. In the navy."

Carol Jean looked funny, like a scribble a little kid might make with big, clumsy crayons. She was kid number three in a big crowd of five happy Spences who lived in an apartment on the next block, on Barineau Street.

I approved of the way Carol Jean looked. Her hair, tar black, flat as a board, lay in bangs across her brows and fell short over her big ears. She looked like Buster Brown, her brows and lashes the same tar black as her hair.

This was the way a good friend ought to look, simple and unadorned, steady as you go, nothing to flare up and take you by surprise.

Erskine "Sonny" Kelly, on the other hand, was better-looking, even prettier, I hated to admit, although tough and smart-mouthed. I resented Sonny. And I liked to have him hanging around, too. There was an ambivalence embellishing Sonny. And it made Sonny, I thought, a little bit more valuable than Carol Jean. He was a man. He had options. He could walk right out of there. Or he could hang around eating up my pink birthday cake frosting. He had the best of things. It made me mad.

Erskine "Sonny" Kelly had always been hanging around. Our mothers pushed us in strollers through the streets of Badin when I had no hair on my head and frowned a lot. Sonny had piles of tight blond curls and a pug nose and smiled at everybody and made everybody fall in love with him. He was a good-looking blond who got everything he wanted.

"Kiss my foot, Sonny Kelly," I used to yell, then let Sonny Kelly chase me all over Badin and up and down trees, even running through big rain culverts when he dared me. Even under the road, where there might be copperheads ready to bite a leg. For thirteen years, Sonny Kelly, a fact of life.

Today we ate the birthday cake and guzzled Coca-Colas and watched my father throw down another inch of bourbon and my mother frown and suck in air and exhale dramatically, "Don't use Titania's birthday as an excuse, Franklin."

"Okay, I'm going to the office." He was out of the kitchen and back to the little chiropractic office he kept across one end of our apartment on Entwistle Street.

"What does Franklin really do to people?" asked Sonny, arching his brows and emphasizing *really*. His Coca-Cola was smeared with frosting. Just the sight of that made me feel superior.

"He gives chiropractic adjustments."

"He smacks people around," said Carol Jean. She cut little neat bites of cake, cleaning crumbs off each bite before forking it into her mouth, so matter-of-fact, so assured.

"He does not," I glared.

Carol Jean continued as if she were teaching a class, so calm, so organized. "He punches people and hits them with the side of his hand and rolls them up and down and that's what knocks the cricks out of their necks."

"Chiropractors are not real doctors," said Sonny, arching his brows at me again, this time emphasizing *real*. "They don't go to real medical school."

"Yes, they are." I rose to this bait. "And he did, too, go to a medical school, isn't that right?"

I turned to Joan for affirmation.

"If you can call it that." Joan pushed on the faucet, washed ice cubes down the drain.

"In Davenport, Iowa," I added for effect. "That's a long way off."

Sonny wasn't impressed. "Come on." He changed the subject, dismissing me and Franklin and Davenport, Iowa. "Come on, outside. I'm gonna show you how to skate without busting your big butt."

Outside in that cold bleak November light, he whizzed rings around me and Carol Jean, his rollers almost sparking fire, a big skate key swinging from his neck. I laced on the shoe skates, drinking in the smell of the new leather, taking time to adjust my socks and tighten the laces.

"I hope you don't get a blister on your ankle," said Joan. "New leather is awful stiff."

11

She stuck a kitchen broom in my hands for balance. "There you go." She shoved me off, smiling as broadly as Sonny and Carol Jean. I thought maybe for a minute, my mother, Joan, really liked the idea of a champeen skater. Just for a minute. I could be Sonja Henie. In the movies.

But Joan had already gone back in the apartment. The sun had come out to welter against the gray sky and reflect off the green enamel of our front door. I blinked my eyes at it. The sun hurt. I was glad for it, but it hurt.

AND SO RIGHT HERE, blinking again, thirty years later, I got up and filled a glass with ice. I had an old beat-up yellow fridge stuck over with photographs and drawings and notes and magnets. My fridge was bigger than the one we had back in that World War II apartment. And it was worn with use and devotion, like a big old pet, still panting in the corner of the kitchen, obedient and reliable. I painted the cabinets the same pale yellow. My mother looked at it, nodded a faint approval, then said, "I never was crazy about yellow. But this is okay."

I settled back at the table with my ledger. Empty and white as fresh-washed sheets, smooth, ruled across to each edge in blue lines. It continued to talk back to me without a word on it.

IN THREE DAYS I could skate alone, requiring neither their hands nor Joan's broom. Carol Jean applauded, "That's real good, Ti."

Sonny proposed a test. "Let's skate," he tempted, narrowing his eyes at me, "all the way to Badin Lake and back."

"We can't go out there," objected Carol Jean, "it's too far. We can't go out to the lake, up and down hills! On skates!"

Carol Jean turned to me. "Don't pay any attention to him. He's just trying to get you to fall."

I loved Sonny for thinking up such stuff. Damn Sonny Kelly. So rascally and wonderful. I'd skate all the way up and down hills to Badin Lake and back, of course. I smiled at him, latching on to the whole thing, taking it over as my idea.

"Sure," I flared. "Let's go."

"Well, just remember I told you." Carol Jean put both hands on her hips and skated a graceful little circle around both Sonny and me. "Just remember I said it was too far."

Sonny shrugged. "Miss Priss," he said to Carol Jean.

And we took off. Had Franklin known it, he'd have predicted, "You'll all three fall in that water and sink straight to the bottom with those skates on and drown your little asses."

Joan would have added, "You'll fall and break your neck. You'll fall in front of a car and get run over, Titania Gentry, and then what do you think we can do about that?"

I didn't care. I rose to Sonny's temptation the way I always did when he grinned and narrowed his eyes and made me grin back, narrowing my own eyes. I didn't care if I killed myself to do what Sonny said. I paid attention to men. To Sonny Kelly. And to my crazy drunk father, Franklin Gentry.

For example.

I watched the way Franklin Gentry threw down his bourbon, then I poured an inch of Coca-Cola in my own glass and threw it down, first cutting my eyes slyly right and left, as if I expected to get caught. I tossed it off behind Joan's back in the kitchen, then exhaled a loud satisfied "Ah."

I paid attention also to a third man, entirely unknown to the others. Sebastian McSherry. Off in the paratrooper corps. I'd learn from him as I'd learned from them. I planned cozy little entertainments for Sebastian McSherry when he got back home, battle-scarred and thirsty for tenderness and sex. I looked at the glossy pictures of women kissing soldiers and sailors in *Life* magazine. The way the men bent the women over at their waists, the women yielding at the knees, graceful as dancers, skaters. The smudgy lipstick. The closed eyes. Those dark seams down the back of each smooth leg.

Titania Anne Gentry would know how to do that. How to bend and yield, close my eyes, taste the smudgy lipstick from my mouth.

So I practiced twirling the baton, practiced how to win, making all the fancy moves, and how to do this without getting sick or falling down to hurt myself in front of people.

When I got it right, I knew I'd twirl fire. Burn both ends of my cheap chrome-plated baton, already dented from failed aerial pitches, dented hard from bouncing off Badin sidewalks. I'd begged for the baton after seeing twirlers on the Movietone News leading a Rose Bowl Parade. Those flashing circles tossed into the mild California air, the twirlers catching their batons easily, smiling, prancing through Pasadena, all those floats covered with roses gliding behind them, crowds of people waving. I went crazy, my hands dying to take hold of a baton and pitch it, catch it, smile and prance on down the middle of Pasadena.

Joan Gentry ordered it from Sears. "I don't know why you had to have this, Titania," she scoffed when it came. "It's not going to get you anywhere. It's a toy."

I stripped off the paper, dazzled by the bright chrome and the white rubber tips. I studied the little instruction manual, mimicked the twirlers posing on each page, and learned their routines from the footprints sketched into the captions. On the last page, the picture of the girl twirling fire excited me beyond anything ever thought up by Erskine "Sonny" Kelly.

I'll do that, I promised, smoothing the page. It'll get me somewhere, I don't care what Joan says, and that's why I had to have it.

That's what I planned and lied to myself about. The shoe skates and the silly birthday. The baton. Sebastian McSherry. And I thought about it all the time and how I had to choose just the right moment.

I was already thinking about it before the birthday, before the lake and what happened there to us, me and Sonny and Carol Jean.

But way back before that particular moment, I had settled against the scratchy backseat of Uncle Morton's Ford, the one my mother would later use to spy on Franklin, and dozed the rest of the way to Salisbury. I was still twelve then.

In Salisbury, Morton and Della kissed, then he got on the train with a lot of other sailors. I alarmed pigeons in the depot yard and twirled my baton and winked at the sailors and people. They clapped, winked back.

"Quit showing off," scolded Joan. "Get in the car."

She drove us back to Albemarle and to Harmanco's for a hamburger and a milkshake. Aunt Della kept crying in her hamburger napkin. "I don't care if he gets killed. I don't care."

I traced the frosty sides of my milkshake glass. The soda jerk mixed up things in a big silver machine I imagined to be a big silver cup I'd won for twirling the baton and turning cartwheels through blazing fire.

"He won't get killed, Della," soothed Joan Gentry. "I know Morton Trueblood. He'll come back to Albemarle and everything will go on like before. Believe me, Della. Nothing bad has ever happened to Morton and it never will. You'll see."

She snuffled the last of her milkshake, tapped her straw on the rim. "You'll see."

So Joan got to keep Uncle Morton's black Ford, even if she didn't drive it very well, gunning the motor on the hills of Badin, rolling back and yelling at the car, jerking the gears, "I hate this car, I hate Fords!"

So she drove herself and me through the dark streets, the tight little network of back alleys. She turned around in tar and gravel, alarming dogs who barked and made lights come on in apartments and people look out.

"I just want to catch him," Joan gritted her teeth. "In just one great big lie or another. I just want to get him in a place where he can't get out and he'll have to lie to me and I'll catch him in it."

"What are you going to do," I always meant to ask, "when you catch him like that?" But always the car bumped along and I kept dozing off and then at the end of these treks, I fell back in bed like a brick and slept so hard I felt dazed the next morning.

Sometimes I wasn't sure it happened.

There would be Joan washing clothes on the back porch. There would be all our neighbors on Entwistle Street talking, dogs barking, babies crying. I could hear Mr. McSherry wheeze in his apartment, hear Jettie Barefoot start up quarreling with her high school boys, then burst out laughing at them.

The treks through the night in Uncle Morton's black Ford could have been some ornate dream I had. I just couldn't be sure. And the uncertainty angered me. I looked for people to blame, to beat up. When Sebastian McSherry gets back here, I vowed, I'll make him take out his gun and shoot people, make him fasten on his bayonet and cut their throats. Then we'll sit on the sofa and kiss.

For the moment, though, like always, I had to get through both Joan and Franklin and it took all my attention.

I COULD CRY GREAT big tears on demand. And for this talent, my mother meant to put me in the movies.

"Titania can cry," Joan bragged. "Just look at that. I'm going to send her to Hollywood."

She set her hand on my braids, examined my face, my eyes, looked in both my ears.

"If I'd had my way, I'd have named you Scarlett. For *Gone with the Wind*. I just loved that." Joan sighed, lifted her hand from my braids.

"If you'd been a boy," she added, "you'd be named Ashley or Rhett or something."

"I'm a girl," I reminded her. "And it's not my fault."

"It would be goddamn tacky naming your own child after a movie star," sneered Franklin Gentry.

"And that's why she didn't get her way." Franklin leaned over, poked my ribs. "I named you, Ti Baby. I picked out that name."

He winked. "That's from Shakespeare."

"Shakespeare, your ass," said Joan Gentry. "When did you ever read Shakespeare?"

I winked back at Franklin, then slipped from both their gazes, ran out to the front sidewalk and twirled my way down Entwistle Street.

"Titania!" I beat a rhythm. I tossed the baton. "It's Shakespeare. And she didn't get her way."

Joan Gentry got her way, though, about plenty of other things. When she got it through her blond head that she didn't have a chance of becoming a movie star, or of playing the piano in Carnegie Hall, she went after the best-looking man she could find, Franklin Gentry, marrying him when she was already pregnant. He knew it, too, so there was no deceiving anybody. They drove across the South Carolina line to York, returning late, worn out with each other already, driving back to Morton's house in Albemarle.

Uncle Morton cut a watermelon in honor of the occasion.

"Look at that," he bragged. "Perfect. Just right." He held out a dripping wedge to Joan, another to Franklin.

Joan detailed the story to me many times. "That was the best watermelon I ever ate, Titania, and I don't even like watermelon," she qualified the facts.

"And Morton and Della stood out there in the yard with us, and we ate up Morton's perfect watermelon. And then later on, Morton, when he found out you were on the way, Morton went around telling everybody that stupid joke about swallowing a watermelon seed. 'Happened in my backyard,' he told everybody. 'I was the cause of it. It was my fault.' Morton is such a big mouth."

17

Joan thought my daddy was going to be a big-league baseball player when she married him in York, South Carolina. Then she thought he was going to be a wealthy chiropractor, calling himself Dr. Gentry, and getting cards printed up to advertise that. But Franklin failed at both endeavors, settling finally into the payroll office at Carolina Aluminum in Badin.

Joan Gentry, blond and angry, had believed and lusted for such things. The big-league games, Franklin's name on the sports pages of national newspapers, his spring training reported in Movietone News, tricolored bunting, cleats, bats, gloves, their pictures together.

When that fizzled out, Joan went to work on her idea of a handsome smart chiropractor with loyal patients who paid good money to get their spines adjusted and their blocked bowels knocked loose. Dr. Gentry, they could brag, he used to play for the Boston Red Sox.

Gone with the wind.

Franklin never recovered from those days pitching in front of hollering drunk crowds in Wiscassett Park, Great Falls, Granite Quarry, Albemarle, Badin. He was the best they saw in the textile bush league, a league into which Carolina Aluminum was allowed even though it did not make textiles. Franklin's job as payroll clerk was contingent in the beginning upon his playing baseball for Carolina Aluminum. And it was one way he could hang on to his big-league dreams. He kept his caps, his uniforms, his grimy and mean-looking little baseballs rolling around in his bureau upstairs on Entwistle Street.

"Let's throw a few," he would invite me on a mild day into the backyard on Entwistle Street and for a while it would be wonderful, Franklin throwing, Titania catching.

Then, warming to the thrill of his pitch, the hard thud in the glove, warming, too, to the pitch of the bourbon inside him, Franklin Gentry threw the mean little baseballs too hard, hurt my hand, scared me, made me get so mad I hated him. I ran off and left

18

him hollering, "I'm sorry, Ti Baby. Come back here. I won't throw it hard again, honey."

Joan would come to the back door and yell, "You're going to ruin her hands, break her arm, bruise her, knock her eyes out, knock her in the head and kill her. Can't you leave her alone one minute?"

Franklin never recovered, likewise, from the two winters he spent at Kincaid Chiropractic College in Davenport, Iowa, before he ever thought about playing baseball, just picking at cadavers and memorizing the skeletal system, the cardiovascular system, the urogenital tract, and the properties of three types of muscles.

Shutting my eyes upstairs in my room on Entwistle Street, listening to Joan and Franklin quarrel downstairs, I imagined Franklin learning chiropractic. It could be like making love, I thought, Franklin's fingers probing, his palms firm and assured, all his skillful adjusting and pommeling and his smacking people up the side of the head, as Carol Jean Spence said.

And the result for those people was clear, pure relief. Franklin Gentry, my father, could adjust pain, assault and vanquish disease. He had a healing touch to his fingers.

I shivered, tightened my eyes. It was a touch Sebastian McSherry would have to his fingers, too. Here, I would say to him, right here, under my arm, and here, too, inside my left leg. He would assault and vanquish my agonies, pommel and rub away my terrible angers.

Who cared if you went to real medical school when your fingers had such healing?

Franklin kept all his cards printed *Dr. Franklin Gentry, Chiropractic Adjustments*. He flicked through them in his dark hours when he most despised himself and Joan. He received patients after a day spent in the payroll office at Carolina Aluminum, but mostly on weekends, sometimes even at night. In the little office arranged across one end of our back porch. They called him "Dr. Gentry." He told them about baseball.

And at night, week nights, again on weekends, Joan Gentry, as pretty as any movie star, gathered me in a crocheted afghan and stuffed me in Uncle Morton's black Ford and trekked around Badin looking to catch Franklin in his infidelity. And even after Morton came back from the navy and took back the Ford, Joan still schemed to catch Franklin, gritting her teeth, exhaling dramatically.

"I just wish I knew what you're going to do to him," I continued to want to ask her, drowsing off, falling off deep in a dream with Sebastian McSherry's arms around me.

Let's throw a few, Ti Baby, he whispered, smacking the glove. Right here. That's it.

No, I said, I've got to get Franklin Gentry out of this before she catches him. Look at him in there walking that hussy right to the bathroom. Look.

Yes, Sebastian narrowed his eyes, curled his lip. I see him. That's your daddy.

It's a full-time job, I exhaled loudly.

SUCH REMEMBERING IS time-wasting. I smacked shut the blue ledger and brushed cracker crumbs off the table. I had eaten a whole stack of crackers just sitting there remembering, writing nothing.

2

Everybody in the family has things to do.

My mother polishes her sterling. My father knocks the cricks out of people's necks even though he's been retired from Carolina Aluminum for five years. My two girls relentlessly pursue their curious and private lives with me, not in Badin but in Lake Waccamaw, a hundred miles south. And Kelby, the man I love, perhaps the most relentless and curious and private of all, Kelby stays out in California.

I must deal with Kelby. He fits into the design of things I want to spread here before Sarah and Hannah. They called me a born loser, giggling, thinking I'd giggle, too, when I found the little Post-it note stuck to my head in the picture. And I did. But I couldn't get rid of the thought. *A Born Loser.*

It's the kind of thing that swamps you with scary feelings. Makes you worry you've gone ahead and lived half your life and just now noticed it. Physicists talk about things having a half-life or a half-half life. When I found *A Born Loser* stuck to my head, I was afraid I'd lived something like a half-half life. I wanted that unlived part back.

This big blue ledger makes me self-conscious.

I want to write everything out in blue Scripto ink, the old-fashioned kind in a bottle, blue as the ledger's binding. This requires using an old-fashioned ink pen, the kind with a little rubber siphon inside a barrel. I like to plunge the nib into the blue Scripto and squeeze the rubber siphon and listen to it drink up the ink. The faintly acrid smell pleases me, almost intoxicating.

If I write about those times, remembering what I tried to do and how I tried to win, the truth and the strange improvisations of the truth could dazzle me. I believe I'd like telling about it. Like thinking how Sarah and Hannah would read it. How they would know I have had things to do.

Real things, not the mindless barreling around in a yellow VW, around and around a Wal-Mart lot like that old lady I saw. If there's one vision that torments me, it is the vision of myself ending up like her, hair like dandelion fuzz, cigarette bobbing from my tight mouth, and no place to put the car.

I want to dazzle my girls.

Still, the dazzle of it, just the telling of it, might summon up visions too long laid away. Like pulling old clothes out of a cedar chest. You like the oily smell of the cedar. And you trusted the heavy lid and sides of the chest to protect the things you folded inside. But they unfold in yellowy, limp wrinkles. And the moths must have gotten to them anyhow. Little holes everywhere.

I ALWAYS WANTED JOAN to leave me behind in her pursuits of the notorious Franklin. I wanted to stay asleep and undisturbed in my bed. I didn't care what Franklin did, what hussy he could be surprised with. I just wanted to sleep, sleep. *Please, leave me alone. Please, leave me behind.*

One time she did. Only because she hadn't far to go, just out the back door and down the gravel alley to intercept a ridiculous tryst in an old garage apartment at the far northern end. And, even more delicious, what Joan did not know was I was still awake, sitting up in my window in the dark, gazing into the long backyard. She didn't think to turn and glance up where I was supposed to be sleeping. So certain was she I would be sleeping.

But I saw her slip from the screened porch down the path and past the row of hollyhocks brushing against the garage. It was the dead of winter and the hollyhocks stood stiff and brown, their seed pods shriveled up tight as buttons, and their leaves like torn leather. The garage, painted a hideous aluminum bronze, a paint people in Badin seemed to prize, glowed like sick neon in the cold moonlight. I took note of the hollyhocks and the aluminum bronze just as I took note of Joan.

There was nothing tight or torn or shriveled up about her. But there was something nagging at me about her, something as sick and annoying as the aluminum bronze paint on the garage. I knew she was in the right, a woman wronged, an avenging angel. Still it nagged. Just to watch her slip straight toward her target.

I had a panorama of the whole thing, a sharply defined God's-eye view, and neither she nor Franklin nor Dixie Cole, the particular hussy of the evening, ever suspected.

Dixie Cole, a plumpish sort of young woman, sweet and blank as a doughnut, was married to a foreman in the ingot yard, a frustrated skinny man called Buster. I used to study Buster and Dixie picking out things in one of the three little Badin grocery stores. Dixie clasped fruits and vegetables to her full bosom, to her pink nose, shut her eyes, inhaled. Buster stood staring for long periods of time at the meat display, the hamburger, the chops, the piles of organs some people fancied. Then slowly, very slowly, he tapped a finger against the glass and indicated his choice to the butcher. He showed his ration book and proved he had enough stamps to get whatever it was he wanted. Then Buster took it away, wrapped in white paper and tied with string. This meat he clasped to his bosom and to his nose like a pungent treasure. And there was nothing full or pink about Buster.

It was eerie. So why did Franklin want Dixie with a husband like the skinny Buster around? I knew they had been sneaking out to meet in that garage apartment at the far end of the alley for weeks. I'd sat up in my window and watched it all unroll a section at a time, like a history lesson, like the development of a civilization, and all so ridiculous. After supper, Franklin would cough and groan and make excuses how he had to go put in some extra time at the office.

"The war effort, you know, Joan," he'd lie, winking at her and grinning, his moustache quivering like a bird's wing. "Bad as double daylight savings time, you know."

She pulled at her hair, twisting strands around a finger, then letting them spring free in a long blond bounce. "I know, Franklin," she said.

He might as well have sent out invitations. Anybody could see right through those lies. I used to wonder, and I still wonder, did he know that? Did he just put out the bait for her?

And why did I, after watching him sneak around the block twice, then steal down the alley from the east exit, going straight up the stairs to that garage apartment on the far northwestern slope— all of this I could see without impediment from my window with the light out—why, I used to wonder, and I still wonder, did I want to rescue him?

I should have been downstairs rescuing Joan.

I should have been out in the alley rescuing Dixie Cole.

Poor Dixie. She did not know what plummeted toward her that cold winter night. What crept up the stairs and pushed open the door. I could see it, but I couldn't hear it. I had to imagine it.

Joan pushes wide the door. Dixie Cole stares, a hand to her fresh sweet lips, her hair fluffed and caught in a net snood just like those worn by Linda Darnell and Vivien Leigh.

"He's not coming," says Joan. "You better go back and wait for Buster to get off shift work. You better be glad I didn't tell your husband what you've been out here doing with mine. Get out now."

And she pushes the door wider for Dixie to escape. As Dixie hurries by in a soft breeze of talcum and fear, Joan hisses, "And I might still tell Buster. I just might like to tell Buster. Personally."

Then she shuts the door and settles down inside like a big spider to wait for Franklin. She fluffs her own hair. Freshens her own lips. Outside the streetlights cast a strange lemony hue along the aluminum bronze of all the garages in the alley, including the apartment Joan lurks in. I see the skyline of the old Badin Theater, the turrets and domes of various churches, and down the alley, finally, steps Franklin Gentry. I know everything.

"She's not here, Franklin," says Joan as he opens the door and pokes his head in and looks around for Dixie Cole. "But I am."

He blinks, he grins, he twitches his moustache. "I can explain."

"No, Franklin," she contradicts, "I can explain."

And so she does, never raising her voice, but hissing and biting each word. "What do you mean with something like Dixie Cole! Dixie Cole? More like Dixie Cup!"

She would end up taunting Franklin with "Dixie Cup! Is that the best you can do?"

Dixie Cup, the popular ice cream. I liked to get a Dixie Cup at the Olympia Cafe. You could hold a Dixie Cup in your hand, striped blue and white with a paper lid you pulled off and licked. Then you scooped out the vanilla ice cream with a tiny wooden paddle. It was good. I could taste it sitting up in my dark window watching.

It seemed to me the whole episode took less than a heartbeat. Joan in; Dixie Cole out; Franklin in; Joan out, Franklin following down the steps. He followed her all the way back to our garage, the dry withered hollyhocks casting shadows against the aluminum bronze. He followed her down the path and into our apartment. They did not come up to bed before I fell asleep.

THE WAR WAS EVERYWHERE. The war raged in Europe and Asia, with reports every day in the newspapers and on the radio, with horrific shots of flames and explosions in the newsreels. But I ignored it and told stories to myself about Sebastian McSherry. I never really took into consideration that the war actually killed people, that people were blotted out in the blink of an eye and never came back.

I centered the world on myself. I was an insignificant thirteen-year-old, a small-town North Carolina baton twirler who thought about winning things. I never even thought about the invasion of Normandy.

Then a light reconnaissance aircraft crashed in Badin Lake three days after my birthday. My legs still wobbled from the long zoom down Pomona Hill, straight through the middle of Badin. Sonny Kelly yelled all the way, "Hurry up, you two chickens! Come on!" Carol Jean Spence complained, "Shut up, Sonny Kelly! You're going to make us all fall!"

I concentrated on maneuvering curbs and big jagged cracks in the Badin pavement, watching for irritable old ladies with shopping bags and little kids toddling and the ubiquitous Badin dogs that barked and chased.

"Kiss my foot!" I yelled at Sonny. "I hate you!"

Pomona Hill zoomed straight down through town, so I could coast for long stretches and save myself for the curbs and big jagged cracks.

But toward the end, I worried I couldn't slow down, that I might zoom straight on into Badin Lake, sinking, as Franklin would have predicted, straight down to the cold black bottom, and drown. *I told you!* Franklin would exult. Then I remembered to zigzag and brake.

Past the Olympia Cafe, past the gatehouse of Carolina Aluminum where our fathers worked, past the zebra-striped Dead Man, we coasted and zigzagged, our wheels grinding and growling down.

The Badin Lake pavilion, under a peaked roof of cedar shakes, was constructed of lashed-together peeled logs, stockade fashion. As bleak as the November afternoon, the long gray wooden pier stretched over the rough lake water and looked ready to break from its piling.

I plopped on a long bench under the pavilion, the wheels of my skates still spinning, my feet throbbing. I had a feeling like I got at Myrtle Beach each time I waded out from a strong thrashing surf and stood on the sand. There the sand always receded and gleamed as the sea sucked between my toes and I felt the surge of the Atlantic still threaten my legs. Everything in the world was out of breath and throbbing.

"Look at the whitecaps," said Carol Jean. Her face was full of scribbly smiles and little white teeth, a clown face with black button-on eyes.

"Hey, it's just like the beach!" exclaimed Sonny.

I loosened the laces of those stiff shoe skates. I rubbed my ankles and looked where Sonny and Carol Jean both pointed.

The waves broke along the shore and slapped at the pier. Like Carol Jean said, they were whitecaps, crested in a bleach-white foam as they spilled over, then boiled back out on each other.

"I never saw anything like this over here at Badin Lake before." Sonny took out a wrinkled pack of Lucky Strikes and lit up.

I watched his smoke curl. "Give me a cigarette."

"You don't smoke," he sneered.

"Give me a cigarette, anyway."

Carol Jean stood up, her skates still on her feet. The wheels left little ruts in the dirt under the pavilion. "Here comes a car. Y'all better quit smoking."

Sonny swung from the lower peeled logs of the pavilion roof. His skates made a soft little squeak-squawk. "I see it." He flipped his cigarette toward the water.

A big heavy maroon Packard rolled to a stop in front of us. Three people got out and walked on the pier, a man in uniform, a girl who rolled her eyes and giggled, and one old fat lady with a fur collar. The collar was one of those with two foxes' heads dangling. I hated that kind of fur collar. The foxes with their teeth caught in throes of pain and hate, their eyes shiny and hard and dumb as marbles, made me feel sad and guilty, as if I were to blame.

I considered any old fat lady who wore foxes' heads deserved to get bitten on the neck and get rabies and run mad through the streets of Badin, foaming at the mouth, and then die of lockjaw with everybody looking. The old lady waddled grumpily, stopping once to spit into Badin Lake. The pier creaked under her.

"I hope she falls in," I hissed. I began hating those people for spoiling my chance at a cigarette.

"That's a Seabees," said Sonny Kelly. He gazed after the man in uniform. "See that jacket he's got on? That's a Seabees."

"I hope he falls in, too."

"That's a navy jacket," said Carol Jean. "I know what a navy jacket looks like. My brother Bobby's in the navy."

Sonny swung closer to Carol Jean. He pushed her back on the bench beside me. "That's a Seabees."

"Nope." I squinted down the long pier. "That's a paratrooper."

"You both are butt brains," said Sonny.

When the three people reached the end of the pier, all three, as if on signal, like birds settling to roost, sat down on the slatted green benches nailed around the T-shaped promenade. They looked up into the gray sky and they watched for something.

"I don't care what you say," said Carol Jean Spence, "it's navy."

Dizzied by the thrashing whitecaps, the throb of the heavy new shoe skates, I began to feel I was on the brink of something. Good or bad, I couldn't say. It was definitely there, gathering itself to barrel down on us.

"I don't care, either, butt brain," said Sonny Kelly, getting ready to swing against us and knock us both in the dirt.

Then Carol Jean announced solemnly, her eyes black as buttons, "Here comes a plane."

Carol Jean had one finger up her nose, something she ordinarily wouldn't have done because Carol Jean was very prissy and precise and careful. She pointed with her other hand at the sky over Carolina Aluminum. A stiff wind scudded across Badin Lake and into the cold dark woods on the far shore.

"That's a light reconnaissance aircraft," said Sonny Kelly, and nobody disputed him.

I shivered, continuing to feel oddly uneasy. I could be glowing, giving off rays the way my bones, my lungs, my blood seemed to flash and collide and then beat against my cold skin, *This is for real, watch out.*

The wind pulled through my childish, braided hair and chilled my ears. I saw the bare trees begin to bend. I felt them bend. Little goofy phrases from my parents' 78 records picked up in my mind, leaving sudden flashy trails. The Mills Brothers singing about Miss Otis who couldn't come to lunch. She had such regrets, such dark regrets.

"Hey!" Sonny hailed the plane laboring over the rough water and looking as flimsy as the bending trees. "Who would fly a light reconnaissance aircraft right over Badin?"

The whole Carolina world appeared to bend and shimmy. I rubbed my eyes and blinked as the pilot made his plane do tricks over the rough water. The three people on the T-shaped promenade clapped their hands and cheered. I could catch the girl's long horsy giggles. And see the foxes' heads bouncing on the old fat lady's shoulder.

"Why's he doing that?" asked Carol Jean.

"I don't know!" Her question alarmed me. I shoved Carol Jean, "Quit picking your nose!"

We were no more than three simple children. We all saw the thing coming and we couldn't stop it. We could only sit and watch the thing coming, gather itself to barrel down on us there. I was so scared, I burst out singing the goofy melodrama, told how Miss Otis pulled a gun out of her long velvet dress and shot her boyfriend and then everybody grabbed her and put her in jail.

The light reconnaissance aircraft flew low over the dark water. It flashed toward the waves colored like Coca-Cola and banked to turn for more tricks. Then it fell. Straight through some crazy hole in the November air, it fell as neatly as if the pilot had made it fall. His best trick, the big surprise: death.

Just one hard awful plunge. Then gone.

The three people on the end of the pier jumped up and gaped at the water. Their eyes, I quickly imagined, were as dumb and hurt as the eyes of the two dead foxes. Carol Jean stood up again on her roller skates, open-mouthed, her finger still stuck up her nose. Sonny Kelly swung off the beam and landed on his butt in the dirt.

"Goddamn!" he said. "Did you see that?"

The first swells from the plane's impact broke against the pier, then piled along the shore, knocking cold spray. The three people on the end of the pier woke up, looked from one to another, then turned and hurried back to the pavilion. The old lady puffed. One of the foxes' heads trailed, bumping her hip. She threw it back with absent-minded cruelty.

"We have to tell the law!" declared the man in uniform. He

rushed the women, the girl sobbing now, into the maroon Packard and backed away from the pavilion. For the first time he noticed me and Carol Jean and Sonny. He rolled down his window.

"Hey! You kids stay right here and if anybody comes before we get back, you tell 'em what just happened out yonder in the lake. You hear me! Tell 'em we went to get the law. You hear me!"

Sonny shook his head, started toward the Packard, his skates lugging in the dirt. "Wait!" Sonny yelled. "Who was that out there?"

The man spun the Packard around and struck off in a shower of gravel and dirt. I sang louder, more stuff about how the people were going to hang Miss Otis off a willow tree and she was really sorry she couldn't come to lunch. But not sorry she shot the boyfriend. Such regrets, such dark regrets.

"What're we going to do, Ti?" Carol Jean's feet looked so clumsy stuck in her skates, the dirty wheels, little steel ball bearings and splayed leather straps. In view of what we had all just clearly witnessed, the skates were ridiculous. Everything was ridiculous. Yet it brought us back into the hard world.

"What're we going to do?" she asked again.

Carol Jean's innocent questions made me cruel. I grabbed her back down beside me. "Listen," I hissed, "we're not going to do anything. We're just kids. We're just here."

Carol Jean trembled. "Ti?" She looked around to Sonny Kelly. "Sonny? Will that man get out? Down in that plane?"

But before he could answer, Sonny whirled around on his skates. "Look!"

The gray dirt sprayed my legs and settled in a film over the white shoe skates.

"Look!"

A wing tip bobbed up in the middle of Badin Lake, then dipped. The big wing of something shot down and left to drown in the cold water. Down in the awful dark and silence. The water swallowed,

31

covered it with the white-capped Coca-Cola waves, then parted again, together, apart, together, apart. The wing tip rose and sank.

"I can't stand this kind of thing." I shut my eyes hard. "I can't stand this kind of thing. This kind of thing is killing me."

"That guy won't get out," said Erskine "Sonny" Kelly. "Nobody could get out. I bet you that guy's head popped like a light bulb when he hit the water." He smacked his hands together hard.

"Shut up, you, shut up." Carol Jean dissolved into hoarse sobs.

I felt the breath go out of me. I collapsed, my body thick and dull, no thrills left, no sensations. Limp as rags. Only my feet had nerves enough to throb against the soles of the skates.

"Carol Jean, I'm sorry," I whispered, "come here." When I felt my friend settle inside my arms, I began crying harder than Carol Jean. This made Carol Jean cry more than before, her clown face and tar eyes hidden behind her hands.

Sonny Kelly watched us cry awhile, then he got disgusted, looked away and scrubbed his skates in the dirt. "Shut up," he said, "you two damn girls, shut up. The law's going to come and take care of this."

He lit another Lucky Strike and dragged on it deeply, the line of his chin sharp.

I held my arms around Carol Jean Spence, squeezing out tears, feeling them run down my face and drip to my sweater. I pictured Sebastian McSherry, his head popped like a light bulb, knocked open under Badin Lake, his skull that was as thin and precious as my own. I heard again the smack of Sonny's hands.

He could die. He could get killed before he got back and I had any use of him. I held on tighter to Carol Jean to lock out Sonny Kelly's scorn. I fastened my mind on Sebastian McSherry. He hovered over the plane's little dials and needles still glowing as his sweet handsome body wafted on the dark cold currents of Badin Lake.

His face was turned away from me. I couldn't see him good. *Look at me, Sebastian. This way.* Then his face floated loose from his skull. His face turned around and grinned at me like an old man, old Mr. McSherry, grinning in his sleep, his mouth twitching in a cold dark dream, *Tell 'em, you kids, I went to get the law!*

Erskine "Sonny" Kelly was saying the army would come haul up the plane, the army would send divers down to get the secret bomb-sight out of the plane so the Japs and Hitler would not find out about it and use it against us.

"Nobody just crashes a light reconnaissance aircraft in Badin Lake and gets away with it," he promised, adding, "I don't even know what he was out here for in the first place."

I sat and noticed how sharp Sonny's chin looked against the thickening November evening, the bright ember of his Lucky Strike. This was war.

CROWDS GATHERED ALONG BADIN Lake. People stood on the pier and under the pavilion. It seemed to me they hung around for days just watching the water, staring out at that mid-channel where the plane went down. Babies were lifted to their fathers' shoulders and told to "Look!"

People wanted anything, a piece of the wing floating, then sub-merging again, gasoline slicks radiating in rainbows over the muddy water, a body washed ashore.

Sonny, Carol Jean, and I got lost in this. Nobody paid any atten-tion to us. Back in the apartment, Joan had said, "Showing off. That's what he was doing."

"I'd like to know how he got his hands on an army plane," said Franklin, "and how he thought he could get away with that."

Nobody seemed sorry, not Joan and Franklin, none of those people with babies on their shoulders at Badin Lake. The people in the maroon Packard had come back with the police and cried and carried on, explaining everything over and over. Then they got back in the Packard and tore off again.

I was sorry only to the extent that I might lose Sebastian McSherry in some similar stupid accident. I didn't care about the man in the plane. I had cried because I was scared, because I was cruel, and because I wanted something.

This shocked me to the core.

3

Shock has been an intimate part of my existence. I find myself forty-three years old looking back on that aluminum-smelting town and my fire baton and the war. I wonder why I didn't shower into a million little pieces then, like the showering embers of a cigarette.

Maybe I had a built-in protection. Maybe those shocking and perilous times were also innocent times. I took it for granted that I'd survive. I was a kid. Kids always think the world includes them in its plans.

My daughters look at me in disbelief when I tell about Erskine "Sonny" Kelly and Sebastian McSherry. If I say anything about smoking cigarettes or sneaking a taste of Franklin Gentry's bourbon, they roll their big eyes—such tender-looking eyes to be so cynical. Golden-hued eyes that, had those two girls stayed in the pot a minute longer, might have honeyed over into a definite brown.

They say, "Is that the meanest thing you could do back then, smoke a cigarette? Sneak a snort of liquor? God, Mom!"

And they swish off to their sophisticated lives with sophisticated boyfriends, roaring around on motorcycles, motoring around in BMWs, top down.

I'm glad my girls are tough. They won't end up like Titania Anne Gentry, or Joan. They won't end up like Franklin. They'll always be strong, cool-limbed, and sleek girls. Their brains tick like Swiss clocks, a perfect jeweled precision. And I'm relieved.

Sarah is a park attendant. Off to work each morning wearing heavy woodland boots, thick socks, and dark green shorts. Her strong tanned legs and arms keep her comfortable with the world. She has an impressive badge with her name engraved on it. Hannah takes college-parallel classes at South Columbus Tech and combs the classifieds for unusual Help Wanted.

"Listen to this." She rattles the paper. "Dental Ceramics Lab. They want somebody to help make false teeth. You think I'd like that?"

"I thought you were going on to East Carolina. I thought you were strictly liberal arts." I put down my coffee mug and study Hannah a long time. Her fingers are smudgy from the newsprint and she sneezes.

"The liberal arts are dead." She sounds congested behind the classifieds. "I want a job to make money."

She sounds like my mother. Joan Gentry wanted money. But she wanted it from Franklin, not from false teeth. Or from a job of her own. She wanted him to pay for everything. For my piano lessons, for my piano. For her complete sets of sterling silver, her Spode, and her crystal. She declared many times, "Franklin should have to pay to keep me up. I mean that, Titania. He should have to pay."

Hannah flattens the paper and folds it beside her breakfast plate. Her hair falls in a pale blond ruffle and I see she looks like my mother, too. The blond hair, the disdain, the expectation that the world will fall in place around her if she insists long enough and gives it enough proof.

How do children do this?

* * *

I HAD STRAIGHT SHOULDERS, skin that tanned without burning all summer, green eyes sometimes deepening toward blue, and plain brown hair Joan kept braided like Margaret O'Brien's in the movies. She intended keeping me a little girl as long as she could, doggedly French-braiding for thirteen years. I casually put up with it for the time being because that was easier. I'll cut it, I promised myself, wincing as Joan tugged, I'll cut it off over both ears when I'm ready. I'll make myself look like an urchin. I liked the sound of that word: urchin.

"I want to be an urchin," I ventured.

Joan brushed the hair back from my ears, twisted it into French braids. "Don't be silly."

"Well," I pulled back from Joan's brush, "I like the sound of that. *Urchin.*"

Joan straightened the long brown hair in her hard grip. "The sound of something doesn't mean anything. Don't say that again. I don't want to hear it."

Joan Gentry's hair was ash blond. She rolled it on big metal curlers, trying to look like June Allyson. "June Allyson wears a pageboy," she explained if I watched her from the bathroom door. "And you get that with these big rollers."

Joan went around half the day with her head tied up in a kerchief and when she took the rollers out, she had a long smooth pageboy. She glossed it with her hard brush, patted and tucked each blond wisp until they hung together over her shoulders and shone.

People with blond hair seemed to get what they wanted. I resented it. Resented Erskine "Sonny" Kelly. His mother never went off without bringing something back, a foot-long flashlight, a ball cap, a bag full of Tootsie Rolls, for Sonny.

There was a towhead back in the fifth grade I'd been so jealous of. Poor old Rachel. Born on the Congo. Even Sonny Kelly was impressed by the Congo. *I was born on the great and mighty Congo,* wrote Rachel. *The Congo is a great and mighty river.*

Rachel wrote that every time we had to write little paragraphs about ourselves in the fifth grade. And she said it a lot, too.

"You probably don't know where I was born." Rachel would gaze across the Badin School yard, taking in the shabby swings and see-saws, the weedy perimeters of the ball court. "I was born on the great and mighty Congo."

She took out a wrinkled Kleenex and mopped her nose. "That's in Africa." She squinted at me and Carol Jean Spence. "I bet you didn't know that."

"I did." I pushed Rachel against the monkey bars. "I know everything."

"Oh, yeah?" Rachel squinted again, fastening herself tighter to the bars. "What do you know that I don't know already?"

I was jealous not only because Rachel had blond hair, but also because I'd been born in no place but Badin, North Carolina, and felt cheated. There was nothing great or mighty about the Carolina Aluminum company hospital, two blocks beyond Badin School.

Rachel's parents made me jealous, too. No big-league baseball players, no movie stars or chiropractors. No June Allyson pageboys. Rachel's parents were Baptist missionaries. That was what caused Rachel to get born on the great and mighty Congo. They came back to Badin on a furlough. That was what caused Rachel to stroll into my fifth grade each morning pale and fat as a slug, her coarse blond hair pinned back from her ears by plain black bobby pins and her fingernails cut short across the ends.

Rachel didn't even try to look the part as I thought she should. Rachel should have been exotic, olive-skinned, with big hoop ear-rings, a touch of Yvonne de Carlo or Rita Hayworth, red lips, red fingernails, and her blond hair, frowzy and lush, should float from a purple veil fringed in gold.

"Tell me," Rachel insisted, "what do you know that I don't?" She put a stout foot on the bars and waited.

"I can twirl a fire baton."

"What's that?" Rachel kicked at me.

Rachel stuck out her tongue. I saw with disgust that even Rachel's tongue was bland and inferior. Her tongue ought to be long and pointed and red as a pimento. That's what my tongue would be. I felt vastly superior.

"Don't pay any attention to her, Ti," advised Carol Jean. "Rachel doesn't count, anyhow. She's leaving next month. She won't even finish the fifth grade."

Years after Rachel had gone back to Africa with the Baptist missionaries, I still thought of her, especially when I was hanging around with Sonny Kelly and happened to study his bright curls. Sonny kept his hair clipped close to the skin, but curls ringed around and sprang up behind an ear, straggled down his neck.

"You remember that old fat Rachel?" I once asked.

"Yes," he said, then mimicked, "I was born on the great and mighty Congo. The Congo is a great and mighty river."

"Oh, shut up." I threw a rock at him and we tangled like cubs.

But when I was alone in my room, I unbraided my plain brown hair and let it hang over my bare shoulders. I drank in the feeling it made against my skin, tipping down to my two ridiculous pats of breasts. What do you need an ash blond pageboy for? I chided. You like your hair the way it is, the way it ripples and waves from all that tight French braiding. You could be on an island. You could be on Tahiti and wear a sarong and shells around your neck.

Listen, Titania, I assured myself, you can be Dorothy Lamour and make Joan Gentry and all those ash blonds look sick as a dog. You make Sonny Kelly look like a clown.

I grinned, licked my lips. I flexed my right little finger, the one truly exotic appendage Titania Gentry had. Mine alone in the whole town of Badin, North Carolina, not another one like it anywhere, not in Badin, nor in either family of Gentrys or Truebloods.

I flexed it, snagged it through the long brown hair. My right little finger curled. I could straighten it and extend it as well as anybody could straighten and extend a little finger. But when I didn't exert this pressure, the finger went back into its curl, tucked around neatly as a babe in the womb toward my palm.

This didn't hinder my baton twirling. In fact, I could flash out a Figure 8 or go into a Pancake quicker than most twirlers. My finger stayed out of the way. But when I needed it to grasp hard, it was there, strong as an eagle's talon.

Franklin Gentry, the chiropractor, assured himself it was not a debilitating flaw. Such a finger would have been great on a boy. Think of the knuckle ball he could have taught that kid to throw!

But Joan, the movie star, Joan, already plotting my career as a famous pianist, felt the finger was a handicap. She asked doctors what to do.

"Break it," they advised. "Break it, and it will grow back straight."

"Break it! Break a perfectly good bone!" Franklin sneered. "Joan, if you let them do that, you're crazier than I thought."

"I don't want my finger broken!" I screamed. "Leave me alone!"

"Don't you want to look pretty?" Joan asked. "Don't you want a straight finger like everybody else?"

Then Joan betrayed her own ambitions. "Don't you want to play the piano?"

"We don't have a piano," I pointed out.

"We can get one," said Joan.

"Leave me alone!" I repeated. "It's none of your business." I put the finger in my mouth and glared.

"Leave her alone," agreed Franklin Gentry. "There are worse things."

"I should've done this when she was a baby." Joan gave her best long exhausted and dramatic sigh. "Then she never would've known the difference."

I took the finger out of my mouth and straightened it toward my mother. "See, my finger's as straight as yours."

Joan Gentry spread her fingers, each nail polished brilliant red, across the kitchen table. "Well, someday, Titania, you'll look back on this. And you'll wish you'd got it fixed."

I will look back on this, *Yes!* I thought, and I will wish I'd got things fixed, *Yes!* But my finger is not one of them, *No!* I put it back in my mouth, chewed the nail. I'll get things fixed. First, as with everything else, I had to get through something.

For example.

Going to church with Uncle Morton and Aunt Della.

Braided and stubborn, impatient for Sebastian McSherry, the paratrooper, to get home and help me get things fixed right, I sat in the front seat of Uncle Morton's old black Ford in front of the Badin Methodist Church. The woolly seat rubbed my legs until they burned. Morton and Della hemmed me in on either side. They took me to church, to the Badin Methodist Church, not First Street Methodist in Albemarle. "If we take her down here," they said, "she'll be with her school friends and maybe it'll sink in."

They gave Franklin a hard look.

"I like a child raised in the church," approved Franklin Gentry. "But I'm not going myself. I don't need to believe in a dominant power."

Most of the time, neither did Joan. She recognized, though, the value of the Badin Methodist Church, the social payoff such an association brought, the birthday party invitations, the dances, the hayrides. She easily saw my future in shiny snapshots pasted in Sunday School scrapbooks. And she was delighted to go along to set an example, the four of us filling a pew, good people, Methodists.

This particular Sunday, Joan did not accompany us. She had a headache. Franklin was back in the apartment adjusting his patients' tensions and easing their vertebrae.

Uncle Morton scoffed, "I wouldn't let Franklin touch me with a ten-foot pole. I'm not lying. I wouldn't care if I was half-dead."

Aunt Della declared, "Look at the kind of people that go to him."

Morton agreed, "White trash. I wouldn't be surprised if he had some niggers."

"You all shut up," I bristled, and added, "and if he had any niggers, it's none of your business. So, shut up."

"Don't tell me to shut up." Della popped my leg. "Don't say niggers, either."

I scrunched down on the woolly seat thinking about the people who came faithfully each weekend to get smacked and pommeled around by Dr. Gentry. They left looking as if they felt a lot better after he had knocked them around on his adjustment table.

They came to the back of the apartment, shook the screen door, and I showed them to the little office. They wore overalls, print cotton dresses. I never saw anybody who looked rich. Maybe they were trash like Uncle Morton had sneered.

And while Dr. Gentry attended to pinched nerves and slipped discs downstairs, I knew how Joan Gentry sprawled upstairs in her bed with the pink satin comforter, looking at new magazines. I knew Joan assured herself her blond pageboy could have been pictured there on those slick covers, her face and her figure described by Parsons and Hopper, if *only!*

I understood both my parents were spoiled rotten. I didn't care. That was their business, sorry as it was. I had other business. But I also protected them both, silly and sorry as they both were. I wouldn't tolerate Uncle Morton and Aunt Della saying any bad things. So already riled up by both Uncle Morton's and Aunt Della's attacks, I sat ready for a fight, just daring somebody to start something.

I hoped Sonny Kelly would come by so I could jump on him and pinch him and pull his hair. I hoped Carol Jean Spence would come by, too, so I could make fun of her, make Carol Jean cry. I didn't care if Morton and Della beat me to death for it, I would do what I wanted from then on. I would be good-looking and rotten like Franklin and Joan.

With my plain brown hair braided, ribboned in yellow gros-grain, my body elegant in a yellow pongee embroidered around the neck and across the shoulder by the clever hands of Joan Gentry, I was the only good-looking thing in that ugly black Ford. I look as good as Margaret O'Brien, I congratulated myself. Maybe something was getting ready to happen.

We were too early for church. Nobody else there yet and as we waited, a rumpled, grubby man walked through the Badin morning, right past Uncle Morton's Ford. His shirt sleeves were rolled and on each arm were tattooed coiling serpents, red and black with green forked tongues.

Aunt Della stiffened. She pulled in her chin and put both arms around me, squashing my yellow pongee and the French braids.

Uncle Morton pulled in his chin, too. He sat like a toad watching the tattooed man pass. "Yonder goes Hootchie," he hissed. "I thought he was still on the chain gang."

"Must've got out," Della hissed back, "got parole." She squashed me some more. "It's a disgrace."

"Who's Hootchie?" I pulled out from under Della. "Who's he?"

Hootchie approached the white doors of the Badin Methodist Church, paused, turned his bald head from the breeze and lit a long cigarette, tossing the match into the church boxwoods. Without the slightest concern for Uncle Morton and Aunt Della, without the slightest notice that anybody watched from the Ford, Hootchie casually hiked a leg and farted hard.

Loud, sharp. A whir as exciting and abrupt as the takeoff of par-tridges breaking cover. There was no mistaking the sound. The report carried to the open windows of the Ford at the curb.

43

Uncle Morton snickered, then shushed when Della elbowed him.

Della smothered me again. "Titania, Hootchie is a wicked man. That's how he got that ugly name. I mean it! Don't you laugh!"

"What kind of name? What's Hootchie mean?"

I watched admiringly until Hootchie reached the end of the street and went inside the Olympia Cafe. My little finger tingled.

"I like him."

"Shut your stupid mouth. He's a bootlegger." Aunt Della popped my leg again.

"Well, it's the truth." I strained to peer over Della's big arm.

"Shut up," echoed Uncle Morton, then snickered again.

I rubbed my little finger. I straightened it perfectly, folding my other fingers firmly under my thumb. I wanted to dash down there, burst through the cafe door and find Hootchie and his tattooed snake arms.

I'm an urchin born on the great and mighty Congo, I'd tell him, twirling a long cigarette, the Congo is a great and mighty river. Look at my little finger. My stupid mother wants me to get it broken so it will grow back straight. Then she can get me in the movies to play the piano with José Iturbi.

Hootchie would bend down and light my cigarette, smirking.

Look at this ash blond pageboy, I'd keep on. June Allyson has one of these.

We would sit on the Olympia barstools upholstered orange, our Badin hair turned blond, our Badin eyes exotic as tigers, our Badin skins tattooed like mosaics. Then we would leave Badin, North Carolina, behind, far, far, I promised myself right there on the front seat of Uncle Morton's car.

We would tell each other things.

For example.

"My mother wanted to name me for *Gone with the Wind*, for the movies," I whispered, puckering my lips for a little kiss.

44

"I heard that already." Hootchie ignored my lips, took a deeper drag off his cigarette, flicked ash on the Olympia counter.

"But my daddy named me. Titania. That's Shakespeare. My daddy played big-league baseball. My daddy is a chiropractor. My daddy," I lowered my voice dramatically, dragging at my own cigarette, "has run around with every woman in this town."

"I heard that already, too," Hootchie smirked, dropping his cigarette to the floor and grinding it out underfoot. "You ain't told me nothing I don't already know." He fixed me with a bald rude stare.

I stared back, taking in the red and black snakes coiling along Hootchie's arms, his hair curling over their green forked tongues and hooded eyes. "You'll see," I sneered, "when Sebastian McSherry gets here. You'll see something you don't already know."

Hootchie shrugged. "McSherry, your ass, little girl."

4

Children believe anything. In their strange and fascinating world of half-truth, half-lie, they will go with you to any level of fantasy, any level of pleasure, even pain.

When my girls were four and five, they believed if they just had an Underdog cape, like the TV cartoon dog, they could fly. Sarah ran about with a beach towel tied around her shoulders, jumping off the back of the sofa, off the kitchen counters. "Never fear!" she shrieked. "Underdog is here!"

And down she would swoop, making Hannah squeal with admiration. Then Hannah had to do the same, aping the wonderful Sarah, off the same sofa, the same kitchen counters. "Never fear!"

The beach towels billowed, green dolphins grinned and yellow seahorses chortled, and on and on Sarah and Hannah ran. "Underdog is here!"

When they took to jumping out the windows, I stopped it. Nobody can fly with a beach towel around her shoulders, I lectured, besides, they might get hurt. I had a horror of them snagging a fingernail or a lip or a nostril on the window latch.

Sarah and Hannah stood staring at me, flushed with their game, breathing hard as little engines. "We won't get hurt," insisted Sarah.

"Yes, you will." I yanked at the beach towel.

Then their father, the splendid Kelby, the handsome, the charming and enigmatic Kelby, stopped me cold. "Let 'em alone. They're just kids."

I loved and misunderstood Kelby. He encouraged madness. A gentle madness was Kelby's. That's why he's not around anymore to encourage it. A sincere misunderstanding.

I had a madness, too, in those old World War II days. Not necessarily gentle, not at all encouraged, and sincerely misunderstood. The blue Scripto ink flows so fast across these pages, you'd think it was hungry for white paper. But the words I write are not these. I trail blue ink. Curls and tendrils. My writing spirals into infinity. These are not words. I try to make notes. I try to make lists. I put down the pen and drift away from notes and lists into one delicious wallow of a thought, then into another, get tumbled around, diving under and coming back up as in a surf.

Each word has a bittersweet undertaste, and I can't help tasting and retasting each one. Yet I know I don't really want to eat them all up. Have my cake and eat it, too. That's what I want here.

I intend to cut and paste my life for my two girls. The Wal-Mart ledger has turned into a scrapbook like those Joan used to stuff full of my piano recital pictures, my bubble-bath pictures, the write-up of the baton competition. Only mine has Kelby in it. And Rory Flynt, the one man I betrayed Kelby with and somebody I have to talk about soon. And Brenda, the woman in California.

I want to write it out straight like a testimony. But the memories are too daunting. I am a newspaper woman. I like facts. I like things to be clear. And it is clear, I now see, I will not write this story out like a testimony for Sarah and Hannah to read. I go back awhile to making lists, to cutting and pasting. Jot down names. Put things in order by number and alphabet. But in between all this busyness, those memories roll out. They stack up like white cumulus in the sky.

I always liked to see those white towers standing over Badin, especially in the summer with the boom of the smelter in the background, and Joan out hanging wet clothes in the backyard, laughing with Jettie Barefoot. And Sonny Kelly coming down the sidewalk with a hidden pack of cigarettes and—there, see I'm off again. And the page cannot hold me back. And no testimony gets written. Just long and short lists. Sharp spurs to what I remember.

I hear the car drive up in the sandy yard. Sarah and Hannah get out laughing, complaining. They are coming right into the house, so I put this Wal-Mart ledger away, hide it deep under the cotton T-shirts I sleep in. Every T-shirt is the same, gray with short sleeves, a left breast pocket. An oversized XXXL so I can stretch them down to my knees and turn over comfortably. I wear them all night, then maybe half the next day over shorts or jeans.

I don't need to hide the ledger. Nothing in it, not yet. But I just want to hide it. I like the solid feel of it lying flat against the bottom of the drawer.

I left the pink Post-it stuck to my picture in the living room. I wonder if the girls will take it off. I'm so glad it's Sarah and Hannah coming back to fill up the house with their perfume, Giorgio for Hannah, Anais for Sarah, nothing cheap. I hear them pile groceries on the kitchen counters, hear the whoosh of a pop-top. And I'm just so glad.

They don't know any of this.

I COLLECTED A LITTLE box of old socks and underwear in that Badin garage, shivering with my own melodrama, *Soon, soon!* I'm going to bandage up the baton, strike a match to it and twirl real fire, *yes*.

I poked in the box. I lifted out a torn and faded flannel nightie and rubbed it across my arm. The underside of my arm was bruised blue from the thumping of the baton's rubber-tipped shaft. I still fumbled too many twirls, dropped and dented it. I sighed, what did I know, anyhow, about twirling real fire?

Nevertheless, I would twirl myself to a fiery glory, I would win all the prizes, every cup and ribbon and crown I could find, I would strut through stadiums, coliseums, ballparks full of applauding, adoring people. I would lead the Rose Bowl Parade through Pasadena.

Not only this, but Erskine "Sonny" Kelly and Carol Jean Spence, Franklin Gentry and Joan, everybody, would be there to watch. And Sebastian, yes, smiling, kissing me on the mouth.

I threw the nightie back into the box, shoved it farther into the garage corner. Soon, yes. The little stories sustained me like shots of adrenalin. How could they harm?

I went outside and got to work again. I posed and strutted, twirled and pitched the old Sears baton. I caught it gracefully, bowed to my audience. I knew Joan Gentry could dream up more practical glories, like playing pianos and looking pretty and getting the doctor to break my finger to grow back straight. I knew Joan wanted beauty and a full value for her money. I dreaded her.

In our Entwistle apartment, polishing silver, waxing linoleum, Joan dreamed of recitals and the London Palladium, Carnegie Hall, the Hollywood Bowl. I wore long sequined gowns and old men with wild hair rushed up to me, kissing my hands and stammering, "Ah, Titania, ma chere, thank you, thank you! For the way you have played my sonata, thank you!"

Movies about Titania Gentry's life would be shot. Movies starring Titania Gentry playing concert grand pianos, all my fingers long and straight, every nail polished, my brown braids loosened in a glossy pageboy, everything about me sheer gold, first-rate. My music would be flawless, seamless music, the touch of an Olympic gold medalist, a champeen figure skater.

"That's the way to get yourself out of here," Joan pointed out a million times. "Get out of a place like Badin, North Carolina, and make something of yourself. Who wants to stick around here all the time? Learn to do something!" Joan emphasized her determination, tapped a hard red fingernail on the table.

But outside and away from Joan, stubbornly marching up and down the Badin sidewalks, I envisioned red-sequined costumes, tight as my skin, genuine leather white boots with bouncing silk tassels. The only way I saw out of Badin was to strut, strut, pose, twirl, fumble, recover and smile. A plastic whistle between my teeth, the chewed cord damp around my neck, Titania Gentry acted out her own escape furiously, teeth clenching the whistle, a fresh bruise every day on her arm.

And if this did not work, there was Sebastian McSherry. There was Hootchie, for God's sake! At the very worst, I could learn to play that big ugly black York piano we borrowed from Jettie Barefoot last summer.

What an embarrassing occasion. After Jettie offered to let Joan borrow it, everybody else on Entwistle Street agreed the piano belonged in the Gentry apartment. Jettie didn't play it anyhow and she wanted to put a French Provincial armoire in its place. So everybody would get what she wanted in the deal.

It took Jettie's three big Badin High School boys and old Mr. McSherry to roll it from the Barefoot apartment, at the east end of the row, to our apartment in the middle. They had to come down Jettie's sloping front yard, corner the boxwood hedge, and enter Joan's front door up two flights of wooden steps.

I sat under the front yard trees chewing at the rubber tip of my baton, scornful of the whole thing. "I can't stand this kind of thing. This kind of thing kills me."

Madine Ponds came out of her apartment across Entwistle Street, swept a path down to the curb and then stood, a hand shielding her eyes, to shout silly suggestions over at the movers. She waved her broom at Jettie Barefoot.

"Jettie! They're going to tip over into the street! Jettie, you need a rope!"

Jettie followed behind the big York, anxious and excited. She pushed branches out of the way, reminded her boys not to bump it.

"You have to get it tuned," she warned Joan Gentry. "Pianos don't like moving around. Get that piano-tuner from Albemarle to come out and tune it for you."

Joan nodded, flushed with the success of her scheme. She had planned the whole thing, marked days off the calendar, figured out how much it would cost Franklin to pay for a new piano. And then, not wanting to wait until she had the money in her hand, she accepted Jettie's offer to borrow the York.

Mr. McSherry, wheezing and complaining, sucked at a big cigar. I caught a whiff of him as they went by my trees, tackling the first flight of steps.

Even in my embarrassment, I saw things clearly. The lending of Jettie Barefoot's piano didn't simply mean music lessons, nor having to wait for Franklin Gentry to make enough money to buy Joan our own instrument. It meant, I saw clearly, recitals and concerts, white gowns, bouquets of roses, New York, Los Angeles. The horse-drawn carriages clattered through the boulevards of Europe, counts and viscounts quaffed old champagne from my slipper, kings kissed my crooked little finger.

"Eventually, Titania," Joan had announced, "we will get you a piano of your own, a Betsy Ross spinet with mahogany veneer. Right now, we can't. But soon."

A Betsy Ross spinet! I shook my head at the thought. Why not a big-league piano? A real champeen affair, my very own concert grand, an impressive Steinway or Baldwin, with solid mahogany body, a raised harp-shaped lid and heraldic ball-and-claw feet at the bottom of three solid legs.

Veneer, indeed.

But first there was Jettie Barefoot's York to get through.

I SAT UNDER THE TREES and pictured myself as a player of big black pianos, etudes and cadenzas tumbling from my fingers, my crooked

52

little finger hooking the keys with precision, my body fixed on the dark oily piano bench with the hinged lid. *God, it's going to pinch the hell out of my legs.*

Then I pictured my hands crossing over each other in graceful arcs, the candlelight softening my face, the sweet old men with their wild hair and tears, the counts and viscounts kissing me, the champagne rapture, *Ah, Titania!*

That wouldn't be so bad. All those men loving me, doing things for me, and me playing the piano like a champeen.

And somewhere waiting in the wings would be my special moment, the twirling of real fire. *Watch!* I'd say, slamming down the lid on the concert grand, jumping on top, *Watch, all you sweet old men!*

And then Titania Gentry would bring out the fire baton, blazing. They would love me all the more.

I tried to believe these visions.

Her big boys trailed back out of the Gentry apartment and Jettie bustled down the steps. "Lunch. Come on." They flocked away.

Madine Ponds swept another path back to her apartment. Mr. McSherry sneezed on his dark shady porch and blew his nose. His cigar lay cold and reeking on the porch railings. Then the noon whistle from Carolina Aluminum shrieked across the sky and I responded as to a signal.

"Hey! Mr. McSherry! Mrs. Ponds!" I jumped out from under the trees and made a big parade entrance, pacing down my side of Entwistle.

"Hey, watch!" I gave them my best Figure 8's, my most dazzling Pinwheels.

Mr. McSherry and Madine never so much as wiggled. Even when I flung the baton and caught it, eyes shut.

Later I sneaked into the apartment. I always liked to pretend I was sneaking. I felt it gave me an edge on Joan. The big black York reared against the southwest wall of the living room, in the alcove between the fireplace and the stairs. Joan was arranging things to complement its enormous presence.

I sneaked across the Olsen Mills carpet, its pile brushing my bare feet the way Franklin's moustache brushed my cheek when he kissed me, making a slow red itch flood the backs of my legs. I sneaked up to the piano and opened its ugly black lips and looked at all its ugly cold teeth.

"Titania." The sound of my name in Joan Gentry's mouth was so smooth, I didn't know if I'd been questioned or cautioned.

"Yes, ma'am?" Joan liked me to say "ma'am" to her.

"Titania, I hope you appreciate how nice this is of Jettie Barefoot to let you have her piano to learn to play."

Joan stood with both hands on her hips. Dust motes frolicked in the late summer afternoon light around her ash blond pageboy. She was June Allyson with a halo.

I struck a key. Middle C, I later learned.

"I appreciate it, ma'am," I smiled, arching my brows in what I hoped was a winning smile, feeling the dimples throb in both cheeks.

Joan Gentry liked my dimples as much as she liked the way I could cry. "As cute as Margaret O'Brien," Joan would point out to people, to Morton and Della, to Franklin. "Look at her, dimples in both her cheeks, and she cries great big tears. I'm going to send her to Hollywood."

"I do appreciate it," I repeated, "but I'm too old to start piano lessons. I'm almost thirteen, ma'am. I'll be a big grown girl still playing baby pieces."

Joan Gentry could surely see how much I appreciated Jettie Barefoot's generosity. And how much it embarrassed me, taking piano lessons with those little kids.

Joan gazed at me awhile, the eyebrows, the deepening dimples. She listened to the massively echoing Middle C.

Then Joan continued, "You are not too old, Titania. You can catch up quicker than the other beginners, anyhow, just because you are older. When school starts, you are going to take piano lessons from Miss Beaupine, two days a week. It will cost us a dollar a lesson, that's eight dollars a month. And someday, soon, soon, we are going to get you a brand-new piano, a Betsy Ross spinet. Until then"— Joan turned back to arranging things—"you be careful how you touch Jettie Barefoot's."

She zigzagged her magazines across the coffee table. She straightened the gilt-framed oval mirror over the sofa. She emptied all the big square glass ashtrays. She even steadied the chandelier.

I remained quietly on the piano bench. Joan's data washed over me like a green Atlantic wave, breaking bubbles in my nose, smelling faintly rotten and stinging a little. I struck Middle C one more time, firmly, admiring its resonance.

Glancing around the living room, assured she had everything in place, Joan Gentry said, "Now, I am going upstairs and take a bubble bath. This has been an exhausting day, Titania. I need to relax before Franklin gets here and starts tearing everything up again. And I want you to be quiet down here."

She climbed the stairs and soon water began to fill the tub over me. I closed Jettie Barefoot's York. Rubbed a finger along its black music rail. "Okay," I agreed, "I'll be a big grown girl playing baby pieces, embarrassing myself to death. But!"

I rose and paced from the living room, double time, the old baton tucked high under my arm. I felt I was on the brink of something again, soon it would be barreling down on me, just like the light reconnaissance aircraft crashing into Badin Lake. *Soon!*

The long French braids would come off. The music I might have to play in front of people, those silly baby pieces, would burn away like fog under the bright sun. And there would be a big handsome man. I didn't know his name yet or the color of his eyes. He would bend to slip off my shoe, kiss the tender sensitive skin of my instep, lick between every toe until I died from the tickling of it. We would run off together from the poor old men and their sonatas, from José Iturbi and "Humoresque," from Joan and this ridiculous black York piano.

MISS BEAUPINE, BY THE age of fifteen, had sailed through every piano competition in the state of North Carolina, defeated all challengers in the Southeastern Regionals from Florida through Delaware, won medals struck from gold and filled her arms with bouquets of roses. I liked to think about it. Those roses, I imagined, no doubt trembled, their petals fragile and cool from the florist's bin, and tightly furled. As pink and tight as Miss Beaupine.

And here she was now, a sweet old virgin, fading to death in Badin, North Carolina. It was her own fault, too, I sneered. Because after Miss Beaupine had won all the medals and stood with her arms full of the roses, Miss Beaupine had won a full scholarship to Juilliard in New York. She went to New York at fifteen, stayed there six months, then, in what remained a mystery to Badin, Miss Beaupine came home to teach piano lessons.

She had been a champeen. She gave it up to show Badin boys and girls how to place their fingers properly, to strike the keys crisply, and to lust after the genius buried on the sheets of clef and staff.

I sat there smelling Miss Beaupine's perfume. I watched Miss Beaupine's gray eyes, clear as ice, rove the music, her lashes like inky notes, and her lips a constantly curving Cupid's bow. I wanted Miss Beaupine's perfume, her gray eyes and her delicately lingering old maid's beauty. I hated her for giving up. All the crowns and burning batons that might have been Miss Beaupine's had darkened and died in Badin, as year after dulling, deafening year she listened to some Badin child's fingers stammer over her piano.

Nobody in Badin knew how to say her name right. And neither did I, until I went to college and took French. Then I knew she was not Miss Bew-Pine. But Miss Bo-Pin. I felt it an awful waste. Even she did not know and lived every day of her life answering to Bew-Pine.

It was as if she lived in an eclipse, behind a veil, a girl with no hands to wave it aside, raise her window and turn on the lights. I chafed on the piano bench beside Miss Beaupine. I'd go to Juilliard and stay. I wanted to rage out at her. I'd turn on the lights! I'd make them call me Bo-Pin.

Instead I sat and felt ashamed when Miss Beaupine smiled at my clumsy scales, gently correcting my fingers on the keys, and then marked off my exercises with a generous red check when I finally played straight through one without error.

"I like that. Titania, darling," she encouraged, "you're putting some feeling into it now. That's good."

At night Miss Beaupine floated back to me in bad dreams, gently smiling, icy pink and tight as a bud, trapped inside a big glass bowl. Her long fingers tapped against the glass and just as I got ready to smash the glass and let Miss Beaupine out, I saw that I myself had no hands. I woke breathless, in a sweat.

Across the upstairs hall, I heard Joan shift in her own sleep, sighing under the pink satin comforter and Franklin beside her giving little melancholy grunts. I sat up, pulling aside the curtains from the windows right beside my bed, and rubbed my fingers over the glass. I spat on the glass, smeared it.

"Miss Beaupine, Miss Beaupine," I intoned, "why didn't you do something to get yourself out of here?"

The 11:30 whistle blew at Carolina Aluminum. I thought of the men clocking in for the graveyard shift. If I were the boss, I'd have Miss Beaupine play for them all night, Vivaldi, Bach. And when the men changed shifts, they would hear the piano, close their eyes, forget the hot dirty dangerous smelter, whisper, "Ah, Miss Beaupine! She went to Juilliard."

In the daylight, though, when I practiced on the York, Franklin threw down his newspaper, gritted his teeth under his dark moustache and declared, "Goddammit, shit! I can't stand that banging. Joan! She's giving me a headache. Goddammit! Joan!"

Joan, her ash blond hair smooth, announced from the kitchen, barely raising her voice, "Go to hell, Franklin, and take your headache with you."

My fingers stumbled octave by octave, up scale, down, making harsh, discordant errors, starting over again.

"Goddammit, Joan. I'll just leave! That's what. I'll leave!"

The walls shuddered as Franklin slammed the front door. The gilt mirror over the sofa glimmered. Its reflections bounced off the wall on either side of the big York and hurt my eyes.

"Ma'am?" I explored the possibility of escape. "Ma'am, can I quit?"

"No." Joan stood in the kitchen door and flicked a dish cloth at me. "One whole hour. You know that. It hasn't even been fifteen minutes since you sat down. Don't ask if you can quit."

My little finger stretched, flexed, curled and pulled toward High C, sounded the fullness of the chords. My finger had been no more a handicap to me with the keyboard than it had with the baton.

Miss Beaupine said, "You might have to stretch a little harder playing your arpeggios." And she smiled, patting my right hand.

Oh, Miss Beaupine, let me play arpeggios like an angel! I ground my teeth. One, two, three, resoundingly, four, forcefully, five! *Arpeggios!*

I banged and hammered, hours, days, weeks, until one afternoon Mr. McSherry began to beat on the apartment wall with his stick.

"You hear that, ma'am?" I looked at Joan. She sat on the sofa,

House Beautiful and *Modern Screen* in her lap. Mr. McSherry beat again, a rude and impatient clatter, punctuated by his wheezing, then the sound of hawking up something unpleasant from down deep inside him.

"I heard, Titania," Joan said. "Don't stop. Keep playing." She narrowed her eyes, turned a page. "It's just that old man. Keep on, I said. Pay no attention to him. We can do what we want over here in our apartment. Keep on, now."

So, deliberately, with prickles rising on the back of my neck, frizzing up the short hairs of my braids, I struck a long thundering barrage of chords. The plain sober Tonic, then stretching with ambition, Dominant-Seventh, finishing with the satisfying deep distortion, Sub-Dominant! One right after the other. Their notes blended, lifted with fury through the beaverboard apartment wall to Mr. McSherry.

Joan said I could! Joan said keep on! I giggled, banged them out again, again. Mr. McSherry yelled, "Shit fire!" He hammered against the wall like a woodpecker gone mad. "Shut up!"

The gilt mirror over Joan shook, the light wavering in its big oval.

Joan's eyes blazed. "Did you hear him say something, Titania? Did you hear him say shit fire and shut up?"

"Ma'am?" I asked, carefully rounding my eyes innocently.

"Nobody's going to cuss my kid. Not in this place. Nobody, and I mean it!"

The front door slammed and the walls around me shook. My chords throbbed away to small echoes deep inside Jettie Barefoot's big piano. My fingers pressed the keys and my little crooked finger held down High C.

I waited.

I heard the fury of my mother break all over Mr. McSherry next door, his stinking cigar, and his stick. I thought of long sharp splinters, shards of china plates, then bright jagged pieces of glass shattering in endless rows of windows through the whole town of Badin, apartment after apartment.

I imagined Joan impaled the old man and left him to bleed to death in his own mess. I imagined the startled expression on his dumb face, the cigar falling from his mouth, the stick rolling to a corner.

I began to pity Mr. McSherry.

Joan breezed back into the living room and took her place on the sofa, her face bright red. The mirror was hanging sideways. I wondered if I ought to point that out.

"Ma'am?" I asked, already knowing the answer, but risking it anyway. "Can I quit now?"

"Titania," Joan exhaled her long dramatic sigh of exhaustion, "I have told you and told you never to ask me if you can quit. Keep on."

She sank back against the cushions, smacked a fist on *Modern Screen*. "Practice!"

Her nostrils quivered. The reflections from the mirror spread over her hair until it resembled bright rippling blond water.

I struck a key, tried an arpeggio, then stormed through scales and chords. Mr. McSherry was quiet on the other side of the wall. I felt as subdued as he.

Joan said, "Somebody ought to do something about that old man. He's got a grown son. Somebody ought to write him about that old man. Get him to come straighten him out. Put him away somewhere."

I looked around. "What grown son?"

Joan jabbed a thumb toward the wall behind her. "That boy ought to come home and have him put away. He aggravates me so much, I could kill him."

I sat up straighter. The reflections bounced over my braids, making my hair, I hoped, now look like dark braided water. Mr. McSherry with his stinking black cigar and old stick knocking on our wall, he had a grown son, a grown man? I didn't believe it. I had to find out for sure. And this was my first approach toward claiming Sebastian McSherry.

THE NEXT SATURDAY MORNING, I went out with my baton and over to Mr. McSherry's. He sat on his porch, his stick propped against the steps at his feet. The sun blazed straight in Mr. McSherry's eyes. He never blinked or moved out of the way.

"Hey!" I called, striking a Knee Flat pose on his bottom step, looking, I hoped, pert and cheery enough to erase Joan Gentry from his mind. "Hey, Mr. McSherry!"

The old man squinted, grunted something I took to be friendly, and waved a hand.

"Mr. McSherry, you got any kids?" I eased up his steps. I got close enough to catch his stale smell in the hot sunlight. I wondered if he might shrivel, melt away. He pegged a cold cigar between his gray teeth.

I held the baton like a divining wand. "Where's your grown son?"

Mr. McSherry roused. "What's that? Hah?" He chewed his cigar and took out his plaid handkerchief. He wiped his eyes, his nose, scoured into both his ears. I noticed long white hairs curled from his ears.

"My grown son, hah? What about him?"

"Yes. Where is he?"

"Who wants to know? What's he done?" Mr. McSherry eyed me.

"I want to know, Mr. McSherry. Just me, Titania Gentry." I eyed him back.

"Oh, he's in the army. In the paratroopers. I forget where." Mr. McSherry blew his nose. "You know what a paratrooper is?"

"They have a parachute. They jump out of airplanes." I shivered. "Of course, I know what a paratrooper is. When's he coming back?"

"Christmas, I think. Sometime. Maybe it's Christmas." Mr. McSherry folded his handkerchief. He picked up his stick and, still chewing at the cold cigar, poked at me. "Why do you bang on that old piano all the time?"

"I don't know. Because my mother makes me." I poked back at him with my baton.

"Why don't you get a broke finger?"

"I already got one. Look." I showed him the little finger curled into my palm.

He snorted. "Ain't broke. Just growed that way."

"That's what you think. Watch this." I lifted the baton, tightened every muscle and threw off some high-flying Pancakes all around his porch. Then I did a quick Wrap-Around twirl, ending with a sassy little Lunge pose.

Mr. McSherry snorted again, settled back in his swing. He drummed the stick on the floor. The stale smells of cigar and old man blended.

"You can't do that, Mr. McSherry," I taunted him, tucking the baton under arm. Dimples tugged in my cheeks.

"I don't want to do that." He sniffed.

I gave him my best smile. "What's his name?"

"What's what?"

"Your grown son. What's his name?" I pulled one leg back into an Arabesque pose, pointing my toe, twirling Pinwheels. I was a shameless show of smiles and dimples, as manipulative as Shirley Temple.

"Oh." Mr. McSherry rocked the swing. "Sebastian."

"Sebastian?" I dropped my pose. "That's not anybody's name. Sebastian?"

"That's his." Mr. McSherry rocked on. His eyes roved Entwistle Street.

"Sebastian," I repeated, tasting and exploring it.

"Sebastian McSherry."

"That was his mother's name. Maiden name, as they say. She named him that. I wanted him named after me, Rudolph McSherry, Junior!"

Mr. McSherry pounded the porch with his stick, said it again, "Rudolph McSherry, Junior! That's what I wanted. But I never got nothing I wanted. She named him Sebastian. I never got used to saying it."

He stopped the swing and listened a moment to Entwistle Street's Saturday morning noise. Women whistled in their kitchens, stood in their backyards and giggled over clotheslines. Children cried out. Madine Ponds was digging in her yard and Jettie Barefoot's big high school boys hosed off their car.

"I never got used to it," he said again. "And I never thought she'd raise that puny youngun, standing out in our yard, hollering all day. But she did. She lived to see him get sixteen, bossing him and me around both. Then she died with a cancer. He went in the army."

Mr. McSherry drew a long breath and took out his plaid hand-kerchief again. I shivered at the sight of it, so filthy it was stiff. It swarmed with years of his old germs.

He blew his nose a second time, making low, oily, obscene snorts. I swung my left arm in time to Mr. McSherry's snorts and strolled off his porch. The sun flashed and rinsed his old stale stink from my clothes and dark braids.

Now I knew. His name was Sebastian, a name like nobody else's in Badin, North Carolina, except maybe for mine. He was a soldier, a fighting paratrooper. He wore big lumpy boots. He jumped out of thundering airplanes, his parachute foaming over him.

I pictured the cords and the harness hooked to the jump guide, the long aluminum wings, the dark door sliding open in the plane's fuselage, then the foamy bright billowing of the parachutes. They blossomed first over Sebastian, then me as we jumped. Sebastian caught me. The hard ground rushed up to meet us. We rolled over and over, tangling in the cords and the parachutes. Then Sebastian kissed me. On the mouth.

He killed people.

He got shot at by the enemy, speared, clubbed, kicked, spat upon by the Japs and Hitler. But Sebastian rose up again, and lived for me, Titania Gentry. He was the one. My little shameless stories bloomed like bright flowers and succored me.

I'd be the delight of his life. I'd bring cool drinks and hold them to his bloody lips while bombs fell and bullets spattered. People all over the world bled and blew apart and rotted in the dirt. People got torpedoed. Their ships sank to the bottom of the ocean. Their airplanes spiraled straight down and burned. But Titania Gentry saw nothing of it, paid them no attention. Only Sebastian McSherry made any difference.

And only because of Jettie Barefoot's big black York piano. Only because Joan Gentry had made me practice and keep on banging the piano after Mr. McSherry hit the wall and hollered "Shit fire!" and "Shut up!"

If it had not been for Joan and Jettie and the piano and Miss Beaupine and the banging and the "Shit fire!" I'd have never found out about Sebastian.

Things were connected.

I glimpsed that precious network when I next struck chords and stretched my crooked little finger through brilliant arpeggios, rising by octaves to majestic apogees of music, and then descended with thunderous authority to Great C, Contra C.

Once through the opened apartment window, the weather still warm for October, I caught a faint but definite low-pitched, oily, nasal, and obscene sort of mournful sound. Mr. McSherry was singing on his porch, keeping time with my etudes and cadenzas.

Again I knew I was on the brink of something important. I didn't know what, for good or for bad, but I felt it grab at my innards, give a little lurch, then grab again. It was like being on the top of the Ferris wheel when it suddenly stopped and I found myself swinging, swinging, locked in, but definitely hanging up there in thin air, vulnerable and exposed.

I liked it. I went for my piano lesson and Miss Beaupine patted me, exclaimed, "You are showing real feelings! I can tell. I can hear it, Titania! That's good. You must always show real feelings."

Miss Beaupine's pale old maid's skin, without a mole or a wrinkle or even a stray hair anywhere to ruin its surface, deepened to the pink of a sweetheart rose. I blushed in response, gave Miss Beaupine a clumsy snuffling grin and wiped off my nose, wishing my nose and my skin were Miss Beaupine's.

Old-maid perfume wafted over the music room. I worked my fingers through every note on the pages Miss Beaupine set before me, *Sebastian, Sebastian. Oh, I love you.*

I understood, pounding out big loud piano music, that I would not, as had poor Miss Beaupine, falter on the brink of whatever it was out there, for good or for bad, whatever it was that was barreling down on us.

First I had to get through all this till Christmas.

5

Christmas is the time for having babies. Both my girls were born in December, on bitter cold mornings but bright with sun, no ice on the trees, no snow on the ground. Joan Gentry wanted me to name the first girl Merrie. "Since she's a Christmas baby," she said. "It'd be appropriate. Merrie Anne," she added, "for you and for the season."

Kelby had already named the girl, Sarah Anne, for me and for his mother. He left Joan and the season out completely. The next time, when Hannah came on December 23, Christmas Eve's Eve, Joan really had a fit. "Angela," she argued, "Angela Joy."

But we'd already decided to let Sarah name her. And Sarah called her sister what she called her teddy bear, something that sounded like Hannah. I added Joan to please my mother. "Hannah Joan," she repeated, bending for a better look at the baby through the nursery window. "Sounds like a Pilgrim."

These days, with Kelby across the country in California, living with a woman with blue hair, I wonder if he ever thinks about what Joan said. I let both the girls fly out to California to visit Kelby when they graduated from high school. He sent them the plane tickets. Sarah went, came back, didn't say too much. Then one day, as we were dividing the dark clothes from the whites for washing, Sarah said, "Kelby's living with a woman with blue hair."

"What d'you mean blue hair?"

Sarah balled up the washcloths, threw them one by careful one into the mouth of the washer. "She dyed it blue, like a little bird's wing or something, right across the front. Yellow in some places. And a little place she dyed rose-color. But mostly blue."

"Did you like it?" I was careful how I asked. I didn't want Sarah thinking I was jealous.

She just snorted, kept on throwing the washcloths.

Hannah wasn't there to hear this. I didn't mention it again. Then it came Hannah's time to fly out to see Kelby. She didn't wait until she got back, but called me one evening from Ventura Beach, where they'd gone for a weekend. "Brenda's got this weird hair," she started. "She said I could get mine done, too."

I didn't say anything. It was Hannah's hair. But when she got off the plane in Charlotte with the same pale blond rufflings, I was relieved. Hannah Joan the Pilgrim.

Christmas was always the time for having babies, when Kelby was still around and things were easy and sweet and I never thought they'd change. Not like those old Christmases in Badin.

BACK THEN I PEELED tangerines and watched Joan and Franklin put up the Christmas tree.

"Why do you always have to go get the biggest tree you can find? You know it never fits in this cheap holder. I cannot stand this, Franklin. Every year it's the same. I'm going to scream."

Joan plopped on the couch, leaving Franklin holding one side of the bushy cedar. The tree leaned all over Franklin, swallowed him up.

"Then scream," he snapped. "Ti Baby, get me that ashtray."

I lifted the heavy glass square off the coffee table and toward the cedar branches and watched Franklin extract a hand from the tree and stub out his Philip Morris.

"Goddammit, shit." He ground his teeth. "Joan, get back over here and help me. You said you wanted a big tree. You said you wanted a great big fat cedar tree, Joan, and I got just exactly what you said you wanted."

Joan Gentry fluffed her pageboy. She narrowed her eyes. "Franklin." She let her breath out in her familiar long, exhausted, dramatic manner.

"Franklin, you are the only person in this house who celebrates Christmas. You put that tree up. Yourself."

I watched them hold each other off for a while. They passed hard hot eyebeams across the living room. Their eyes grew narrower and narrower. Joan gave another dramatic sigh, rose from the sofa. "This'll never get done unless I do it."

Then, "Titania," she directed, "stand over by the front door and tell us when we get it perfectly straight."

I stood by the door. I felt the cold outside air seeping around the jamb and I put my fingers there, relishing the cold. I touched my cold fingertips to my face. My fingers smelled like tangerines.

"I said *tell* us," Joan insisted.

"Okay." I turned back to them. "Go right. Some more. Okay. No, too much. Back left a little."

They straightened the tree and quit yelling at each other. Franklin measured himself many little shots of bourbon, walking around admiring the tree while Joan and I put on the lights. The strings glimmered red, blue, yellow, green, white, like Life Savers, I thought, all five flavors. Cherry, lemon, lime, pineapple, but what was blue?

And orange was missing. No orange-flavored lights. Blue could be a mint. I whistled. Minty blue. I threw on a frizzle of foil icicles.

Joan stood back to look at it. "I wish we had a set of those new bubble lights like Sue Kelly. She gets these new things. I don't know where."

"It looks great, Joan, darling, just great," Franklin toasted the tree. "Sue Kelly wouldn't dare have a tree as good as this."

Joan shrugged. "Don't drink up all that bourbon," she said. "I want some left to put on my fruitcakes."

"Joan, darling," Franklin toasted her gallantly, "those old fruit-cakes'll get as drunk as me. Ain't that right, Ti Baby?"

He winked at me, holding up his glass to toast her next.

I stuck a finger in the bourbon, stuck the finger to my tongue. It spread a sweetish warm film across my tongue. Franklin grinned. "Don't start drinking liquor, Ti Baby," he warned, waggling a finger at me. He threw down the last of the bourbon. He quickly licked the rim of his glass, wiped his lip.

"Now, remember what I just told you." He grinned at me again. "Say it back to me."

"Don't start drinking liquor," I repeated.

"God," said Joan, "that's a joke."

The next day a deep snow covered the town. It hushed up Entwistle Street, cold and white. Madine Ponds swept the snow from her door all the way to the curb. Jettie Barefoot's big high school boys squalled their car around in the snow, fishtailed, bottomed out, and got stuck, spinning their tires all the way down to the red mud. They sat scowling through the steamy windows, shivering and turning up their collars.

Keeping flannel pajamas on under my blue jeans for extra warmth, I pulled on floppy galoshes, then tobogganed and gloved myself and trudged through the snow to Erskine "Sonny" Kelly's house up on the top of Pomona Hill. People were already sledding Pomona. They whizzed over the packed snow, laughing and yelling. School had closed and everybody went to Pomona, the steepest hill in Badin.

Sonny had an old dog Toto, named for Judy Garland's dog in *The Wizard of Oz*. Actually, it was Sue Kelly's dog, an ugly mottled slick-haired rat of a dog, with claws and teeth like the edge of a saw. Sonny stood in the yard with Toto while the old dog peed on a snowy bush, his breath puffing little clouds.

Sonny lived in a bungalow, three bays wide, four bays deep, clapboarded, hip-roofed, with a wide front porch. Exactly the kind of house I'd lived in the first seven years of my life in Badin, North Carolina, the Gentrys living next door to the Kellys then. Sue and Joan had strolled me and Sonny together, Toto trotting behind, growling, peeing on things.

Carol Jean Spence lived down the hill in her apartment on Barineau Street. I didn't meet her until the first grade at Badin School.

Only Joan Gentry wanted to move us to Entwistle Street. It was all her big idea. She thought the apartments were more chic, more modern, than the French Colonial bungalows on Pomona Hill. Closer to the school, in walking distance of the country club: Joan pointed out the advantages of Entwistle Street. Franklin didn't care. I didn't know what was going on.

Sue Kelly hadn't been impressed. "I like to walk all the way around the outside of my house, Joan," she said. "Look, down in those apartments, you are stuck in a box. Only if you get an end apartment can you go outside and walk around, and even then, it's only around one side of it."

She lit a cigarette. "You're nuts, Joan, to move out of a bungalow and into one of those boxes."

But Joan got her way, as usual. We had moved to Entwistle.

This snowy day as I stamped into the yard, Toto growled and scratched backward in the snow. "Hey!" I greeted Sonny, then scooped up a snowball and threw it, catching him on the shoulder.

"You just played hell, Ti!" He tackled me to the ground and sat on me. Sonny rubbed my face in the snow. Toto growled and scratched backward and then peed again on the bush.

"Get off me," I ordered, "get off me right now, or I'll tell your mama."

Sonny leaned to mutter in my cold ear, "You know you like it," and then dry-humped me hard twice before he got off and let me up.

"I hate you," I glared, brushing off the snow.

We tramped inside his house. Sue Kelly stood at the kitchen window smoking a cigarette. Toto shot into the kitchen and rubbed against Sue's leg, then began to lap water from his bowl. I shivered at the way his claws scratched across the linoleum.

"Look at this." Sonny plugged in their tree and I watched the little bubble lights shaped like little candles, all of them blue, spring to life as the fluid inside them warmed.

"Like that?" Sonny was eager for me to admire his tree and its bubble lights.

I stamped my cold feet. The little bubbles floated to the tips of the candles, blinked, disappeared. Others floated up. I imagined I could hear each one gurgle, soft blue and warm as oil.

"That's pretty, Sonny," I said. "Where did you all get bubble lights?"

Sonny shrugged. "Mama got it."

Sue Kelly came into the living room and lit a fresh cigarette. "What's Santa Claus bringing you, Ti?" She squinted through her smoke.

"I don't know."

"I'm getting a racing bike," bragged Sonny. "Ten speed, and turned-down handlebars."

Sue Kelly flipped cigarette ash into her palm. "You don't know what you're getting, Sonny. You might not be getting anything."

"Yes, I am." He rolled his eyes at her, then at me. "And I know what else. A .22 rifle."

Sue turned her attention back to me. "I bet you're getting a baby doll." She dragged on the cigarette and smiled.

"I'm too old for a doll." I stamped my cold feet again.

Sue frowned in mock sympathy. "Ah," she chided, "you ought to get just one more."

"I'm thirteen," I said, "a teenager." I felt offended. I had little titties growing off me, for God's sake. Baby doll? "A teenager," I said again.

"That's what I mean," said Sue Kelly, "you ought to get one more baby doll, just for old times. Now you're a teenager, God knows what you'll get next."

Toto trotted to the tree and curled beneath. The little blue bubbles blinked and disappeared all above him, reflecting on his ugly pelt. Toto sighed, lowered nose to paws and began to snore.

"Well, what are you going to get for Christmas, then?" Sonny asked.

"I don't know. Stuff. A surprise, I guess."

"Well." Sue Kelly blew smoke through the tree. "Just so you're surprised. Whatever it is, you'll get it. Sonny," she ordered, "unplug the tree. I don't like for those lights to get too hot."

Back out in the snow, Sonny took my arm and hissed between clenched teeth, "Listen, I *am* getting a racing bike and I know where it is, too."

He nodded toward the garage. "They tried to hide it behind some old pieces of plywood and put a old sheet over it. God, they're so stupid, Ti. It's in there. I already rode it, too."

Sonny turned loose of my arm. I grinned in spite of myself. Erskine "Sonny" Kelly was so brazen, standing there in the cold white snow, his blond hair creeping out in little ringlets from under the aviator's helmet he wore all the time in the winter.

"And the .22 rifle is upstairs in their closet," he added. "They are so stupid."

"God, Sonny." I was delighted, envious, that he had gotten away with something like already riding around on his Christmas bike. Something I would like to get away with.

"God, Sonny, you are the hatefulest person in the whole world."

"I know it." Sonny snapped the chin strap of his helmet and pulled the imitation goggles down over his eyes. "And I'm still getting that bike. *And* the rifle."

He knew what was going on in his life, Erskine "Sonny" Kelly. He didn't tell stories to himself. Things happened. Things came true. No half-life for Sonny, no half-half life, no waking up to the sick feeling that you'd already lived half of everything and never knew it. No born-loser stuck to Sonny's head.

CHRISTMAS MORNING, I EMPTIED my red stocking of English walnuts, peppermints and tangerines. I unwrapped the presents that were socks and nighties, bubble bath and a birthstone ring, topaz for November, exotic as a tiger's eye, and a subscription to *Classic Comics*. Inside a box of stationery with poodles all over it and a little gold pen with a poodle on top, I found a note from Joan promising, "Titania, we are going to redecorate your room after Christmas. We are going to paint it and get you a new bedspread, new curtains, a rug, and fix a vanity with a mirror. You are going to love it all. Merry Christmas from Mother and Daddy!"

Under the Christmas tree, twinkling its strings of red, blue, yellow, green, and white, sat General MacArthur. The one last baby doll of my life. I glared at him, glaring next at both Joan and Franklin. "Where did that thing come from?"

"It was in the Sears catalog," said Joan. "I thought it was kind of unusual."

"It's the ugliest thing I've ever seen. It's got to be a joke," I declared. "Nobody would give this to a person for Christmas."

"I told you she wouldn't like it," Franklin exulted.

Joan sighed. "It's unusual," she explained. "It's something you get because it's unusual."

Something plaintive in the sound of Joan's voice made me relent. Maybe this ugly thing had value, like the sterling silver Joan counted, the piano lessons. I kissed General MacArthur's cold beaky face, caressed his olive uniform, and propped him on the York piano.

"That doll is going to be a collector's item one day," Joan pointed out, encouraged by my attentions to General MacArthur. She sliced her fruitcakes. "When this war is over."

"When this war is over, shit." Franklin took a slice, pinched off a chunk of candied pineapple. "When this war is over, General MacArthur will start another war."

He popped the pineapple in his mouth and chewed.

"All I mean," Joan brushed at the sticky crumbs, "is she ought to be careful with that doll and not play with it and tear it up. It might be worth something someday."

"Shit," observed Franklin again.

I studied General MacArthur. He didn't look quite right. Too prissy. Even with a uniform and cap, he was no sexy endearing paratrooper. He looked more like a scarecrow, an imperial and holy scarecrow, than he did a soldier.

"Aw, the poor old thing," sneered Franklin watching me undress General MacArthur. "Got it shot off in the war."

He measured out his bourbon, threw it down and grinned at Joan.

"Shut up, Franklin," she said. "Now, see, that's what I meant about not tearing it up. Titania, put General MacArthur's clothes back on. He's not to play with. He's going to be a collector's item."

I pulled the uniform back over General MacArthur's neutered body, brushed the brim of his cap. I didn't even know, I admitted with great contempt, what I was looking for when I took his clothes off. Did I expect him to have a big dick? Erskine "Sonny" Kelly had an unimpressive but fair-sized worm of a dick. He had showed it to me, jeered, "You want to hold it?"

But I paid no more attention to Sonny Kelly's dick than to a baby's. Than to a dog's in the yard, old Toto. No, I declared, I want a man to jump out, lay claim to me, punch Franklin in the mouth and pinch Joan's arm and say rude things to the both of them.

I want you, Sebastian McSherry, to get back here from the war.

I pushed the topaz ring over the finger next to my crooked little one. I straightened and flexed my crooked finger, liking the friction of the ring against it. The topaz glowed like an ember, an eye. *Burn, yes, twirl.*

THE NEXT SUNDAY WAS communion. I knelt at the Badin Methodist altar with Uncle Morton and Aunt Della and sipped juice sour enough to water my eyes. Franklin Gentry's bourbon would have tasted better. I set the tiny glass back in the ring of purple velvet, lush as Joan's fruitcakes, and while everybody around me prayed, I told myself little comforting stories about Sebastian McSherry. He'd come to me, helmeted and harnessed up to parachutes, right there in the Badin Methodist Church. He would put a hard heavy boot on the chancel rail, maybe step on Uncle Morton's foot.

"What do you want, babe?" he'd ask, the candles glinting off his boots.

"I want you to sit on the porch and watch me twirl the baton. I can twirl fire, you know." I smiled, unfastened my braids and let them fall down my naked back like darkly waving water. They smelled like rich fruity flowers. My skin was as tanned and smooth as a Tahitian's. I wore a sarong. I was proud I looked like Dorothy Lamour and not June Allyson. "Watch this."

"What's your uncle doing here?" Sebastian pointed at Morton

praying in front of the flags. "Why isn't he off fighting the Japs and Hitler like me?"

I smiled, lifted a brow. "The navy sent him back. He's already done fighting. He's too old, anyhow."

"And your daddy? What's his excuse?" Sebastian's eyes roved over the three flags, North Carolina, Old Glory, and the banner of Christ. He shook his head, disgusted.

"My daddy works for Carolina Aluminum. He got excused. You know that." I rubbed his arm. I brushed his bright paratroop insignia. "Franklin got excused from the war."

"Excused like hell."

I felt faintly offended, the way I had when Sue Kelly asked me if I was going to get a doll for Christmas. I didn't like Sebastian making fun of either Franklin or Uncle Morton. It made me feel inferior if he did. Like I was the same as Uncle Morton and Franklin.

Things were getting out of hand in this daydream. I shut off the little stories and returned to my pew with Morton and Della and sat there with a worried frown for the rest of the service.

BUT THE TIME WAS right for Sebastian McSherry's appearance. The snow had melted and I practiced faithfully on Jettie Barefoot's black York. I grew more agile with the baton. I added to my box of rags in the garage, stockpiled matches.

He did not appear.

I met him in dreams. He looked blank-eyed, had a broken nose. He held out both his hands to me, twirled fire from the ends of his fingers and smiled. He rode a ten-speed racing bike with turned-down handlebars. Star clusters burst from the end of his .22 rifle. Little warm blue bubbles rose all around him, blinked and disappeared with a gurgle.

I was good and polite and well behaved, saying "Ma'am" to Joan all the time. And still Sebastian didn't appear. I took Mr. McSherry a plate of Joan's fruitcake, luscious slices thick in cherries and raisins. He gobbled up the whole plate, never offering me a bite. I walked around his apartment, fingering the crumbs in my pocket, a dry raisin, slivers of pecan, knots of lint.

"Did you like that big snow we had, Mr. McSherry?" I was determined to be polite to him. I wanted news of Sebastian.

"Hate snow." He snuffled over the last of the cake. "Cup of coffee would go nice with this, don't you think, Titania?"

He wiped off his face with the plaid handkerchief and got up, carrying the empty plate.

I followed into his kitchen. It was exactly like Joan's on the other side of the beaverboard wall, only furnished differently. A sink in the corner, one enormous cupboard with glass front built against the long side of the room, a cylindrical water heater reaching the ceiling and painted the same dull cream as the walls. A light bulb dangled on the end of a black cord.

Mr. McSherry grabbed at the bulb, pulled a chain. His kitchen appurtenances were simpler than Joan's. A wooden table with three painted chairs, the seats woven with white oak strips. Greasy-looking electric stove, small refrigerator humming in the dim back. He had no curtains, though. Joan Gentry kept crisp white swags. Mr. McSherry kept naked windows.

I sat down, feeling the white oak strips stretch under me, and watched Mr. McSherry rinse off the cake plate. He filled a coffeepot with water and took down a can from his cupboard. As he measured out coffee, I asked, "When's your grown son, Sebastian, coming back from the paratroopers? You said he was coming Christmas. Christmas is half over."

He pressed the lid back on the can, returned it to the cupboard and put the pot on the stove before answering.

"Any day, I reckon, any day. I can't keep all his stuff straight. He got wounded. Over in France. Sebastian got wounded bad. Had to be in the army hospital. He got sent back. Any day, I reckon, he'll walk in here on me."

Mr. McSherry turned the heat down under the bubbling pot. I sniffed greedily at the rich nutty fragrance. I watched him pour a cup and asked, "Can I have a cup of coffee, too?"

He wheezed, blew his nose and wiped it slowly. He studied me over his cup.

"Kids don't drink coffee."

"I do," I said. "I drink a whole cup of coffee every morning. Ask my mother." I glared at him.

He snorted, glaring back. "Aw, get a cup down. They're back there, next to the bread box. And don't knock nothing over."

The cupboard door swung loosely on one hinge. The shelving sagged. Mr. McSherry needed some good repair work. Even the kitchen floor buckled under me just as the white oak strips of his chair had done.

I chose a yellow cup. It had a tiny dark crack down one side.

"Don't burn yourself on that pot. I seen kids scalded to death on coffeepots."

I sat down carefully and blew across my hot cup. Mr. McSherry shoved over the sugar bowl. A spoon stuck out, tipping the lid. "You have any milk, Mr. McSherry?" I asked.

"You see? What did I just say, what did I just tell you? Kids don't drink coffee! They have to sissy it up."

He thumbed disgustedly toward his refrigerator. I got up to get the milk. When I opened the refrigerator, bright polar light flooded the dim back of his kitchen. I sized up everything, all the weird contents and smells, and then dug a fingernail in the thick rime hanging from the freeze-box. Mr. McSherry's small refrigerator amused me. All the delicacies of his life displayed on wire shelves, his half-eaten cans of pork-and-beans, plates of congealed soup.

I took the milk bottle to the table. Its paper plug announced *Sunshine Dairies! Wake up fresh as a daisy with us!* I sat watching the cold milk curl into my hot coffee and I sniffed the little tendrils of steam wisping from the yellow cup. I felt sheltered. Even Mr. McSherry's snufflings and smackings across the table did not annoy me. Even his stale old-man smell, his dead cigar, did not offend Titania Gentry in this warm moment. What did Sebastian smell like, I wondered? The thought froze me up in a little stinging fright. Surely he wouldn't smell or look or act like Mr. McSherry?

"Remember to put that milk back," the old man reminded me.

We finished our cups in silence. Then I took the cake plate and started back through his living room to the front door. I noticed Christmas presents still piled on the sofa, unopened. I stopped, picked a little one out and shook it. It rattled with a crisp wooden clack against the sides.

"Mr. McSherry," I accused. "You didn't open all your Christmas presents. Why not?" I shook the package again.

He came in behind me and stared at the holly-print paper. No ribbons on the presents. Every one was slick and flat in the holly paper.

"Aw," he complained, "that ain't nothing. Christmas is for kids. All that mess came in the mail from him, from Sebastian, and I had to carry every blessed piece of it home from the post office."

"In all that snow," he added, then shrugged and poked the stick at me.

"You open that one, if you want to. You can have it, too. I don't know what it is. Just junk he sent. You can have it."

I sat down on Mr. McSherry's cold floor—no Olsen Mills carpet in his apartment—and ripped off the holly paper, thrilled through with lust and curiosity. Just junk he sent. From him, from Sebastian!

It was a plain pasteboard box tied with string and the string popped under my finger. I slid off the top, and in a wad of tissue paper, I found two little wooden shoes. Dark and hollow, they clacked like castanets in my hands, little wooden heartbeats, the carved toes as pointed as little hooks. I thought a person might bleed to death just looking at them. I touched a finger to the little points and the thrill radiated through me.

"Look!" I marveled to Mr. McSherry, who stooped to look over my shoulder at the little shoes.

"What did I tell you?" he snorted. "What did I just say? Just junk. Junk he picked out and sent and paid the postage on to get here. What did he think I wanted them little things for? You can have them, Titania. I said you could already."

He straightened up, still snorting. "And tell your mama I said thank you for the fruitcake."

"Thank you, Mr. McSherry." I patted the little shoes. They were as slick as satin. They glowed in the middle of Mr. McSherry's ugly old living room. There were no others like them in the whole world. Pride shot through me and I jumped up, Joan's cake plate under arm, and swaggered out of Mr. McSherry's apartment. I had something of Sebastian now, something he had picked out and handled and breathed all over.

That evening, when the air got bitter cold around the street-lights on Entwistle, I sat at the York and played "White Christmas" especially for Mr. McSherry. I tried to put in little flourishes. Stretched my crooked finger into arpeggios and grace notes, trilling high treble notes into what I hoped resembled sleigh bells. I hoped he heard.

The wooden shoes sat beside me on the black bench. I was delighted to see Joan Gentry wanted them to go on her what-not shelf.

"Those came from France, I bet. They're called *sabots* in French." Joan fingered them, positioned them with her paper-weights and her one piece of Wedgewood.

"Mr. McSherry gave them to me," I took them off the what-not shelf, adding generously, "ma'am." I deepened my dimples at Joan.

I took them upstairs and set them on the windowsill beside my bed, breathed on them, polished them to a high gloss with the hem of my flannel pajama shirt.

Now Titania Gentry met Sebastian McSherry in dreams wearing dark sabots from France. He limped a little bit, held one arm in a sling. A bloody bandage trailed from his head.

I got wounded bad, he muttered. I forget what, but bad.

I twirled my fire in a wide and generous lantern beam to show him how to get back home to Badin. I changed his bandage and I kissed him on the mouth.

It's about time somebody did, he said, settling closer to me.

6

The first time I met Kelby, I felt the same way as in the dream, as if I'd come home.

It was a pleasant recognition, a welcome from somebody you'd been missing, or been homesick for, all your life. He was a short-order cook in a place I went to in Greensboro, The Corner, as it was called by the girls of The Woman's College of the University of North Carolina at Greensboro. We could sneak beer in paper cups there. Kelby made the best french fries I ever ate. And when he wasn't cooking, he was out front, talking to us over the counter.

He had what Joan Gentry's magazines called classic features, a long slim nose, ears close to his head, and eyes evenly spaced. And surprisingly scuppernong green, same as mine. Joan didn't like people to say scuppernong green. She preferred a more exotic description, like greeny-amber. I got in the habit of saying things like greeny-amber. But really the color was scuppernong green, rich and deep as a September harvest of scuppernongs, the wild and naturally sweet grapes of Carolina.

And Kelby's hair was light brown, very curly. I found myself reaching a hand across the counter at The Corner to touch his springy cushion of hair. Soft as a baby's hair, yet with a definite, an almost defiant, springiness.

"Leave my hair alone," he grinned, and put his cook's cap back on.

I found out he was majoring in accounting at Guilford, a Quaker school right outside of town. Joan Gentry liked that about Kelby, the accounting major, not the Quaker. "Accountants make a pot of money," she declared the first time I brought him home to Badin.

He just smiled a lazy way and then lifted his brows at me. Kelby wasn't going to make a pot of anything. I already knew that. He was impressed by Franklin's chiropractic equipment. He stretched out on the adjustment table and sighed. "Get up here, babe," he said. "Let's make it right here."

I shoved Kelby over and sat beside him. I didn't stretch out because my parents were both in the apartment, right in the next room, and I didn't want them walking in on us. Sometimes, the way it turned out with Kelby and me, I wish I had stretched out on the adjustment table.

He never finished his accounting degree at Guilford. I never finished slogging along in the journalism program there at WC. We went to the beach that Easter and I got pregnant with Sarah.

But I didn't care. And if Kelby cared, he didn't say. He went to work in the First National Bank. We set up housekeeping in an old house on the other side of Guilford Battleground. And it was okay for a long time, long after Hannah Joan came.

Things can last.

And then they can't last anymore. The world is too hard, the light too bright, a flashlight turned full beam into your eyes, hurting. And it's probably better when you don't know the truth, when you keep going along fashioning little stories about people you love, people you want to stick around and help act out the stories. You

84

scratch things on paper, then you scratch things out. It's better, you admit, just to think things up. Nobody is accountable for thinking things up.

I know now I was too passive, too placid about Kelby. I know now, too, that Kelby was always strangely dissatisfied, though he never really talked about that. And I never really asked him. Why didn't I do more to keep Kelby? Why didn't I just demand things in a loud voice?

He never told me much about his family. His father died in an industrial accident, fell off a catwalk. This was in Roanoke Rapids, a city in the far northeast of the state. His mother, soon after, Kelby said, dropped out of things, pining away, that old-fashioned nineteenth-century sort of thing.

"My mother, on a fainting couch," said Kelby, "pining, with a hand to her brow." He did not sound scornful. He never wanted to visit her, never took me to Roanoke Rapids.

But his mother, Sarah, for whom he named our first daughter, and his older brother, Vincent, came to see us once in Greensboro. Sarah was toddling. I was pregnant with Hannah. Kelby's mother lay on our rump-sprung sofa and smiled at the energetic Baby Sarah. Vincent, too, smiled and watched her play, arranging toys by color and size, then dropping them into her toy bin with a bang. "She seems to know what's going on," Vincent said, like some great pronouncement of Sarah's ability.

When Joan asked me about Kelby's people, I said his father was dead and his mother was emotionally distressed. "That doesn't sound good," she said. She looked at Sarah. "I hope it doesn't get into the children. You know, like in the genes."

I hoped a lot of things didn't get into Sarah and eventually Hannah. I wanted them to be, though, like Kelby. Once when we were walking in a meadow in Greensboro, a wide swath of pure green, the girls yammering and frolicking around us, we surprised a big skunk digging for grubs. It was nearly dark, the streetlights just glimmering on.

Kelby called softly to the girls to shut up, quit jumping around, be still. He pointed at the skunk, which was standing up staring at us, his tail spread like a big black feather. I picked up a rock and balled it in my fist ready to throw. I could throw pretty good. If that skunk decided to charge my children, I'd hurt him somehow.

In the middle of my hateful thoughts, I saw Kelby, too, had picked up a rock. But he rolled it firmly underhand, as if bowling, straight toward the skunk to frighten it off. The rock bowled along and the skunk watched it coming a minute, then he waddled away, stood up one more time to look at us, then dropped and waddled completely away.

Nobody had said a thing.

I looked at the rock still balled in my fist. My crooked little finger was tight around its sharper point. I realized Kelby's first move had been to intimidate. Mine had been to destroy.

"Did you see that?" Both girls rushed to us. "That was a big, big skunk!"

"Yes," said Kelby. "He was big, but now he's gone."

CAROL JEAN SPENCE'S BROTHER came home, a sailor in dark blue wool, carrying a sea bag stenciled with his name. All the Spences shrieked, "Bobby! Bobby Spence!" They ran out to kiss him and have a picture snapped beside Bobby and the sea bag. He brought Carol Jean a grass skirt. She carried on as if it were the most wonderful present she ever got.

"That doesn't even look like real grass," I sneered. The fronds fell in a dry rustle the color of straw, stitched to a tie-around sash.

Carol Jean pushed off my hand. "It does, too."

"It's not even green," I kept up. "It looks like straw. That's what it is, a straw skirt!"

86

I raised my brows, wrinkled my lips, did everything I could to show Carol Jean my disapproval. Make her feel bad. Reject the grass skirt.

"I don't care." Carol Jean tied the sash and began to dance. "Hula Hula Girl," she sang, "on the beach at Waikiki."

Carol Jean Spence hulaed all over her yard, grinning at me. She knew how jealous I was. I felt murderous. I kicked at the wet dirt.

In March 1945, the snow had melted off months ago, the Badin days were windy and wild, with buds showing color in the trees. Life was so strong in Badin, North Carolina, right then that for all I knew, Carol Jean's dry straw might easily turn green, thick and lush as new wheat, and swish against her scrawny legs.

I felt sorry for myself and angry that I succumbed to it. I didn't have anything like Carol Jean's grass skirt. No trophy of any kind, except for the little wooden sabots. I hadn't twirled fire. Sebastian McSherry hadn't come home. And when, for God's sake, was the last time I'd seen Hootchie with his marvelously wicked tattooed snakes? Or heard him fart?

There was Carol Jean Spence, blind to all such sufferings, merrily doing the hula in a tacky grass skirt. I worked up to a good crying fit, yelled at Carol Jean, "I don't care about your old grass skirt!"

Carol Jean rounded a big forsythia bush, its bright yellow spikes bouncing in the March wind. She stopped, studied me. "What?"

"I said I don't care about your fucking old grass skirt!" I ran out of the yard and halfway down Barineau Street before I stopped and turned.

"Fucking grass skirt!" I yelled and ran on, sobbing as theatrically as I could.

"I'm going tell your mother you said fucking," yelled back Carol Jean. "You said fucking!"

Back on Entwistle, I sat in my upstairs window and asked myself why I'd never really seen Sebastian. "Where is he, anyhow? And why didn't anybody tell me about him before?"

The wooden sabots gleamed on the sill. *Because,* they answered me, *you are too dumb to know about him.* I wiped my face, blew my nose and threw the Kleenex on the floor.

"Yeah," I agreed with the sabots, "I am too dumb."

I stared glumly out the window at the back alley of Entwistle. The tar and gravel paving looked wet. The two garbage cans beside the garage glistened. I realized it was raining a fine little mist all over Badin. "See," I pointed out, "I'm too dumb to know when it's raining."

Then I tried to cheer myself a little, pointing out other things. For one, it was not really my fault about Sebastian's failure to appear. And as for my failure to twirl a fire baton, well, I'd hardly found out about Sebastian. I'd hardly any time left to practice twirling. I was all the time practicing on that damn big York, for another thing.

I stretched my fingers, straightening the crooked finger until it ached. And, I continued, ever since the light reconnaissance aircraft crashed into Badin Lake three days after my birthday, I'd tried to pay attention to the war. But it still took me by surprise. Even the mildest things, like Bobby Spence coming home from the navy. Even though every day Franklin listened to the war on the radio, read *The Charlotte Observer.* And complained about the blackouts every night.

I relaxed my fingers. I liked the blackouts, even though they worried me. The harsh sirens screeched in the middle of supper or the middle of *Amos and Andy* . Franklin would throw down his newspaper and curse, flicking off the radio.

We had to put out every light in the apartment. I sat on the cold kitchen linoleum, the smell of our supper still in the air, water gurgling in the drain. I clenched my fists and waited for the bombs to start dropping all over Badin, North Carolina.

Or I huddled on the itchy Olsen Mills carpet in the living room, my braids falling over my shoulders as I tried to make out the frames in *Classic Comics* by the one little candle Joan kept lit on the coffee table.

All our drapes and curtains were drawn shut and then safety-pinned together. I had the feeling of being buried alive, locked in forever with Franklin and Joan. What if we never got out again? What if the all-clear sirens never blew?

I kept the holy imperial General MacArthur under one arm and my baton under the other. I kissed them both, prayed to them, *Don't let the Japs and Hitler bomb us. But if they do, then let me get out first.*

Franklin smoked cigarettes and his smoke thickened against the drawn curtains, making me cough, sneeze, gag. Joan glared at him until he stubbed the Philip Morris. "Well, goddammit, shit! I'd just as soon they dropped a bomb. Get it over with."

Joan tried to read her magazines as I tried to read the comics. The feeble beam of her flashlight failed. Joan shook it impatiently. "Oh, hell."

The batteries rattled.

I gazed at the little candle and squinched my eyes to blur out everything else. I know where we will hide, I assured myself, if the Japs and Hitler land in Badin and come sneaking down Pomona Hill and slide like snakes up our steps.

In Erskine "Sonny" Kelly's basement.

SONNY'S HOUSE ON POMONA Hill was built against a rocky toe that eventually sloped into one of the Uwharrie hills surrounding the town. A shallow basement with a dirt floor ranged underneath Sonny's house, a dark place of spiders and roaches. Sonny and I stepped on every bug we saw, exulting in the crunch under our feet. We watched for snakes or rats, either of which could come out of the dark corners of the basement and bite us at any minute.

Carol Jean Spence wouldn't go in the basement. She didn't trust either me or Sonny Kelly down there. She would rather stay in the yard and fend off Toto.

"I know what you look like," Sonny said. He narrowed his eyes and focused on my blouse front, then the crotch seam of my blue jeans. "Without your clothes on."

"No, you don't," I snorted. "And I don't care even if you do."

Sonny's basement was sprinkled with white lime. The walls next to the rocky slope were studded with thin brown-shelled snails. I flicked a snail off the wall and smashed it, then turned back to Sonny. "I said I don't care even if you do."

"Get Carol Jean to come in here, then," he said.

"Why?" I inspected the shelves loaded with canned tomatoes and peaches, each jar sealed with a red rubber ring and enamel lid.

"So I can take all her clothes off. So I can take all her clothes off and yours, too, and fuck both of you." Sonny narrowed his eyes even more.

"I'll stick it in you so deep, you'll both cry." He leered at me. And in the dim spiderwebby light, his blond hair took on a sort of aura. Sonny glowed in the dark. I didn't care if he threatened to stick it in me, but I was very angry that he thought I might cry.

"Sonny, why don't you shut up?"

"Oh, hell." He fell back, kicked at an old wooden sprung-bottom rocker. "You don't know nothing about real fucking, Ti."

I'd started to say "How do you know I don't?" when Mrs. Kelly let Toto out in the yard. He barked and growled at Carol Jean so fiercely, Sonny had to run out of the basement and make him shut up.

So—remembering Sonny Kelly's basement during the air raid blackouts, I grinned again. Nobody, not Japs, not even Hitler, would follow us there. And it had enough room for everybody, Carol Jean Spence, Sonny and his family, even Toto, Franklin and Joan and me.

I grinned, squeezing General MacArthur, rubbing the long baton. I will choose, though, I declared, who gets the best place, and who gets pushed into the snails, and who has to lie like a sardine in the dirt, and who bumps her blond June Allyson pageboy on the joists of the floor.

I will decide, furthermore, who takes off whose clothes and who fucks who. Such conceited thoughts sustained me through all the blackouts of World War II.

And months later, still angry and envious, I wanted to spoil Carol Jean's brother's homecoming for Carol Jean. I wanted to spoil the grass skirt Bobby Spence brought back to her. I was ashamed. So I cried.

General MacArthur had been abandoned during those months under clothes and shoes and *Classic Comics* in the debris of my closet. Now I exhumed him, kissed again his cold beaky face. I straightened his uniform, brushed his cap, and saw, with genuine sorrow, that the tip of his nose had broken off. I felt true pain looking at the dingy pulp inside General MacArthur's nose. Joan had wanted him to be valuable someday, a collector's item. Now he was junk.

I kissed his broken-off nose, then set him up on the windowsill, next to the wooden sabots. Drab and cold as he was, broken-nosed, he would serve as Sebastian McSherry, I decided, my lover by proxy, every morning and every night, until the real thing got there.

General MacArthur wouldn't fail me. I had a strange melancholy and sweetish sort of feeling, like being homesick. I leaned back on my bed, gazing at General MacArthur. "This is like being lost from your people," I told him. "Like learning to walk all over again after you broke your leg, maybe, in the war."

I'D LEARNED TO WALK across the front porch of our first house up on Pomona Hill, the French Colonial bungalow that Joan exchanged for the Entwistle Street apartment. It was a wide front porch with plain wooden posts. I walked along holding out my arms for balance and tapping the posts for assurance. I could still recall sitting down on the top step of that bungalow when I was a baby and looking down Pomona Hill, taking in the whole horizon of Badin.

Carolina Aluminum had boomed in my left eye while Badin Lake sparkled in my right eye. And between the two spread the town, straight down to the Olympia Cafe.

"Downtown," I'd said, "go get me a beer."

The first words. Joan exclaimed, "The baby's talking! The baby's talking and walking both!"

"What did she say?" Franklin pushed open the screen door. "Did she say a real word or just make a noise?"

"She said a sentence." Joan bent over me. She gazed in my face. "Say it again, Titania. What did you say?"

At thirteen, sitting in my old room—as today at forty-three sitting in my house at Lake Waccamaw, a hundred miles south—I could recall every detail clear as a photograph.

I'd scanned the horizon off Pomona Hill. "Downtown, go get me a beer."

Joan sat back hard on her heels. "She got that from you," she accused Franklin, still waiting behind the screen.

"Aw, she didn't even say nothing. You just think she said something." And he slammed the door.

I recalled the bungalow, the sounds of their voices, the color of the sky. I had walked by myself. I had said a whole sentence. Joan Gentry had accused Franklin of teaching me to mimic him.

I could just as easily have said, "Look in there. He's walking that hussy to the bathroom. See him? That's your daddy."

And the day we moved to Entwistle Street, seven years later, I came home from school, said good-bye to Carol Jean at Barineau Street, walked all the way up Pomona Hill with Sonny Kelly. Sonny went dashing inside his bungalow and I heard Toto go into his familiar irritable barking frenzy.

Our bungalow was empty. Cleaned out. Not one thing left in it.

I rambled through all its rooms and listened to my echo in the bare space. I called, "Where are you? Ma'am?"

I sat down on the top step and leaned against the posts. All of Badin spread below. And I wondered how Joan and Franklin lost me.

How I, maybe, lost them.

They'll come back, I comforted myself, picking at splinters in the step. They'll miss me and they'll run back up here and get me.

But the longer I sat, the more I understood, *No*, they are not coming back. They are *not* missing me.

I looked down at Carolina Aluminum to the left, Badin Lake to the right. The familiar landmarks. How could Joan and Franklin not miss me?

I sat awhile longer, then remembered, with anxiety and shame, Entwistle Street, the new apartment, what Joan wanted. You won't have to walk up that hill anymore, Titania, she'd pointed out. You can walk right around the corner to Badin School, Titania. You can ride your bike downtown. Look how close it is to the country club.

I felt foolish, betrayed by my own forgetfulness. And when I finally got down to the new apartment on Entwistle Street, Joan and Franklin were impatient and tired, unpacking stuff, criticizing each other and everything else.

"Where have you been? We told you to come right to the apartment after school. Titania, you'll have to be punished for this. We told you to come straight to this apartment."

"I went," I said, trying to explain all the ridiculous things that had happened, all the ridiculous feelings I'd been having, trying to behave as if it mattered to either Joan or Franklin, "I went home."

"Well, this is home, now," said Joan, a sharp line between her brows. She was worn out. "I told you to come straight home here. Isn't that what I told you?"

The wind ruffled my braids. I felt big hard goose bumps rise on my arms. The sun was going down behind the mountains, sliding off Pomona Hill into Badin Lake. I nodded at Joan. "Yes."

***

A BORN LOSER. I ponder the words, the letters hooked together by blue Scripto. The rest of the page in the ledger book is slick and fresh, as white as if I'd bleached it with Clorox. These three words are all I've managed to write, to mimic the joke my daughters made. It's not fair for Sarah and Hannah to say that, to stick that on my head. And back then, in Badin, it wasn't fair, either.

"Was it?" I had to shake my head back then at General MacArthur on the windowsill.

Sure, it was, he replied. The same old hard goose bumps rose on my arms and I rubbed them. "Well, it didn't feel fair." I got mad at General MacArthur. He was as dumb as Joan and Franklin.

What I wanted to tell him was that I went home and it didn't feel like going home anymore. It felt like going where Joan and Franklin lived.

I switched my mind off of General MacArthur. Summoned the spirit of Sebastian.

"And where were you, Sebastian McSherry, when I got lost on Pomona Hill and had to walk all the way back down to Entwistle Street and get punished?"

Suddenly, I wanted Sebastian to take the blame for everything, for my getting punished years ago, for my rejection of Carol Jean's grass skirt that day. "Where were you?"

You tell me, said General MacArthur, his broken nose darkening, and his uniform dampening in the misty spring rain. *I'm not the one who gets lost. I'm not the one too dumb to know when it's raining.*

"That's right," I agreed, my mood both sad and vicious, "you're not the one who misses me."

And Sebastian McSherry wasn't the one, either.

I was missing myself. Which I did up until the time of Kelby.

7

One of the happiest times Kelby and I had was a picnic at the Battleground. Sarah and Hannah were still running around in those beach towels, still trying to fly like Underdog. Kelby took a day off from the bank, just walked in the house and said, "Let's have a picnic."

It was a sunny windy April Tuesday, the spring peepers hollering in the creeks, and the sky as showy as a movie—first bright, then dark, then bright again as the wind blew big banks of white clouds along. Even the roaring traffic of Greensboro had calmed.

"I don't have anything for a picnic." I was halfway mad at Kelby for surprising me like that. I'd lost all that delight in spontaneous adventure I used to relish so much in Badin with my friends, Sonny Kelly and Carol Jean Spence.

Kelby smiled his lazy way, lifted his brows, and opened the kitchen cabinets and started piling stuff into our hamper, saltines and a jar of jelly, little packages of Sugar Pops and some Vienna sausage.

"Okay," I grinned, "wait a minute." I boiled some eggs, cut up celery and carrot sticks, and added a thermos of coffee. We got

lemonade for the kids from a Quik Chek on our way to the Battleground.

Kelby was so funny that afternoon, swinging the kids around by
their skinny little wrists through the bright April air. Sarah and
Hannah laughed so much, they got the hiccups.

We spread the food and afterward lay on the blanket and stared
up at the trees while Sarah and Hannah pretended to fish in the
lake. It was the best thing, just lying there next to Kelby, the raggedy
little meal finished, the sounds of our children drifting back to us.

"I don't like the bank," he said. "I want to quit."

I'd been lying there loving the sounds of the children and the
April winds brushing over me and the healthy wonderful smell of
Kelby, sort of sweaty and grassy. And I'd thought nothing, absolutely
nothing, would take it away.

Kelby sat up, shook the thermos and poured the last dregs into
his paper cup. I didn't want him to say anything else. I didn't want
to consider anything else. I lay looking at how swiftly the wind
bunched his curly hair, making it more of a cushion than ever. I
instinctively reached up a hand to press that cushion.

And then what was really happening swirled around in my head
like a glass ball you shake until the little snow pieces flutter and boil
and then settle again to reveal a scene as sharply perfect as you could
imagine.

He's going to leave me, I warned myself. *He's already gone. This is
a man I don't know.*

The little snow pieces fluttered all over us. The scene perfectly
settled down: Kelby, Titania, Sarah, Hannah. Sealed inside a glass
ball.

And then I thought next he must somehow know about Rory
Flynt. For several months, I'd been working a few days a week,
mostly Mondays and Fridays, at the *News Gazette*, doing some stories, some copy editing, a bit of photography. Kelby thought it a

good thing for me. It was, after all, what I'd planned to do, what I'd gone to school for. Rory Flynt, though, wasn't what I planned to do.

He had thick carrot-red hair, dark eyes and brows, and freckles all over the like of which I never saw anywhere else on a person, except on Ginger McSherry, the woman who, I have to admit, eventually married my Sebastian right out from under me in those silly and adventurous Badin days.

Rory was no paratrooper, no Kelby. He had a Volkswagen the color of Campbell's tomato soup. With a sunroof you cranked open. He was the first man I knew who wore sandals all the time, even in the cold with thick woolen socks. Something they made him stop at the *News Gazette*. "You're gonna drop something on your toe," they complained, "and then sue us!"

We shared a corner office with a big light you had to turn on by a long cord. Rory had a terrible cold, and then I got the same cold, and all the time we were yanking on that long light cord.

"You gave me your cold," I said, "your germs are all over this cord." The first thing I said to him, an accusation. Rory Flynt, the man I had an affair with in Greensboro, behind Kelby's back, sneaking about the same way Franklin Gentry did. Except that it wasn't the same as Franklin. Nothing silly or funny. No nightly pursuits in a black Ford.

And it was over as quickly as it had started—not with a bad cold, but with vigorous, almost savage, lovemaking. I was not Franklin, I vowed, I would never be Franklin, sneaking up and down back alleys, telling lies to Joan. And Kelby would never be Joan. He would never play such a game as theirs.

And Rory Flynt? I think he actually tried to help me. We took our clothes off in Greensboro motels. We went to bed and explored every nuance of infidelity. Except in Rory's case, there was no wronged wife back home with a little girl wrapped up in a crocheted afghan. And I knew from the start, gazing at motel neon blinking across the painfully anonymous walls, that I'd have to separate myself from Rory, that we'd go back into our own identities. What I didn't know was that Kelby would separate himself from me when he found out.

But now he had begun by saying, "I don't like the bank. I want to quit." And now he'd work up to Rory and me and those motel rooms. Then he would leave and disappear into the state of California. He would find Brenda, the woman with blue hair, and he would stay with her.

Until that time the scene would be perfectly sealed, snowflakes settling over us all. Inside a glass ball.

AS PERFECTLY SETTLED AND sealed as I used to imagine Sebastian McSherry.

I asked Bobby Spence, "You ever heard of Sebastian McSherry?"

He said, "Sure. I graduated with Old Sabby. Why?"

Bobby Spence grinned at me out of a wide shiny face exactly like Carol Jean's, the same straight black hair and tar eyes, the scribbly mouth. He smelled as fresh as she did, scrubbed up clean. All the Spences smelled that way.

"Old Sabby?" I couldn't stop myself grinning back at Bobby Spence. *Old Sabby?*

"Yeah, that's what we called him. And he liked it. Wouldn't you, if your name was Sebastian?" Bobby grinned more broadly, asked me again, "Why?"

"I don't know." I felt a flush. "Old Sabby," I whispered. I twirled my old chrome-plated baton down the Spences' sidewalk. "Come on," I yelled back to Carol Jean.

I wondered how Old Sabby would smell. Clean and scrubbed up like Bobby? Like a dead cold cigar, maybe. Old Sabby, indeed!

Carol Jean caught up, panting. "Where are you hurrying off to, Ti?"

"Nowhere." I sat on the curb and when Carol Jean sat beside me asked, "How old is Bobby?"

"Twenty-something." Carol Jean picked at a hard scab on her knee. She winced, picked more delicately. "He's graduated. Through with the navy, now, too."

"Don't do that, Carol Jean." I pulled Carol Jean's hand away from the scab. "Has Bobby got a girl?" I balanced the baton on my palm.

Carol Jean studied the flecks of scab under her fingernail a moment. "He's getting married. I'm going to be in it, too. I'm going to be a bridesmaid." She glanced up and waited to see what effect this might have on me.

I made a face, passed the baton to my other hand. "I'm never getting married. I'm just going to have affairs. With all kinds of good-looking men, old ones, too. Old as Bobby."

Carol Jean snorted. "Well, I'm getting married. I'm getting married in a big wedding."

She blew away the flecks of scab and then turned on me her tar-black round eyes, her Buster Brown bangs falling thick as paint over them. "Don't you want to have kids?"

"No."

"Mama's having another baby." Carol Jean was proud of the announcement.

"I know that," I said. "Your brother just got back from the navy and is getting married and you're going to be a bridesmaid in the wedding and your mama's having another baby. How can you stand that? I'd be embarrassed. You're old enough to be its mama yourself!"

Carol Jean sucked in her breath. "Titania," she said, "you don't know anything. You don't have anything, not a brother or a sister. Just you."

"I don't care." I shook my head. "Look, Carol Jean," I changed the subject, inspected all my fingernails, then declared casually, "I'm in love with somebody I never told you about."

Carol Jean straightened, moved closer. "Who?"

"Sebastian McSherry. Old Sabby. Who graduated from Badin High School with Bobby."

Carol Jean cackled, moved away again. "That's the craziest thing I ever heard you say, Ti. You never even saw him before, Ti. You don't even know what he looks like. And besides all that"— Carol Jean slid back closer to me and gazed self-righteously in my face—"Besides all that, Ti, he's too old for you. He is over twenty. You're not but thirteen."

Carol Jean convulsed with her cackles and stamped her feet on the tar and gravel of Barineau Street. Then she leaned closer. "What do you know about being in love anyhow?"

"I know a lot." I shoved Carol Jean away. "You think I don't know? Just shut up."

Carol Jean didn't shut up. She rolled and cackled, her black button eyes tight shut, her clown face crinkled.

"I can't wait to tell Bobby! I can't wait!"

"Tell everybody, tell the whole world!"

I left her still laughing, "Old Sabby! Old Sabby!" I did not venture back around Carol Jean Spence for a long time. Not until Mrs. Spence had the new baby and I went over to see it.

I thought it was hideous. A big bald head, weak neck, ugly sucking lips, and eyes that rolled backwards and sideways. But Carol Jean was as pleased with this new little baby sister as she had been with the grass skirt Bobby brought her.

"See Pam?" she bragged. "See my new little baby sister, see Pam?"

Carol Jean rolled Pam up and down the Badin sidewalks, stopping for people to admire her. She pulled back the blanket so they could get the full effect from bald head to curled toes. Carol Jean beamed while they admired Pam. "Is it a he or a she?" people asked coyly, then protested, "Wait! Let me guess."

Carol Jean loved the game. But the baby was so plain and ineffectual, I was glad it didn't belong to me and Joan Gentry. If Pam had been born to us, I'd have slung her against the side of the apartment.

Any baby I have, I vowed, will not be like Pam Spence. Sebastian McSherry, I promised myself, will bring me beautiful blond babies in picnic baskets, picking them like ripe strawberries from a French meadow and they will all wear little wooden sabots. Sebastian and I and the babies would all drink wine in long green bottles.

"You're jealous," insisted Carol Jean. She pushed Pam's carriage and I twirled my baton alongside. Carol Jean clenched her tongue between her teeth with the effort of keeping the carriage steady over the big cracks in the Badin pavement.

"I am not." I flashed off some brilliant Pancakes, swaggered around and about-faced. The big cracks in the pavement didn't threaten my maneuvers. I went into a wide Figure 8, both feet far apart. "I don't have time to be jealous of you, Carol Jean," I explained. "I'm going to be a fire-baton twirler, a champeen fire-baton twirler."

"You might," Carol Jean admitted crustily, "and you might not."

Pam whimpered. "Okay, baby," Carol Jean soothed her, "don't cry. I'm taking you back home."

"I'll be a champeen fire-baton twirler," I insisted. "You'll see."

Carol Jean bumped the carriage off the curb and started across Barineau Street. Again she admitted, "You might. And you might not."

INSIDE OUR APARTMENT, JOAN Gentry polished her pieces of sterling, Briar Rose. The silver lay in a big gleaming fan on the kitchen table. Joan worked at each spoon, each tine of the forks, with a dark rag and a pot of polish. She glanced at my face.

"What's wrong with you?"

"Nothing. I had a fight with Carol Jean."

I opened a Coca-Cola and sat thumbing its frosted neck, watching Joan work. "I don't think we have anything in common anymore, me and Carol Jean."

Joan rinsed a spoon. "I had a little friend when I lived in South Carolina, near Spartanburg. Did I tell you this before, Titania?"

I shook my head, swigged at the Coca-Cola.

"Mary Crump. I liked to spend the night with Mary Crump as much as I could. Mary Crump's daddy would hold us, me on one knee, Mary Crump on the other, and tell us stories."

Joan dipped the rag in the polish and scrubbed a butter knife. Briar Rose gleamed under her fingers. I watched each petal brighten.

"He had a big moustache, not like Franklin's, but a real old-fashioned handlebar moustache. Do you know what I mean?"

Joan smiled at me, running her rag over the silver handles. On Sunday she would put silver beside our plates and our plates would be on a white cloth with eyelet scallops. Joan always made our table pretty.

I swigged the Coca-Cola and smiled back at Joan. Joan was giving me something here in this little story about Mary Crump, I realized, and it was something I never knew Joan Gentry had to give. The whole thing struck a melancholy, yet proud, feeling.

"He was nice. I liked to lean against Mary Crump's daddy and listen to his voice coming through his shirt. It was deep, and nice, you know. And his handlebar moustache twitched under his nose when he talked, told us those stories. I just loved that."

Joan stopped abruptly. She slapped the table with her rag, left a dark smear on the surface. The Briar Rose clanged against each other.

"I don't even know where Mary Crump is now. I don't even know if her daddy is still alive."

I first thought Joan was going to cry then. But she didn't. And as I sat thumbing the cold Coca-Cola bottle, I understood that, had I ever wanted it, I could have made a good friend out of Joan Gentry. It would have taken some real effort, but I could have done it.

Joan's story was done. She collected her bright silver together, wrapped it in Pacific cloth and closed the drawer.

"I'm leaving you all this sterling, Titania," she assured, turning to smile again. "Briar Rose. Eight place settings. And the serving pieces, too. You will get everything that we have, me and Franklin."

Joan appeared pleased with that. The Briar Rose was valuable and she could give it to me, hand it over like a special power, a definite magic. Joan could count every piece, all the spoons and forks and knives, and be assured they would pass, intact, to her daughter.

She had no doubt her daughter would value the sterling silver as much as she did.

"Ma'am?" I finished the Coca-Cola. "Why don't you have another baby?"

Joan didn't flinch. "There will be no more babies, Titania. Don't ever ask again."

Joan gathered the rag and the polish. "Put that empty Coca-Cola back in the carton on the porch," she said.

I had enough sense at thirteen to see what troubled Joan Gentry. Her story about the one little friend she'd had. Mary Crump and Mary Crump's daddy were not as durable and tangible as the Briar Rose. Mary Crump could be dead, more than likely her daddy was.

But the Briar Rose, ah, now there was something you could count on. Nothing to hurt you. Nothing to die. It stayed right there in the silver drawer, wrapped in Pacific cloth. You could take it out and count it anytime.

And babies? Well, having babies was no guarantee either. You never got what you wanted. Then they grew up into people you never recognized again.

I was thirteen. I knew about people. I knew about sex and falling in love and binding someone to me forever. My little friend rolled her new baby sister around the bumpy streets of Badin. My beautiful angry mother polished her silver spoons.

I had to overcome all of them.

LONGINGS, LONGINGS. BIG-LEAGUE DREAMING. I practiced until the dented baton slipped through my fingers as smoothly as a skein of silk. Joan polished her sterling. She tallied Franklin's paydays, building toward the Betsy Ross spinet she could shove into the alcove and show off and say, "This is Titania's piano. We got it just for her."

I tallied raindrops bouncing on the roof, each clear bead attached to the eaves of the apartment and along the Entwistle Street tree limbs. I gazed for whole afternoons out of my windows across the long backyard to where the raindrops tattooed on the garbage cans.

I gnawed at the baton like a bone.

The awful waiting and the not knowing what the wait might bring drove me crazy. Drove us all crazy, Joan and Franklin and Titania. We wanted pretty much the same things. The things were related, even if nobody knew it yet. Franklin Gentry riffled through his chiropractic cards, went out in the backyard and pitched hard little baseballs. He got drunk. Joan polished silver. She got angry. I practiced arpeggios, practiced twirls, stretching my fingers. I tried hard to be more than just a big girl doing baby things. All this big-league dreaming drove people like us crazy. We were selfish and uncertain people and locked away in our separate agonies.

I looked back from the windows into my room, ran a hand over the smooth beaverboard walls. The first year we lived in that apartment, I'd glued pictures of little girls on the walls of my room, cut them out of the Sears catalog.

The Carolina Aluminum painter came to freshen the Gentry apartment and when he got to my room, he put down his brush, motioned me over.

He pointed at the little girls glued on the walls. "I don't want you to do this no more, honey."

He began tearing them off the wall, their bright skirts, their smiles, the long drools of amber-colored glue that had hardened around their legs. I was fascinated by the way he tore them, hooking a fingernail under their edges.

"When I get your room painted pretty, you better not stick stuff on the walls no more. If you do," he turned and grinned, "I'll come back and get you."

He rolled his eyes.

"This is my room," I said.

"I don't care whose room." He grinned again. He flicked a bright blister of glue off his thumb straight toward me.

"Those are my little sisters," I added.

"I still don't care. You put them back on the wall, I'll come get you." He winked at me.

I liked him winking at me, rolling his eyes. The faintest moustache like tiny fish spines glistened on his lip. I felt like telling him, Hey, my daddy, Dr. Franklin Gentry, has got a big black moustache, bigger than yours. My daddy played big-league baseball. My daddy can give adjustments and knock the hell out of you, if you need it.

There was a lot the painter didn't know.

He didn't leave a shred of the little girls sticking to my walls. Then he loaded his brush and swept creamy new paint across the places they had been. I liked the paint as much as I liked him, the smell of it, the little bubbles riding the sweep of his brush, the bristles of his brush like the spines of his moustache.

"My mother doesn't care if I stick stuff on the walls." I added again, "This is my room."

He just chuckled and swept the walls over and over. After a

while I forgot the little girls. My little sisters. I forgot why I cut them out of the Sears catalog and stuck them up there in the first place. I only wanted to stand and watch the painter sweep his brush.

But when my room was done, all the walls dry and bare as a bone, my bed again under the two six-over-six sash windows, I remembered, before falling to sleep, Those *were* my little sisters. I remembered, too, the painter with his good-looking face I liked, threatening, *You stick stuff on the walls and I'll come back and get you.*

I knew he was a liar.

But I liked it. I felt the painter and his casual threat would keep me from doing bad stuff all my life. He would clump up the stairs to my room, wherever I was, in Badin or anywhere in the whole world. He would scratch off the little girls, hooking a fingernail under their fragile edges, and then masterfully sweep his heavy wet brush over and over.

He would threaten me again, his moustache thin as an eyebrow, a fish spine, again and again. I knew he was a liar. He wouldn't come back to Entwistle Street or to any place I was. But I still liked it. He would keep me good all my life just by making me think about him coming back to get me.

And one day, if I was bad enough, he would show up as promised and hook his fingernail under my own fragile edges and rip me right off the wall.

When that happened, I would thrill straight through from the pain of my casual destruction, the thrill radiating like fish spines. That would be the end of me. Titania Gentry? She's gone, nothing.

BUT THAT WASN'T THE way it was with Kelby and the picnic. He finished off the coffee and when I realized he wasn't going to lie back down on the blanket, I rolled over on my stomach and pushed up.

"What're you going to do, then?" I asked, shading my eyes, squinting up at Kelby. "Are you going to quit?"

This was scary. This was falling off a cliff. This was pulling yourself right off the wall, peeling your skin right off your bones.

I had put everything on Kelby. He took care of me, of Sarah and Hannah. I didn't stay home polishing Gorham silver the way Joan Gentry did. I didn't push my girls to practice a big black York piano. I went down to the *News Gazette* and worked. I went to motels with a red-haired man, Rory Flynt. I indulged myself in sex. Then I came home and I took long baths, made myself beautiful for Kelby. I cooked the best of dinners for him. I showed his children how to be confident and at ease in the world. I felt I had it balanced, under control.

But now he was saying again he didn't like the bank, wanted to quit. I listened to the sounds of Kelby's voice as through a long tunnel, its echoes and reverberations. I didn't separate the sounds into anything else. I was tumbling.

8

After that picnic, Kelby smiled all the time, lazy and yet determined, but nothing cynical. He is making his plans, I realized, with
plenty of accurate forethought but no malice. He'd still said nothing
about Rory Flynt. I didn't know what I was supposed to do. This was
no forbidden fire I longed to twirl at each end of a chrome baton,
the dents flashing bright as stars. This was no Sebastian McSherry I
groomed in my teenage imagination until I actually believed I could
control him. Sebastian, a man impossible to capture, indeed, already
captured by Ginger, a force I didn't reckon and certainly never even
suspected might exist.

Rory Flynt and I bumbled through Greensboro pursuing human
interest stories, fillers and sidelines, taking dozens of pictures that
turned out glossy and trivial. One week we pasted up supermarket
specials, then went out to Safeway or Kroger's and shot ordinary
Guilford County shoppers to add a local flavor. I liked riding in the
tomato-soup Volkswagen with Rory. He cranked open the sunroof.
The sudden shafts of hot light lit up his hair like a corolla, a bright
dahlia, a halo of redemption.

I felt the illumination was a signal to me. So, stepping up to the brink, "You know," I said, "we can't keep on doing what we do. It hurts too much."

"Who?" Rory turned a corner, sending a spray of loose gravel against the low curb. His corona dimmed, the fiery redemption lessened. "Who does it hurt, Ti?"

I considered a moment, then, "Kelby loves me."

Rory shook his head, the last of the red dahlia disintegrated. He didn't look over at me, but he patted the gear knob as if my hand. "He doesn't love you, Ti," he contradicted. "He just doesn't know what to do with you."

It was a shock to hear that. Came right out of the proverbial left field. No warning. A bombshell. Hit like a ton of bricks. And it got worse inside the sunny, bumbling little car. Rory led me through one of the hardest lessons of my life. *He just doesn't know what to do with you.*

He told me a story from his childhood. His birthday party and all the kids coming in through the front door with their little wrapped presents. "And my daddy, the old coot, you see, Ti, he hadn't paid the gas bill and they'd turned it off."

Rory pulled in the Safeway parking lot, switched off the car. "And Mama'd nagged him all week about my birthday party and how the house would be cold as hell and I'd be embarrassed and all my friends coming. And he never said a thing back to her, to me. He just went out and found a big dead tree somewhere in the neighborhood and dragged it up to the yard. I thought he was going to chop it up in logs and we'd have a fire burning for my birthday. I would've liked that. But, you know what?" Rory turned and this time he did pat my hand. "On the day of my party, he dragged it through the front door and across the living room and stuck one end in the fireplace. No ax, no saw. He broke off a few scraggly branches and stripped off some of the dead leaves."

Rory shook his head as he'd done before when I said Kelby loved me. "Daddy just poked the tree in the fireplace and set fire to it. The crazy coot sat there, huddling in his old gray sweats, tending the fire. It smoked pretty bad. The chimney never did draw too good. So the living room was full of smoke and a big tree all across the floor, and my daddy not looking at anybody."

I listened to this. I thought how Rory must have felt, the doorbell ringing and his friends coming. I thought what those kids must have thought seeing his daddy huddling around that tree, one end burning in the fireplace.

"What did you do?" I asked.

Rory drew a long breath, smiled with just a faint regret. "That's just the point here. I asked Mama sort of the same thing, what was she going to do? And she said, 'I don't know what to do with him.' And that was it. We went on and had my birthday party around him and his tree. I blew out candles. I opened presents. Mama cut the cake. Then they all went home. And he was still sitting there poking at the tree. Not looking at anybody. Not saying a damn word."

I felt sorry for Rory Flynt after that story. But it was obvious Rory did not feel sorry for himself. Just bewildered by it still. I gathered up my camera and got ready to get out of the car. "Do you think I'm like that?" I asked him. "Like your daddy?"

"You might be," he said, "to Kelby. He'll go on and work around you and ignore you, maybe." Rory gathered up his own gear, got out of the car and shut the door.

I stood outside and looked at Rory over the top of the tomato-soup Volkswagen. "I don't understand it," I said, "and I think you're wrong."

"Maybe," he said, just like Carol Jean Spence of so long ago, "and maybe not."

Whatever it was Rory was trying to tell me, teach me, I refused to accept any false comfort, his, mine, anybody's. When I got home that afternoon, Kelby was pulling Sarah and Hannah in a red wagon they'd gotten for Christmas, the kind with polished pine slats set in a crib along the rim. The pine gleamed like precious oil in the late sun. Hannah trailed an arm through the slats. Sarah trailed an arm over the slats. I thought how all day I'd been presented with such striking scenes of red and sunlight, cars the color of soup, a man with sun lighting up his fiery hair—and now my children in their wagon, patiently and lovingly pulled by their father. And everywhere the generous sunlight.

Rory Flynt could not compete with this. I did not love Rory. I knew I could go back to the *News Gazette* and work alongside him and never touch him again. I could even get a bad cold again from yanking on the same long light cord. Never make love, never play games, never deceive Kelby or Sarah or Hannah.

I rushed to embrace them all three. Kelby paused in his pulling, smiled in his old familiar lazy way. "How's Rory?" he said. And so I knew.

That night we went out to look at the Perseides showers, rousing the sleepy girls from their beds, much as Joan had once roused me to pursue Franklin through the streets of Badin. They grumbled, then curled together in the backseat of the car as we drove out of the city toward Yanceyville, seeking any wide vistas beyond the interference of harsh lights, out where we could view the meteors. It was the second week of August and the night air was muggy.

Kelby parked the car down a dirt road with cornfields on either side. We climbed on the hood and lay back, scanning the sky. The girls slumbered so peacefully in the backseat, we didn't rouse them anymore. I had about given up on spotting a meteor when just to the right of me, like a bright swift smear, one fell, then another, then a blazing bouquet of them. I sat up, pointed. "Oh, Kelby! Look!"

He nodded, then lifted himself close beside me. We gazed a long time as the stars blossomed and fell all across the sky. And I became aware of the thick fragrance of the cornfields, a heavy greenish sort of smell, rich with earth and health. "Smell the corn?" I asked Kelby. "It smells so strong."

"Yes, it's because the sun's gone down. You can smell things better then. I think the sun saps the smell of things all day. But at night, when it cools off, you can smell everything again."

We sat awhile longer gazing. Kelby spoke softly, firmly, "I know all about it, Ti." I knew what he meant.

"I know," I said. "I'm sorry, Kelby."

We drove back to Greensboro, put the girls back in their beds, and went to bed ourselves. I fell asleep with the smell of the August cornfields still clinging to me, with the bright showers of the Perseides filling my brain, and believed that it had all healed both Kelby and me.

But it ended with him leaving Greensboro. I didn't really know anything more until I got a letter from California. Kelby didn't say for me to come out.

I took the girls to Joan and drove halfway across Tennessee before I realized what I was doing. I pulled off and parked in a rest stop between Nashville and Memphis. The mountains rose all around me and the winds blew like that day at the Battleground.

"I'm out chasing Franklin through Badin," I announced to the mountains. "I'm trying to catch him in something. Just like Joan."

And with that, I turned around and drove back to Badin, some four hundred miles east, pulling in around three A.M., the town sleeping gently and prettily under a late summer night. I slipped upstairs and into bed with my girls, one on either side of me, and fell into the deepest sleep of my life.

The next morning Joan asked, "Well? Why'd you start after him in the first place, Titania?" She slapped pancakes onto her best china plates for me and Sarah and Hannah Joan.

"I don't know," I said. "I thought I could do it. But I can't."

Joan settled into her old place at the table. Her hair, still fresh and blond as Hannah's, floated up in a kind of crown, shorter than the old days, and impressive. I thought of Rory Flynt's red hair, of Kelby's springy curly cushion, then quickly erased the thought. I looked at my mother and envied her, admitted, Well, she's still got her husband and I don't have mine. It troubled me, like a very bad joke. She and Franklin Gentry played games all their married life, sneaked around, laid traps, pursued, accused, and confessed, and still came out intact.

Chasing a man across Tennessee was the most and all I could do. I would do no more than that. It sapped me. I was finished. Instead of a very bad joke, it was, for me, a very bad dream.

IN THE OLD DAYS, Joan Gentry troubled Entwistle Street with screaming nightmares. She let out bloodcurdling yells. Jettie Barefoot, Mr. McSherry, even Madine Ponds across the street, woke up and listened and clutched their sheets to their lips. "God a'mighty! God help! Did you hear that?"

I tried hard not to drop off each night. I waited for Joan's screaming to start. I felt suffocated, buried alive. As the weather grew warmer, stickier, I tried not to sleep at all, afraid Joan would scream me right over the edge into God knows what.

I always fell asleep. Joan always screamed. I woke up, about to scream myself, grabbing at General MacArthur. The little wooden sabots knocked together, fell off the sill. And long after my return to consciousness, my anxiety stayed in bed with me.

I began to sit up in the windows as long as I could, the stars faint as powder over the dark rings of the mountains. Some nights I imagined I could hear things growing out in the dark town. Blades of grass, each individual leaf on the trees. My whole body sprouted antennae. My body listened to the night.

It even listened to itself growing, the ridiculous little titties, pale pubic fuzz, thick braids of brown hair, a little crooked finger. I'm going

114

to rise up, I grinned, listening to my body stir inside, deep warm blood-red sounds, sweet and melancholy and furious. Rise up and break through this apartment and swell up and hang over the whole world, the whole town of Badin, like a big airplane, a parachute.

Sebastian.

That is so stupid, I chided. Sebastian McSherry is off in the war, in the army hospital, already died, probably, already buried, too. Who cares?

I don't care. I tossed General MacArthur to the end of the bed. I don't. I shoved the wooden sabots behind the curtain.

These were the windows that gave me the long view of the back alley. Joan Gentry slept on the other side of the hall from me. I knew how her ash blond hair splashed over the pink satin comforter. I knew how Joan's sleeping shape reflected in the mirror over her dressing table.

Things were peaceful. Badin turned in its orbit. My eyes drooped. My hands relaxed. Then I heard Franklin Gentry whistling through the back alley, singing like he thought he was all of the Mills Brothers put together, four guys and a guitar on that blue Decca label, adding little special flourishes to his favorite song of theirs, adding, indeed, I fancied, little special flourishes to the middle of the night.

"Oh, baby! I'm gonna buy a paper doll to call my own!" Then his little sly rhyme, "Not like you, Joan! But one all mine!"

His voice threaded a bright path through my screen. It rushed right through my ears, then back out the screen, melting into the big sky over Badin. I stared down at the alley until I picked out Franklin bumping into light poles, trampling on people's gardens, stumbling over boxwood hedges.

I decided to go downstairs and let Franklin in the front door. He would stumble down the alley, circle the length of the quadruplex. He would come back around to Entwistle Street and parade down the middle of it. I knew the routine.

115

Joan had locked him out before we went to bed. "Let him get back in the best way he can, Titania," she declared. Her satin gown rustled up the stairs. I watched it float away like a bright pool of silver.

I envied Joan her gown. I wanted to sleep in a silver gown, too.

By the time I got downstairs, rippling my fingers across the banisters, unlocked the front door and stepped out, I heard Franklin whistle around Jettie Barefoot's end of the quadruplex. He puffed and whistled and tossed off more little flourishes of the Mills Brothers. "I must've had a million dolls or more! I've played the doll game o'er and o'er!"

I noticed how warm the porch floor was under my bare feet. I had expected it to be cool.

He kept on, "I'm through with all of them! I'll never fall again! Hey! Joan, here's what I'm gonna do!"

But what could he do?

I stood with my nose pressed to the screen, my fingers ready to lift the latch when he got close enough to me, maybe an inch. He made it up the two flights of wooden steps. I was proud of him for that. Then, just as Franklin Gentry put out a hand to take hold of the screen, and just as I tightened my fingers to lift the latch, just as our two faces came within an inch on either side of the screen door, upstairs, right directly over us, Joan Gentry let loose her most horrendous scream, loud enough to crush bone.

Our two bodies thrown off a ten-story building couldn't have made a more thundering impact than her scream. Joan's scream fell down over us and drowned us together, tore off our arms and legs, raised every hair on our heads.

Franklin jumped backward the whole two flights of steps and collapsed flat on his back, gasping like a fish there in Entwistle Street. I shook, my skin prickling into goose bumps and my heart jackknifing.

Joan screamed and screamed. Then I heard the bedsprings creak

116

as she turned over, mumbled something and fell away into quiet sleep, for the moment purged and healed.

Franklin lay in the street a long time, gasping, staring into the Badin sky. And then Erskine "Sonny" Kelly's old dog Toto, on a nightly reconnaissance, clattered down Entwistle Street, straight up to Franklin Gentry's side and barked in his face. Toto nosed Franklin, raised a leg and peed on him in the middle of the street, scratched backward a big shower of tar and gravel and growled.

I waited for a hundred years, I thought, on the porch. The box-wood hedges of Badin could have grown to cover the apartment roof, my teeth fallen out, my braids turned gray, before Franklin got up again. But he did get up and he climbed the steps, wet, pale, sober.

I unlatched the screen.

And as he passed by me, unseen in the porch shadows, I felt a big compassion for my father, selfish and ridiculous as he was. I wondered if people ever pointed him out on the streets of Badin, *Franklin Gentry, Boston Red Sox, he's that rubbing doctor, you know, the kind that knocks you around and fixes cricks in your neck.*

If I was going to keep these people good, as effectively as that painter with the moustache threatened to keep me good, I needed help. I needed Old Sabby. And I'd given up on him. His wounds and bloody bandages, the way he limped in and out of my dreams, the way the straps of his helmet hung down against the hair of his chest, his bare arms tattooed with snakes. All that had faded. Now I had no dreams, sitting in my windows, listening for Joan to scream.

Sebastian McSherry?

"Shit," I snubbed General MacArthur, "soldiers are liars, like the painter who tore those little girls off my wall."

Shit, people don't show up. They promise you everything, they expect you to be good, and then they don't show up. They tear pictures off the wall. They push you over cliffs.

9

Near the end of May, I began practicing my baby piece for Miss Beaupine's spring recital. Just as I predicted, I'd gotten a baby piece. There I was, a big grown girl playing a baby piece in front of the whole world.

"The Song of the Bobolink" tinkled up and down the big black York, full of bright trills. I gave myself to it, pulled the best music I could out of the bowels of Jettie's piano. *Oh, little bobolink, please sing! Long and sweet your merry notes must ring!*

What was a bobolink, anyhow? Who ever heard of a bobolink in Badin? No matter, I sang with the York, thumping and bouncing on the bench. The old piano bubbled. I felt happy, generous, grateful, perfect. I was a player of big-league pianos. I would be, I knew, a twirler of big-league fire batons.

Then, as easily as one octave dissolves into another, as one clear octave pitched higher or lower, just as the merest progression between C and D, do and re, I summoned a man straight through the apartment wall and into my arms.

There came the clump of heavy boots next door. A low hoarse "Hello, Daddy? Where are you, old man?"

The bobolink shut up, my fingers fused to the keys, the little hammers trembled inside the York. Pure as air, pure as fire burning, pure as aluminum poured in the potrooms, *Old Sabby!* The back of my neck prickled. Warmth flooded through my stomach, grabbed hold of me and held on. My toes curled.

"Old Sabby, is that you?" I looked straight into the notes of Miss Beaupine's bobolink propped on the piano. *If you don't be good, I'll come back and get you.*

"Old Sabby, that *is* you."

Mr. McSherry began to caterwaul, hurrying down his stairs and, I imagined, jerking out his filthy plaid handkerchief, snuffling tears, mopping his rheumy eyes.

The floors of both apartments shook.

That is you!

I grinned, feeling my mouth spill into my ears, and then I pounded out my recital piece with new energy, trilling every bobolink note. I sang and bubbled over like boiling in a kettle. I was a migratory songbird. I sported garish plumage. So what if it was a baby piece? I'd make it sound better than it was, more difficult and more valuable.

Joan came to the kitchen door. "Are you sure it goes like that, Titania?"

I grinned, lifted my fingers pertly from Jettie Barefoot's keyboard, and waggled them at Joan. "You bet!" I said. "It goes just like that."

My song flew through Badin, from apartment to apartment, up Pomona Hill through all the French Colonial bungalows, out on the country club golf course, down under Badin Lake. I commanded armies. Ordered conquests. And at the finale, I stood, a resplendent grande dame on a golden stick, a flaming baton. Old Sabby was back. I had brought him.

But I didn't see his face for real for another day. I stood with an ear against the apartment wall, straining to catch all his words, his noises, his body movements. The low hoarse tones of Sebastian

McSherry struck my fertile ear, vibrated my tympanic membrane. They swirled like warm, fragrant and exotic oils through my cochlea, semicircular canals, eustachians.

He thrilled me.

His tones mixed with Mr. McSherry's ugly shrill ones, peeled them apart, combed and smoothed them. I, too, felt peeled, combed, and smoothed. I paced down the stairs, up again, back down, fondling the little sabots in my pocket, stopping at the top landing to twirl a perfect Figure 8, march smartly in place, one, two, three, four, and *Halt!* giving the sassiest of majorette parade salutes.

General MacArthur looked on, glum and holy as ever. "What do you know?" I sneered at him. "Who do you think you are? You don't even have a dick. Don't tell me what to do anymore."

Old Sabby still had his dick, I bet. I saluted and smiled, then back down the stairs, up again, while I imagined big bands played. Big American flags unfurled, snapped in the Badin wind, and big shiny planes roared by, dipping their aluminum wings.

I kept this up, grinning and looking stupid, until Joan demanded, "What are you doing? What are you grinning about? Titania Gentry, what have you done behind my back?"

"Nothing," I said, adding, "Ma'am," my grin breaking out again.

That evening I hurried over to Barineau Street to brag to Carol Jean Spence. She wasn't impressed. "Did you get to see him, Ti? Is he as cute as Bobby?"

Carol Jean's clown face infuriated me. Her questions actually hurt.

"No. What do you mean 'as cute as Bobby'?"

"Well," Carol Jean dismissed Sebastian altogether, "if you didn't get to see him, you don't know if he's as cute as Bobby Spence is."

I stared. "Carol Jean," I threw out, "Bobby Spence is not cute. And if he was, I would hope and pray Old Sabby wasn't."

"Oh, shut up," Carol Jean said. "Let's go downtown and get an Eskimo Pie at the Olympia Cafe, okay? Have you got any money?"

"No. But I'll pay you back."

As we went out, I called to Bobby Spence, "Hey, guess what? Old Sabby's home from the paratroopers."

"That right? Old Sabby? You better watch out, then. Old Sabby'll get you!"

Bobby grinned like Carol Jean, a generous clown, scrubbed up and healthy to the core. And without an idea in his head of how deep down inside he had just thrilled me. *Old Sabby'll get you!*

Erskine "Sonny" Kelly was not so thrilled or generous. We ran into him at the Olympia, lounging in a booth, sucking at a Coca-Cola.

"What the shit you care about a guy like that?" he sneered. "Just because he lives next door to you, Ti. That's all."

Then he slid up closer to me. "He's probably already married anyhow. Those old guys are always already married."

"I don't care about him," I said. "I don't give a shit. And he's not already married, either." I pretended to scan the bar lined with slippery orange stools. The stools twirled on their shiny pedestals the way the old baton twirled in my fingers.

I looked for Hootchie. I wanted to point him out to both Sonny and Carol Jean. Maybe swagger around in front of him, do a few twirls.

"That's not what you told me." Carol Jean took the Eskimo Pies out of the freeze box, paid the man behind the counter. With a look of mild reproach, she handed one to me. "You just got through telling me, Ti, you were in love with him."

"Shut up." I peeled the Eskimo Pie.

Sonny Kelly sucked up the last of his Coca-Cola, pulled the paper cone out of the black plastic holder and flicked it at me. Tiny shards of ice stung me. A bigger lump slid down my shirt, trickled between my two blind nubs of titties. "I hate you," I said.

"Well," he said, "I'm coming down there tomorrow to your house. We'll smoke a cigarette or something. Mess around. We can shoot the .22."

"No, you will not." I followed Carol Jean out of the cafe. "I got to practice my recital piece tomorrow. All day."

"You ought to be ashamed," said Carol Jean, biting her Eskimo Pie.

"I don't care," I snapped. "I hate you, too, and I don't care what I do anymore."

We munched through the mild May evening, watching Badin settle down, curl up and go to sleep. Streetlights eased on. Dogs yawned. Carol Jean and I walked along, glancing at lighted windows, catching pieces of cozy conversation through opened apartments. Badin sounded healthy, satisfied with itself.

I chewed the stick of the Eskimo Pie. The splinters tasted thin and sour. "See you," I left Carol Jean at the corner.

In bed, I took out General MacArthur. "You get one more chance." I examined his broken nose, imperial eyes, neutered sex. I put an ear to his chest and listened for Sebastian McSherry to speak.

I woke hours later out of a wild dizzying dream where the Olympia Cafe's jukebox bubbled in my ears and Erskine "Sonny" Kelly laughed at me. He pointed between my legs where there was nothing but a blank place, limp as sawdust, while Carol Jean Spence in a grass skirt sniffed, "You ought to be ashamed."

I woke to another sound, a low growling snuffling noise behind my head. I sat straight up, the sheets pinched in my fingers. A quick hoarse snort. Some softer snarlings. Then the low growling started again.

I grinned, rubbed the sheets over my face and giggled until I choked. I jumped up and stood on my bed and pressed my naked throbbing ear to the wall.

Sebastian McSherry, the paratrooper, Old Sabby, was snoring.

KELBY DID NOT LEAVE us for Brenda, the woman with the California blue hair, the exotic hair with gold wings and rose wings in it, but mostly blue, as Sarah had described years after.

Kelby just left. Made a quiet departure, no traps, no confrontations. He'd always had a mystery about him. A vague dissatisfaction with something. My affair with Rory Flynt, perhaps, though not the real root of this, certainly brought it to the fore. I had behaved like Franklin. Kelby, however, had not and never would behave like Joan. If Rory was right, saying Kelby didn't know what to do with me, then Kelby's leaving might have been the proof.

But I couldn't admit it. I never have. I refused to blame anything or anybody. I refused myself any false comfort. My parents, my girls, nobody can put a finger on anything. All they know is Kelby just cleared out.

My mother said, "Well, he must not've loved you and the kids very much." She didn't mean to sound so superior and insulting. That was Joan's way. I smiled at her. She stood watering the azaleas and the spray shot around in rainbows, cool and smelling like cut grass. "What're you going to tell Sarah and Hannah?"

"There's no point in telling Sarah and Hannah anything right now. They don't know what's going on," I said. "Just leave it like that."

"Well, you got to tell them something." She placed a thumb on the nozzle, making wider and finer spray. "I mean, sometime."

I collected the girls and drove to Greensboro, through the rolling back country of Davidson County, Randolph, Guilford. We crossed over a long trussed bridge and the sun winked through the girders and off the muddy Yadkin River below. I thought about my drive through Tennessee, heading for the Mississippi River I'd never seen. Now I'd never see it. I'd never go to California and bring back Kelby. He went there. Let it be. I can make no apologies for me, for him. I got through it. Kelby, too.

Sarah and Hannah went to sleep in the backseat. I remembered how peacefully they had slept when Kelby and I drove out and parked in the cornfields and looked at the meteor showers. I remembered the heavy fragrance of the corn, the earth, the hot August.

Somehow I felt peaceful again, even though I had just lost Kelby, good-humored, handsome, gentle and splendid Kelby, the father of the children curled behind me.

I let him go. And despite the very acute and often returning pain, I loved something about that letting go. Like it was an aria in an opera Kelby and I were destined to finish together, some big scenario, some efficient and important acting-out, both of us rushing on stage at the last minute, throwing roses and daggers, swooning to the ground.

I thought of his father falling from the catwalk in Roanoke Rapids. His mother Sarah pining away on the fainting-couch. His brother Vincent. These were once my people. Now no more. They belonged now exclusively to my daughters.

I hated it, too. It was hard and real and natural as an avalanche. No prowling around Badin with Joan in an old black Ford looking for Franklin Gentry. That was soap opera, that was vaudeville, appropriate for them.

This thing with me and Kelby, with, I allowed, Rory Flynt, though I'd never see either one again, was something so exquisite and awful, my mind couldn't frame it at one time. I had to deal with it in little pieces, like Sarah and Hannah playing with Tinkertoys.

A big silence opened around me as I crossed the Yadkin River bridge. A silence as flat and deep as the water below us.

You always do your worst living by yourself.

DEEP INSIDE BADIN, NORTH Carolina, Old Sabby snored. I loved every syllable, every snort and snarl. I sucked it through the beaverboard wall as I stood on the bed, my arms and legs hanging out of light plisse pajamas, the elastic sagging around my waist.

Behind me the organdy recital dress billowed from a hook on the door. A silly little bridal gown, white and frothy as meringue. Not something a grown girl ought to be wearing in public. My black patent shoes, polished up with Vaseline, gleamed on the floor. "Nothing puts a gleam on patent leather," Joan pointed out, "like plain Vaseline."

I'd been ready for Miss Beaupine's piano recital, resigned to playing a baby piece in front of everybody. I would try to make it sound elegant and difficult. But after I stood on my bed half the night, soaking up the vivid snoring of Sebastian McSherry, I lost "The Song of the Bobolink." Old Sabby blasted it out of my system and left my fingers as stiff as matches. I'd have dropped the chrome baton had I tried to twirl.

No matter, I fell deeper in love with Sebastian snoring on the other side of the apartment wall, my big ear warming it up. With his jagged face and steely eyes, his broken nose and bloody bandaged head, Sebastian had limped home to bed on the other side of my wall. And there he snored with abandon. Suddenly, I loved my life.

The next morning I tried to play my baby piece. My fingers fumbled on Jettie Barefoot's keys. Joan stood over me, frowning. "What are you doing? Can't you play your piece? What's wrong with you, Titania?"

Music had left me. A cruel trade-off had occurred. I'd finally gotten Sebastian McSherry home from the paratroopers, but I'd lost my baby piece. I showed a sick face to Joan Gentry. "I don't know what's wrong with me."

I kept on fumbling and trying until time to go to school for the last day of the seventh grade. There I sat at my desk and watched the streets outside. I watched for Sebastian to come out of Mr. McSherry's apartment. I would know him. I would. Just as I would know "The Song of the Bobolink" again.

Sebastian never showed himself until three o'clock, when I walked home with Carol Jean Spence, both of us holding our report cards, Carol Jean prattling about going to junior high school next year, being in the eighth grade.

"You can go out for majorette with the band, Ti," she said.

"I'm not a majorette, for God's sake. I'm a baton twirler."

"It's the same thing," said Carol Jean, "and they have those white satin uniforms and white boots."

I shook my head, but before I could object, I don't want white satin, I want red sequins all over me tight as my skin, wicked as Hootchie's tattooed snakes, Carol Jean asked, "Aren't you nervous about the recital tonight? I'd be nervous. I bet you are, too."

"How could I get nervous? It's just a baby piece." I flexed my crooked little finger. The bobolink would return, yes, fly right back down into my blood and muscle.

"Well, I'd be nervous," admitted Carol Jean. "I wouldn't like getting up on stage in front of all those people and playing a piano. Even if it is just a baby piece."

"Well, I'm not nervous." I set my chin harder. I was sicker than a dog and definitely nervous. Tonight I had to walk down the long corridor of Badin School, enter the auditorium, pass through the audience, climb to the stage and seat myself at the piano and deliver, unerringly, the merry notes of that cursed bobolink, a baby piece. A grown girl, just promoted to the eighth grade, playing a baby piece and wearing baby clothes.

Carol Jean waved good-bye at the corner of Barineau Street, wished me luck. "Oh, goddammit, shit!" I stumbled on down Entwistle Street, squinting tears and gritting my teeth so hard, I never noticed Sebastian sitting on the porch with Mr. McSherry, sitting in the swing beside his old stale dried-up daddy, dwarfing him.

Never noticed until Mr. McSherry yelled, "Hey, Ti! You remember my grown son in the paratroopers?"

Mr. McSherry properly embarrassed me. I could smell his cigar from the sidewalk. "Well, Ti, this here's him! Come here and say hey. I'm not lying, neither."

A slow red wave swamped me. There was no part of me it didn't color. I wanted to go kill that old man, embarrassing me.

I went, nevertheless. I pulled open Mr. McSherry's porch screen door and looked Old Sabby full in the face, red as I was.

"Titania Gentry," said Mr. McSherry proudly, "this is my son, Sebastian. What did I tell you? What did I say?"

I grinned. "Hey."

Sebastian sat in the swing with one arm slung over Mr. Mc-Sherry. The other arm he had propped under his chin. *Old Sabby.* Old Sabby sprawled over that swing and over the whole porch until he filled it all up, I felt, every inch with health and power. Filled it up until there was not a whole lot of air left for me to breathe.

He was not pretty. He was not blond. His blue eyes burned like asterisks in the shade of the porch. He was better than General MacArthur, better than Franklin with his dark moustache, better than Erskine "Sonny" Kelly, better, even, than Hootchie with tat-tooed snakes on both arms.

I was so pleased. I stood there, and I drank him in.

"Hey," he returned. His voice was as hoarse as I'd expected from all the snoring. He noticed my report card. "What grade are you in, Sister?"

"Eighth grade. Next year." I handed him the card, appalled I did it so easily.

He glanced the card over, nodded, and handed it back. "Not dumb, are you, Sister?"

"Not dumb," I agreed, lifting my chin a little. I hoped it had some of Joan Gentry's firm beauty in it. I deepened both dimples.

"No, not dumb a bit." Sebastian gave the swing a push. I went all funny inside, feeling imposed on but liking it. The easy half-love, half-hate I sometimes felt toward Sonny Kelly. The familiarity star-tled me just a little, then I ignored it.

"I got to go. My mother makes me practice the piano a whole hour."

"That's the truth," affirmed Mr. McSherry. "A whole blessed hour she bangs on that thing."

He gave two heavy syllables to the word blessed, the way some old people do when they pretend profanity. *Bles. Sed.* I hurried away to our apartment, the sound of Sebastian's laughter flooding behind.

"Do you know your piece any better? Has it come back to you?" Joan demanded as I ran in.

I pushed by her and upstairs to the bathroom, where I blasted on the cold water and splashed big sparkling gouts all over myself. I drenched my blouse, my braids, making a mess on the floor. Joan came in and ordered me to quit it.

"I've got to roll your hair, Titania."

"I can't stand for you to do that. Just let it hang down loose. Straight down, loose and plain."

"Don't be silly. You don't have hair hanging down straight and plain for a piano recital. Come on, sit down here."

I had to sit on the toilet lid. Joan unloosed each braid, brushing out my long brown hair. Joan divided it into little strands, wet each one and rolled it on her big metal curlers. She turned them sideways so I'd have springy curls, not a smooth pageboy. I'd be, according to her plan, Shirley Temple, not June Allyson. Not an urchin. Not Dorothy Lamour with a sarong.

"You're going to look pretty, Titania," she promised. "Your hair and your dress. Everything will be pretty."

While looking pretty, being pretty, was not one of my major goals, right then I really wanted to believe her. It seemed so silly and so innocent and so without danger. I went down to the York and stretched my fingers, warming them. I whispered sweet things to them, kissed them, bit them.

But the bobolink had flown.

Joan stood in the kitchen door. "Titania Gentry," she warned, "if you don't get up on that stage and play your piece tonight, I'm going to be mad as hell."

I wanted sympathy, kisses. Joan gave no sympathy, and she had never kissed me much. When Franklin came for supper, she told him, "Titania can't play her recital piece. She's overlearned it, or something. It won't come back to her now. She's going to make a fool out of herself tonight."

"Oh," said Franklin, looking into the living room where I still sat in front of the York, striking the keys, unable to conjure up the simplest scale, the easiest arpeggio.

"Oh," he said again, "is she?" He snickered.

Franklin loved having Joan thwarted in this way. There'd be no big-league piano recitals for her to gloat over tonight. White organdy dresses and shoes polished up with Vaseline wouldn't change it, either. And after all she had put us through, too, him and me, Franklin was delighted.

But after supper, he came upstairs to my room, knocked. "Hey," he said. "Here's something for you, Ti Baby."

He dropped a little corsage on my bed. Pink rosebuds and some dark fern tied with pink ribbon, finished off with a pearl-headed pin.

I held it to my nose, and smiled. "Thank you. This is the first corsage I ever had in my life."

"I can't go to that thing, Ti Baby." Franklin raised his brows. "I got some people coming for an adjustment. You know."

I nodded, "It's okay," and sucked up the fragrance of the rose-buds, the faint bitterness of the fern, the tang of Franklin's bourbon breath. He slipped away, relieved.

Joan dressed me, pulling the crisp organdy over me, slapping my hands when I tried to scratch. She tied the long white sash.

"I'm going to sit on that sash," I reminded her. "I'm going to step on it and fall when I get up on the stage. And I know it'll get wrinkled before I even get out there to play. We have to sit in Miss Beaupine's music room until it's our turn. I'll sit on that sash and wrinkle it. I'll step on it and fall."

"No, you won't, Titania," said Joan. "You just remember to brush it out of the way before you sit down, just a little graceful brush. You hear me, Titania? You just remember to arrange it. You won't step on it, either. You will not fall down, Titania. I mean it. Look at me."

Joan Gentry gazed steadily into my eyes, then took down the curlers and brushed my hair into long soft curls. I felt a cloud floating over my shoulders. I hated the occasional glamour it represented. This was not me. This was not my regular hair. Only my green eyes looked the same. And my crooked finger. I kissed my special ugly little finger, *Help me, I'm thirteen years old, and she's making me look like a bride doll!*

"Now," Joan pinned Franklin's corsage to my shoulder. The fern tickled my ear lobe. The fragrance drifted over me again and I felt momentarily comforted. I felt "The Song of the Bobolink" might live again.

If only Old Sabby might come over and kiss me right now, I thought, kiss me right on the mouth. Walk me down the corridor to the stage and hold out my sash. Save me in front of all those people. *Not dumb a bit, are you, Sister?*

I shuddered.

Joan took me into her bedroom and sat me before the dressing table mirror. Bottles and powder boxes covered the table. A little picture of Titania as a baby gleamed there, my dark fuzz coaxed into a kewpie curl, my eyes round as Carol Jean Spence's.

Joan turned me about and inspected. "Just this, I think is what you need, Titania, just a little color." She picked up a lipstick, unscrewed it, daubed toward me.

"Don't," I pulled back. "I can do it myself." And I took the tube from Joan.

"Okay, good." Joan turned me back from the mirror and inspected again. "Yes, now you look real pretty!"

I looked at myself. She curled and daubed and frocked me in organdy. Thirteen years old and still she made me a little girl. Joan's little movie star. Joan's little champeen piano player.

131

I've got titties starting! I wanted to shriek. I know how to smoke a cigarette, for God's sake! And this is what you do to me!

In a sudden spate of courage, I asked her, "Why are you doing this to me?" But Joan had gone downstairs.

"Good-bye, good-lookin'!" whistled Franklin.

Joan shut the door hard. "Probably tie one on good while we're gone. Probably get drunk as a lord."

I wanted to get drunk as a lord, too.

I walked stiff and dumb down Entwistle Street. The late evening air fell over Badin, softening the edges of roofs and eaves. I tried to look as soft and appealing as the air felt. Joan brushed at the dress, muttering advice, "You remember to brush away that sash."

I gritted my teeth and walked with my fingers pressed together in an attitude of prayer, thinking, This kind of thing kills me. I tried to smile, sneak a look at Sebastian's porch. It was dark. I couldn't see his sprawling figure. Couldn't smell his health and power up there still laughing at me, *Not dumb a bit, are you, Sister?*

I needed a fire baton. The roar of crowds in coliseums, every tier ringing with my name, *Titania Titania Titania.*

At the entrance to Badin School, Joan reminded me again, "Whatever you do, Titania, don't stop in the middle of your piece. Keep going. When you get on the stage, make up something if you have to. But keep going."

"Yes, ma'am." I tried to give Joan a winning smile.

Miss Beaupine greeted her performers with warm little kisses, holding them at arm's length to admire the girls' dresses, the crisp suits and ties on the boys. The boys pulled at their collars. I was the oldest and biggest one, the only teenager among them, and I'd never felt so out of place.

"Now, children," said Miss Beaupine, "before we begin our recital, we want to say a little prayer. Bow your heads."

And while Miss Beaupine prayed, I bargained shamelessly, God, if you just give me "The Song of the Bobolink" back, I will not ask for anything else as long as I live. I swear.

Except for one thing. I want to hold Old Sabby in my arms and kiss him on the mouth. But first let me do this thing tonight without messing up.

"Amen," said Miss Beaupine and we sat down in the music room, smelling her old-maid perfume, and waited. The school auditorium didn't have wings for entrances and exits to its stage, actually, just a raised platform across one end of a long assembly room. So we had to wait our turn to walk down the corridor, cross through the people, climb on stage, and play our pieces.

I sweated inside the white dress. The tips of Franklin's corsage kept tickling my ear lobe and its sweetness began to make me sick. Here I am, a big grown girl playing a baby piece. I'm a big grown girl who can't even remember how to play a baby piece.

My turn.

I walked the black corridor, smelling chalk and pencils from the classrooms on either side, and entered the bright grotto of staring faces. I saw Carol Jean, Joan, Sue Kelly, and Erskine "Sonny" Kelly, their faces like goofy familiar moons.

I mounted the stage.

I watched my Vaselined black patent shoes climb the steps and I petitioned God again, shamelessly, Turn me into a striptease dancer on a runway, let me wear a G-string and spin pasties in the face of everybody sitting out there staring, if you want to, God. Let me play this one shitty little baby piece and be done.

I stared at the keys. I lifted somebody's cold hands, not mine, over the keys. I glanced quickly at the front row where Miss Beaupine sat smiling at me. She raised her soft brows, smiled more insistently. I thought her lips trembled. I thought her right hand, folded in her soft lap, gestured, Start! Darling, Titania, start!

I knew now I very definitely stood on the brink of something.

On a runway, maybe. At a crossroads. Things were gathering to barrel down on me alone, one grown girl the target. And as I sat waiting for impact, miserable, my two silent hands poised over the keys, I became aware of a big healthy body sprawled not two seats away from Miss Beaupine.

And next to him, I caught the unmistakably sensuous and boneless shape of a hussy. Hadn't I seen enough of them through the lighted apartment windows of Badin, after all, to recognize one? Thirteen years of hussy-hunting had made me an expert.

The stage lights bounced in my eyes and I blinked hard, frowning directly into the audience. I thought I saw the flip of bosoms, the twist of hips, but that was impossible. This was Miss Beaupine's piano recital, and no hussies could get in here. Isn't that right?

I frowned. Old Sabby? What's he doing at my piano recital sitting next to a hussy? *See him in there? Look. That's your daddy, Titania.*

Fury boiled inside my organdy and wilted the fern in my corsage. I suddenly stood back up, yanked out my long wrinkled sash and spread it hot as a comet's tail over the piano bench.

I heard a soft collective sigh flood through my audience, as right then *goddammit, shit!* the brink barreled toward me and dissolved. Titania Anne Gentry gritted her teeth, flexed both dimples, and muttering *Not dumb a bit, Sister! Not dumb a bit!* released the merry notes of the bobolink loud and clear from every finger she had.

When the last arpeggio bounced from the back of the auditorium, I stood and bowed, descended and exited through the applauding people, looking neither right nor left, my crooked little finger pulsing as bright as the Olympia Cafe neon, *Not dumb! Not dumb! Not dumb!*

10

Sarah and Hannah noticed Kelby was gone in different ways. Sarah suddenly got jealous of everything Hannah did or said or had. It came out in murderous little attacks. They were calmly playing with puzzles and I was lounging on the sofa making notes when Sarah grabbed a pencil off the coffee table. A pencil I'd just sharpened to a terrible point. She jabbed it into Hannah, piercing Hannah's left ear lobe, just missing her eye.

I jumped off the sofa and smacked Sarah, whisking Hannah to the bathroom and some merthiolate. Her ear never bled, but the merthiolate stained her ear and her cheek for weeks.

"Why'd you do that?" I yelled at Sarah.

She just sat there on the floor, still jabbing the pencil, this time into the braided rug we had, a rug Kelby got on sale at Sears.

"Sarah!" I demanded. "Look at me!"

She fixed me with a hateful stare. She never said a word.

Hannah responded in like violence. But her violence wasn't addressed to Sarah. She addressed our whole house. I'd find piles of Kleenexes shredded across the floor. Boxes of Sugar Pops dumped into the heating vents. It was as if Hannah wanted to destroy the site. She ignored the people.

One night I woke up to find Hannah piling every can of Campbell's Soup, Chef Boy-ar-Dee, and Chicken of the Sea in bed with me. She was cleaning out the kitchen larder. I just lay there, the cans rolling down the coverlet, clanking off to the floor, denting. I listened to Hannah's little feet padding down the hall, out to the kitchen, back to me.

My girls were mad as hell.

For myself, I raged and cried, my anger and my grief as pure as a candle flame, perfectly pointed against a black night. I left the *News Gazette* and got a job with *The Greensboro Pilot,* working my way up toward Feature Editor. Sometimes I saw Rory Flynt on assignments. He was always friendly, helpful. Nothing unpleasant. He knew Kelby had left. He said nothing. I thought, well, despite all my trouble, I really did have a sort of good luck in choosing men. They didn't hurt me. Were gentlemen. *Gentlemen.* I raged anew over that word. I'm sure I put the same emphasis on it as Joan Gentry.

But it was indeed true. Both Rory Flynt and Kelby were gentlemen. I lost one, and did not love the other. It continued to annoy and needle me.

Then, as abruptly as Kelby going off to California, one day I moved us south to Lake Waccamaw where I took over a little Columbus County paper and started stringing for the Wilmington and Raleigh papers. It was okay. It's still okay. I like what I do. I've got awards and commendations all over the walls of my office in Whiteville.

For years I dreamed of meeting Kelby, of getting a phone call from him, and in each dream I ask him, "What're you doing in California, Kelby?"

And in each dream he replies, "Working for Wells Fargo."

Then I'd be so mad, I'd want to kill Kelby, raging and cursing in my dream, pounding him, banging the phone against the wall. "But you said you didn't like the bank, Kelby!" I'd try to reason with him. "You said you wanted to quit, Kelby!"

It took me awhile to understand the significance of this dream. Kelby didn't leave the bank—he left me.

Actually, not to refashion the old truths here, Kelby runs a land-scaping service in California, plants green spaces for malls and hospitals, even for Wells Fargo.

But that dream of Kelby leaving our North Carolina bank for a California bank gave me years of exquisite torment. It's the dreams, the stories, that keep you stuck, even when you need them.

THE CRISP THWACK OF my mallet on the croquet ball accented my perfect secret torment. Carol Jean winced. I'd knocked her ball down to the ditch at the end of Entwistle Street.

"That's not fair!" Carol Jean threw down her mallet. Her clown smile soured on me.

"Well, go get it, then. Put it down anywhere you want, back up here. Put it right up here at the goal! Shit, I don't care." I surrendered generously.

The game was mine. I could knock Carol Jean Spence's croquet ball ten miles, if I wanted. And with reckless fury, too. Carol Jean knew that. Our game, though, was wrecked.

"What are you so mad about?"

"What are *you* so mad about?" I mocked her.

"I'm mad because you're mad, Ti. Every time I come over here, you boss me around and knock my croquet ball too hard and holler at me."

Carol Jean put her hands on her hips, drew herself up. She reminded me of Joan Gentry. "I'm going home," she said. "I'm not sticking around anymore."

"Go home, then. I don't want you sticking around."

Carol Jean stalked back to Barineau Street. She didn't bother to retrieve the croquet ball, so I fished it out of the ditch that was running full after a night of heavy June showers. The water was glassy cold and numbed my fingers around the ball.

I piled the mallets under the front yard trees and as I began tugging up the wickets, I heard hammering in Mr. McSherry's kitchen. That old man never lifts a finger to do anything, I smirked. It's Sebastian.

I tugged the last wicket and threw it under the trees, then sneaked under Mr. McSherry's kitchen window.

"Looking for something, Sister?"

Sebastian sat on top of a ladder and hammered at the cupboard. He could see me perfectly, though I crouched under a lobelia bush full of thick blossoms.

Sister. Nobody called me Sister. I liked it, the easiness it opened between us. *Sister.*

"Yeah. A croquet ball. An orange one. Did you see it?"

He hammered quick steady strokes. "I thought you only banged on the piano, Sister. Not on croquet balls, too. Huh, Sister?"

The blush swamped over me again. The bees in the lobelia bush bumped my head. Probably smelling how embarrassed I was. I sat back on my haunches.

"I don't bang on the piano all the time." I drew deeper breath, fluttering the blossoms. "I twirl a baton. That's what I am, a baton twirler."

"Oh," said Sebastian, never missing his stroke. "Well, Sister, that is real interesting. A baton twirler. A baton twirler right here in old Badin, North Carolina."

He sounded as impertinent and exasperating as Franklin Gentry. As know-it-all as Erskine "Sonny" Kelly. But I kept on, even agreed with him.

"Yeah, really. I can twirl good."

Old Sabby stopped hammering. He shifted around to inspect the cupboard. He pressed on the shelving, clicked his teeth. "Rotten as all hell. I got to replace every one."

He laid down the hammer and took out cigarettes.

The way Old Sabby smoked fascinated me. Not the same as Franklin smoking. Or Erskine "Sonny" Kelly's mother. Or Hootchie in the Methodist Church yard. Sebastian's smoking was exotic, a passionate combination of fire and air, streaming through his lips and lungs, oozing out his nose and wandering, finally, out the window to me under the lobelia bush.

I sucked his smoke up my nose, making sure Old Sabby could see. I wanted to tell him I knew how to smoke a cigarette. I wanted him to know I smoked Sonny Kelly's Lucky Strikes all the time.

"Well, Sister, let's see you twirl something. What can you show me?" He struck a fresh match.

I watched the thin smoke rise. "Just a minute!" I dashed toward our apartment, calling back, "Just a minute, now! I'll be right back. Wait!"

What could I show Old Sabby?

Dazzle him, pose and pace, show off like mad, yes, twirl, and don't drop it, *no, not dumb a bit,* that's right. I tried not to get upset. I grabbed the old baton, knocking General MacArthur to one side of the closet in my hurry.

I grinned, polishing the baton on my shorts, rubbing at the dingy rubber tips. I'd dazzle Old Sabby all right. Then remembering the ridiculous piano recital two weeks past, I had a slight sinking spell. But that wasn't anybody, I reminded myself, that wasn't him sitting out there. What would he be doing at a piano recital?

I kept on soothing myself, descending the stairs two steps at a time. And even if it was him there, I'd knock the thought of it out of him forever. I'd woo Old Sabby right now and win.

He sat on the ladder, looking at me through the window, calmly smoking his cigarette. I stood safely away from the lobelia and the clumsy bees.

"Now," I instructed, "you have to use your imagination, okay? You have to imagine I'm doing this with a band or something, okay?"

"Okay, Sister." Sebastian drew on his cigarette, squinting with the smoke. "I'll imagine the whole United States Marine Band playing 'Stars and Stripes Forever.'"

"Okay." I put the chewed plastic whistle between my teeth and blew a bracing note.

Standing at Majorette's Parade Attention, hands on hips, baton cradled upon right arm, and through the count of eight, I smiled, flashing dimples at Old Sabby on the ladder.

A strong pose, it built my confidence and I went as easily as dye swirling into hot water into my best Pinwheels, underarm Flings and crisp Figure 8's. Next an arm roll, a neck roll, and a flashy once-around-the-body twirl, finishing with another flashy jump-and-between-the-legs maneuver. The old baton gleamed, responded to my thrust and grab.

Back to my first Majorette's Parade Attention pose, with hands on hips, Titania Anne Gentry gave Old Sabby a big winning smile. I wanted to give him a Chinese Split, a Majorette's Salute, and a dazzlingly complicated Parade Lunge. But I'd already pushed my luck and was starting to feel embarrassed.

Then I abandoned all caution and did a quick little aerial pitch. The baton spun up. I prayed I could catch it. The chrome flashed as it went up in front of Old Sabby's surprised blue eyes. He stuck his head out the window to follow it.

The baton turned, spun down. I stood ready, opened my hand to grab. Right. Perfect. I paced in a neat circle, returned to the first pose, paced in place through the count of eight, then came to rest again, hands on hips, *Smile, Smile, Smile!*

Sebastian laughed. He threw his cigarette stub out the window. "That's okay, Sister. You keep that up. I mean it. Really."

I flushed, then did a crisp about-face and with the wet whistle between my teeth, strolled away from Mr. McSherry's window and down the sidewalk.

Toto, reconnoitering Entwistle Street, was lifting a leg against the pile of croquet mallets. I blew a vicious blast calculated to obliterate his mottled brain. Toto laid back his ears and scrambled fast away from me, pausing to pee on every bush and tree trunk along the street. Leaves and bark glistened behind him. At the corner, Toto stopped, turned to see where I was. He growled, hackles raised, and scratched backward in the tar and gravel. He peed again.

"That's for Franklin Gentry," I hissed, "the time you peed on him in the street." The whistle clattered from my teeth, fell damp against my neck.

Sebastian chuckled and hammered in his daddy's kitchen.

He kept hammering nearly every day of the summer. I waited for the war to take Sebastian back, pull him off the ladder and stuff him back in a plane with a parachute and harness and helmet, make him fly over the Japs and Hitler and jump, fire blazing at his boots, blood oozing off his bayonet.

But Old Sabby didn't go back.

He stayed in Badin and nobody explained and I never asked. That was the way I wanted it. That was the way my stories wanted it. No facts to interfere. I watched Sebastian repair shelves, floors, screens in his daddy's apartment. He climbed out on the roof to replace tiles. He tarred around the chimney. He painted the porch.

I cataloged the hammer and nails, the adze, the lathe, all the smells of wood and glue and paint. I cataloged the smells of Old Sabby, his sweat and cigarettes. He let me watch. He didn't care, I imagined, if I made love to him right out in public with my eyeballs.

Sebastian no longer looked like a paratrooper. He dressed in old jeans, old faded shirts, usually with a carpenter's apron tied around his hips, and kept his feet inside the ugliest old brown leather moccasins I ever saw.

I wanted flashy uniforms on his body, chevrons, jumpsuits, goggles. I wanted him to jump out of a plane, throw a bomb, shoot

141

somebody, spill blood and guts all over the world, all over Badin. I wanted Old Sabby to kill for me. Then come straight home to the apartment and kiss me on the mouth.

I watched him improve Mr. McSherry's apartment. I swatted flies off his sweating body and stirred his cans of paint, handed up his shiny new nails, helped steady his ladder.

Soon I came to prefer the jeans, the apron, the old moccasins. I didn't think about uniforms anymore. I grew viciously intolerant of people criticizing or interrupting, of anything that threatened the little stories I made up around Old Sabby. I came, eventually, to forsake Carol Jean Spence. Carol Jean was right when she had accused me of being mad at her all the time, of hollering and bossing her around and knocking her croquet ball too hard. Carol Jean represented something I wanted to obliterate, my old self.

We stopped visiting. Carol Jean became as remote to me as Rachel on the great and mighty Congo. I saw Carol Jean rolling Pam and I waved. Carol Jean waved back, rolled on.

Erskine "Sonny" Kelly, though, was another thing. He came whistling for Toto and watched me pining over Old Sabby.

"You are such a moron, Ti," he sneered, "following around behind that old guy like a puppy dog."

"He's not an old guy," I blazed up like a little brush fire, then died back down. I chewed at the rubber bulb on the baton. "I don't follow him around. He's doing some work in our apartment. For Joan and Franklin. He's painting my room, too. It's part of my Christmas present, what they promised to do."

I hated the irritating whine in my voice, the shallowness of my excuses. It made me both furious and sad to admit it, but I wanted Sonny's approval. Wanted him to wait while I worked through this thing with Old Sabby. I wanted to show Sonny how wrong he was.

It was true, too, I reminded myself, Joan had hired Sebastian to fix the things Franklin Gentry ignored. Joan got him to paint my room, the first move toward fulfilling those Christmas promises Joan had made about redecorating the whole thing, new curtains, new rug, a vanity with a skirt and a mirror.

Sonny threw a rock at the lobelia bush, disturbing the bees, and showering white petals to the ground under Mr. McSherry's window.

"Let me tell you something, Ti," he said, "you are a fool to hang around him all summer. Let's go to the lake and go swimming. Let's go to the cafe and get a Coca-Cola. Hey." Sonny moved in a little closer, winked. "I'll give you a Lucky Strike."

"Sonny." I brandished the baton. "Sonny, I don't want a damn Lucky Strike!"

"Sonny? Shit," he interrupted, walking off. "My name's Erskine. You better call me Erskine."

And he was gone.

I felt then some goofy kind of surprising homesickness for Sonny Kelly—No, you better call him *Erskine!*—welling up right before I dropped off to sleep at night.

But there was all the baton twirling to get through before I could do anything about Erskine "Sonny" Kelly.

I had to deal with the baton twirling first. I twirled while Old Sabby hammered or sawed, always twirling and posing and letting him get a good look when he stopped fixing stuff long enough to smoke a cigarette and look at me.

Sebastian studied me. "Hey, try twirling with two hands, Sister. Get you two batons. Can't you do a backbend, Sister? A handspring? Good God, any decent baton twirler can do a handspring! See if you can't throw that baton up as high as the roof. Throw it, Sister! Thata girl!"

He didn't scold me when I dropped the baton and bruised my arm. Sebastian just shook his head and laughed and turned back up the ladder, a cigarette in the corner of his mouth. "Oh, Sister, you got to do better than that."

I'd have twirled the glittering loops of my guts to make Old Sabby look again, to make him say, Good, Sister, good!

I could win him, yes. I could win this man. Unlike Joan Gentry, there would be no wrapping kids up in crocheted afghans and driving all over Badin in Uncle Morton's black Ford to catch Sebastian in some other woman's bed.

Joan and Franklin could keep on playing games, what did I care? They did what they wanted. They showed off for each other much as I did for Sebastian. We were all desperate people, blood-kin.

For example.

Franklin Gentry opened our front door the next Saturday to a bony young man with sandy hair clipped close to the skull, his eager face red from the June heat.

I lay on the Olsen Mills carpet reading about William Wallace in the new issue of *Classic Comics*. Wallace was surrounded by evil English, the cries of innocent Scots ringing in his ears.

"Hey, good afternoon, sir," began the young man at the door. "My name is Benny Sikes, and I'm selling the good word."

"What's that?" interrupted Franklin, annoyed. He'd hoped Benny Sikes wanted a chiropractic adjustment.

"What?"

"The *good* word?" queried Franklin, a mean little smile working across his jaw.

"The Holy Bible, sir." Benny Sikes returned the smile and patted the top of his display case, a bulging green leather creation with impressive straps and buckles. "God's own good word! Which I'd just love to share with you, if you'll give me a minute, sir."

"God's own good word? In a *minute?*" Franklin Gentry opened the door wider. "Buddy, I have to see that."

I put a thumb on the frame where Lady Wallace, her long blond hair blowing in the wind, shrieked as the evil English cut down her

144

sweet blond bairns. *Courage! Courage, dear heart!* shouted William Wallace as he was dragged off. His tartan flapped in the melodramatic Highland gloaming.

I turned to watch Benny Sikes come inside and go to the sofa. Franklin took a chair across from him. I could hear Joan Gentry running bathwater upstairs. I pictured the hot steam and the fragrant bubbles. Joan pinned her June Allyson pageboy high on the crown of her head, and then lay against the rim of the tub, shut her eyes and basked. *Basked.* I liked the sound of that word. The meaning of that word was Joan Gentry in a tub of hot bubbles, everything smelling like Elizabeth Arden, *basked, basked, basked.*

Benny Sikes snapped buckles and flipped straps. He assured both me and Franklin, "You are going to love these. I knew soon as I saw you that you'd love these."

The display case opened on several big Bibles nested in red plush. Benny Sikes pointed to one. "This is my most popular. I sell more of it than all the others put together."

He began to lift it out with tender pride.

"Why?" Franklin swung a leg over his chair. "I mean, God's good word ought to be as popular in one Bible as in another, don't you think?"

Benny Sikes hesitated, cut his eyes nervously at Franklin, taking in the leg swinging. Franklin grinned encouragingly.

"It's the price, sir. This one is only $9.99. The others are higher."

"Then why don't you sell them all at $9.99?" Franklin stopped his leg and leaned forward. The smell of bourbon flowered the room.

I sat up straighter myself, wrinkling my nose. Franklin rolled his eyes at me and I looked back down at William Wallace and his blond lady, *Courage!*

"I can't do that." Benny Sikes coughed, took a handkerchief from his back pocket. The handkerchief was bordered in brown and green, monogrammed B.T.S. The T stuck up higher than the other

145

letters, and I thought how lucky it was for Benny Sikes he had a middle name.

"Why not?"

"I'm not supposed to, sir. That's the rules."

Franklin Gentry fixed the young man with a stern, measuring look. "You know what I think, Mr. Sikes? I think you're not supposed to sell God's word, God's *good* word. I think you're supposed to give it away. For free. That's the rules, dammit, the *Golden* Rule, Mr. Sikes. You know that rule, huh?"

Franklin Gentry leered from his chair. "Do unto others, you think?"

The running water cut off upstairs, the reverberation in the pipes rumbling like long rolling thunder. I pictured Joan stepping into the tub, stretching out under the hot perfumy suds, sighing, leaning against the rim, shutting her eyes, Lady Wallace rescued, *William, darling, come take a bath with me. Come bask.*

"Sir, I did not come in your house to be cussed at, or reviled." Benny Sikes gave Franklin a tight smile. "I will not let you provoke me, sir."

I gazed at the ceiling, boring my eyes right through the chandelier's candle-shaped bulbs, right into the tub with Joan Gentry. A slurry swoosh accented Joan's shift in the tub. "Uhmm."

I knew how it was all perfumey and warm up there, all naked up there. I knew how I would do it right there in Joan's bathtub with Old Sabby. I gazed and gazed. Lady Wallace rescued by Old Sabby, all the blond bairns, too. *Sebastian, darling, kiss me here, and here, and inside here, too. Let's bask.*

"Let me tell you something before you get mad, Mr. Sikes." Franklin set both feet on the Olsen Mills carpet. His hands clapped firmly on his knees. "Listen, chiropractic is my good word, buddy. Dr. Franklin Gentry. My card."

He laid it on the display case. Benny Sikes stared at it, but he didn't take it.

146

"And in the spirit of Christian charity, I will give you a free adjustment, if you give me a free Bible."

Benny Sikes blinked, folded up his monogrammed handkerchief, jabbed it back into his pocket. "I'm not supposed to do that," he said again.

"Look," pressed Dr. Gentry, "look, I'm not asking you to give me one of those expensive Bibles. I'll take the popular one, the cheap one. But I promise you one thing, buddy."

Franklin Gentry narrowed his eyes the way he always did, the way Joan always did, when moving in for the kill.

"I promise you the best adjustment you ever got in your life. The top of the line. Come on."

Benny Sikes shut his case and stood. "Sir," he said, "I won't bother you any longer."

He started to the door. I got up, too, William and Lady Wallace sprawled on the Olsen carpet. Spiked English helmets glittered. Swords lifted. *Traitor! Scots pig!*

"Aw, come on, be a good sport, buddy." Franklin put a hand on Benny Sikes's shoulder.

"Listen, I'll give you a free adjustment anyhow. Even if you won't give me God's good word. Come on. My office is right out back here."

"No. Sir, I'm going." Benny Sikes stepped over the doorsill.

"No, goddammit, shit." Franklin tightened his hand on Benny Sikes. "I'm going to give you an adjustment, you little hard ass, if it kills you and me both. You can't throw away a free adjustment from me."

Franklin Gentry pulled Benny Sikes back into the apartment. His display case banged the wall. Franklin hustled him through the living room, the kitchen and out to his office.

I followed, fascinated and a little scared. Even a little jealous. I wondered if Old Sabby heard any of it next door.

Before Benny Sikes realized what happened, Dr. Gentry had

him flat on the adjustment table, another impressive leather display with buckles and straps. He hit a lever and the table swooped down, all the blood rushing to Benny Sikes's head, turning him redder than the June heat had.

Then Franklin went to work, pounding and shoving and pommeling, popping joints and rearranging tensions all over Benny Sikes.

Dr. Gentry hit another lever and the table swooped back up. Benny Sikes gasped, gathered air, "You son of a bitch! You fucker! Turn me loose a' here!"

"Listen to that, Ti Baby," Franklin applauded. "God's own good word speaking in tongues now." Then he hardened, bent closer to Benny Sikes. "You watch your mouth with my little girl."

"What are you doing, Franklin Gentry?" Joan stood in the door of the office, her aqua chenille robe tied at the waist, her ash blond hair turbaned in a yellow towel.

"I said, what are you doing?" She watched Benny Sikes struggle around on the adjustment table to glare at her.

"Giving an adjustment," said Dr. Gentry.

"Turn me loose a' here, asshole!" screamed Benny Sikes.

Franklin unfastened the straps and let him off the table with a hearty back slap. "Feel better now, don't you, buddy! No more stiff neck. No more hard ass. And that, buddy," Franklin beamed, "is God's own good word."

Benny Sikes slid off the table and shot through the apartment, grabbed his display case, and slammed out the front door.

"Hard ass," observed Franklin. He began wiping off the adjustment table.

"Franklin, you're too crazy for your own good," said Joan. "I heard all this commotion down here and I thought somebody was killing you and Titania, and when I get out of the tub and get down here, finally, it's you and Titania killing somebody else. Franklin, someday somebody's going to sue you."

148

"I wasn't doing a thing," I said. "I was just standing here minding my business."

"You weren't trying to stop it either," said Joan. "Who was that, anyhow? He wasn't anybody from Badin, was he?"

She unwound the yellow towel and began sopping at her hair. The sweet clean scent of Halo shampoo came out in my face. I wanted to take big fists full of Joan's wet hair and rub it all over my face, absorb it, steal it.

"Some little shit selling Bibles. I gave him a good deal, Joan, honey. I told him he could have a free adjustment, if I could have a free Bible. But the hard ass wouldn't take me up on it."

"What do you mean he wouldn't take you up on it?" Joan giggled. "When I got down here, it looked like he was taking you up on it, okay."

Franklin giggled, too. "That was after I decided to give him an adjustment anyhow, whether he gave me a Bible or not."

He motioned us out of the office, fastened the door behind. We went into the kitchen and Franklin pulled his bourbon from the refrigerator.

Joan watched until he had poured it. "What would you do with a Bible, Franklin?"

"What would you, darling?" Franklin eyed her over the shot glass.

She eyed back.

I just waited there, another part of the kitchen, white and sterile and dumb as a stone. They paid me no mind.

"Let me give you an adjustment, Joan," he said, licking his lip.

Her drying hair made a blond cloud around her face. She didn't have on a dab of lipstick, but her clean unadorned face was the brightest thing, I marveled, in the kitchen. Joan Gentry pulled Franklin right across the kitchen with one raised eyebrow, one curl of her lip.

149

"Franklin," she mocked, "I've got more free adjustments than I can stand."

He wrapped her up in his arms and kissed her. He rubbed the aqua chenille. He rubbed the ash blond pageboy. The scents of Halo and bourbon mingled.

I wandered back to the living room and my *Classic Comics*.

Joan and Franklin Gentry went upstairs and as I followed William Wallace's daring escape from the evil English, his recapture and betrayal and heroic death, they bounced their bed on the floor over my head.

I looked at the ceiling. I bored my eyes through the chandelier. The pink satin comforter slithered between the footboard and the mattress.

Who do you think you are? I sneered. This kind of thing kills me. Stop!

After a while, Franklin Gentry got up, opened their door, announced shamelessly down the stairs, "I reckon it would be cooler for a nap with the door open. Ti Baby," he yelled, "you call me if any-body comes for an adjustment."

I rolled up the comic book and held it like a telescope to my eye. I trained it on the windows, the door, the sofa where Benny Sikes had displayed his good word, the chair where Dr. Gentry sat swinging his leg and plotting.

"God's good word is this," I said. "Sebastian McSherry. Old Sabby. And me. We are going to do anything we want in the middle of the day, with the door closed or the door opened, and we are going to have blond bairns."

I rolled the comic book tighter, tried to twirl it. It was too clumsy, so I pitched it against the stairs, adding, "I'll twirl fire, too."

Then I sat straightening out my ugly little finger, smiled at it and kissed it. "And nothing's going to get in the way."

11

There was a deadly side to these games, tempting and poisonous. Something you couldn't keep your hands off. Something that laid out the limits, allowing just so many lies, then jerked you hard back to the starting line.

Franklin got up some Saturdays during the summer, made himself efficient and endearing. He perked the coffee, made waffles, and served Joan in bed, smoothing her pink satin comforter.

"I'm going over to the park awhile with Ti Baby, honey. She wants to practice her baton tricks over there. I know she's been getting on your nerves all week, hanging around here, staying right up in your face. It's enough to make anybody nervous, twirling that baton all the time."

Franklin winked at Joan. Poured thick Karo syrup over the waffles. "You stay in bed, relax awhile."

Joan Gentry wasn't fooled. Listening across the hall, I marveled at how Franklin used us both.

"What about your patients, Franklin?" Joan cut the waffle, swirled it on the end of the Briar Rose fork. A bright drop of Karo trembled from one tine.

"I don't have anybody coming this morning. I'll be back in time, anyhow. Don't you worry. Eat your breakfast. Go back to sleep. Won't anybody bother you, Joan, darling."

He stuck a finger to the Karo, licked it and winked at her again.

Joan waved a hand. She wasn't fooled. But for some reason I couldn't figure out, Joan let Franklin go off and get himself in trouble those Saturdays. He played one part of the game and she played another. They knew their parts.

Franklin and I walked six blocks to the Carolina Aluminum park, green as a jewel, in the center of Badin. I practiced every twirl I knew, marched and about-faced all over the grass and along the graveled walks. And when I was tired of that, I played on the swings recklessly like a little kid.

Franklin was meeting Renee Ames in the park those Saturdays. Renee Ames, just out of Badin High School, took other people's babies to the park while they had breakfast in bed or went shopping or engaged in a thousand other conventional activities, entrusting the safety of their babies to a cow-eyed girl with illusions of going on to a career in modeling, in New York. Renee Ames talked always of the Powers Agency in New York and how to walk and how models were supposed to be tall and willowy and have perfect skin.

"They're supposed to be limber, too," put in Franklin. "They can't be stiff. Have to keep their joints loosened up."

He smirked at Renee Ames. "I can keep all your joints loosened up. A little adjustment here." He pressed her hip.

"Get rid of a little tension over here." He massaged her shoulder.

"You're crazy, Dr. Gentry." Renee Ames shook out her long straight blond hair and her earrings flashed.

She sauntered over the park, the crying soggy babies in tow. No June Allyson pageboy on Renee Ames. A lot of honey-toned blond hair cupping her shoulders was pulled back to show off a dramatic widow's peak.

I hated Renee Ames for that widow's peak. I rubbed at my own hairline, encouraging a widow's peak to sprout there.

I hated Renee Ames for the earrings, too. She wore the same ones always, little dark blue stones dropped in gold. They dangled like the prisms on Joan's chandelier.

Franklin Gentry, challenged by Renee Ames's disdain, tugged his moustache and swaggered off after her and all the babies. I gritted my teeth. "Hey! Where're you going?"

"I'm going to see if Renee Ames needs an adjustment," he called back. "You keep on practicing your baton twirling, Ti Baby. Back in a few minutes."

I managed a few Figure 8's, then stamped my foot and about-faced into Old Sabby coming across the grass with a newspaper. Not dumb a bit, are you, Sister? I had to grin at such good luck.

"Hey," I greeted him with the same question I'd yelled at Franklin, but in a friendlier tone, "where're you going?"

Sebastian sat down on the grass and opened the newspaper. "Right here," he said and lit a cigarette.

I twirled a few more Figure 8's, then sat beside him. "You know what?"

"What?" He just grunted at me, not listening, deep in the paper.

"My daddy is out there somewhere probably fucking somebody named Renee Ames." I narrowed my eyes and gazed hard at Old Sabby, ready to measure the effect of what I said on him. "Fucking Renee Ames."

He rustled the paper. "What did you say, Sister?"

"Oh, forget it." I saw Franklin Gentry returning, stroking his dark moustache, his cheeks flushed, his eyes stupid.

"Where's Renee Ames?" I demanded.

"Listen." Franklin ignored the question. "I'm going to go buy you an Eskimo Pie, okay?" He beamed in my face.

Sebastian lowered the paper. "Hey," he said to Franklin. "How's it going?"

153

Franklin nodded. "Okay, you know. You do the best you can."
Franklin turned back to me.

I dragged my baton across the grass. Bad temper exploded against my temple like blood beating against hard bone. Then I jumped up.

"Hey! I want two Eskimo Pies and an Orange Crush." I stared hard in Franklin's eyes, hard green bottle-looking eyes, the exact color as mine.

We got to work hating each other. We didn't care if Sebastian McSherry sitting on the grass with his newspaper knew it, either. This familiar mutual hatred was a skill we polished.

Joan fooled nobody, not even herself, lying back in the apartment with her pink satin comforter and her magazines and her June Allyson pageboy, wasting her life making plans about concert pianos and movies starring Titania Anne Gentry. *She can cry real big tears! She's got dimples, too. Look at that, cute as Margaret O'Brien!*

But she did it anyway. This was Joan Gentry's part of our game. She let Franklin run around awhile, then she pulled him back in hard, dumb as a fish on a line.

He depended on it.

For Franklin, strutting around as foolishly as me with my baton, twitching his moustache—*Dr. Franklin Gentry, Boston Red Sox!*—was sneaking, touching, feeling his way back to something he thought he lost, when was it? And what was it? If he got too far afield, Joan, he knew, would be there to point the way back.

So these little dalliances were all the more refreshing.

I'd watched him meet Renee Ames on the corners of Badin and in its back alleys. I'd sat in my upstairs windows and spied, picking at the putty in the window frame, breathing on my old baton.

I didn't have to be wrapped up in a crocheted afghan and hauled around in the middle of the night to witness this hussy. They'd gotten so brazen as to flirt right in front of me, as if I were no more than a piece of shrubbery or one of the stupid babies Renee Ames took care of.

Now there was Sebastian McSherry to witness my family's humiliation.

I pushed my tongue against my front teeth and waited, planning a move.

"Well," shrugged Franklin. "I'll be back in a minute. Hey, Sabby," he turned to Sebastian. "How about a cold Blatz? I'll bring back a few, okay?"

"Fine, man." Sebastian folded the paper and grinned at Franklin. "Okay."

Renee Ames came slinking around the shrubbery with her long model's legs and her cow eyes and her blond widow's peak. She moved herself with little effort, hardly breathing.

The babies toddled through the grass and one plopped down on Old Sabby's newspaper and began trying to pull it out from under himself.

Renee stood almost a head taller than Franklin and she looked past him at Sebastian. The meaning of such a look was not wasted on me.

"Ti Baby," said Franklin, "you help Renee mind these babies." He jingled the change in his pocket. "I won't be a minute, darling," he added to Renee.

I watched him disappear across the park. I moved closer to Sebastian, limbered my arm and twirled some rapid-fire Pancakes, gazing directly at Renee Ames.

Renee Ames said, still looking at Old Sabby in the grass, "You could be a majorette with the band. In high school."

She walked over and picked up the baby who was ripping Sebastian's newspaper and stuffing it in his mouth.

"Quit that, Ricky." The baby's chin was inky.

Renee turned back to me. "Do a backbend. Stand on your head. Do some tricks."

"That's what I told her." Sebastian grinned at Renee Ames.

155

"I don't do tricks," I sneered. "And I'm not a majorette. I don't want to go march around with a band. That's shit stuff."

Renee Ames observed me a moment. She wiped off Ricky's drool and sat down beside Sebastian. "I'm going to tell your daddy you said that."

"I don't care what you tell him."

"I'm going to tell him you said that, too."

She only had to tolerate me until Franklin got back with the beer. Meanwhile, Renee could close in on Old Sabby, too. I saw Renee Ames's bare arm brush his elbow.

"I don't believe I've met you." Renee Ames smiled. "Are you from around here?"

"Sabby." He smiled back, offered his hand.

"He lives next door to us," I interrupted. "And he's a paratrooper."

"Renee." She ignored me, squeezed his hand. "Renee Ames."

I hated Renee Ames right then worse than I hated Franklin for going off and leaving this mess to brew. I began to calculate all that I had to fight in order to protect what was mine.

Renee Ames wore straw sandals. Her toenails painted shell pink, like her fingernails, her lips. She had a spot of rouge in each cheek. She did not have, I flushed with joy, dimples in both her cheeks. She could not, I exulted mercilessly, cry great big tears.

If Franklin comes back here, I narrowed my eyes, I will give him to you, Renee. Back off from Old Sabby. I gripped the baton, choked it hard. Take him home with you, Renee Ames, marry Franklin, run off with him to South Carolina. Just get your bare arm off of Sebastian.

The earrings dangled like heavy blue seeds from Renee Ames's tanned ears. How did she get her ears tanned? I sulked. Blue stones the size of popcorn kernels. I studied the earrings, how could Renee Ames stand them being screwed into her lobes? I rubbed my own.

Flashing darker blue, the earrings snagged in Renee's long hair and she tugged at them, wincing.

Oh, I hope it hurts you bad.

One of the other wet whimpering babies staggered up to clutch at Renee Ames. She stood up and noticed me staring at her ears. "What are you looking at?"

Her tone was hateful and condescending. The baby collapsed on Renee's straw sandal. I thought what it would feel like having a wet soft baby sit on your foot. The baby stared at me now.

"Your earrings." I smiled admiringly. "Do they hurt? I never wore earrings. Could I try on just one, please, please?"

"Oh, okay," Renee Ames relented, smiling over at Old Sabby, tugging back her blond hair. She unscrewed an earring and, rubbing at her lobe, handed it to me.

"This is my birthstone. It's a sapphire."

She smiled at Sebastian. "What's your birthstone?"

"I don't know," he said. "I don't keep up with stuff like that."

"Well," said Renee Ames, "when's your birthday? I can tell you what your birthstone is if you tell me your birthday."

"Mine's November," I blurted, hurrying to say "that's topaz" before Renee could. I extended my hand with the birthstone ring.

"I got it for Christmas." I flashed it at Sebastian.

"January," grinned Old Sabby, beginning to enjoy the confusion.

"That's a garnet," said Renee, glancing to see if I was going to challenge her.

"Oh, this is beautiful." The earring felt warm and sweaty in my hand. My earlobes throbbed.

"You think I'd look good with earrings?" I arched my brows, flexed both dimples. I tried to look as much like Franklin Gentry as possible and win Renee Ames to me, away from Old Sabby.

"Sure." She arched her own brows.

"Can I try them both on?" The sapphires flashed in the middle of the park, hot little pieces of blue, mean enough to cut.

"Sure," Renee repeated generously and unscrewed the other earring and helped me fasten both to my own lobes.

I smelled Renee up close, felt her warm sweaty arm next to mine, saw up into the tiny dark hairs of Renee's nose.

I turned my head slowly side to side. The earrings tapped my neck lightly. I felt strangely transfigured, exotic, precious. *Born on the great and mighty Congo, the Congo is a great and mighty river. Look at these snakes tattooed on my arms. Hootchie, where are you? On the chain gang?*

"You think they will stay on okay, not fall off?"

"Sure, they'll stay on," said Renee Ames. "They're screwed tight."

She bent over the baby who was still staring at me, his mouth a round rosy drooling O. The other baby had resumed eating Sebastian's newspaper.

"Ricky!" Renee scolded.

"Good," and I sprang off, my baton tucked under arm, and dashed toward Entwistle Street, six blocks away, toward Joan Gentry under the pink satin comforter.

I ran right past the astonished Franklin, a paper sack of cold beers in his arm, the two Eskimo Pies smashing down into the grass. Renee Ames ran behind me cursing, "You little bitch! Come back with my birthstones!"

Old Sabby, raised up on an elbow, stared a moment, then stretched back full length in the grass and burst out laughing. The babies, wet and crying, staggered behind Renee Ames.

Titania Gentry, the piano player, the delight of two continents, the darling of the counts and the viscounts, had been profaned, marked by Renee Ames's birthstones. This was no bland sweet Dixie Cole in the dull garage apartment. No tame vanilla Dixie Cup belonging to a gaunt and angry Buster. No. This had to be Franklin's worst infidelity of all.

I meant to show Joan.

I meant to bring pain and confusion.

I stood on the wooden steps, calling for Joan to come look at what Franklin had done to me. I dangled the earrings, feeling my ears bloom larger, and throb more wildly. I wanted all of Entwistle Street to be witnesses, Mr. McSherry, Jettie Barefoot, Madine Ponds across the street. The whole world.

Renee Ames stopped chasing me after the first steep block. She must have realized I was up to something and she had all the babies to gather up. When she stopped running and bent down, Renee was immediately surrounded by them, howling and complaining, clustering to her like big soggy bouquets. Renee Ames collected them and huffed back to the little green park, angry and determined.

I imagined the scene she caused back there, Sebastian looking on.

"Listen, Dr. Gentry," she probably said, "you better get back my birthstone earrings from that little bitch. And if you don't, Dr. Gentry"—she leaned over Franklin, who still blinked and gaped—"if you don't, I'll tell everybody what you've been up to."

And Renee Ames, all the soft whimpering babies sticking like aggregates to her hips and thighs, probably smiled over at Sebastian and then stormed off.

Franklin probably just stood on the curb, blinking, the cold Blatz making wet rings through the bag and through his sleeves.

"I think, man," said Sebastian, "you just been screwed."

"Well, then." Franklin sat down beside him. "Have a Blatz." He flipped off the caps with the bottle opener he kept on his key ring. He opened the Orange Crush he brought back for me, then poured it out, watching it sizzle through the dry grass.

But all this I just imagined.

What really happened was Joan Gentry came outside and looked at me. She had her aqua chenille robe pulled tightly over her satin gown. "What're you carrying on about?" she snapped. "What's all this hollering?"

"Look." I pointed at both ears.

Joan examined the ears. She turned my head with one firm hand. "Who did that?"

"Franklin," I lied with flourish. "He said I would look like a real movie star."

"Where did he get them?"

"They're Renee Ames's." I rounded my eyes. "He gave 'em to her." I lied and I loved it.

Joan Gentry unscrewed Renee Ames's birthstones from me. She took them inside, up the stairs, and flushed them down the toilet. I was shocked Joan did that. Just took them without so much as batting her eyes or even thinking about giving them back to Renee. It saddened me to think of the sapphires flashing through the plumbing, sinking away in the dark, tumbling finally to silt over, lost forever in the offal of the Badin sewer.

I thought Joan would give the earrings to Franklin and bless him out. I honestly thought the earrings would get back to Renee Ames okay, yes.

This was my first error. I fingered my topaz ring, ashamed.

Joan washed her hands. She confronted Franklin when he came in, beginning on a low calm note.

"Listen, Franklin, I can take shit, and I can take shit. But when you start trying to make me eat shit, Franklin, I've had enough."

"What're you talking about?"

She hit him hard across his mouth, smacking his lips against his teeth, bringing bright red blood.

Franklin looked wild then and I was afraid, not of what he would do back to Joan, but of what he would not do. Defend him-

160

self. Make it all up. Forgive me for robbing Renee Ames. Forgive me for lying about him.

Franklin didn't know I lied. He didn't know the birthstones were at that moment sinking to the bottom of the sewer.

Franklin moved out. He stayed gone two weeks, living in a boardinghouse on Highway 740. He telephoned once and asked to speak to me. When I answered, Franklin, in a sort of vague strangled voice, asked, "Ti Baby, which do you like the best, me or your mother?"

"I don't know," I said.

Franklin, clearing his throat, said, "Oh," and hung up.

I WAS SORRY I lied, but wouldn't admit it. My second error.

Old Sabby, stringing fence, watched me twirl the baton in the backyard. "You did it, you know," he said. He wrapped wire around a cedar post. "You did the whole thing, Sister."

"I don't care." I lifted my hard chin. I touched a finger to my ears. They burned, they felt as heavy as when Renee Ames's earrings were attached.

"Well, you know, it really doesn't make a whole lot of difference, Sister, anymore, whether you care, or you don't care. It's your mama and daddy having to go through it. Not you."

He cut the wire, twisted it over with needle-nosed pliers and bradded it to the top of the post. "It could get a lot worse, Sister," he warned. "It could get real ugly around here."

I stopped in mid-twirl. "What do you mean?"

"They could split up for good." Old Sabby gathered his tools and went inside, leaving me hanging there somewhere between good and evil, rebuked.

He was right. Joan decided to get a divorce and I, still contemplating the shock of what I'd caused, listened to her call up Franklin

161

and announce, "My lawyers are going to take you to the cleaners, Franklin Gentry. This is it. You've had it."

Joan circled a date on the kitchen calendar. "That," she told me, "is when our life changes for the better."

I looked at the circle around some remote day in the middle of August. "That's when the legal separation goes into effect," said Joan. "And Franklin can't do a thing about it."

He did, though. He walked right back into the apartment, hissing at Joan, "Sugar, don't you dare try to leave me. Don't you dare try to take off my little girl."

"Your little girl!" Joan yelled. "What do you mean your little girl? Your little girl who you dragged to the park while you fucked anybody you wanted, but fucked in particular that eighteen-year-old Miss United States Pussy!"

"Shut your goddamn mouth." Franklin narrowed his eyes, tugged at his moustache.

"Shut yours." Joan narrowed her eyes back.

I listened, then went out to find Sebastian. "They're fighting."

"What kind of fighting?" Sebastian leaned against the side of his daddy's garage.

"The hollering kind. The 'goddamn' kind." I felt sick telling him. "I can't stand this kind of thing. This kind of thing kills me."

Sebastian didn't say "I told you," but I wished he had. It would open the wound and let me bleed until I was pure.

Joan called up Uncle Morton in Albemarle. "Morton," she cried and beat the wall beside the telephone, "Morton, I have taken shit and taken shit, and now I'm going to give him some shit, Morton."

Joan took a big sobbing breath, wiped her eyes. "I am going to kill him, Morton. I want you to bring me your gun out here, Morton, so I can shoot his ass off. I cannot stand it another minute, Morton. Are you listening to me?"

I pictured Uncle Morton with all that in his ear in Albemarle. I imagined his ear blooming big and red and heavy.

Joan beat the wall again. "Oh, Morton," she declared. "That's not the point! And, no, Morton, I don't want to talk to Della. Oh, dammit, Morton!"

She hung up the telephone, cursed, beat the wall some more. I stood quietly in the kitchen. I'd brought all this on. I wondered what I ought to say to Joan Gentry. What I could say.

The long baton was cold under my arm. My fingers smelled of chrome and rubber. I felt again as if I were on the brink of something barreling down. It was like being on a big Ferris wheel while it loaded passengers. I felt the hard dizzying lurches of the wheel, the grab of the brakes.

When Joan finished beating the wall and sobbing, she turned and glared. "How long have you been standing there?"

"All the time," I said, adding, "ma'am," to make her feel better. I wanted Joan to feel better.

"Titania," Joan Gentry said, "men run the whole world. And when you try to talk to one of them, even if he's your only brother, they just want you to talk to another woman."

She tightened her lips and shook her head. "Morton wouldn't even believe me. He just wanted to put Della on the phone. Damn Della. Damn Morton. Damn Franklin."

She turned again, narrowed her eyes. "Damn you, too."

I blinked at the shock of this vicious pronouncement from my own mother. Then Joan declared, "I can't even breathe in here," and stalked out of the kitchen and up the stairs. I listened to her feet cross the bedroom to the window. I chewed the rubber tip of the baton.

"All I wanted," I whispered to the baton, "all I was going to say was to tell her, Joan, I love you and I love Franklin and I don't want you to shoot him. Or yourself. Or anything."

But then Joan had narrowed her eyes and said, *Damn you, too* right at me.

She didn't mean that, I told myself, she's just still mad at Franklin.

I heard Joan jerk down the curtains. The rods bounced across the floor and then the window got raised with a loud slam, bang! Joan pushed open the screen and climbed out on the roof.

I listened to the tiles crunch under Joan's feet a second, then I ran outside, yelled up, "Don't jump off the roof! Don't! It wasn't Franklin's fault! Not all of it! Don't!"

Madine Ponds came out with her broom across the street. She gave off high thin screams, shaking the broom at Joan Gentry on the roof. Mr. McSherry, asleep on his porch swing, woke, stepped in the yard and looked up to see what Madine was shaking her broom at.

"Mr. McSherry!" I hollered, jumping down the steps and into the street. "Where's Sebastian? I need him to help me get her off the roof!"

Mr. McSherry blew his nose on the plaid handkerchief. He folded it carefully and stuffed it back in his pocket. "Mrs. Gentry," he called up to Joan. "Don't jump off. Please?"

Joan crawled to the edge of the roof and looked over. "I'm not going to jump, you old fool," she told him. "I'm just out here to get a breath of fresh air. To clear my head of all the bullshit that goes on in my house. Don't tell me not to jump, dammit. Mind your own business."

She noticed me for the first time. "Titania," she called, "get out of the street."

Jettie Barefoot, alarmed by all the hollering, came out of her end apartment and, seeing Joan Gentry on the roof, added her own shrieks to the confusion.

"Joan," she yelled, "I'm going to call the law to help you. Don't move. They can get you down. Or the fire department."

"Shut up, Jettie," said Joan. "I'm not going to jump. This is not what you think. You people are crazy. Mind your own business!"

Where was Old Sabby! I looked up and down Entwistle Street.

I was afraid to go find him, afraid Joan Gentry would jump off the roof. But Old Sabby could catch her.

"Where is Sebastian?" I yelled at Mr. McSherry again and shook the baton. "Where is he?"

"I don't know." Mr. McSherry turned up both hands. "Gone downtown to get the groceries, I think."

"Ma'am!" I ran to the boxwood hedge bordering the front yard. "Listen, I'm going to find Old Sabby and he can catch you, or climb up there and get you down. Ma'am!"

A tear caught in my throat and I hoarsed out my last sloppy plea, "Please, please, don't do nothing till I get back with Sabby."

"Titania!" Joan frowned, crawled closer to the edge of the roof. "Don't you go get anybody! You hear me? This is ridiculous, all you people. This is none of your business. I can get out on my roof if I damn well want to! You hear me?"

Joan Gentry, flushed, angry, ready to shoot, if she had a gun, the ass off of everybody standing then in Entwistle Street and looking at her, gathered herself up and balanced over them all a moment. She pointed at me. "I said, already, this is none of your business." And she stumbled, tried to recover her balance, but fell off the steeply pitched roof into the boxwood hedge anyhow.

My mouth froze open, the baton fell to the ground. Madine Ponds and Jettie Barefoot shrieked together. Mr. McSherry took out a cigar and chewed off the end of it, his eyes round, his nose dribbling.

The boxwood was thick and healthy, full of sharp little twigs. Joan pitched down into it. She knocked the breath out of herself. She twisted her ankle and scratched her face and arms.

The neighbors gathered, Jettie puffing to kneel and scoop Joan into her bosom. "It's all right! It's all right! You're still alive, honey!"

Madine ventured, her broom held stiffly in front of her, all the way across the street. "Jettie! Jettie! Is she dead?" And Mr. McSherry pulled out his plaid handkerchief and dabbed at Joan's bleeding scratches.

"What's all this?" I turned to see Old Sabby on the curb, his arms full of grocery sacks.

"My mother," I began to cry, "jumped off the roof!"

Sebastian put down the sacks and made everybody get back. He looked at Joan in Jettie Barefoot's arms. He was the first thing Joan screamed at when she finally got her breath back. "This is my business! Leave me alone!"

"Can you move your legs?" asked Sebastian. "Can you move your arms?"

Joan tried to pull away from Jettie's bosom, but Jettie hugged her tighter. "I hate all you people!" declared Joan. "Let me up!"

"Ma'am?" I crept close to Joan. "Ma'am, I did it. It was me. I took Renee Ames's earrings. It wasn't Franklin. I told a lie. It was me, ma'am."

Joan brushed at the boxwood twigs in her pageboy. "Titania," she snapped, "I already know that."

"Let's get you in the house," Sebastian soothed. He lifted Joan out of Jettie Barefoot's arms and carried her inside the apartment and put her down on the living room sofa, me following. Mr. McSherry and Jettie and Madine stood for a while staring at the apartment, then shook their heads, wandered away.

"You know," Sebastian pointed out to Joan, "you ought to call the doctor, make sure you didn't break anything."

"It's my business," she insisted. "Thank you."

Sebastian looked at her. "Sister," he turned to me, "can you handle this?"

"I'll call the doctor. I'll call my daddy, too."

Joan huffed. "Call the devil."

She lay back on the sofa pillows. "I did *not* jump off that roof. I did *not*."

The Carolina Aluminum doctor came, tended Joan's ankle and gave her some tablets for the pain. He swabbed all her bleeding scratches with the household merthiolate. Some of it got on her ash blond hair and that struck me as particularly humiliating for Joan.

"I fell," she told the doctor, "that's all I did. *Fall*."

Franklin left work in the middle of the afternoon, came straight to Joan's side. He smoothed his moustache and was charming and kind, plumped pillows for Joan, cooked supper, pitched baseballs easy to me in the backyard, and didn't complain about any banging on the piano. He massaged Joan's ankle, gave her every shred of his attention, his chiropractic skill, his special touch.

He and Joan resumed, after a pleasant short peace, the games. She slept late on Saturday mornings, warm as a baby under the pink satin comforter, while Franklin swaggered off, murmuring into somebody's—was it Renee's?—pretty ears, "Did I tell you I used to play big-league baseball? I wasn't always a chiropractor just on the weekends."

He didn't take me with him anymore. But I knew what he was saying, his sparkling extravagant little stories. I knew the sound of his voice.

"You don't believe it? It's true, sugar. It's true. Watch this." And he would go into his showy professional windup, pitching the imaginary ball hard and fast, *wham!* right past the idiot batter. *Whatsa matter, you blind!*

"And, sugar, if your neck gets stiff, trust me to work it out of you. Lean back here. What did I tell you, sugar?"

I stayed home, looked up the birthstone chart in the encyclopedia. All the colors glittered, but nothing there was as tempting as Renee Ames's sapphires. I pulled off my birthstone ring and tied it around General MacArthur's neck.

"I thought Joan would give them back. That ought to make a difference, don't you think?"

No, you did it, he glared back. *You did the whole thing, Sister.*

167

12

I'd always considered my life with Kelby to be quiet, serene, safe. No jumping or falling off roofs into boxwood hedges. No cursing, no infidelities. He was nothing like Franklin, I was nothing like Joan. And he was nothing like Old Sabby. Nothing like Erskine "Sonny" Kelly. I had escaped the past and its little stories, its loneliness and its disappointment.

Kelby might be a complete mystery to me, but he was better than the clear farce of Joan and Franklin. I could see right straight through them. I welcomed the mystery of Kelby, the unpredictable quality of him.

But Kelby left for California and never came back. And I lived in Greensboro for a year after Kelby left, then moved us south to coastal Carolina, to Lake Waccamaw, about forty-five minutes from the Atlantic Ocean. It is a big freshwater lake the color of strong tea. In fact, that's where its color comes from, tannic acid, percolating off the leaves and peat that form its bed, percolating through the swamp springs that help feed it.

So I raised Sarah and Hannah beside a big lake the way I was raised beside a big lake, except this one was natural and organic and that one, my lake, Badin Lake, was man-made, and red-dark most of the time. Often muddy. In summer it could clear up toward a golden-green, something like the color of ripe scuppernongs.

Sarah got interested in bugs and trees, all the time bringing home baby squirrels fallen from their nests. So she ended up, at nineteen, working as a park attendant for Waccamaw State Park, a beautiful green swamp area where Spanish moss festoons the trees. I tell her all the time to go to college, go to NC State in Raleigh and get a degree in biology or something.

She smiles, that same old lazy smile of Kelby's, says, "I don't like going to school. It makes me nervous."

"But," I insist, "you can take something you might like okay. You can take this." And I hold out the catalog, point at the slick page with its photos. "Parks and Recreation. That's a legitimate degree. That wouldn't make you nervous."

Sarah sighs. "I can't believe you, Mom. You sent off for that catalog." She slides next to me on the porch glider. "You go to State and get that degree."

Sarah nudges me. She hugs me like I'm an old raggedy teddy bear. Then she's gone, off the porch, across the sandy pine-needled yard, straight to the ripplings of Lake Waccamaw, where I know she will inspect the shore debris, collect mussel shells and driftwood and bring it all home to pile in the yard with her other finds.

My girls know they can stay at home with me forever.

I ought to be kicking Sarah and Hannah out the door. I ought to criticize and yell, make them tougher and more cynical than they are. They stay at home, Sarah with Kelby's old smile and Hannah with Joan Gentry's blond hair licking over her shoulders, and I like it. Maybe I think it keeps Kelby here, too, though Kelby's been gone years to California. His casual quiet defiance stayed behind. His stubborn honesty.

That defiance and honesty showed up early in Hannah. Right

170

after Kelby left and I got the job with *The Greensboro Pilot*, I had to return to the *News Gazette* to pick up some things. Sarah was in first grade, but I had Hannah with me. She was supposed to be in kindergarten, but she was sticking tight to me. Not only did she empty the kitchen of all its tinned goods and cereal boxes, but she also stuck to me, wouldn't let me out of her sight, cried loudly at the kindergarten door.

Her teachers, all affectionate young women getting degrees in Early Childhood Development at Guilford Tech, recommended leaving Hannah with them. "Just go on," they said, "she'll stop crying soon as you're around the corner."

I couldn't do it. I felt so guilty. It overwhelmed me right then, so I gave in to Hannah, told myself it was for just right then, until she got over Kelby. Until I got over Kelby.

We walked into the *News Gazette*, into the corner office with the long light cord dangling down. Rory Flynt stood riffling through the file cabinet. Yellow pages and old picture proofs tumbled on the floor. "Hey," he said, looking at Hannah, "who's that?"

He bent down, held out a hand to her. "What's your name?"

He knew what her name was, knew who she was. Rory just wanted to hear her say it. "Hannah," she said.

She gazed at his bright carroty hair. Quite seriously she told me, "Mommy, that man's got orange hair."

Rory grinned. "No," I said, "he's got red hair. That's red."

Hannah gazed a bit longer, then, "No, that's orange."

Rory pulled up a sleeve. "And look, he's got a big orange spot on his elbow," Hannah said, pointing to a place where a lot of freckles merged to make a big patch.

She moved closer, still gazing in her serious and clinical manner. She put out a finger, her nail the size of a sequin—painted Panther Purple just last evening by Sarah—and she daubed the patch gently.

I got my stuff and we left in the car. Hannah still held her finger

171

out, studying it, a tiny purple sequin glinting in the light, the tip, maybe, tingling from the touch of Rory Flynt's freckles.

Hannah was not about to believe anything you just told her. I took hold of the finger, kissed it.

"I HEARD YOUR MOTHER jumped off the roof," Erskine "Sonny" Kelly said. "Tried to kill herself."

"That's not true," I hissed. I kicked his ankle under the pew of the Badin Methodist Church. "That's a lie."

Sonny smiled. "That's not what I heard. It's all over Badin." He slid up closer to me, put an arm around me, breathed in my ear.

"Your daddy was catting around and she couldn't take it. Huh, Ti?"

He was mean as a snake, Erskine "Sonny" Kelly. Hardened as a criminal. Despite the blond curly hair. I felt the tight muscle of his arm around me. What you need, Sonny, I thought, is two tattooed snakes on your arm and a big cigarette.

"I hate you," I said. "You know I hate you."

For two weeks I'd had to sit in the Badin Methodist Church and help with Vacation Bible School. Joan made me do it. Joan herself directed a class in embroidery. Aunt Della came out from Albemarle every day to help with refreshments.

"I'm glad you're finally taking a real interest in the church," Della had said.

"It's nothing," said Joan Gentry. "Just something to do, to *get out of* that miserable apartment, that's all."

There I sat on the pew during the opening services with Sonny Kelly beside me, alternately squeezing my shoulder and hissing insults about Joan jumping off the roof trying to kill herself over Franklin. His breath tickled my ear and I swatted at him the same as swatting at a bug. "Leave me alone."

The guest evangelist, Reverend Percy, a man so grotesquely fat I couldn't see what kept him from falling flat dead over the pulpit, delivered the revival message.

Miss Tiny Bodeen, his big muscular wife, was a former lady wrestler, a near champeen, who had received the call of God just as she had pinned her most formidable opponent to the mat in a Charlotte, North Carolina, arena.

Miss Tiny Bodeen, until that moment a heathen, obligingly converted to Christ. She fell upon her stout knees and accepted Him as her personal savior and lost her only chance at the North Carolina title for champeen lady wrestlers.

Her opponent, another heathen, jumped up from the mat and pinned Miss Tiny, nearly strangling her, and won the title for herself.

But Miss Tiny Bodeen—Reverend Percy smiled at his wife indulgently, waved a fat hand at her—received something far more glorious. She won the champeen title to heaven itself, a genuine conversion experience!

"Hallelujah!" declared Reverend Percy and wiped his eyes. "And now she is my right-hand helper, ready to stand before you this evening and give her testimony."

I glowered next to Sonny Kelly. What a fool Miss Tiny Bodeen was. She could serve Christ far better, I considered, winning the title for champeen lady wrestlers. She could then stomp around wrestling rings all over North Carolina, flex and pose and give her testimony to the newspapers. After all, I pointed out as I sat there shoving Sonny's knee, kicking his ankle and swatting off his breath in my ear, after all, God gave Miss Tiny the muscles to do it.

I considered that God ought to be mad as hell over this.

I certainly would be. You only get one chance, *one*.

After the service, Sonny Kelly walked out with me, his arm still lightly around my shoulder. "You're not mad at me, are you?" He smiled.

"Yes, I am mad at you."

"I'm coming over tomorrow," he said, "I'm coming to your house and we'll hang around, do something."

I pulled away from him. "Who do you think you are, Sonny Kelly? Talking about my mother that way and then saying you're coming over?"

"Erskine," he smiled again, "not Sonny. That's who I think I am." He walked off, turned, reminded me, "Erskine. *Erskine* Kelly. Tomorrow."

The next day Reverend Percy brought his evangelistic message to the whole town of Badin. He drove through the town in a big car, its wide rear end festooned with red reflectors. When Reverend Percy put on brakes, Old Sabby said, the car looked like a baboon in heat.

"Look out yonder, Sister," Sebastian nodded, "here come those missionaries."

Reverend Percy oozed out of the car, belly first, then left leg, arms, then right leg. "What's your religion, son?" he hollered up at Sebastian, on a ladder wire-brushing the gutters.

Old Sabby looked down at Reverend Percy a moment. "I don't know, daddy. Maybe I'm a Jew. Maybe I'm a Catholic."

He pulled out a cigarette. "Wait a minute. I know, daddy, I'm a high Quaker. I'm probably the only high Quaker left."

"You playing with me, son?" Reverend Percy glared. "Well, let me tell you something, son, you can't play with the *Almighty!*"

He separated the last word, accented each part, *awl might tee!*

Old Sabby let the smoke dribble out his nose in little thin gray snakes. I blessed him for that smoke and those snakes.

"You saved, son?" Reverend Percy squinted.

Sebastian smiled. "You might put it that way, daddy."

"Well, you take this tract anyhow, son." Reverend Percy whipped out a fistful of papers.

"You, too, little woman," giving one to me, reaching another up the ladder to Sebastian.

Then with amazing speed for a big fat man, he stuffed himself back in the car and was off down Entwistle Street. The wide red baboon hiney winked as he braked to slow and yell at people, "Madam! Are you saved?"

Sebastian and I looked at the tract. Like Reverend Percy, it yelled in shrill flaming letters, *Are You Saved?*

On the other side, flames exploded in the middle of people running and screaming and trampling each other, their arms thrown over their terrified faces.

Are You Saved? the tract yelled again. Then it leered, *We may think we are saved if we have an air-raid shelter to get in. But no one is saved until they have accepted Christ as their personal savior! There is no air-raid shelter you can get in, no place you can hide in, when the Almighty comes.*

I ran a thumb down the border of flames.

You must be ready! The hour of redemption draweth nigh! Accept Christ as your personal savior, know the power of His healing love! He is the only Lord Protector! And remember always you know not the hour, nor the day, nay, not even the place!

There is no air-raid shelter against God!

He comes again soon!

Are You Saved?

Saved? Saved? Saved?

I exhaled, looked at Sebastian. "This is scary." I felt dizzy and steadied myself against his ladder.

"Persistent sons of bitches, aren't they, Sister?" Old Sabby folded the tract neatly, creasing every corner. "Don't believe that bullshit, Sister. Don't listen to that old tub of guts preacher. Stuff like that can give you bad dreams at night."

Sebastian folded Reverend Percy's tract down to the size of a

175

matchbook. The fragrance of his cigarette wavered in the air. Old Sabby's tobacco was alive, vibrant, delicious. Never cold and black and dead like Mr. McSherry's cigar. Sebastian smoked Camels.

I drank in that smoke. I rubbed my hand over the pack wherever he left it out. The camel, the pyramid, the faint silver lines printed across the white, the blue seals and North Carolina tax stamps, the shreds of tobacco sticking to the ripped paper. I drank it in.

"I don't believe in that bullshit," I assured him, crumpling my tract to a ball. "But my mother makes me go anyway. And for two weeks, I have to help up there with the Vacation Bible School."

"The whole shebang is nuts, Sister." Sebastian flipped his folded tract toward the lobelia. I threw my paper ball after. Madine Ponds swept her path, attacking every crevice in the pavement. She leaned on the broom, shaded her eyes toward us across Entwistle.

"Fuckers and bullshitters, Sister. Fuckers and bullshitters," he declared.

Madine pricked up her ears. "I heard you say that!" she shrilled, shaking the thick dry broom. "Don't you talk down religion to that child! Those missionaries may be strange, but they're carrying on God's love in the world, and that's more than you do, and you know it, too, Sebastian McSherry! I don't care if you were in the army."

That was the most I'd ever heard Madine Ponds say.

"I admit it, madam," smirked back Old Sabby, lifting a hand and saluting her. "They're carrying on God's love in the world."

Then he climbed down, folded up the ladder and carried it around the end of the quadruplex. I followed, looking back at Madine. How in the world did that woman hear all the way across the street?

"Damned old bitch," Sebastian said. "This town is full of damned old bitches, Sister. And damned old sons of bitches, too."

He banged the wire brush against the cedar fence posts with fury.

That night I dreamed myself in bed with Sebastian McSherry. The cozy Badin night wrapped around our two bodies, warm and black. The air pinpointed little starry hot asterisks. I snuffled closer to Old Sabby, drinking up his snarls and snores. Then in the dream, somebody started banging on the front door.

It was our front door, mine and Old Sabby's.

I sat up. I could feel my full naked breasts jiggle under the sheet. "Somebody's at the door."

He pulled up. "Go see who, sugar."

"Oh, okay."

I slipped my silver satin gown back on my shoulders. Both my nipples stuck up hard through the satin. I opened the front door and saw two people.

"Is our Lord Protector here?" they asked.

"What a stupid thing to ask me in the middle of the night!" I hissed. "Of course the Lord Protector is here, you bullshitters, you fuckers! He is in bed with me, his Lady, sleeping."

I blessed them both out good, just as they deserved.

"Would you get him, please, ma'am?" they asked.

"Is this an emergency?" I lit a Camel, picked the little shreds of tobacco off the tip of my long pointed tongue, red as a pimento.

"Yes, this is a big emergency. We need our Lord Protector."

"Okay." I tossed my ash blond pageboy. "You're probably lying, but I won't take a chance and have you sue me. Wait just a minute."

"Thank you, ma'am, bless you," they said. "Thank you."

In my delicious dream, I got back in bed with Old Sabby. I nuzzled his ear. I put my lips close to his snoring lips. "They want you. It is a big emergency. They want you to come right now."

I slipped the satin off one shoulder, lifted a hard nipple to his lips, traced them with it.

Sebastian opened his eyes then and I could see, even in the dark, their erotic blue.

"Well." He sucked my nipple to a long point, then got up. "Persistent sons of bitches, aren't they, Sister?"

Old Sabby went off dressed in jeans, his hairy legs striding

177

through Badin, his old moccasins slapping the tar and gravel. He left me alone in the warm burrow of our Entwistle Street bed.

I fell away again, dozing and dreaming inside one more dream. In this dream it was raining. Drops fell on my face, gentle and cool, the good familiar Badin rain.

I opened my eyes in this new dream and saw Old Sabby out on the roof, shaking the window screen, hissing, "Sister! Sister! Let me in, sugar."

I stared at him a minute, dazed, all my lust rising off my skin like steam off a hot wet Badin pavement. Then I got up and opened the screen.

"I had to kill a snake for those sons of bitches." He climbed through.

"Huh?"

"That old girl, Tiny Bodeen, got in the shower and there was a snake in it, in the corner. Don't you know she got back out again damn quick, the old fat ass!"

The bedsprings creaked as we settled back into the warm deep loving dream. In the next room, I heard all our blond children turn over in their sleep, sighing. I pictured their hair splashed on the pillows, their fingers flexing, every little finger on each right hand as crooked as mine.

"What kind of snake was it?"

"I don't know. A big one. Too big to take a shower with!" Sebastian laughed, sneered. "She wouldn't turn on the light. Afraid somebody might see her naked. She got in the shower and turned on a little flashlight, you know those kind the size of a fountain pen? And there he was, all piled up in the corner. Poor old snake."

I grinned, shutting my eyes, snuggling closer to Old Sabby. I saw Miss Tiny Bodeen, lady wrestler, jumping out of the shower, naked and white as lard, clutching her shower cap and her towel, fleeing the snake.

Then a long kaleidoscope took over and rotated through my dream, changing patterns with every turn, all the bright symmetry delighting me, the tumbling bits of loose colored glass.

I saw Madine Ponds shaking her broom at me and Old Sabby.

I watched Renee Ames dig through the Badin sewers. "Where're my birthstones, you little bitch? I know you put them in here someplace."

I frowned next to see Erskine "Sonny" Kelly slide into bed with me and Old Sabby. He threw an arm around me, easing me away from Sebastian, who, I was annoyed, didn't do anything about it but continued to snore and flutter his eyelids.

"What are you doing here, Sonny Kelly!" I hissed.

"Get out of this bed! Go home!"

"I heard your mother tried to kill herself," he smirked, squeezing hard. "And I came over to hang around in case she does it again. Give me a kiss." He puckered his lips.

I hit him full in the face with General MacArthur, then I heard Joan Gentry downstairs clanging the skillet and spoons. I smelled the morning coffee and jumped awake.

Are you saved, *saved?*

Don't believe that, Sister.

13

Franklin always drank the same bourbon, J. W. Dant. "When I get to be trash rich," he affirmed, "I'll drink Jack Daniels Black, but for steady drinking, a poor man has to drink J. W."

He lifted the shot glass, pretended he could see through it. "Ti Baby," he instructed, "always drink pure liquor. Don't drink that blended shit. It'll make you sick as a dog. Drink *pure* liquor."

He threw it down masterfully, then patrolled the apartment, up and down the stairs, through every room. He paused to gaze through the white swags of the curtains, parting the blinds and peeping.

"Oh," he sighed, then brightened up to sing his favorite Mills Brothers, the wry and sorrowful "Paper Doll," and he never got the words right, changing them around to suit his situation. He drove us crazy.

"Listen, when I come home at night, she'll be waiting. She'll be the truest doll in all the world. Not like you, Joan."

He stopped, sighed again. He sang the whole thing over to the creamy walls, recently freshened by Sebastian's brush, to every riser of the staircase, patting the banister Sebastian had tightened and balanced. He went over to Jettie Barefoot's York piano, struck a note, sighed again. "Boys, it's tough to be alone. Tough to love a doll that's not your own."

A long woeful hesitation.

Then a hiccup, a giggle.

"Look, Franklin." Joan had no sympathy for his sighs, hiccups, or giggles. "Look, just drink it all up and be done. Go on and feel sorry for yourself, but I'm a busy woman. I'm helping with the Vacation Bible School this summer. So drink it all up and don't let me find a drop when I get back this afternoon."

Joan and I left the apartment for the Badin Methodist Church, Joan fairly certain she had won, fairly certain he would drink up the J. W. Dant and be done. She slammed the door, certain.

Franklin sterilized the apartment behind her. He gathered all the pots and pans from our kitchen and carted them to the garbage cans beside the garage. He got to work with brush and bucket, scrubbing and scouring the kitchen, the bathroom, his little chiropractic office. Franklin bleached sinks, unclogged drains, disinfected and sterilized every surface, gouged out every blob of grease, every crumb in the cracked linoleum.

He even defrosted the refrigerator, refilled the ice trays.

We came back to a shining and gutted kitchen, a pile of ice cubes melting in the sink, the mop dripping over the back steps.

"What in the hell have you done?" Joan opened each cupboard, then smacked it shut. She washed the ice cubes down the drain.

Her face grimmer than Reverend Percy's and her eyes narrowed, Joan drew in her breath, then let it out in her familiar dramatic exhausted way.

"I'm waiting, Franklin."

Franklin Gentry whistled, sighed, gave his little hiccup and giggle. He beat time on the table with his shot glass. "Gonna get me a li'l paper doll all my own."

He beamed at me, winked his green eyes.

"I said, Franklin, what in the hell have you been doing here?"

Joan stood over him, hands on her hips, the June Allyson pageboy tossing. Her chin stuck out so smoothly, I admired the curve of her bone beneath the skin.

Franklin cocked his head back to look at her. He lifted the shot glass in salute, snickered, "Joan, darling, I threw everything out, by God, sugar. That's what I did."

He downed the J. W. Dant, sighed, lifted the glass in a second salute. "Goddammit, Joan, sugar, I threw it all out the door. Right there," pointing.

Continuing, "And you know something, darling, we are going to start all over again, sugar. That's right. Brand-new, Joan. And that's and that's," he winked at me again, "and that's a goddamn fact, Ti Baby."

"Franklin," corrected Joan Gentry in a tone as firm as her perfect chin and ash blond hair. "That is not a goddamn fact. This is."

She whirled, went out the back door, heading straight for the two garbage cans beside the garage. Joan exhumed each pot and pan, every last slotted spoon, sieve, and clanging eggbeater. She made me help her lug them back to the kitchen and shove them back in the cupboards. Joan smacked all the doors hard shut each time another one was filled.

She marched grandly up and down the backyard, bending over the garbage cans, jerking out her skillet and mixing bowls, roaster lid, grater, kettle, her pageboy blowing like a horse's mane.

I thought about all the palomino horses I'd seen in the movies, running wild through California canyons, standing on the top of the Rocky Mountains, stamping and neighing. Joan Gentry was like that in her purest anger. I hoped Old Sabby was somewhere seeing this. My mother, I hoped he saw, is the most beautiful woman in Badin, and the meanest. She could kill somebody.

At one point, Joan stopped short. She balled up both fists and lectured me, standing loaded with a stockpot and three pie plates.

183

"Listen to me, Titania Gentry," she huffed, "you better get everything you can when you can. Get a pile of money, get a good education, get you a good job, oh, get anything, it doesn't matter. Just so it's yours. Just so you won't have to put up with what I've put up with. Remember that. *Remember that.* And remember I told you."

I nodded. A summer wind scattered Badin dust in my eyes, brought tears. Franklin stayed at the kitchen table, whistling good-naturedly, then singing with flourish, "Hey, hey! I don' need no real-live girl. I need a paper doll."

He grabbed at Joan's skirt. " 'Cause a real-live girl, she jus' bitch the whole worl' and hey, hey!"

He announced his intentions to start all over, brand-new. "A chance, sugar," he offered Joan, "to change all this, me and you. Whatcha say?"

She clattered around him. She filled up the kitchen, tracked grass and dust, crumbs of tar and gravel, dead bugs, across the clean linoleum.

"Shut up, Franklin," she hissed as she went by.

"Hey, hey! Ti Baby." He pulled at me and I dropped an armful of muffin tins. "Listen, did I ever tell you I played big-league baseball? Did I tell you that? Hey, go get the baseball. I'll show you. Hey!"

He grinned, winked, twitched his moustache at me.

I grinned back, sidestepping his reach.

"Hey, Ti Baby," he begged, "come sit on my lap."

When she was done, Joan stood in the middle of the kitchen, her face flushed, hands on hips again, and glared at Franklin.

I scratched my sweaty legs, waited.

Franklin quit grinning. He gave one long sigh, peered solemnly into his shot glass, made a sort of summary, "Well, I tried to show you, Joan, sugar, that I could start all over the same as anybody, but if you don't want to, well, what can I say, sugar?"

Joan shook her head. "Too late, Franklin," she said. "You lose." Moving closer, she added, "Tomorrow, Franklin, when Titania and I get back from the church, there better not be anything like what we found today. You think?"

He didn't reply, just continued to peer into his glass, then gave a little hiccup, a giggle.

The next day I helped serve Aunt Della's refreshments, raisin cookies and lemonade, to the Vacation Bible School kids. I stirred the lemon rinds floating on top of the big tubs of ice and sugar water. I felt generous, comforted somewhat by the Eucharistic passing around of cookies and paper cups. I even felt affectionate toward Carol Jean Spence's baby sister Pam. I offered her a big raisin cookie.

"She can't eat that," said Carol Jean, taking the cookie out of Pam's fist. "Don't you know anything about babies, Ti? Here, you eat it."

"I don't want it now. She slobbered on it."

Carol Jean shrugged, exasperated. "I wouldn't be scared to eat after a little baby. God, you're so dumb."

Carol Jean crumbled the cookie, rolled the raisins over her palm, then stuffed it all in her mouth. "See, I'm not afraid to eat after a little baby."

I polished my own deep generosity and pardoned Carol Jean everything. It was possible, maybe, to love and be loved in this brutal world. So long as there were Methodist cookies and raisins, I could offer the world my love feast, I could save everybody.

Then we got back to the apartment.

We discovered Franklin had somehow captured and somehow bathed, in our own tub, Erskine "Sonny" Kelly's old Toto. Franklin had dried him on the best white towels, combed and brushed his old mottled rat fur and clipped, somehow, Toto's ugly claws with Joan Gentry's manicure set, the scissors and file made from the finest Swedish surgical steel.

Franklin Gentry had somehow greased the old dog's butt hole from our own personal jar of Vaseline, the same Vaseline used to shine my patent leather recital shoes.

"Hey, hey!" Franklin beamed. "That poor old dog looked at me, Joan, sugar, you just would not believe this, darling. He looked at me and wagged his tail and barked like he was trying to tell me, 'God-dammit, man, that feels good!'"

Franklin, enthralled with his generosity, in love with himself and admiring his own humane concern for Sonny Kelly's Toto, clicked his tongue and winked at me. "Hey, hey! Ti Baby, aren't you proud of me? I had a hard time catching that damn dog, too!"

Joan looked stunned, paralyzed.

I stared at the jar of Vaseline. A neat tunnel glistened where Franklin's finger had plunged, driven by his burning zeal to bring relief to Toto.

"Hey, hey! You both saw how that old dog's wiped his ass all over the grass in our yard, hell, in everybody's yard lately?" Franklin launched into a generous exposition. "Well, when I finished giving him a bath, he jumped out of my arms and started wiping his ass all over this apartment. So I said, 'Hey! I know what you need, old dog, and I know what I'm talking about because I am a chiropractor, Dr. Franklin Gentry, goddammit! And what you need is a little Vaseline to help you overcome that problem!'"

Franklin belched, then beamed more brightly than ever and clicked his tongue at me again, winked.

He put me in mind of a big red Humpty Dumpty with a black moustache, winking and belching and grinning at me.

I tried not to laugh at him and make it worse, make Joan mad at me, too. So I stared into the Vaseline.

"So, you see, Joan, sugar, I got this trusty Vaseline, and like I said, that old dog was tickled to death. I had to catch him, too, all over again. And that was not easy, I can tell you, darling. No, that was not easy to catch that damn dog again."

Franklin lifted his shot glass in salute to Joan Gentry, still paralyzed in the bathroom door. "Now, Joan, sugar," he admonished her, lifting not only the glass, but also his brows, "you have to remember to treat poor dumb dogs, poor dumb old Badin dogs, the way you your ownself would want to be treated, if you was a poor old dog, darling."

He took a deep snuffling drink. J. W. Dant spilled over the rim. "And if it was all changed around, sugar"—he took another swallow—"and if you, Joan, was the poor, poor, *poor* dumb old dog, and he was you."

At that Joan Gentry came back to life. She picked up the jar of Vaseline. She looked into the tunnel left by Franklin's finger. She let loose one of her exhausted dramatic sighs and walked toward the little trash can under the wash basin.

Dog hair was still in the bathtub and a thick dog smell all over the room. Joan stood a moment, balancing the Vaseline on her palm. Then she turned and threw it back at Franklin, who, blissfully confident he had won this time, had turned himself and was strolling away, humming again about his infernal paper doll and how he had to find her.

The jar, hard and cruel as a grenade, caught him between the shoulders, bounced down and shattered on the bathroom floor. Franklin staggered, reached to grab the door knob as he went down on top of the broken glass. I watched his fingers slide in the clear blobs of jelly.

Joan never flinched.

I watched, the back of my neck prickling, as Franklin Gentry groaned and maneuvered very carefully to face us both. He lifted his shot glass, still intact, a smear of J. W. Dant jiggling inside, and he saluted.

I saw he was cut.

"Ma'am?" I pointed out, "He's bleeding bad."

"Oh?" said Joan. "Just rub a little Vaseline on him."

I put out a foot to touch one of the blobs of jelly. I heard Toto barking and growling in the street and I hoped that dog would die horribly before the morning.

And in the morning, Franklin was not humane, not at all generous. He cursed at Joan across the table, his teeth clenched, "You brought the blood, you bitch! You threw that goddamn jar of Vaseline and you meant to hit me. You brought the blood!"

She put down her coffee cup, clenched her own teeth. "Of course, I meant to bring the blood, you asshole."

"Hey, hey! Remember this, Ti Baby," he charged me, never taking his hot green eyes off Joan. "She meant to bring the blood!"

I shivered inside my summer plisse pajamas and spooned up cornflakes. I was not afraid of either Joan or Franklin anymore. I didn't care anymore, either, how much blood they brought or what they threw at each other. I knew they were liars. Just like the handsome painter in my room, the one who pulled the paper dolls off my walls.

I'll come back and get you! If you do this again!

Franklin slammed out without eating any breakfast. Joan settled back, shook out *The Charlotte Observer,* and took her time drinking her coffee. I watched the tips of Joan's fingers trembling against the cup.

Joan and Franklin wanted me to keep them good, define the limits, set up the game and keep score. He'd ask, "Which one do you like the best, me or your mother?" She would be pointing out, "See him in there? That's your daddy."

I rinsed out the cereal bowl and set it on the drainboard. Joan poured another cup of coffee. She never looked at me when I went out the door.

"You know what?" I told Old Sabby in his backyard. "My mother and daddy hate each other. They'd kill each other if they didn't have to go to jail for it."

He grinned. "No," he said, "that's just true love. That's the real thing, Sister." He mounted the blade he had just sharpened for the push mower and squirted oil in both wheels.

"Come on, Sister," he encouraged, "get your old baton and march down the path I'm getting ready to mow through this grass here. You need to march this morning."

Sebastian pushed off through the long weedy backyard, a Camel bobbing in the corner of his mouth. I gazed after him a minute, drinking in the smells of cut grass and machine oil and cigarette smoke.

I considered for a moment that there might be things Old Sabby didn't know. Like how it really was with Franklin and Joan Gentry. Like how I had to play these infernal and tiresome games with them every day of my life.

I forgot Franklin and Joan and followed him. My old baton flashed for a moment like some fiery defiant wheel.

KELBY WAS DEFIANT, GENTLY defiant, as I've said. He never fussed with people, never forced them. When Kelby didn't like something, he just walked away. He wouldn't discipline the girls when they were little. Left it to me to do the yelling and the enforcing. Then one Saturday, when Hannah was about three years old and pitching the worst fit if she didn't get to go barefoot in the yard, I told Kelby I was tired of it and he better do something or I might kill Hannah.

It was too cool to go barefoot, the middle of March, a sunny morning but with air sharp enough to raise goose bumps on bare skin. Hannah screamed and kicked at us, trying to kick off her Keds.

Sarah dangled from the swing set watching. She hoped Hannah would get the spanking of her life right there in the yard. "I mean it," I told Kelby. "You do something."

Kelby picked up Hannah, turned her upside down and held her

by her ankles at arm's length. Hannah was chunky, a squirmy handful, screaming and kicking. But Kelby was stronger, more determined, and without saying a word, he held Hannah like that until she shut up. Then he flipped her back right side up and set her on the yard. "It's too cold to go barefoot, Hannah," he said.

She gulped and blinked at Kelby. She didn't scream another thing about going barefoot. Sarah giggled, pushed herself on the swings. I gulped and blinked as much as Hannah.

Kelby spread out in the hammock we'd tied between two big pines. Hannah went over and stood looking at him. After a while, he settled her in with him and they rocked together a good long time.

I didn't know what to think about Kelby holding her upside down like that. But I knew it had something to do with power and defiance, with confidence and love and trust.

He held Hannah straight out by her ankles. He could have dropped her at any minute, splattered Hannah on the ground. I'd have dropped her, probably, because I was so mad at her, so worn out with her screams and her kicking at me.

Kelby just waited it out.

Hannah trusted him.

14

Showy morning-glory vines covered Mr. McSherry's garage. The concupiscent blossoms, loud as trumpets, cavorted pink and naked in the hot sun. I half-expected the morning glories to pick up the aluminum bronze building, shake the gray dust and snails from its foundation, and fly off with it over Badin like a big pink shooting star.

Sebastian worked at a rough table inside the garage. Pink light from the vines at the one small window threw mottled aureoles over him. The garage's opened double doors showed a sprawling vista of alleys and tiled roofs and a bright nervous line of Carolina poplars. As always, Carolina Aluminum hissed and boomed at the farthest horizon of the vista.

I had followed the orbit of Old Sabby all summer. I didn't care who knew it, so glad was I to put his big healthy body between me and anything that threatened or criticized. I often felt as riotous and pink as the morning glories climbing his garage, healthy and shameless, loud and full of color.

That morning I looked up from the wood shavings that fell in sticky yellow curls, faintly sweetish, from Old Sabby's plane into my fingers, to recognize Miss Tiny Bodeen, followed by Madine Ponds and her broom, mincing down the alley toward us.

Big and muscley, Miss Tiny was nevertheless dainty. She side-stepped all the slick black tar bubbles that pocked the alley's hot surface. Madine imitated her gait.

A peculiar dread crawled through me watching the two ladies approach. This is it, I thought. They're coming to get Old Sabby, take him back off to the Japs and Hitler. They are going to make him go back to the paratroopers.

I sat with my mouth hanging open and my fingers itching in the sticky wood shavings. I waited to see what the two ladies wanted.

They wanted to ask Sebastian a favor. "Oh, Mr. McSherry," they trilled. I cringed to hear them call Sebastian "Mr. McSherry." I thought it aged and weakened him. It put a filthy plaid handkerchief to his nose and turned all his erotic snores to rheumy wheezes.

"Oh, Mr. McSherry, sir," they repeated. Madine waved the broom as if she expected him, obviously sensuous and profane, to attack Miss Tiny.

"Do you think you could do us a little favor? We are planning a Galilean service, yes, a Galilean service for this coming Sunday evening, not tomorrow but next Sunday evening, for the inspirational benefit of our fine young people here in Badin where we preached the Lord in their Vacation Bible School for these last two weeks."

They paused. Miss Tiny fluttered her lashes and included me in her generous smile.

"We were thinking of having it down by Badin Lake, on the pier. And we were wondering if you couldn't make us something. Sister Ponds has been seeing how handy you seem with building stuff, always fixing up things over here. Could you make us something?"

Miss Tiny flashed Sebastian a big smile. She plumped up her pale frizzled hair with a hand so fat, the knuckles looked like dents in dough.

Sebastian stayed the plane. A curl of wood writhed before the blade. "Sure," he said. "What?"

"Well," Miss Tiny fluttered her lashes again. Madine clenched the broom, squinted at me on the floor. "We were wondering if you couldn't make us a cross?"

Miss Tiny beamed. She was as naked and showy as the morning glories. I imagined they actually shriveled some in her presence.

"A what?" Old Sabby flared his eyes, his nostrils.

I spilled all the wood shavings, causing a big sticky cloud of yellow dust to fly up. I sneezed three times, quick and hard.

Miss Tiny took out a Kleenex and handed it over. "A cross," she reaffirmed, a greedy dramatic emphasis in her voice, her eyes shining.

Miss Tiny and Madine Ponds clearly appalled Sebastian. He gaped, blinked. "How big?"

Then he blinked again at Miss Tiny, taking in her muscley wrestler's girth, said, "Well, look, I mean, now what in the hell are you really talking about?"

Old Sabby took out a Camel and put it to his lips. He regarded the ladies with deepening amusement. His eyes took on a curious shade of blue.

The ladies stiffened. "It is not necessary to cuss, Mr. McSherry," scolded Madine, advancing two dainty steps with the broom. "I told you." She looked back at Miss Tiny. "I told you he had a mouth."

Miss Tiny swept her aside. "We need a cross big enough to see from far off," she explained eagerly. She looked at Old Sabby, measuring him. Her eyes nearly disappeared in her gobby face with the effort, like two buttonholes sewn together.

She bubbled out cheerily, "We need one your size. *Man* size!"

Miss Tiny Bodeen beamed and punched Madine's frail shoulder. I marveled that she didn't crumple to the floor. Instead Madine added, "You can make us one, Mr. McSherry. We would appreciate it with all our hearts. And it would make such a good example for all these young people!"

She fished out a dry little smile for me.

I waited to hear what Old Sabby would say.

He drew deeply, thoughtfully, on the Camel, still regarding the both of them. He gave a little shrug. His eyes colored deeper blue. "Okay, ladies. I'll make you a cross. Anything else? You want me to nail anybody on it?"

He turned back to the plane.

They ignored this last remark, consulting busily. Miss Tiny cleared her throat. "Oh, yes, we just about forgot. We want you to wrap it up thick with rags and paper and stuff like that. We want to burn it, you see."

With that, they beamed and turned and minced their way up the tar-bubbled alley. The pink morning glories curled tight shut, hanging in pale shriveled convolvuli along the eaves of the garage. They put me in mind of little furled-up pink umbrellas. Madine and Bodeen, I mocked, Madine and Bodeen. One so dry and skinny, the other so gobby and fat.

"Galilean service! Did you hear that, Sister?" Sebastian hissed over the plane. He shoved it with deliberate recklessness. "I told you they were bullshitters and fuckers. Didn't I tell you, Sister?"

He argued and carried on, but he built the cross. I watched it emerge, rough-hewn under his unfailing adze, to a thing six feet upright, with a crossbar reaching a span of four, T-shaped, like two giant sticks of kindling some giant might rub to spark a fire.

I thought he touched it sometimes with true love, at other times with murderous hate. He stood on the cross and hacked at it between his feet. I shivered, watching the blade whistle down.

He wrapped it in rags and sacks stuffed with newspapers, strips of thick dirty burlap, stuff which Miss Tiny and Madine Ponds brought to the garage. They tittered and giggled and admired the progress he made. "Oh, Mr. McSherry, you are making it just right! You could've made the real cross, Mr. McSherry! The one Jesus had."

Miss Tiny put a hand over her heart. "Oh," she said to Madine, "this makes me feel so much closer to the Lord."

He was always in a worse mood after they visited. I asked, "Why are you doing this, if you hate it so bad?"

He shrugged. "I don't know. I'm just doing it, Sister." He changed the subject, attacked me, "Why do you bang on the piano, why do you stay in the house with your mama and daddy? Shit, Sister. Nobody knows why they do a thing. Nobody knows why they make a cross."

Sebastian wrapped the rags tighter, until they hugged the raw pine, whispered to it of the hot flames to come, the pure clear joy of their martyrdom, the ecstasy of sainthood. It would be some great big splendid pungent orgasm of kerosene and a plain old sulfur-tipped kitchen match. *Burn!*

He made me feel uneasy, like I'd better not turn my back on him.

When it was finished, Old Sabby loaded the swaddled cross onto the back of a pickup truck he had recently bought. With me sitting beside him, he took the cross to the edge of Badin Lake to set up for the Galilean service.

We bumped along. The seat covers had cracked open and straw stuck out. I wondered why he bought such an ugly old truck. Sonny Kelly's ten-speed bike was better.

"You know, Sister," Sebastian glanced over. "We are privileged to get to do this for those sons of bitches. I say privileged, Sister, because Jesus Christ himself couldn't get a foot through their front door."

I nodded. I got a headache from bumping in the hot truck. My legs itched from the straw. "Are you a Christian?" I asked him. I was immediately shocked at myself. I didn't mean to ask that. I didn't even want to know that. I sounded like one of Reverend Percy's exclamatory tracts.

He threw back his head and laughed hard. I watched the muscles throb in Old Sabby's throat, the hairs in his nose tremble. Old Sabby made me want to throw back my head and laugh, too, feeling my throat muscles throb, my nose hairs tremble.

We dumped out the cross and it lay on the shore of Badin Lake waiting for its glorious Galilean launching. I poked it with a big toe. Sebastian set out a garbage can of sand and bailed lake water over it.

"What're you doing that for?" I watched the dry sand darken.

"Wetting it down. What does it look like I'm doing, Sister?" His voice was suddenly hateful. He hurt my feelings. He was mad about something I couldn't figure out. In short, Old Sabby seemed as selfish and unpredictable right then as Joan and Franklin.

"Are you a Christian?" I asked him, this time not caring if he laughed and not shocked that I asked.

"Are you, Sister?" He packed the wet sand, dragged the cross closer to the can.

"Everybody's a Christian. Even if they don't believe in it. They're still a Christian."

"Oh, Sister!" Old Sabby sat back on his haunches, then lay back full length on the shore. "Oh, Sister!" he exclaimed. "This place has got you in spite of yourself!"

I frowned. I felt diminished, betrayed, as if Sebastian had misunderstood me on purpose. I got back in his truck. When Sebastian had anchored the cross in the wet sand, he got in, too, and drove us back to Entwistle Street.

Before I got out, not looking at him, I said, "Nothing's got me in spite of myself."

He reached a hand, tugged my braids. "Okay, Sister," he soothed. "You're right, nothing's got you, not a thing."

Inside the apartment, Joan had everybody's embroidery pieces from the Vacation Bible School classes spread on the kitchen table, judging them. Mine was the ugliest one, twisted and spotted. Joan planned on giving a prize. It irked her that I couldn't win, that I hadn't even tried to win.

"I told you to wash your hands before you worked on your embroidery, didn't I?" she reminded. "Look at that. See that thumb print?"

"I don't care. I don't want to embroider."

"Look here, at Carol Jean's." Joan picked up a bureau scarf. "See? Perfect."

"I don't care." I went to the York and made a fist and banged it hard over the entire keyboard. I stomped upstairs and yanked open my closet. I scrunched into the dark back corner, clattering empty wire hangers and rumpling my fresh clothes hanging there.

I held the old baton to my face and broke into a soft steady weeping. General MacArthur stared while I hoarsed out, "What'd he mean, what'd he mean? And who'd he think he was, saying that to me? Sebastian," I snuffled, "you're as hateful and selfish as Erskine 'Sonny' Kelly, as Franklin Gentry. As Joan."

I WAS NOT A candidate for baptism. Nor was I a member of the Glad Tidings Choir, but Joan Gentry made me stand with the rest of my Sunday School class out on the Badin Lake pier that Sunday evening for the Galilean service. I wanted to be with Old Sabby back on the shore. I wanted him to make me a fire baton with as much skill and love and murderous hate as he had made the cross for Miss Tiny Bodeen and Madine Ponds. I wanted Sebastian to stand on it and hack it out with his sharp adze, then swaddle it with rags. At the right moment, when all eyes were glued to the center of a big stadium, the American Legion Ballpark, Old Sabby would strike the match and hand it, burning like a comet, over to me.

I would twirl hoops of fire. Throw fire around my red-sequined body, step in and back out of pure hot fire. I would convert all sinners.

Old Sabby would be converted to me.

My little stories were delicious and encouraging.

I stood in my white recital dress next to Carol Jean Spence. Carol Jean's face was the face of a stranger now, its tar-black eyes, its black Buster Brown hair and clown grin. I felt I'd known this person a hundred years ago. The memory made me sad.

Carol Jean Spence didn't feel sad. Didn't behave like a relic left over from a hundred years ago. She giggled, whispered, "Ti, this is fun. I can't wait to see all this."

Those giggles, those words, *this is fun, I can't wait,* did not come out of somebody who had seen a light reconnaissance aircraft sink in the middle of Badin Lake. Don't you remember there's a man out there? I wanted to yell at Carol Jean. A man crashed and drowned right in front of our eyes, don't you remember?

The Galilean service began calmly enough. About a hundred yards from the pier, two Badin policemen sat in a rowboat loaded to the gunwales with life rings and ropes, big cushions, oars and long reaching poles. This was for safety, they had persuaded Reverend Percy, and this was their job, Badin Lake being a public-use area, in case the people got carried away and fell in Badin Lake and tried to drown each other as they accepted Christ for their personal savior.

Reverend Percy had announced throughout Badin that he would be sure to get several conversions and testimonials during the Galilean service, to say nothing of all the baptisms right there in Badin Lake, exactly as the Lord Himself was baptized in the Jordan River.

A big crowd had assembled on the shore. They came, Sebastian had predicted, to hear people confess all the stuff they had done in the past year, who slept with whose wife, who killed who over a poker game in the back room of the Olympia Cafe, and who got

198

drunk. They came, also, he said, to see if somebody would get drowned in the lake by that big fat preacher and his big fat lady-wrestler wife.

I ran all this through my head as I looked at the two policemen waiting in the rowboat, oars in hand, pistols gleaming. The sun struck their visors. They sat lined in fire.

The candidates for baptism filed quietly through the twilight, led by Miss Tiny Bodeen, her head bowed over her fat clasped hands. The candidates wore pajamas and nighties under bathrobes. They looked rather victimized and a little anxious. I was embarrassed by their shabby, vulnerable postures, their old chenille robes. A pile of fresh towels was heaped under the pavilion. The candidates would dry off there after they passed through Badin Lake water and got saved.

I was embarrassed by their towels, too. These people should be clothed in shining robes, dried off and garbed again in more shining robes, maybe given a crown.

Everything got on my nerves at once. What got on my nerves the most was Erskine "Sonny" Kelly, who was hanging around on the shore, waiting to help Old Sabby launch the burning cross at the right moment, having first drenched it in kerosene.

I glowered at him over there with Sebastian, hanging around the way I wanted to. I wanted to drench kerosene on the cross, smell the kerosene, smell Sebastian's match, his Camels, his sweat. Nothing, I pictured, shutting my eyes and making fists, nothing burned as pure as plain kerosene soaked into old rags swaddling a six-foot cross hewn out of fresh pine.

Even the oily black smoke would seem pure, precious as incense, a sweet exotic resin.

And Sonny got to do all that! God knows, too, what he might be telling Old Sabby about me! *I took her into the basement under my house, he could lie and brag, and took all her clothes off, and she let me,*

199

and we did it right there in my basement under the kitchen with my mama walking back and forth over the top of us and the dog barking.

I opened my eyes, gritted my teeth and stared hard over there. Sebastian had wired and anchored both the cross and the can in an old skiff. At the right moment, Sonny Kelly would wade in Badin Lake with Sebastian, take hold of the tow ropes and after Sebastian struck a match to the cross, he would help him guide the whole conflagration around the shore into the adoring view of the people on the pier.

I glanced over the people again, embarrassed now not only of them, but also of myself and my impatience. I wanted to scratch under the white organdy into both my armpits, dig deep next to my bones, boldly, with abandon and flourish. Show myself a complete savage.

Carol Jean Spence stood there perfectly calm and quiet, suffering no torments. What did she care about Old Sabby over there with Erskine "Sonny" Kelly? What did she care about not getting to help Old Sabby? What did she care anymore, I sneered, that a man crashed and drowned in the middle of the lake and that we had all three stood there on roller skates and watched it and Sonny had been smoking a Lucky Strike?

Carol Jean Spence was indeed shallow, indeed a disappointment.

I concentrated on the water, the darkening sky, the summer air. I drank in the breeze blowing across Badin Lake, its scent of ripe flowers, the heavy greenish odor of cut grass and the faint muddy and fertile odor of Badin Lake itself.

Streetlights winked in town, reflected along the rippling lake at the far end across from Carolina Aluminum. Carolina Aluminum kept booming and hissing and shrieking the way it had all my life in Badin, North Carolina, oblivious toward the people who tended it and lived beside it, the people who at that moment stood on the pier across from it and waited to receive the Lord.

Reverend Percy met the candidates for baptism at the promenade end of the pier. He grabbed each one, shook hands, stared into their eyes. "Bless you, child! Welcome to the Lord! Praise God, hallelujah!"

He had arranged special music for the service, two tubby guitar players and one banjo picker. Madine Ponds, robed like the people in the Glad Tidings Choir, took a place next to the musicians on the promenade. I was surprised. I'd never heard Madine sing, never heard her make more than furious little dry shrieks, shaking her broom, warning the neighbors of Entwistle Street to get off her path. She had never even been a member of the Badin Methodist Church.

But here she was, converted, ready to sing in front of people.

Reverend Percy raised his meaty hands, prayed over them on the pier and signaled the guitar players and the banjo picker. They struck up and Madine, standing absolutely alone, without even her old broom to bolster her, opened her dry pinched-up mouth and sang lustily about joy and blood and blessed Jesus.

I realized Madine Ponds, in that moment, was another kind of genuine champeen. When she had finished singing, my mouth was hanging open. I felt a thread of drool start from the corner of my lips. I was even more ashamed than before, swallowing clumsily and scrubbing at my red face.

Never again, I scolded, will you make fun of Madine, threaten to blow off her head like an old dried-up dandelion with one puff of your mighty breath. Never will you make fun of her broom again.

The special music done, Reverend Percy delivered his message. He stood up on the benches of the promenade and his voice bounced over Badin Lake, bumped against the two policemen in their rowboat, splashed the dark rocky shore. He bellowed about the same things Madine had sung, joy and blood and blessed Jesus.

Then he struck a new note, ultra-high and shrill. He left blood behind, put joy and blessed Jesus on hold, as he tackled stronger stuff. I was again enthralled and again felt the drool spin from my open mouth.

"You young women out there," he screeched, "it is to you I want to reach out this evening. It is you who holds the home together. And it is to you, young women, that I cry so pitifully this wonderful summer evening here in Badin. Young women," he begged, "don't dance!"

Daince! Don't daince!

His accent echoed flat and nasal. I wondered what dancing had to do with holding the home together. He went on.

"Because if you dance, young women, you will smoke cigarettes! And if you smoke cigarettes, young women, you will drink liquor!"

Likker!

He lost the *q* entirely, gave it two long vulgar *k*'s.

"And if you drink liquor, young women!"

Reverend Percy nearly pitched off the pier into the darkening air, nearly exploded with delivery, "If you drink liquor, young women, you will be loose with men!"

The people on the pier, under the pavilion, and along the shore applauded. They swayed with his message. I felt envious of Reverend Percy, fat and dumb as he was. I wanted people to applaud and sway with me. With Old Sabby.

Reverend Percy's eyes roved the promenade, lighting accusingly on several people. Madine Ponds stood with her thin hands locked over her robe, her face transfixed. I looked toward Joan Gentry standing under the pavilion. I wondered if Joan heard what Reverend Percy said. If she thought of Franklin and Renee Ames, of the little shots of J. W. Dant, and Vaseline on the bathroom floor, of Franklin's blood, *You brought the blood, you bitch!*

If she thought of Titania, and what she said to me, *And damn you, too.*

I wondered if Joan ever thought about Sebastian McSherry next

202

door, of Old Sabby snoring behind my bedroom wall. Or of me, Titania Gentry, listening to it, my thirteen-year-old ear flowered into an enormous whorish petunia, absorbing his noise, *I am not a little girl, I am thirteen years old, I have titties, I can smoke a cigarette, I know about sex.*

Joan Gentry, I concluded, didn't think of anything. I fastened my whole attention on the benches of the promenade where Reverend Percy stood. They bounced with his weight as he bent forward, then backward, with the ecstasy of his message.

Daince! Cigarettes! Likker! Loose with men!

Reverend Percy gathered fresh power and started all over. The tubby guitar players and the banjo picker twanged and frammed. The policemen rocked in their boat. Then Reverend Percy made his final Parade Lunge, his Majorette's Fancy Strut toward God.

"These words in my mouth, people," he thundered, "these words in my mouth come straight from the *Almighty!* He told me to dwell among you and seek out His enemies in Badin, to drive out Satan and the lechers who are among you! To drive out the despoilers of young virgins, the wicked moneylenders in His temple! He told me to tell you this tonight, people!"

Reverend Percy right then, his fat finger jabbing toward heaven, fell off the benches of the promenade backward into Badin Lake. He spluttered. He thrashed the dark cola-colored water to a suds.

The Glad Tidings Choir and the candidates for baptism and all of my Sunday School class watched with unabashed delight and horror as he beat Badin Lake to pieces. He bobbed like a big fat cork, choking with each rising and falling, until he passed into a more dangerous depth of Badin Lake, thrashing and spluttering and carrying on until he had maneuvered his hulk close to the policemen and their rowboat.

The policemen sat smirking like two green toads on a lily pad, plainly in no hurry to save Reverend Percy. Who was he, anyway? Just some fat old son of a bitch from out of town.

"Throw out the lifeline, brothers!" gasped Reverend Percy. I could see his eyes roll. I could feel the spin of my drool down my chin a third time, falling finally to blotch the white organdy.

At this moment, exactly the right moment, as the sun completely dropped behind the horizon of Carolina Aluminum with its impressive smokestacks and catwalks, the burning cross floated around the curve of the shore, towed by Sebastian and Sonny Kelly. The water glistened on their thighs. I watched their strong legs push through Badin Lake. I hungered to be there towing and pushing with them.

Nobody else watched.

Everybody else watched Reverend Percy. The policemen, blinking and smirking, reached out the long pole to him and he grabbed it, nearly tipping them over.

They made a procession back to shore, one policeman rowing, grunting in rhythm, and the other policeman holding the pole with Reverend Percy hanging to the end of it. He accepted that pole, I mocked, for his own personal savior.

Meanwhile, the burning glory, all six feet of it, floated up to the pier, and was upset by the thrashing water. And just out of my finger's reach as I, the recital organdy crumpling around my ankles, bent over to welcome it. The cross bowed once, twice in its garbage can. It flared brightly and tipped over and sank, skiff and all, sizzling to the dark muddy bottom of Badin Lake.

I snapped my fingers, *what!*

Reverend Percy lay beached, dripping and gasping. He sucked up the sweet Badin air as fast as he could in his fat mouth. Miss Tiny Bodeen knelt beside him, praising God and giving her testimony.

"Snatched from the jaws of death! Hallelujah, praise God! A miracle!"

Madine Ponds hurried down the pier, followed by the two guitar players and the banjo picker. She peered at the sodden man. "Just like Jonah out of the belly of the whale!" she added.

I was mortified. I knew for a fact that gods and heroes ought to come floating up out of the dark water of Badin Lake. They ought to come like Old Sabby, home from the Japs and Hitler, from fighting our enemies and driving them out with bombs and guns. Wounded, maybe, spilling their own red blood, breaking their noses like General MacArthur.

They ought to rise from the middle of Badin Lake like the pilot should have from the light reconnaissance aircraft, faintly apologetic for not making that last trick, wiping off his face and saying, "Well, it was an easy error to make, you know. I looked left when I shoulda looked right. That's all."

They didn't lie around like big fat whales sucking air and hollering for Jesus.

I heard thunder across Badin Lake. But when I looked for the clouds, I only saw the winking lights of Badin, North Carolina, and the throbbing red sparks thrown out by Carolina Aluminum. And then I saw Sebastian swimming through the dark cola-colored water. His arms made beautiful swift strokes, pull, pull, as he covered the distance easily. He was as powerful as the silent stars over my head, all of them swimming in rhythm.

He was all by himself. "Old Sabby, Old Sabby," I murmured, "Sebastian McSherry," my eyes following his body through Badin Lake.

Where was Erskine "Sonny" Kelly? Oh, who cares where Sonny is? I smoothed my white dress, smiling. Then I jerked back, sharply alarmed.

Sebastian strode out of the water and straight into a woman's long bare arms. Where'd she come from? Did Sonny know about this? It would make me so mad if Sonny Kelly already knew this. I would hate him forever. Who? I couldn't see who. She's tall. She's got long strong arms. She can wrap Sebastian McSherry up inside of her. The back of my neck prickled. I rubbed my eyes hard. I tried to part a path through the thick summer night with both hands, *Who?*

15

When I took Kelby home to Badin to meet Joan and Franklin, they insisted on showing him every picture they had ever made of me, from a bald baby right on up to me standing beside the hollyhocks by the garage, posed in my graduation cap and gown. Kelby was very generous about it, smiling his old way, making funny little remarks.

After Franklin had a few more bourbons, he dragged out our old projector and showed Kelby the movies he'd made of me twirling the baton. These were in color. I was fascinated at how the color had taken on a rosier and more golden hue, as if it had ripened like fruit or flowers.

The movies were without sound, of course, and they struck me as downright eerie, possessing my childish energy and enthusiasm, legs kicking, fancy struts, high wild aerial pitches, the baton flashing like a needle in the 1940s sunshine.

Joan could be caught not looking at the camera. Franklin sneaked up on her watching me instead of him. And when she realized the film was capturing her, she turned and scolded Franklin, laughing the same time she was frowning. Her June Allyson pageboy was tied with a ribbon. She looked so girlish, I couldn't believe she was my mother. She had on a pink halter-top, her middle bare over a dark dirndl skirt. The halter-top was knotted between her breasts, and her shoulders shone smooth as gold in the old film.

Joan had never seemed girlish to me before—and I'd looked at the old home movies a thousand times. She had always seemed imperial, like General MacArthur. Suddenly, I felt a bit sad, as if I had lost something.

There was one little part of me playing the old black York. Mostly shots of my hands roaming the keyboard. An arpeggio stretched my crooked little finger. I flashed a quick smile up at Franklin, then it blurred off.

"I was trying some inside shots there," Franklin said. "Borrowed some guy's lights. It was like a real movie production."

I couldn't remember it. It was easier to look at the baton pitching up into the Badin air, then tumbling back to my skinny bruised and sunburned arms. The twirling was more real to me than the arpeggios.

"Run it backward," suggested Kelby, "let's see what she does backward."

Franklin ran it backward. We laughed at me marching down Entwistle Street backward, throwing the baton backward, smiling and bowing backward.

That should have been a dark clue to me about Kelby.

That should have shown me something about my future with Kelby.

The futures of our daughters, Sarah and Hannah.

WITH EVERY CITIZEN LODGED behind smooth beaverboard apartment walls or in the French Colonial bungalows, each bungalow and apartment exactly alike, I pictured Badin, North Carolina, as one of the old walled cities of Europe with towers and belfries full of roosting pigeons. The pigeons cooed. The sounds spread like soft gurgling water over all the tile roofs as I wallowed in my bath on Entwistle Street.

One wall melted into another wall. I can tap on the wall, I shut my eyes, breathing steam and sweet bubbles, Joan Gentry's Elizabeth Arden bubble bath, I can tap on this bathroom wall right here on Entwistle Street and it will be felt all over the town.

Like my heartbeat. Pass it on, pass it on, the walls will say. Beat, beat, pass it on. I smiled, settled beneath the bubbles. I can hear people hollering at each other, loving and kissing each other, getting sick and puking in the toilet. I can hear a baby on the top of Pomona Hill wake up and cry, and Mr. McSherry hit the wall with a stick, *Shit fire! Shut up!*

The blurry reverberations rippled my warm bath. The Badin sun streaked the thin walls around me, and I imagined the baby's fingers on the top of Pomona Hill twitching in his mouth when he sucked himself back to sleep.

I lolled in the claw-footed white tub up to my chin in Joan's bubbles while Franklin squatted on the floor focusing his new camera.

"This way. This way," he directed. He turned the lens, checked his focus.

Joan stood in the door, smiling, but with a deep line digging across her forehead. "Look pretty," she reminded. "Keep your chin up out of the water."

I shifted in the tub, feeling the bubbles break in my nose and spread over my shoulders. I squeezed my toes and thought how shriveled up they were already. My fingers looked like pink peanut shells.

With braids pinned together on top of my head, my bathing suit plastered around my body just beneath the bubbles, I was posing for pictures at Joan's and Franklin's request. Joan beat the Elizabeth Arden bubbles into a luscious froth, piling them higher and higher, like sweet egg whites, like the Alps.

"We can sell this picture to *The American Home,*" she promised Franklin. "They run pictures like this all the time. Kids who don't look half as good as Titania get in there all the time. Or in *Photography.*"

She stepped back, inspecting me, the braids, the bubbles.

"You're going to look like a movie star," encouraged Franklin. "This will be the best picture I've made with this camera yet, Ti Baby."

"I'm getting shriveled up! It's cold. I want to get out."

"Just one minute. Smile."

The flash went off in my face.

"You can get out now." Joan shut the door behind them.

I turned the hot water on full force. I warmed myself in the quick gush and started pointing out things in a self-righteous manner. "Joan didn't want a picture of me twirling a baton."

I lifted a foot to the hot faucet. "Joan didn't want a picture of me playing the old black York." I pushed the faucet back to a slower flow.

Joan had wanted Elizabeth Arden bubbles and my face like some kind of babyish Valentine with braids pinned on top, just a tease of bare shoulders, just a whisper of little thirteen-year-old bosoms under the white froth. She got Franklin to come in there and make the pictures. After he got the enlargements back from Jack Rabbit Photo Finishing in Spartanburg, South Carolina, they would send them all off to *The American Home,* to *Photography.* They would make everybody famous.

I settled lower in the tub. A chipped oval on the bottom showed through the water, looking like a broken oyster shell with pearly layers of grit. I stroked the chip with my shriveled fingers and glanced around, feeling suddenly generous and cozy, admiring everything my eyes touched. Damp towels, Joan's aqua chenille robe hanging from a hook in the door, mineral oil and bars of Ivory and Franklin's Old Spice, a tube of Ipana worming over the washbasin, the ridged oval bottle of Halo shampoo with a bright aqua cap, a brighter aqua than Joan's robe.

Maybe, I thought, if I poured a whole bottle of Halo over my braids, I would get up out of the tub blond as June Allyson, smelling like Joan Gentry. I put a hand to the braids, unpinned them and let them drop heavy as ropes into the suds. Thirteen years old and they're still keeping me a little girl.

I wallowed and listened shamelessly at the wall, hoping for Sebastian to come into Mr. McSherry's bathroom right next to ours. I hoped Old Sabby, hot off the desert, handsome and mean as the Sheik of Araby with a white robe and a curved sword, would come crashing through the wall and jerk me out of the tub and run off with me, wet and slippery, under his arm.

I grinned. If that happened, Carol Jean Spence would scream, "Get loose, Ti! Bite him on the leg and get loose!"

Erskine "Sonny" Kelly would sneer, "She's not doing a thing but showing off. She's doing that on purpose."

Franklin, sneering like Sonny, would first measure out a shot of J. W. Dant, throw it down, his moustache twitching. "That's right," he would agree with Sonny. "She asked for it. Strutting around here all the time with that baton you got her, Joan, sugar. Flipping her cute little butt up at him. She asked for it."

And then Joan Gentry, every ash blond hair in place, would snap, "Shut your damn mouth, Franklin. I told you she was hanging around that guy too much, but you said, Franklin, you said, oh, no, that guy was nothing. That guy got shipped back with a goddamn Purple Heart between his legs. Oh, no. Well, you see, Franklin, you were wrong again!"

211

Then she would pick up the shot glass and hammer it on Franklin's head. "And what did I expect, anyhow, when she's got you for such a good example? What? What?"

"Shut up, Joan, sugar," Franklin would hiss back, grabbing her wrist and squeezing it until she dropped the glass, "what did you expect, all the time keeping her hair in those goddamn stupid pigtails? All the time telling her she could be in the movies, cute as Margaret O'Brien with dimples and crying great big tears. Joan, darling."

And here Franklin Gentry would narrow his eyes, clench his teeth. "You've been trying to keep Ti Baby a little girl forever. But she's thirteen years old, sugar. What'd you think she was going to do with herself for the rest of her life? Play Jettie Barefoot's goddamned piano?"

I wallowed in the tub and grinned at all the sensation I caused just by lying there in my amusing stories. I heard Franklin downstairs in the kitchen. His words spurted between his hacking cough. He thumped his chest, strangling on J. W. Dant and Philip Morris.

Joan spoke softer, but definite and assured. She meant to get her way, whatever it was. And she got her way, polishing her nails there at the kitchen table, blowing on them to dry the bright red Revlon.

I looked at my hands, at the ends of my long shriveled fingers. I was in love with my hands. I wondered if they would really twirl fire. I begged them to do this. I promised them more topaz birthstones if they did. I kissed them and ran them down the length of my body, neck to knees.

"When I get married to Sebastian," I declared, drumming my fingers on my knees, "a little girl will come out from inside of me, and she will have my fingers, including the crooked little finger on my right hand."

But she would not twirl batons and play pianos, I vowed. "Old Sabby will buy her a flute and she will play it and her flute music will turn into silver morning-glory vines and choke everything in Badin."

The flute music of my daughter splashed over my shoulder, stammered, then floated down the drain. "I don't want any little girls coming out of me. I don't want to get married like Carol Jean Spence."

I wanted Sebastian, his strong strokes pulling through Badin Lake. Who was that woman he'd walked out of the water to? I kicked the last bubbles, got out of the tub and peeled off my bathing suit, squeezed it and left it hanging over the rim like an old skin I just shed. "What am I supposed to do with myself for the rest of my life?" I asked the fogged mirror over the washbasin.

I opened the medicine cabinet behind the mirror. I took out Joan's Swedish manicure set, the same one Franklin had used to trim Toto's claws, and I selected the biggest, sharpest pair of nail scissors. After unbraiding my plain brown hair, I began clipping it off in little handfuls, steady, steady, clip, whack, until it filled the washbasin.

FRANKLIN KILLED HIMSELF LAUGHING.

"Look at that! I can't believe she did that!"

Joan was outraged. "Stop laughing! It's funny, Franklin, but it's not that funny! Shut the hell up laughing!"

With my hair clipped close to the skull, except in front where I'd cut some Buster Brown bangs like Carol Jean's, I stood there in the kitchen and took all the insults and the outrage while Franklin killed himself laughing.

Joan gave up. "Well, she did it. It's done." She sat down at the table, covered her head with her arms and actually cried, hard.

"Not your little girl anymore, sugar." Franklin patted Joan's arm. "It was bound to happen."

"She's just like you, Franklin." Joan raised up. She wiped off her face with a Kleenex and blew her nose. "Crazy. Hard-headed. She does what she wants to do. I can't see a thing of me in her. Not one single thing."

Joan watched Franklin measure out another shot in his glass. "You like it, don't you, Franklin? It just tickles you to death that she did this."

"Sugar." He lifted the glass. "It's Ti Baby's hair, not yours."

I brushed the short wet hair behind my ears. It smelled like Elizabeth Arden. A little strand fell on the table, and I fitted it around the crook of my ugly little finger.

"I'm not like anybody," I told them both. "I'm not like anybody in this kitchen."

THE MINUTE THEY BROUGHT Sarah to me in the hospital, I examined her fingers, spread each little one out straight. Sarah quickly curled them into a little fist again. She didn't inherit my deformity.

Kelby thought it was funny, my crooked finger. He liked to hook his finger through mine, then pull hard, as if tightening a shoelace or something.

"It makes you sexy," he said. "I can always find you by this finger. If they put me in a room full of women with the lights out, I could find you, Ti, just like this."

Joan ought to have told me that, told me Kelby would like my strange finger instead of all the time threatening to get it broken by some doctor and set straight. She ought to have promised me Kelby would kiss my finger, hook it around his, kiss it again. She ought to have said he would find me.

I checked Hannah's fingers, too, when she was born. Both girls escaped the gene. And they escaped the big black York piano. And the baton. In junior high band, Sarah, who always got to do things first because she was older, actually picked out the flute. I liked to

214

watch her assemble it, fitting the pieces, then testing the pads and valves. She didn't play it very long, got bored or discouraged. Then Hannah took it up and did better.

I listened to Hannah flute the scales and little ditties, no "Song of the Bobolink," no Miss Beaupine. I was pleased, remembering my secrets from Badin, how I'd have a daughter with long fingers who'd play the flute.

Remembering, too, how I got mad and cut off my long braids.

THE ONLY BRAIDS MY girls got to wear were some long yellow yarn fakes attached to little Dutch Girl caps that Joan gave them one Easter. The caps were knitted out of white yarn, snug and pretty. Soft flaps buttoned back like the wings of a Dutch cap. The two braids dangled down on either side from the ears, each tied off in a big yellow bow. Sarah and Hannah didn't really know what was going on that Easter. The braids hung down to their shoulders. I had put the girls in little blue corduroy jackets it was so cold. They were about two and three, stumbling around in the pine straw and leaves in the woods across from the Badin Methodist Church.

Aunt Della was out there with Joan, helping her direct my girls around the egg hunt. Uncle Morton got too cold and stayed in the car smoking a cigarette. Franklin and Kelby stayed in the apartment, Franklin drinking and Kelby watching, amused, absorbing it all for later comments on our way back to Greensboro.

Sarah's and Hannah's hands plumped out of the blue corduroy sleeves like little red stuffed sausages. "Look in there!" enthused Joan Gentry. "Is that an Easter egg I see?"

Aunt Della hurried over, pushing the girls along. "You reckon the Easter Bunny's been in here messing around?"

I was alternately amused and embarrassed. I was even disgusted, to some degree. I felt useless, a fifth wheel. And maybe I was even jealous of my own children. Joan never ran around these woods with me hunting eggs.

She had put the Dutch Girl caps on Sarah and Hannah with immense pride. "Nobody else down at that egg hunt will have little caps like these," she assured them. Sarah and Hannah just stood there blinking, letting my mother adorn them. They fingered the long yellow yarn, the big bows. "Don't pull on that," she added.

"You look like Hansel and Gretel," declared Aunt Della when she saw them at the church. "You look like Heidi, or something."

They had little plastic baskets we got at Rose's, pink woven plastic, with shiny Easter grass foaming over the sides like some kind of green soda pop. Some of the Badin kids showed up with plain brown paper bags for baskets, their names crayoned on the sides. They had stuck Disney Easter decals on the bags, too, Mickey and Minnie Mouse with eggs and bunnies, Pluto and Goofy.

I had never seen that in Badin before, in all those crazy years of baton twirling and lusting after Sebastian McSherry, those days of my little friend Carol Jean Spence and her baby sister Pam, of my buddy Sonny Kelly—I had never seen anybody show up for an egg hunt at the Badin Methodist Church with only brown paper bags.

It added to my sad and disgusted feelings. I told Kelby on the way back to Greensboro. He said, "What's the big deal? They showed up, didn't they?"

"But it was so sad," I insisted. The girls babbled cozily in the back of the car, stuffed on chocolate and marshmallow chicks. They wiped their sticky faces on the long yellow braids.

Kelby smiled. The lights from oncoming cars played over our own faces. He softened his reply. "But it wasn't sad for them, you have to see that, Ti. It wasn't sad for them."

We drove on through the cold Easter night, smelling like chocolate and marshmallow. And another smell, too, something strange, something sad and plain, like a brown paper bag. I just couldn't see then what Kelby saw.

* * *

LIKE I COULDN'T SEE what Sonny Kelly and Sebastian McSherry saw, or what was going on. I couldn't separate what was sad or disgusting or envious from what was perfectly natural and okay. I had to make a big deal.

So I asked Sonny Kelly who was the woman waiting for Old Sabby at Badin Lake the night of the Galilean service. He immediately sneered, with great relish, "That guy doesn't care nothing about you."

Then he changed the subject, looked at my short hair. "You look like a boy. What'd you do that for?"

"Who was it?" I insisted. "Do you know?"

"I might know," he teased. "What's it to you?"

I took hold of his arm. "Sonny Kelly, if you don't tell me who it was, I'll beat you up with this baton."

His arm was hard and tanned. I liked the play of muscle under his T-shirt. "Sonny? You tell me."

"That," he said, "is a secret between me and Sebastian." He grabbed my hand off his arm and pulled me closer, pinned me to him and kissed me a long exaggerated smooch.

"I hate you, Sonny." I broke away.

"Erskine," he reminded, "my name is Erskine. Mr. Erskine Kelly, the one and only."

"Mr. Erskine Shit, the one and only." I marched off, the old baton heavy under my arm.

When Carol Jean looked at me, she marveled, "Ti, I never would've cut my hair off like that. If I'd got my hair grown out as long as yours was, I never would've cut it off in my whole life."

"Well, it wasn't your hair, Carol Jean. You didn't have to live with it. And I cut it and I like it cut, and it's done and I'm proud of it."

Carol Jean continued to marvel, shaking her head, "I never would've, never."

217

"I don't care." I flashed the baton into furious Figure 8's. "I don't care what I do. I don't care about a thing in the whole world."

I lied. I did care. Bitterly. Not about the hair, but about Old Sabby. About the woman who waited for him at Badin Lake. I wanted to march into his garage and ask him who it was. Ask him why he let Mr. Erskine Shit Kelly know his secrets, but not me. "I can't stand this kind of thing," I'd point out. "This kind of thing kills me."

I was sadly embarrassed of myself.

Then I saw the notice in *The Albemarle Herald* for a twirling competition, with categories for fancy strutting and military marching and acrobatics. The grand winner got to march with the Fort Bragg military band. It was a gesture of patriotism to enter.

There was no category for fire baton. "I'll twirl fire anyhow," I promised. "And I will win the whole damn thing and go to Fort Bragg and march with a million damn paratroopers."

It cost a dollar and a half to enter. I had to get it out of Franklin Gentry. After a lot of teasing about showing off and maybe breaking my finger and being a mascot for those stupid idiots at Fort Bragg, he tossed the money at me across his adjustment table. The dollar was wrinkled and the fifty-cent piece rolled on edge, then fell over, *whap!* on the slick upholstery.

"Thank you, oh, thanks!" I scooped up the money. "You are going to be glad you gave me this money when I win, when you see me go off to Fort Bragg to march with that big band!"

I flashed Franklin a real winner's smile, deepening both dimples.

He snapped his fingers. "You just better win, Ti Baby."

"I will, I will!"

I wanted a spectacular costume, nothing cheap or vulgar, no long full sleeves or dangling fringes to catch fire and burn me up in front of everybody. No shakos or busbies made out of polar bear fur, no plumes or shiny visors on the top of my head. Nothing, I knew, must interfere with the fire, the high aerial pitches of the flaming baton.

I wanted a sequined costume cut in one piece like a bathing suit, snug as my skin and blood red. A pair of white genuine leather boots with tassels.

Joan Gentry said I absolutely could not have those things.

So I cried. I beat my fists on the apartment walls and hoped everybody heard it in every other apartment and bungalow in Badin, spreading like ripples from a hard stone, *I want it, I want it, I want it!*

"Titania," Joan pointed out, "there is a war still going on. It is all we can do to buy you your own piano."

"We don't have my own piano yet," I interrupted. "We still have Jettie's."

"Don't change the subject," Joan continued. "Your father already gave you the money to enter this competition and I am going to have to pay both our bus fares to get to Albemarle."

"Get Uncle Morton to come get us," I suggested. "Uncle Morton will come get us and take us to Albemarle."

"I said don't change the subject." Joan shook a finger. "I cannot ask Morton to come all the way to Badin just to take us to Albemarle for this, when he comes out here every Sunday just to take you to church, Titania. And that's why you cannot have a majorette's costume, too. Don't be so selfish, Titania. Do you understand me?"

She pointed her finger at me. I wanted to bite it off. "No, ma'am!" I yelled. "I do not understand you!"

I felt my face turn as mottled as a slice of salami. "No, I don't!"

Look, I wanted to say, I will sew on each red sequin and bite off the thread between my teeth. I will polish the genuine leather boots with Griffin Shoe Polish until they shine. I will comb out the threads of each white tassel until they both hang smooth as silk, smooth as your June Allyson pageboy, ma'am.

It was Joan who didn't understand.

"Besides all this," I added, "I am not a majorette, ma'am. I'm a baton twirler."

Joan got her way. She decided I would wear my best red cotton shorts. "They've got those cute navy blue anchors appliquéd on the cuffs," she said. "You'll look real cute. Real military and patriotic."

Joan Gentry added to these red shorts a navy blue halter-top that tied around my neck and across the back, stopping just over my ribs. "This gives you a bare midriff, Titania," she explained. "And with your good tan, that'll look extra good. A good tan always helps in a beauty contest."

"This isn't a beauty contest, ma'am," I said, "this is a twirling competition."

Bare midriff, indeed.

"Well, anyhow," Joan went on, "you ought to show off your good tan, your shoulders and legs and your midriff."

I collapsed backward on my bed with disgust, rumpling General MacArthur. Joan poked around in the closet looking for more stuff to put on me and decorate me for the *beauty* contest.

"Here." She held up the black patent recital shoes. "Wear these with some plain white socks. The white socks will set off your good tan even more. And patent leather is always in good taste."

I will never, I vowed, never, never forgive Joan Gentry for this. I will never forgive the war, the Japs and Hitler. I don't care. I have to go over there to Albemarle in front of everybody wearing red shorts appliquéd with navy blue anchors, a halter-top showing off my midriff, and black patent recital shoes and white socks to set off my good tan.

I might have cut off my braids to prove I wasn't a little girl, but it obviously didn't count much right now. Joan still gave the orders. I was still her little girl, red, white, and blue.

I assured myself the fire baton would save me, all that bright hot dangerous fire, the pitching arcs of my baton against the Albemarle sky. When the people saw that, they would know then I was thirteen years old, not a baby, not a bride doll playing in a baby piano recital.

I would be purified and proved by fire.

But the fire, the actual honest-to-God burning fire, I'd have to get from Old Sabby.

16

Kelby did not ask for a divorce when he left. We have never divorced. This is crazy, but it is how we are with each other. He sent money, never missed a single month, for Sarah and Hannah. I know how it hurt him to leave them. But he never fought me for their custody. And there are no legal papers on Kelby and me saying we're separated, saying we can keep company freely with whomever we wish, saying we're no longer married.

I'll always be married to Kelby. Sometimes I've had a boyfriend, but I'll always be married to Kelby. That won't explain itself to people. That won't even explain itself to Sarah and Hannah.

Franklin used to say, "You're a good-looking woman, Ti Baby, you can get married again. Get rid of that s.o.b. in California. Get a new husband."

That made about as much sense, real sense, deep down sense, as deep as a bodily organ is rooted inside you, as when Franklin said, drunk and charming, "Why don't you ever twirl your baton anymore, Ti Baby?"

He reached out to pat me, encourage me, I think, in those curious years. My two girls were growing up in Lake Waccamaw. I was settling myself in one place as far from Badin and Franklin and Joan, as far from Greensboro and Kelby and California, as I could get. My father tried to use the one thing he knew I used to love. "Why don't you ever twirl your baton anymore?"

I was in love with the baton, with the fire twirling on each end of it. Then it stopped twirling and burning. It's still there. Kelby is still there, too, just as fascinating, just as perilous.

Twirling a baton is a silly thing, like cheerleading and tap dancing, like piano recitals and big-league baseball yearnings, like the glittery movies. Although, I believe, Carmen Miranda's tutti-fruitti hat and José Iturbi's "Humoresque" make more sense than twirling a baton. Sarah and Hannah wouldn't be caught dead twirling a baton. And they're right. They laugh at the pictures, Franklin's silent Kodacolor movies, a fun-poking gentle laughter. They joke, "God, Mom, you took yourself so seriously!"

In the long grand scheme of things, baton twirling wouldn't save a cat's ass, wouldn't even get you a cup of coffee. I never really thought it did, even when I was going after it so hot and so heavy, wanting to be a number one person in all endeavors, a genuine champeen.

Now I want Sarah and Hannah to see how these things affected me, made me their mother. I want them to see that a sort of ordinary, maybe even a sort of second-place, person like I was, like I am, isn't necessarily a loser. A Born Loser.

Kelby was no loser. He was a power, like those other important men, like Old Sabby. And it seemed in those old days, as it seems sometimes still, I had to fight and scheme around people with power. Or if not power, then some kind of technical knowledge that I had to learn to use for myself. Knowledge I'd never even thought about in the first place, and which, when I did, angered and frightened me. I thought I just had to twirl the baton with fire. My dream would be enough to make it happen. The stories I told myself would provide the fuel. So it would happen. I never figured on how my dream and my stories had to be fitted into a system of facts and measurements, a technical knowledge as dazzling, finally, as the burning fire itself.

That technical knowledge made the difference.

HE FIRST LAUGHED AT me. "Sister, you're asking for trouble. You'll burn yourself."

Then he relented. "Okay. Let me think about it." Sebastian sprawled against the ladder, his eyes sort of sleepy. I thought a blue cloud moved in them, a glacier.

"Let me see that." He motioned at the old baton. I handed it over. And as Old Sabby examined its embarrassing dents and smudged, chewed rubber tips, I felt he examined my own inferior body.

He turned the baton between his fingers. I felt a grab in my stomach, a sharp breath, the old Ferris wheel anxiety, like something was barreling down.

"If you set this on fire, Sister," he said, "it will have to be lots better balanced than it is now. Look."

The baton listed toward the left of Sebastian's palm, toward the heavier rubber bulb at its top.

"It's got to be the same weight on both ends. Otherwise, Sister, the fire will run up the middle and burn you."

He gazed at me. The blue eyes hard, unpromising. He began turning the baton again, slowly.

I gazed back, trying to fit it all together. What was he lecturing me about? Both ends the same weight? The fire run up the middle? I tried to look as hard and unpromising as Old Sabby looked. I stubbed my bare toes in the wood shavings and blobs of dried paint on the garage floor. The air still smelled of the pine cross, the kerosene.

He stopped turning the baton, demanded, "Sister, does your mama know about this fire stuff?"

"Sure," I lied. "She thinks it's okay. Go ask her if you don't believe me."

"I just might do that, Sister." Sebastian knew I was lying to him.

Joan Gentry never dreamed people would do such a thing as set a baton on fire and twirl it in their bare hands. She never dreamed about twirling at all. *I don't know why you had to have this, Titania. It's not going to get you anywhere. It's a toy.*

I could just as well be getting ready to do other crazy stuff, like throwing around big satin flags. Or throwing around big sharp swords, for all Joan Gentry ever dreamed about it.

"Well, Sister, like I said." Old Sabby stood up. He stretched his arms, the old ladder quivered, the wood shavings scattered. "If you do this thing, you better do it right. Don't think you can get away with just prissing around and showing off. Messing with fire is serious stuff. You follow me, Sister?"

"Yes, I follow you. I know what you mean."

"Okay, then listen." Sebastian began to lecture me in depth, the old baton like a schoolteacher's pointer in his hand. "You have to be damn careful, Sister, you have to pay attention every minute. And somebody has to be there to light the thing and hand it back to you, and then take it when you get through twirling, and put the fire out. Right out! Like that!"

Sebastian smacked the floor with the baton. "And that's the worst problem you've got, Sister. Putting the damn fire out."

My mouth fell open. The idiot drool almost spilled. Put it out! I'd never thought about having to put the fire out! I thought it would burn and burn, and when I was done twirling and showing off, the fire would take care of itself, go out on its own.

The magnitude of my silliness flooded me. I felt sick, inept, felt I'd never live up to the demands I myself had designed.

"Now, Sister," Old Sabby was dismissing me, "get out of here and let me think about this stuff some more. And leave the baton here, so I can experiment a little."

I walked out of the garage and down the alley in shock. I rubbed my eyes. Little red flecks peppered the hot summer sky everywhere I looked. This wasn't what I'd planned, wasn't the way I wanted it.

Sebastian McSherry had made me tell him a lie. He knew I lied and I knew he knew I knew. These hard facts turned like the glittering pieces inside a kaleidoscope and made me more dizzy. I practiced acrobatics for the rest of the day, turning and marching with crisp about-faces. I tried to stretch myself into backbends. I turned cartwheels down Entwistle Street, repeating spectacular Parade Lunges.

I got out the Sears instruction manual and studied again all the twirlers. They looked unimpressive and disappointing to me now. I felt a little definite claw of doubt. The page with the girl twirling fire had a deep diagonal wrinkle. As I smoothed it, little specks of paper sloughed off and stuck to my fingers, gray specks, thin as ashes.

"I don't need an instruction manual anymore." I flipped it toward the waste paper basket and missed. The pages rippled open.

"I don't need anything anymore." I wiped my fingers on my shorts.

But I missed the old baton. My fingers itched for the thing. It put me in a strain not to have it close by. The next morning I stalked to the garage and demanded, "Well, did you get it figured out?"

He sat in the same place as yesterday, sprawling on the ladder. Sunlight shot through the window behind Old Sabby, lighting his jagged profile, burning off the tips of his ear and chin. He looked as harsh as General MacArthur, but nothing imperial. Although bright specks of dust floated in the air around his head, Old Sabby didn't have the halo of a saint.

He turned. "Of course, I did, Sister. What did you expect?"

Then Sebastian lectured to me how he would have to punch holes in the baton to keep it from getting too hot while I twirled fire.

"I don't want you to punch holes in it!"

"Okay," he declared. "Then that's it. I'm through. You can't handle a piece of metal, Sister, that is scalding hot, and Sister, believe me, when you fire up both ends of that damn baton, it will be hot."

"And the holes will cool it off?" I relented a fraction, though I didn't like to think about the old baton punched open and disfigured like that.

"It's the only way."

I drooped. I rolled up as tight as the morning glories on the eaves. Sebastian was telling me the truth. I had enough sense to know the truth when I heard it. I picked up the baton and fingered it. The long dented shaft was like a piece of myself. It kissed my fingers. *No*, I declared, the chrome plate *was* myself, Titania's most secret and vulnerable part.

"No, you can't punch holes in it."

"Okay, Sister." Sebastian slapped his thighs. "I'm washing my hands of this business. You're not going to go out in front of everybody and burn yourself up and have your mama come blaming me for it. Hey." He winked. "Look, Sister, go twirl your baton the same ordinary way everybody else does. Forget the fire stuff. Maybe you'll win anyhow."

Old Sabby grinned. He lifted his brows, trying to cheer me. "Hey, maybe you'll win on your good looks."

His teeth flashed white in the gloom of the garage. I wanted to jam them down his throat with the baton. "I want to twirl fire."

I flashed my own teeth in a bigger, fiercer smile. I rubbed the baton. "Fire!"

Old Sabby lit a fresh Camel. "How?" he taunted.

"I don't know how yet." I wouldn't break down and cry in front

228

of Old Sabby in that ugly garage in Badin, North Carolina. I felt my face, nevertheless, going into its familiar salami mottle.

"I'll figure it out by myself. Just wait."

I kicked through the wood shavings and shattered a few morning glories on my way out. Sebastian dragged at his Camel and laughed.

I stormed down Entwistle Street. I will do it, I will. Madine Ponds was sweeping her path as I passed. Dust flew from the broom. I stopped and took a dozen deep racking breaths.

"What's the matter with you?" Madine shrilled across the street.

"Nothing." I waved a hand and then took a hard look at the broom. I caught up several more breaths, cooling off, and watched Madine flick her broom around as easily as she would a baton. The handle was long and sleek. It actually shone.

That was how. I grinned. I will twirl fire, Sebastian. I dashed across Entwistle and hugged Madine. I covered her apron with kisses.

"You just gave me an idea." I patted her broom handle. "You just saved my life."

And while the old lady gaped, I dashed back across Entwistle and around the corner of the quadruplex to the garage.

"Guess what?"

Sebastian looked up from sharpening a chisel. "What?"

"I figured it out, Mr. Smarty. That's what."

"How?"

"A broom handle, a mop handle. You can cut it off to fit my arm, why not? That's how. A wooden baton. Why not? It won't get hot."

I pranced around Sebastian, doing Pinwheels and Shoulder Rolls. Just out the garage door, I stopped and pitched the baton. It tore off the pink morning glories going up, coming down.

He stared at me awhile, then shrugged. "Sure. A broom handle. A damn mop. That ought to do it, Sister. But it won't last. Maybe just long enough. I said maybe, Sister."

"I don't care. Just so I can do it." I lifted the old chrome-plated baton and kissed it. It tasted cold and bitter.

I paced into the alley, confident and proud, promising, I will dedicate the whole performance in Albemarle, everything I do, every burning flame, to Madine Ponds. She'll never know it. Nobody will.

I WAS ALMOST HOLDING the fire in my bare hands, but Old Sabby had a thousand more irritations to solve, things I'd never thought of. I sneaked out an old mop from Joan's kitchen and held the baton to it while Sebastian sawed off the wooden handle to fit. He glued two perfectly balanced tips to either end and wired black asbestos like two black cocoons to these tips. When I held it, the mop handle lay across my palm without teetering, as balanced as a pair of scales.

"You owe me, Sister," reminded Old Sabby. "I got this asbestos from the hardware."

"I'll pay you back," I vowed. "When I win, I'll pay you back everything. Even if I don't win," I added, "I'll still pay you back."

We tried burning rags soaked in kerosene. I hated the thick smoke. I choked on the heavy black stink. We burned pure gasoline and it evaporated, flaming in a quick poof of luminosity that I admired and immediately wanted on the ends of my baton.

"Okay," said Old Sabby. "I think I got it now, Sister. We'll split the difference."

He mixed kerosene and gasoline in the same bucket, dipped a wad of rags, and struck the match. This burned with a pure radiant flame, steady as a beacon. I was delighted. My hands itched to take over.

We got more wooden handles, Sebastian foraging them out of the Badin dump, and me asking around for old mops and brooms. "It's another war drive," I lied to Jettie Barefoot, "like turning in all your scrap iron. This is for old wooden handles."

Jettie nodded, gave up two old string mops and a worn-out broom. Sebastian cut these off to fit me and wadded old rags instead of asbestos at their tips. I had to practice twirling fire and he wanted to save the black asbestos for the competition in Albemarle.

I asked Joan Gentry if I could have her old nylon hose. "They're full of picks and runs, ma'am," I pointed out, "and I need them for a project."

"What project?" Joan rummaged in the closet for her old nylons. She held them up to the light. Her face took on a blush from the nylon and the sun shining through it, the dark seams wrinkling her cheek.

"I'm stuffing a doll for Carol Jean's little sister." I brightened, pleased with the generosity of this lie. "Nylon hose will make a good stuffing."

"Here." Joan wadded up a big pile. She smiled. "I'm glad you're doing something for somebody else for a change, Titania. That's good."

This is for everybody, ma'am, I wanted to say, all of us, the whole world, the whole town of Badin, North Carolina. I'm doing it most of all as a surprise for you.

But the first practice baton Old Sabby gave me, burning at both ends, surprised me when I took hold of it, grinning, and trembling.

I had listened to his warning. "You listen to me, Sister. You have to wipe this thing off, and then wipe it off again. Because if you get one drop of gas on that handle, Sister, the whole thing will go off like a bomb, and you, too, dammit! I mean it, Sister. You hear me?"

I heard Old Sabby, but I didn't believe him. All fear of burning had left me. I felt invincible. I slowly took hold of the wooden handle and began to twirl with my two bare hands, slowly, too slowly. The wood threw off a thin fiery spray. I never believed it would really hurt me until I felt the hot sting. A million burning bee stings, fiery red and deep, over both my naked arms.

"Speed it up! Faster, Sister!" yelled Old Sabby. But I got scared and dropped it, jumping back, staring and rubbing my arms.

I was ready to run off the way I did when Franklin Gentry pitched his mean little baseballs too hard at me.

"Goddammit, Sister!" Old Sabby pounced on the blaze with a bucket of sand.

The flames smothered out as I watched, shocked. My arms hurt. The little burning stings would raise blisters before bedtime. I thought I'd cry, *Shit, I burned my own self right here in front of Old Sabby.*

"Listen, Sister, and I really mean listen this time. You have to twirl fast if you don't want to get burned. I mean fast, fast, fast! Look here. I want to show you something, look, now."

Sebastian struck another match and held it steady. The tall clear flame lifted in a perfect arrowhead. "Watch, Sister." He pulled his finger quickly through the flame. "See?"

My arms hurt and my throat choked back stupid tears.

"Now, you do it, Sister. Fast, now, I mean fast! Through the fire, fast, and it won't burn you. It won't have time to burn you. Do it."

He held the match toward me and I put my finger through the flame, back and forth. My long tanned finger swam in pure fire. It didn't burn. Old Sabby had told the truth.

"You slow down, Sister, even only for a little, and it'll burn the living shit out of you."

I pulled back my finger and stuck it in my mouth. I thought I'd go on and cry anyhow, Old Sabby was working so hard to help me and me being such a fool. I was disappointed and confused and mad at everything. I snuffled over my finger, then crammed the whole right hand in my mouth.

He narrowed his eyes, took hold of my hand and pulled it back. Then he smiled.

"Goddamn, I never noticed that, Sister. How'd you do that?"

He ignored the finger I'd stuck naked into the fire for him. He held on, instead, to my ugly crooked little finger. He laughed and straightened it, curled it back, inspecting it as though it were some sort of creature itself, another Titania Gentry.

"Goddamn, Sister."

"It's my finger," I said, letting him hold it. It was the first time Sebastian McSherry had actually touched me in a personal and interested sort of way.

"I was born with it. My mother wants to get it broken, and then let it grow back straight." I smiled at him, feeling dopey.

Old Sabby smiled back, shook his head. "No, Sister. You keep it just like that. That finger's okay."

And then, just as Kelby would do years later, Sebastian McSherry put my ugly little finger to his own mouth and kissed it, folded it back to its curl and then folded up my whole right hand inside his. "You keep it just like it is."

I thought, I can stand right here in this ugly garage forever with my hand folded up inside of Old Sabby's. People will come out here to find us and throw wreaths on us and say blessings. *God bless you! You're wonderful!*

But Old Sabby, like Joan Gentry, meant to get things done. He broke into the little cozy, dewy-eyed fantasy and reminded me, "Listen, when you get through twirling, you have to hand it to me quick so I can put out the fire. You understand, Sister?"

He waited, studying me. I still stood there soaking up his hand around mine. I didn't care anymore what he said, what he did. I gave Sebastian another dopey smile.

He let go my hand without another thought to it. He was clearly annoyed. "Maybe we ought to just lug a bucket of sand around until you learn not to get burned. Until you pay attention to what I'm saying, Sister?"

I sucked my little finger he'd just kissed. I forgot my burned and stinging arms. "Are you going with me, Sebastian? Over to the competition in Albemarle?"

"I don't know yet, Sister. Somebody's got to put out the fire. Maybe. I don't know yet." He frowned.

He made me go home and put Vaseline on both arms. I had to hide them from Joan. The Vaseline stuck to my pajamas. I leaned against the wall listening for Old Sabby's snores. They never started. He wasn't over there all night. I lay down, uneasy, and the burns twinged a long time.

17

Down in Sheafer's, the most expensive jewelry store in Greensboro, we picked out our wedding rings. John Kennedy was getting elected president. He had been over to Duke and people were talking about it. One of my Woman's College friends actually got her picture made shaking his hand. I thought it was auspicious: Kennedy running his campaign. Me and Kelby picking out rings.

We weren't sure what we were doing but we browsed the display cases in Sheafer's with poise. Kelby said, "It's sort of effeminate for a man to wear a ring. At least, I always used to think it was."

He let the lady measure his finger and bent over the velvet trays of rings with genuine interest. I loved the way he looked, the way he went along with all that stuff. We had our rings, two gold bands a half-inch wide. Then we went to an arcade on West Market and bought Spanish peanuts, hot and fresh, in a paper bag. They were running a special on Spanish peanuts. Kelby was crazy about those.

We leaned against the brick wall of the arcade and looked at the rushing traffic. Greensboro, in my memory, is always rushing and busy and loud. That afternoon it blended the smell and taste of the hot peanuts, the joy of our fingers going into the bag together.

"I don't know if I'm doing the right thing," Kelby said. "Getting married." I wrinkled up my face. But he was smiling that easy way, like a flashlight turned on. "But I know I'm marrying the right woman."

YOU TRY TO MAKE sense of your existence, connect all the moments when things happened to you and when people said things. Kelby meant what he said in that arcade on West Market. Now there aren't any more arcades like that in Greensboro selling Spanish peanuts. Sheafer's is torn down. Now there are multilevel malls with spectacularly gushing fountains where you throw pennies for wishes. And exotic plants, their fronds three feet broad, tower toward the skylights.

Kelby is in California, happy, smiling, healthy. He could still be my best friend, but I don't know. He is a mystery to me. I try to make sense of it, stringing those moments together like beads.

The lady in Sheafer's said, "Don't you want these engraved?"

Kelby looked at me. "You know," he said, "I like a ring just to be a ring. It doesn't need to say anything."

I liked that. So we took the rings in their little boxes and went to get married. That's all.

Kelby said he knew he'd married the right woman. Whatever the outcome. And I knew I was married for life, merged into the Spanish peanuts, the Greensboro traffic. No matter about California years later. No matter about the two little girls. No matter I never asked questions.

SEBASTIAN MCSHERRY WAS A different thing.

Those days I was exactly like Joan, possessive and fractious. I wanted to walk in on him and demand, Where were you last night? What's going on? Who was that woman waiting on you at the lake after the Galilean service? How come Erskine "Sonny" Kelly gets to know stuff that I don't?

Who is she?

What's her name?

Who do you think you are, anyhow, Old Sabby, Sebastian McSherry, paratrooper?

Instead I peeled my pajamas away from the Vaseline and carefully put on a thin long-sleeved cotton shirt, faded from washing. Joan looked across the breakfast plates. "That shirt should've gone in the rag bag long ago."

"I know." I pulled the cuffs down around my wrists. "But it feels good, ma'am. All worn out. And soft."

"It's too hot to wear long sleeves, Titania." Joan frowned. "You'll burn up in that."

I grinned into my toast and jelly. Little did she know. The stings faded from my arms in a few days. I resumed practice with Old Sabby, heeding his every word, now, wiping off the wooden shaft, twirling rapidly, getting more and more accurate.

Nobody knew what we were up to in Mr. McSherry's garage behind all the pink morning glories. Nobody paid any attention. Sebastian could get away with anything, the handyman, the fixer-upper home from the paratroopers, that guy got wounded, did you know that, in France, in the invasion? Anyhow, all he does is piddle around his daddy's place, fixing things. And he's good at it, too. Roofed my house last week.

Titania Gentry, the thirteen-year-old insignificant nobody, had only myself to please and so long as I stayed out of Joan's and Franklin's way, I could do anything I liked. I liked getting away with murder.

Then one morning Sonny Kelly's nosy dog Toto, raising a leg against the morning glories, looked in the garage. He caught the smell of fire and he bayed, rolled his eyes, and ran off, his claws scattering alley gravel.

237

"What you doing in here?" Erskine "Sonny" Kelly stood in the door, his eyes settled accusingly on me holding the baton flaming at both ends.

"None of your business." I turned the baton with one whistling fiery circle, then dropped it in a pile of sand. "This is none of your business. Go away."

"Does he know you're out here doing this?" Sonny nodded back at the McSherry apartment.

Sebastian hadn't yet come out to the garage. On a reckless impulse, I had lit the baton myself, not waiting for his permission.

It was a dumb thing, as I immediately realized. I tried not to give way to my anxiety, especially with Sonny Kelly standing there staring. I already guessed how annoyed Old Sabby would be, if he found out.

"Of course he knows," I flung back at Sonny. "This is our thing we're doing, our business, so go away and leave us alone."

"Well." Sonny settled back against the garage wall. "Just what is this business?" He waited, grinning. "Tell me. Or I'll go right now, Ti, and tell your mama."

Sonny knew already, I could tell just by looking at him, Joan Gentry didn't know a thing about the fire. About me staying out in Old Sabby's garage all the time. I clenched my teeth. Sonny knew a lie when he saw it.

"I hate you."

He kept grinning, waiting.

I wiped my hands against my shorts. "Okay. Okay, if you first tell me who it was he met at the lake, tell me everything you know that I don't." I grinned as viciously as Sonny Kelly.

"I don't care if you know it, Ti." He threw up a hand. "No big deal to me."

"Who?" I moved closer to Sonny, studying his face. If he lied to me, Erskine "Sonny" Kelly, if he lied to me right then, I'd surely know it in the color of his eyes and in the way his blond cowlicks stuck up on the top of his head.

"Who?"

"Nothing but his wife," Sonny hissed. His grin broadened back toward his ears. "His wife, Ti. Old Sabby's a married man."

I pulled back from him, stricken. "Wife!" But even as I rejected the notion, I immediately realized I'd been suspecting it all along. Still, "You made that up, Sonny Kelly," I accused.

"Ask him yourself." Sonny watched Sebastian slam out the back door of the apartment and sprint through the yard. "Ask him, Ti. I dare you."

Sebastian entered the garage, but I couldn't ask him anything, couldn't so much as say "good morning." He greeted Sonny, "Hey, man," then grinned at me. "Guess it's not a secret now, Sister."

I thought for a moment he meant being married, having a wife waiting on the shore of Badin Lake for him and not telling me a thing about it. Then I realized Old Sabby meant the fire baton. I relaxed enough to grin back. "Yeah, Sonny came in and saw me twirling fire."

I stopped, realizing again too late, the wrong thing. I had betrayed myself. I had told Sebastian I lit the baton by myself, reckless and stupid.

"He what?" Sebastian frowned. "You lit that thing up by yourself, Sister? Out here with all this kerosene and stuff? Jesus, Sister!"

He slammed his fist on the carpentry table. "I thought I smelled it when I first got here."

He took hold of me by both shoulders. "Don't ever do such a stupid thing as that again, Sister. You're going to burn up my daddy's garage, and yourself, too."

"The whole place," Sonny added, eating it up, loving it. "The whole town!"

"Shit." Sebastian released me, sat down at the table and took out a Camel. "Shit."

He lit the cigarette and dragged on it deeply several times. "You know something, Sister?" He gazed thoughtfully. "I can't trust you."

I was afraid to cry right there, turn as ugly as a slice of salami again. I caught myself up, recovered, and promised, "Yes, you can, too, trust me. I won't do it again. I mean it."

He shook his head. "No, I can't trust you. This whole thing is now called off. No more fire batons."

"Aw, man." Sonny came over, put an arm around me. "You can too trust her. She means it." Sonny gave me a stupid little brotherly kiss on the cheek. "Come on, man?"

This isn't the way I planned it, I raged, this isn't how I wanted it to be. With Sonny Kelly being a part of everything and hanging around. With Sonny Kelly taking up for me.

But there he was, firmly a part of everything. He convinced Old Sabby to let me do it again. So I owed Sonny Kelly for that. He brought Old Sabby back to my side. I took a big breath and put the business about Old Sabby's wife in the back of my mind for a while.

I had to get through the twirling competition first.

"Okay." Sebastian stubbed out the Camel. "Then let's get on with it. Look." He showed us a long metal tube with a screw cap on one end. Sebastian pointed at the wooden baton. "Drop it in here, Sister, and see what happens."

I dropped the baton in the tube. A perfect fit. Old Sabby quickly screwed the cap on tight.

"There," he announced. "Now we won't have to lug a bucket of sand around, Sister. I figured this one out myself. This puts the fire out, pronto!" And he snapped his fingers in both Sonny's and my face.

"Great!" Sonny applauded, as if he knew everything we'd been struggling through.

I looked at the tube. "How? How does it do that?"

"Aw, don't be so dumb, Ti." Sonny took over. "Look." He picked up the tube and unscrewed the cap, shook out the baton. "No air.

You drop it in here and screw on the cap and you shut off the air."

Sonny demonstrated. He held the tube to me. "And the fire goes out! Pronto!"

I refused to take the tube from Sonny. "But that will get hot, too. That will burn me, too." I hated the long tube. It looked like a telescope. I hated the joining up of Sonny Kelly and Old Sabby. The easy way they shared their practical male science, solving all my problems.

I wanted to go back to where Sebastian and I were before Erskine "Sonny" Kelly butted in. "Can't we just fill up a bucket of water when we get to Albemarle?"

Old Sabby scolded. "Sister, that's the dumbest thing you've said out here yet. Look, I figured out this fireproof tube, easy to carry, easy to get rid of. What's the matter with you, Sister?"

I stood there and lifted my stubborn chin at Sebastian and Sonny. They were right. I knew they were right. After a moment, I said, "Sonny Kelly, I hate you the worst of anybody in the world." And turning to Old Sabby with scorn, said, "Aren't you ever going back to the paratroopers?"

WHEN THE COMPETITION ENTRY forms came in the mail, I studied them a long time before lettering in all the information they required. Name, age, place of birth. My name is Titania Gentry, I pondered, a juvenile, aged thirteen and a half, not quite four months off from a full fourteen. Born in Badin, North Carolina, not on the great and mighty Congo.

I put down all the information. No previous training in dance, acrobatics, or baton. Just piano lessons from Miss Beaupine where I was a big grown girl playing a baby piece.

I entered myself as a solo in the novelty baton category. The rules of the competition promised I'd have two minutes to do it, whatever I did. Two minutes to light the fire and show off in front of everybody in the American Legion Ballpark.

Walking all the way downtown to the Badin post office to mail back the entry forms and the money Franklin Gentry gave me, I felt I had gotten through the first big part of my ordeal. "Now, that's done." I shoved the envelope through the mail slot, heard it clunk to the bottom. "Now," I gritted my teeth, "I have to ask him who she is and what her name is and if what Sonny was telling was a lie."

I waited until after supper. While Joan and Franklin were listening to their Andrews Sisters records, I sneaked out to find Old Sabby. The garage was empty. The metal tube leaned against the ladder where Sonny had left it. I picked it up for the first time, stroked it, lifted it to my lips and kissed it.

Around the corner of the quadruplex, I found Mr. McSherry dozing in his porch swing, his stick across his knees, and the cigar cold in his teeth. His eyelids drooped and twitched with his snuffling wheeze. I made a fist, slammed it against my thigh. Nobody around. No Sebastian. Nobody.

From my own apartment I heard Joan and Franklin laughing, mimicking the Andrews Sisters. It seemed everything they liked was sung by a bunch of sisters or brothers. I couldn't think of a single song they liked that was sung by just one person.

The lyrics came sliding out, Maxene, Patty, and LaVerne chiming such slick harmony, their voices like oil all over something called "Pistol-Packing Mama."

Then Franklin murmuring again, Joan laughing again, then again the silly words about making somebody put a pistol down, somebody called Babe. This Babe laughed and cried and kicked in a car windshield. Was that right? How could anybody kick in a car windshield? Maybe I didn't hear it right. Mr. McSherry's stick slid to the floor. The Andrews Sisters' harmony washed across the porch, laughed into the lobelia bush, somebody wanted to be somebody's loving daddy if she'd just put the pistol down. Babe's loving daddy. I hated it.

SEBASTIAN RETURNED AND HE wasn't alone. The woman was with him, her arms around him. They walked along kissing all the way down the back alley. I watched from the windows, my hands clasping each of the little sabots, their carved toes digging into my palms. The Badin streetlights poured out a tangy yellow glow around Old Sabby's body. She, what was her name? what? stuck to him. She rubbed his arms and laughed in his ears.

Sebastian took her around the corner of the quadruplex, right past the porch swing. I pictured Mr. McSherry still sleeping there, his stick on the floor, his old cigar stinking between his teeth. I wanted him to rise up like some avenging angel, take the stick, and beat Old Sabby and his woman into a pulp.

I felt as wronged as a pistol-packing mama, as hungry for revenge. Maybe I could kick out a car windshield.

Old Sabby took his woman upstairs to his room, right behind my wall. And as I stood on my bed, ear to the wall listening, Old Sabby, the same who had straightened my little finger and kissed it and folded my hand inside his, made love to Who is that? Who? all night long.

They sound like dogs, I sneered, growling and pouncing on each other, wrestling. I was enraged, the idiot drool running from my mouth down into my big ear flattened against the wall.

Sometime during that torment, I fell down hard as a rock on my bed and went to sleep. Through my dreams, his wife laughed and Old Sabby snored. I dreamed Mr. McSherry woke up, heard them, and stomped upstairs to throw the door wide open and drive them both out, naked and ashamed, into Entwistle Street where everybody could see.

I helped him drive them out. I loved taking revenge on Old Sabby. I dreamed I reached toward him to hit him hard, and I saw, with horror, that I had no hands. Only burning stumps at the ends of my long tanned arms.

I cried. Kissing my stumps, I begged them to grow back some hands. The stumps said, *You know something, Sister? I can't trust you.*

18

Thirty years or so later, just thinking about how to write this all down in a big blue ledger from Wal-Mart, I am surprised it can still surprise me. I hope it will surprise Sarah and Hannah, and jar, just a little, their firm golden-skinned cynical demeanor. The way you brush against a bowl of perfect Jell-O, all the fruit cocktail suspended at just the right depths. You brush against this bowl sitting on the kitchen counter, your elbow jars it, just a little, and it gives a little ripple.

I want to see that gentle ripple in my girls.

When they were little, they always bumped their heads on the table getting up from their play on the kitchen floor. They never seemed to learn. Sarah and Hannah scurried around on the floor, building things out of colored blocks, racing little plastic cars—then a quick rise to their feet, the bump against the table, and the howls of pain.

I got in the habit of putting out my hand whenever they were around. I would sit at the table reading, my hand held out over their heads. I thought about fontanels and skulls, concussions, fractures. I had a great horror.

The same in the car, too. No seat-belt laws then. No child car-seats. And always when I put on brakes to slow for a light or a turn, Sarah and Hannah would plunge toward the windshield. I got in the habit of putting out my arm.

I even did this once with Kelby in the front seat. The kids weren't anywhere around, off at kindergarten, and I slowed for a light near Starmount, automatically put out my right arm in front of Kelby.

"What're you doing?" he laughed, pushing my arm away.

"Keeping you from going through the windshield."

Seems prophetic, the way things turned out. Me protecting Sarah and Hannah from knocking their brains out. Me protecting Kelby. But maybe prophetic in a backward way. Nobody protecting me. I barged on along toward oncoming cars, railroad trestles, kitchen tables hard as concrete pyramids.

I homed in on it, the attractive and inevitable collision.

SHE CAME TO THE screen door and looked at me. "Yes?" She smiled, but didn't open the door.

"I want to see Old Sabby."

"Who?" She wrinkled her forehead, smiling more generously.

Sebastian came up behind her. "Hey, Sister," he said, "come in here. I want you to meet somebody." He opened the door.

I stepped across the porch and inside the living room. It was as dark as it had been last Christmas. Sebastian and the woman were the only two things giving off any light in the whole place. Old Sabby put his arm around the woman. "Sister, I want you to meet Ginger, my wife."

He smiled at Ginger, kissed her cheek. "Ginger, this is Sister. Sister is a baton twirler, and she's getting ready to win the big contest over in Albemarle next week."

He took on a conspiratorial pose, lowered his voice, hissing in

Ginger's ear, "She's going to twirl fire. It's a big secret, shhh," looking around to catch somebody, maybe his daddy, maybe Joan and Franklin, eavesdropping.

I hated the way he looked doing that. I felt embarrassed for him in front of Ginger. He made me feel five years old.

Sebastian held Ginger as if to display her to advantage. Then he did the same thing with me, urging us both forward, showing us both off, as if he wanted Ginger and me to admire the value in each other.

"Oh," I mumbled, then smoothed my cropped head and spoke clearly, "I am happy to meet you." I took in Ginger's every feature. No ash blond pageboy. That assured me. No tattooed snakes on Ginger's arms. And her fingers, spread over Old Sabby's hand, I could see were as straight as fingers were supposed to be, but without red polish on the nails. Ginger's nails were pale and short.

Ginger was not Renee Ames. No birthstones in her ears. No widow's peak. Ginger's hair was as plain a brown as mine, curling to the level of her ears. She had freckles everywhere. She was a veritable celebration of freckles. Just as Rory Flynt would be years later.

"Sister," Ginger smiled, "I am happy to meet you, too," and held out her hand.

I took it limply, a warm strong hand, a hand that made my own feel like a wet tea bag. She seemed taller, too, than Sebastian.

"You want some breakfast?" Ginger started back to Mr. Mc-Sherry's kitchen. "We're just sitting down."

"No, thank you. I already ate." I directed myself the opposite way through the front door. Then I stopped and gazed at Sebastian.

He squinted in the sunlight. "Ginger will be as tickled as all the rest of us if you win, Sister."

"When did you get married?" I interrupted his generous negotiation.

He took out a Camel. "A long time ago." He struck a match and held it, studying it a moment before touching it to the cigarette.

"Why didn't you tell me?"

"I didn't know it was any of your business, Sister." He threw his match out the screen door.

I drew myself up and tried to look both disapproving and agreeable as I affirmed, "It's not any of my business, you're right."

I couldn't keep up this hard pose, and went limp again with envy and despair. "But why?" I knew it was dumb to ask, dumb and unseemly. But I wanted Old Sabby to feel the dimensions of my disappointment.

"Look, Sister." Old Sabby guided me out the door and into the yard. The blossoms on the big lobelia had spent themselves and lay drying across the late August grass. "Nobody knows why they do a thing."

He put a hand on my shoulder, holding the Camel between his fingers. I wrinkled my nose at the fragrant smoke, hiccuped.

"Look," he started again, "it is none of your business, but I will tell you anyhow, Sister. We got married at Virginia Beach, when I first got out of the hospital and started back here. We just now, though, decided to live together, to tell people. Are you hearing me, Sister?"

I waved away his Camel smoke. I hated Camels now. "Why didn't she come back with you at the first? Where's she been all this time?"

"You ask too many questions, Sister." Sebastian thumbed off ashes. He sighed. "Ginger's been in Virginia Beach, working. She came down once, the weekend we burned that cross at the lake."

He shook his head remembering. "I had to get things fixed up here in this crummy apartment, had to get Daddy used to the idea, before she could move down for good."

"What about me?"

He stubbed the cigarette. I hated his old moccasins, his jeans. Good Lord, I never realized Sebastian McSherry was so ugly and coarse and terrible. No better than his old daddy blowing his nose in a plaid handkerchief.

"What about me?" I shrilled.

"What about you?" He pondered me a moment, then laughed the way he had laughed in the pickup truck when I asked him if he was a Christian.

I watched the muscles in his throat ripple and my disappointed angry feeling spread like a dark blush. He stopped laughing. He took on a somber look, his eyes like blue steel.

"Sister, I'm not your daddy. I'm not your big brother."

There Sebastian McSherry stopped and shrugged it off. *Not your daddy. Not your big brother.* I gazed back at him, my eyes as steely as his. I felt the ground split open between us.

I mimicked his serious tone. "And you're not my boyfriend, either."

He gazed at me awhile longer, calculating my little attack. Sebastian shook his head. "It's a war. People get married." He went inside to his strong and freckled Ginger.

I took myself home and sat on the sofa under the gilt-framed oval mirror, trying to think it through without getting in a tangle or making a mistake. "I have to twirl fire," I reminded, "I have to have both Old Sabby and Erskine 'Sonny' Kelly to help me do it, too."

Sebastian McSherry's plainspoken wisdom echoed through Joan Gentry's well-appointed living room. *Sister, nobody knows why they do a thing. It's a war. I had to get things fixed up here in this crummy apartment. I had to get Daddy used to it.*

I put my hands to my cheeks, feeling how hot my face was. I shut my eyes, remembering Sebastian's kiss on my crooked finger, his hand folded around my hand. I sat there, hard as a rock, memorizing Ginger's face, her real woman's body, her real breasts.

I had no real breasts, just dumb little titties sticking against my shirt, little pats or flaps of tissue, little blind things growing off of me without permission. I knocked myself hard in the chest, hard enough to hurt and bring the tears, *It's a war. People get married.*

What if Ginger didn't let Old Sabby help me anymore? What if they went to bed and did it to each other all night so good she made him forget about Titania Anne Gentry waiting at the American Legion Ballpark?

It could happen, it could happen! I tormented myself for the rest of the morning. I stared at the old chrome baton and thumped its dingy rubber bulb. "I know who to blame for this," I snorted. "Erskine 'Sonny' Kelly. He didn't tell me when Ginger came down here the first time. It's his fault I'm feeling like this, mean enough to kill people. Erskine Kelly. He knew this was going on all the time."

At lunch, in the middle of Joan's passing around potato salad, the phone rang for me.

"I don't know who this is," mouthed Joan, handing it over. "Some woman."

"Hey, Sister," Ginger brightened the wire. "We're making ice cream this afternoon and you're invited."

I didn't want to go eat ice cream. I wasn't some little girl next door they could feed ice cream to and make her feel better.

"What kind of ice cream?"

"It's coffee ice cream," said Ginger.

"I never heard of coffee ice cream," I relented a fraction.

"Well, come over around four. We'll be in the back."

Ginger hung up and the wire buzzed in my ear, the same ear I'd put to the wall upstairs night after night, drinking in Sebastian's snores, going numb, finally, listening to Sebastian's lovemaking with his own lawfully wedded wife, Ginger McSherry.

You are a fool, I reminded myself. An idiot. As dumb as Carol Jean Spence or Sonny.

"Who was that, Titania?" Joan asked when I returned to the table.

"Ginger," I said. "Mrs. Sebastian McSherry." I nodded at the wall. "Over there."

"Well, when did that happen? Franklin, did you know that? Did you know Sabby got married?" Joan glanced at him forking ham on top of his potato salad.

"No," he said, "I didn't know it. So, Old Sabby's got a wife. Is she good-looking, Ti Baby? Is she from around here?" He winked. "When did you meet her?"

"This morning." I pushed potato salad around my plate. "No, she's not from around here, and she's not good-looking. She's got freckles all over her." But when Joan started to interject, I graciously added, "But she's not bad-looking, either. Sort of in-between, you know?"

I was protecting Ginger, protecting, too, Old Sabby. I marveled at my loyalties moving in such spontaneous ways.

"Anyhow," I continued, "they invited me over this afternoon when they make some ice cream."

"Well, I for one am glad he got married. I am glad there's another young woman on this street. I have had nobody except Jettie Barefoot and Madine Ponds to talk to for years." Joan smiled, shook her pageboy.

"But can you imagine what it's going to take to live over there with that old man?" She frowned. "There'll be some changes made on that account. Mark me."

"Joan, darling, I'm glad there's another woman on this street, too. For years I've had nobody, besides you, sugar, to look at on this street except Jettie Barefoot and Madine Ponds." Franklin leered across the table. "And, no, I can't imagine what it's going to take to live over there with that old man. Or that young man, either." He winked at me. "Right, Ti Baby?"

Joan gazed at him a moment. "Franklin," she warned, "it wouldn't take much for Sebastian McSherry to break your arm."

"Just teasing, sugar." Franklin pushed back from the table. "Just teasing."

* * *

AT FOUR O'CLOCK, THE short hair brushed back over both ears and the bangs glossed just to my brows, I strolled to Old Sabby's backyard. Mr. McSherry sat in a striped red-and-yellow beach chair, giggling, his face flushed and his eyes watering against the sun.

"Hey, Titania!" he yelled. "Did you meet my daughter-in-law? Did you meet Ginger? From Virginia Beach, Titania?"

"Yes, this morning already."

Ginger and Sebastian greeted me. Sebastian cranked the freezer and Ginger sprinkled salt over the ice. "It's going to be good, Sister," he promised. "Coffee ice cream."

"Come over here, Titania." Ginger took me up the back steps. "You can help me get the bowls and spoons. I'm glad I finally found out what your name really was. Titania. That's unusual, isn't it?"

Ginger opened the kitchen door and I followed inside.

"It's Shakespeare." I smiled back at Ginger against my will. I already liked Ginger against my will.

"Well, I don't know much Shakespeare. If you said Juliet, I'd recognize that." Ginger took down four bowls from the cupboards, every door leveled and solid, with spanking fresh paint and shiny chrome pulls.

"The spoons are in that drawer."

I lifted them out, surprised to find sterling silver in Mr. McSherry's kitchen, not Briar Rose. I'd remember to tell Joan Gentry it was something else, heavier, fancier, with a crest on the handle.

Ginger loaded the bowls and silver spoons on a big wooden tray. She added four white napkins. "You know," she said, "Sebastian told me about your secret, the twirling competition, and how long you and he have been working with the fire baton."

I shrugged, looked away from her. So, he tells you everything already. And Erskine "Sonny" Kelly knows it before I do. I'm not surprised.

"I want you to know, Titania," Ginger held out her hand again, strong and warm, "I believe you're going to win, okay?"

I didn't hesitate, but took hold of Ginger's hand vigorously and smiled into Ginger's freckled face. "Okay."

WE WERE ALL A part of the deal, Sonny Kelly and Ginger, too. Old Sabby taught Sonny how to light the baton, drop it in the tube. Ginger encouraged me with new twirls, showed me some dance routines.

"But she can't practice in this garage," Ginger pointed out. "There's no room to really twirl in here. She needs to spread out, really let go with it."

She walked to the garage door and studied the Badin vista.

"Of course." Ginger pointed down the alley. "She can go out and twirl her regular baton all over the place, work up her routine perfect, but she'll never really know until she twirls the fire baton all the way through, and lets herself go, doing everything she's going to do, just one time, with it on fire."

"Where can we go?" Sonny took up her idea, eager to go right then.

"Anywhere we go in Badin," he warned, "people will see her, and then the secret will be out, and her mama won't let her do it. Where can we go, where?" Sonny hungered for the adventure, his eyes roving all our faces for a signal.

I felt like a piece of furniture, one of Old Sabby's tools in the garage. They talked about me as if I were not even there. "I don't care," I objected. "I can imagine what it's going to be, and I can already twirl the fire without burning my arms. It's okay right here."

Ginger and Sonny Kelly ignored me.

Ginger turned to Sebastian. "Where can we go, honey?"

He thought a moment. "Maybe out in the country, out in some field, out in some cow pasture."

253

"Are you kidding?" I said. "In a cow pasture? Not me."

"We need level ground," said Sebastian. "Some place grassy and smooth."

"The golf course," said Sonny. "Out on the golf course, I know, way back on Number 9 fairway. We have to sneak out there at night."

Ginger shook her head. "I'd rather do something in the day. No sneaking around at night. Too much trouble."

"Let me think," said Sebastian.

"I want to stay right here in this garage."

Again they ignored me. So I stalked home in a huff, muttering to my aching fingers, "I'll do what I want. I don't care what I do. There's a war going on. Nobody knows why they do a thing."

But two days later, Old Sabby decided we'd sneak out after all to Number 9 fairway as Erskine "Sonny" Kelly had suggested. Ginger didn't like it, but she agreed.

"Now," said Sebastian, "we have to plan everything down to the last minute, and sneak out there with the stuff and do it just one time, Sister. Just one time so you really get the feel of it, doing the whole routine with the fire. You hear me, Sister?"

"What's the plan?" Sonny's eyes gleamed. "The cops check the golf course at night, you know."

"Sonny Kelly," I reminded him, "I hate you. I hope you get arrested."

They wanted to get me away from Joan and Franklin for the whole night, so Ginger invited me to stay over with them.

"We're going to the movies in Albemarle," she persuaded Joan, "a double feature, and we wanted to go out to eat first, too. You don't mind, do you, if she spends the night with us?"

Joan, charmed that Titania Gentry had made such a good impression on Ginger, somebody from Virginia, agreed, *a Virginian! she's really going to do a lot for that old man and his paratrooper of a son.*

The next evening, the three of us got in Old Sabby's pickup truck and headed to the Olympia Cafe, where Sonny Kelly was already lounging in a booth.

"What movies we going to see?" He slid across the orange upholstery and switched on the little carriage lantern mounted on the wall at the end of the booth.

"Maggie and Jiggs," said Ginger, "and something else. A murder mystery. *The Black Gardenia, The Blue Dahlia?* Something like that. Anyhow, it's got Alan Ladd." She slid along the opposite side of the table and Sebastian followed.

I stood frowning a moment, then slid in beside Sonny. "Hey," he said and pressed my arm.

"Shut up." I studied the menu. "I want a hamburger, no onions, and an Orange Crush."

When the orders came, Sonny opened his bun and raked off the chili and onions and mustard. "I don't like all that goo," he explained, then bit into it.

"Then why did you order it?" Ginger asked. She separated her french fries from her pickles and shook ketchup on the fries.

"Because," Sonny chewed with delight, "I like the way it all tastes on the hamburger, the juices soaking in, all the different things. I just don't want to have to eat 'em."

I swigged Orange Crush and checked the counter. No Hootchie. Hootchie was dead, maybe. Gone back to the chain gang. I pictured him shackled, lifting a sledgehammer, the green forked tongues of his tattooed snakes flexing over his biceps. *Wham!* the sledgehammer pulverized a pile of rocks at Hootchie's feet.

"I'm going to the ladies' room." I slid out of the booth and strolled to the little toilet at the back of the Olympia Cafe. It had the black silhouette of a girl on the door, a pug nose and high forehead, bunches of curls tied at her nape with a long black ribbon.

It smelled of Lysol and ammonia, strong enough to choke me.

Soon as I pulled the light chain, I saw a thick black billfold lying to the side of the toilet. I locked the door and seated myself, scooping up the billfold. It was a man's billfold, stuffed with dollars and I.D. cards. I put it in my drawstring bag, the red leather one Joan made me bring along to the movies. "Be sure you show this drawstring bag to Ginger," she prompted, "it's genuine leather."

Now it held the man's billfold. I finished and got up. I pressed the slimy pink soap out of the glass cone over the basin and washed my hands slowly, looking at myself in the smeary mirror.

I'm going to steal this money, I said to the mirror. I don't care, it was right there, and if I don't steal it, somebody else will. I don't care whose it is, either.

I jerked off the light and went back to the booth. "Want anything else?" asked Old Sabby. "Want a Popsicle?"

I shook my head. "No, let's go to the movies." I gave Erskine "Sonny" Kelly such a generous smile, he blinked.

We jammed in the cab of the truck, me practically sitting in Ginger's lap and Sonny squeezed somewhere in between Ginger and Old Sabby. Halfway to Albemarle, I opened the red drawstring bag and took out the billfold.

"Look. I found a man's billfold in the ladies' room, and it's got a lot of money in it."

"You stole it!" Sonny Kelly accused. Then he grinned. "How much money?"

I took all the bills out and counted them. "Seventy-eight dollars." Dumped out the change. "Three more dollars in change. Eighty-one dollars all together."

"You can't keep it, Ti," Sonny said, still grinning admiringly. "It's not yours, you know."

"I know. But I'm going to keep it."

"You, Sister?" Old Sabby teased. "Stealing stuff?"

"It was just lying on the floor in there." I looked through all the

I.D. cards. "Walter Vanhoy, that's his name." I threw the cards out the window.

"You sure you want to do that?" Sebastian's Camel winked in the corner of his mocking mouth.

"I don't care." I threw out the black billfold. I watched it skip along the shoulder of the road.

Ginger waited until I'd counted the money, thrown out both the cards and the billfold, then spoke up, "Oh, let her keep the money. What was Walter Vanhoy doing in the ladies' room, anyhow? What?"

Ginger shifted under the jammed-tight weights of Sonny Kelly and me. "She found it. Let her keep it. What's eighty-one dollars? It's not going to kill Walter Vanhoy to lose eighty-one dollars, is it?"

Sebastian and Erskine "Sonny" Kelly both looked embarrassed, almost envious. I pictured them finding somebody's billfold, somebody's genuine red leather drawstring bag, in the men's room.

"It's okay, Titania," said Ginger. "You found it. You keep it." And she glowered right back at Sonny and Old Sabby.

"I never stole anything in my whole life," I remarked. I folded the eighty-one dollars into the red drawstring bag and knotted it tight. "Never."

"You have now," affirmed Sonny Kelly.

"Forget it," said Ginger.

"Yeah, forget it," grumped Sebastian.

At the Alameda Theatre, Sonny laughed out loud through Maggie and Jiggs, through all the corned beef and cabbage and Maggie bopping Jiggs on the head with a skillet, Sonny laughed and punched me, encouraging me to laugh, too.

I sat primly, resisting Sonny. I stared through the mystery, too, with Alan Ladd and murder and dewy blonds getting kissed and then strangled or bashed by a disturbed William Bendix in coveralls. I couldn't keep up with the screen. I patted the eighty-one dollars in my drawstring bag and worried about what it meant to steal Walter Vanhoy's money. I also worried about twirling fire out in the open, on the golf course. And after Porky Pig's stuttering "Th-th-that's all, folks!" we drove from Albemarle to the golf course back in Badin.

Out to Number 9 fairway. In the middle of the night. In the thick summer dark. Old Sabby and Sonny got the gear from the back of the truck. "Come on, Sister," hissed Sebastian, "do this right. One time, one time only, then we got to get the hell out of here!"

Ginger wiped off the long wooden handle. "Remember, Titania," she encouraged, "do it the way you're going to do it next Saturday, in the ballpark."

I stepped onto the lush green of Number 9. The little flag flapped on the end of the pole. The sky was webbed in thousands of little specks of stars, high up.

"Here!" Sonny and Sebastian lit the baton and handed it to me.

I grabbed hold, posed, gave myself to Number 9 fairway and the flag on the pole in the center of the green. I marched around the whole great big circle of grass, twirling wild showy Figure 8's, Pancakes, and intricate once-around-the-body twists.

"Get with it, Sister! Go, like crazy!" cheered Old Sabby.

"Yay! Ti!" Sonny copied him, applauding, whistling through his fingers.

"Shut up, quit that!" Sebastian cuffed him. "You want to get the damn cops on us?"

"Shut up, both of you," shushed Ginger. "Go on, Titania, the hard part now, the best part, the part that's going to win you the whole thing! Pitch it up high, Titania, and catch! Go on! You can!"

I remembered to twirl fast, no fiery spray on my arms, nothing to burn or sting. Ginger was right, I could do this. I pitched the flaming baton, a bright burning arc high into the night, whistling up over Number 9 fairway.

It came down just as fast and as spectacularly as it went up and fell beyond me, flat to the green, flaming up, the fire running from each end to meet in the middle.

"Jesus, Sister!" Old Sabby and Sonny both ran to retrieve the baton. The tube was useless.

"Get the burlap! Get the burlap!"

Sonny dashed to the truck and came back with thick burlap sacks which he and Sebastian beat down on the fire until it died. A burned place snaked along Number 9 fairway. I could see it, even in the dark. The grass was burned, ugly, ruined, and I did it. I'd missed the baton. Couldn't catch it. I wouldn't win anything. I wasn't the best. I was no good.

"Go on, get in the truck." Old Sabby and Sonny kicked at the charred grass. They threw the remains of the baton in the back of the truck.

I huddled close to Ginger.

"That's what happens when you steal eighty-one dollars out of a man's billfold," Sonny jeered. "God gets even." He cackled mercilessly.

"Shut up, man," said Old Sabby. "God doesn't have anything to do with anything."

I felt sick all the way back to town.

The truck chugged to the top of Pomona Hill. All of Badin spread below, as webbed with streetlights as the sky over Number 9 fairway had been webbed with little stars. "If I didn't know better," observed Sebastian, idling the motor, "I'd think we were in Los Angeles or New York City, or something."

"Norfolk," chuckled Ginger, "or D.C."

I looked over the quiet town, Pomona Hill, Entwistle Street. I had never been anywhere in my whole life, Charlotte, Salisbury, Myrtle Beach. I felt even sicker.

"See you, man." Old Sabby let Sonny out on his side of the cab, holding the door open wide.

As Sonny approached his house, Toto started up inside, his old frenzy of growls and barks and clattering toenails.

On Entwistle Street, the Gentry apartment was dark. I pictured Joan under the pink satin comforter, Franklin turned on his side, and the electric fan making slow sighing sweeps. No matter how hot it turned, Joan slept under the pink satin with the fan going all night.

Mr. McSherry was in bed somewhere in the depths of his apartment, snuffling and wheezing. Old Sabby stomped upstairs, threw things around, grumbled. Ginger helped me wash off in the bathroom, which opened just off the kitchen.

"Don't think about it, Titania," she comforted. "It was dark. You couldn't see. That's all. Don't even think a thing about it. You'll be okay." She shut the door.

I took a deep breath. I'm alone in Old Sabby's bathroom. I'm going to sleep in the same apartment as he does tonight. I had to make a fool out of myself to do it. I had to steal Walter Vanhoy's eighty-one dollars and drop my baton and burn it up in front of everybody.

I brushed my teeth, pulled off my shorts and blouse. And now I am naked in Old Sabby's bathroom. He's upstairs so mad at me he could kill me, throwing things around, cussing, behaving just like Franklin Gentry.

This wasn't what I planned, not how I wanted it.

I slipped on my pajamas, folded my clothes together with the drawstring bag and the eighty-one dollars. I went back to the living room, where Ginger had spread sheets on the sofa, plumped a pillow for me.

"This will sleep good," she promised. "You hop in and I'll be back down in a minute to say good-night."

I mournfully acquiesced. I felt like a fool. But I crawled into the sheets, rubbing my short hair and my bangs. My hands still smelled of burning. I stuck the crooked finger in my mouth.

Overhead I could hear Old Sabby and Ginger talking, then some low gentle laughter. Good, he's not mad at me anymore. I took the finger out of my mouth, smiled at the ceiling. I love you, Sebastian, I forgive you.

The stairs creaked as Ginger padded back down. She hovered over me. "You okay?"

"Yes." I smelled her perfume. Not Miss Beaupine's old-maid roses and lavender, Ginger's perfume was spicy, fruity, something rich and full of itself. It was the smell of a woman who slept by Old Sabby all night.

Ginger sat on the edge of the sofa, smiling. She lifted her freckled arms over her head. I saw with a sudden sharp shock, Ginger had long curly tufts of light brown hair in her armpits. The hair was exotic, sprawling, and I wondered why I hadn't noticed it before.

It was as if Ginger flaunted her curly armpits.

Ginger yawned, lowered her arms. Her breasts stirred against the long pale cotton nightgown.

"Are you going to be okay now?" she asked. She tucked the sheet around me. "Sure?"

"Sure." I smiled. "I'm going to be fine now."

Ginger padded back up the steps and I lay awhile flexing my toes against the sheet. I put my ugly little crooked finger to both flaps of my breasts. Move! Live! I commanded them. Flesh out and freckle yourselves. Dumb blind little things. Wake up!

I moved the finger to the middle of my hairline, dotted it hard. Make a widow's peak, plain brown.

Then drawing it straight down the middle of my face, over nose and lips and chin, until it hit the top of my sternum, I plunged the exotic finger lightly, but deeply, into each armpit. Curl, blossom, grow thick black fur. Help me.

19

One night, a year after I had moved us to Lake Waccamaw, I dreamed Kelby came to my house. I didn't dream how he got there. He just walked in the front door and looked around him and then started opening cabinets and pulling out drawers, marveling at what I had, at how I had made a home for us.

He was absolutely fascinated with every little detail, the debris between the sofa cushions, the cereal boxes in the kitchen, the melted-down pats of soap in the shower I had tied together in a little net bag.

"You're still saving," he teased, "you're still hanging on to every last thing. Look at this soap!" Kelby threw the little bag toward me.

I smelled the Ivory and Dove, the Irish Spring in my dream, pungent and cozy as anything alive. The little bag thumped on the tiled floor. The dry soap cracked into smaller, more fragrant pieces.

"Kelby," I said, "look, you broke the soap."

"I like it here." He continued exploring my house, amazed and pleased and admiring of everything, including the soap. "Yep, I like it."

Kelby smiled, wide-open, the way a baby smiles at you, giving you everything good, assimilating all healthy and charming things in one place. Smiling, also, as a baby smiles, to any available stimuli, what I read in one of Sarah's textbooks was called the "smile of assimilation." Something that excites the cell assembly and helps the baby learn.

Learn what? I asked in my dream.

"I need five dollars to get back to California," Kelby said at the door. "I got stranded on I-40 West. Have you got five dollars?"

I gave him five one-dollar bills. I counted out each one into his hand, wrinkling my nose at their stale-ink smell. Kelby folded the dollars. He turned to go out the door of my dream. "If you write down your address, Ti, I'll pay you back when I get to California." He held out one of the bills for me to write on.

"That's all right," I said, "I'm not going to write on a piece of money."

He went out the door and I dreamed I would never see Kelby again.

But coming right into this dream was my mother Joan Gentry who said, "You shouldn't have given him that five dollars. He probably had a brand-new car parked outside with a tank full of gas. You are the world's most generous fool."

I woke up then, sat up in bed. The wind was blowing in the old cypress trees along Lake Waccamaw. There was a full moon and I could see the Spanish moss blowing from their long branches and there was a smell of cypress, a green crushed smell of pine needles.

The house creaked and sighed. My girls slept in their rooms. Kelby wasn't anywhere around. But I sat up and said, to Joan Gentry, three hours inland from Lake Waccamaw, "It didn't matter if he had a brand-new car parked outside. I wanted to give him five dollars. And I gave him five dollars."

It made a whole lot of difference to me to be able to sit there in my bed and say that. I watched the wind blow the moss around in the moonlight. I smelled the pines, smelling, too, I fancied, the fragrant little pats of soap I saved in my shower.

THEN THE CALL CAME from Brenda in California. "Kelby's very sick," she said, "can you come? He wants to see you."

Her voice was low and cool, not Southern, but close to it. She made me feel comfortable, even as alarm sprang all through me. Kelby dying in California right now. This, too, is not what I wanted, not what I planned. Why couldn't things just content themselves with second prize or amicable separation or Post-it stickers on a photograph? I would be okay living by myself at Lake Waccamaw for the rest of my life. Kelby didn't have to get sick and die to prove anything. I'd even get the empty ledger back out and write real words on it this time, write every page full, not just the doodlings and drawings and lists I'd affronted it with. Just don't make anybody die.

Especially don't make Kelby.

"Yes," I told Brenda, "I will come. I will come today, if I can."

Sarah and Hannah drove me to the Raleigh-Durham terminal, both of them quiet and kind all the way there. "We hope it'll be okay, Mom," they said. They waved and smiled at me. They thrust brand-new magazines at me and a little box of Coffee Nips.

And then I was changing planes in Dallas, flying on to the Pacific. I had thought so many times of how it would be to see Kelby again. I sipped a plastic cup of bourbon and Coca-Cola. I watched white banks of clouds rush past the wings. The sweetish taste of bourbon reminded me of my father, and for a minute, the sound of Franklin slurring through "Paper Doll" filled my ears, the silliness of him, the terrible, wonderful, human silliness of him.

But Kelby was sick and dying. Everything changed so cruelly. Without warning. In the middle of the night. All the tired and unusable but accurate clichés poured through me. This thing had been lying in wait for me, like a thief, ready to spring. And now dropped its bombshell, took my breath away, kicked, jolted, bushwhacked, and finally opened my eyes.

"Fly into Burbank," said Brenda, "it'll be easier." The plane set down and I looked out at the brown-red hills rising up from clumps of buildings and big palms. This was California. Kelby was here.

Brenda was a small robust woman with a deep smooth tan and eyes upturned, cat's eyes, you could call them, eyes that gave the impression of getting ready to laugh at you, yet remaining cautious.

The rose, gold, and blue streaks in her dark hair were soft wings of pale color, not the garish display I had expected from my daughters' descriptions. She wore long earrings that brushed the shoulders of her jumpsuit, a jumpsuit of stonewashed gray. I felt no animosity as I might once have. This Brenda had been good for Kelby, and, obviously, Kelby for her. And she had called me to his deathbed.

"Do you have some more luggage?" She hurried me from the gate and through the long carpeted concourse. I caught glimpses again of the brown hills through dazzling banks of high windows.

"No, this is all." She seemed relieved, seemed to approve of me, as we made our way out of the terminal and into a parking deck.

"What kind does he have?" I asked her when we were buckled into the car and Brenda had paid the toll-keeper and steered us out into the rushing late afternoon traffic of Burbank.

She hesitated a moment, a frown to her eyes. "It's in the liver," she said, "the bowel, all over. They took out his spleen and one end of the pancreas. But it's everywhere."

I had no reply to this. It sounded clinical and deadly. A widespread invasion. Kelby had no chance. He could not get well, so they had sent him home from the California hospital, his staples removed, his incision a perfect pink scar. But the inside of him still boiled with the angry hunger of cells as ravenous as crabs.

266

Their house was small, stuck into a hillside, accented by the indigenous palms and eucalyptus. A faint smell of cough drops drifted in the air, not menthol, but eucalyptus. It was oddly comforting. Red tiles on the roof. Cream-colored stucco. No chimney.

Brenda unlocked the Spanish door, heavy carved wood with black iron hinges. I was suddenly thrust inside Kelby's house. Just as I had once been suddenly thrust inside the apartment of Mr. McSherry, the environment of Sebastian and Ginger.

A painting of disturbed horses hung on the wall opposite me, their muscles flexed in oily blues and greens, glints of gold. Their big nostrils flared, manes flaming to the tips in dark purple, rose. Genuine nightmare horses, horses that thundered toward me in a breathless beautiful terror. Faintly silly, too, I thought. A painting that took itself so seriously, about two yardsticks broad. My simple Carolina background was catching up with me here in California. The dramatic horses were just two yardsticks broad. Such homey measurements helped me.

Yet the nightmare, the terror, was unmistakable.

Brenda was motioning me down a narrow hall and into another room, Kelby's room, I realized. I walked carefully. I straightened my clothes, running a hand over my plain short brown hair. We saw each other at the same moment and we smiled, Kelby raising himself on the pillows. He was very fragile, gaunt, almost ethereal, the skin merely sketched over his face. And his cushion of curly hair, that springy cushion I'd always loved to press, was diminished to a dark damp web. But his eyes were the same rich scuppernong-green, same as mine, and grinning at me with their same teasing, mocking challenge.

"Hey, Kelby," I said. I took his hand. And his hand, oh, God, Kelby's hand, dry as paper, managed to hook one finger around my crooked one, *That's how I can find you, Ti, in a room full of women, with the light turned out.*

267

He didn't say much, just "I'm glad you're here. I'm so glad you're really here," squeezing my hand, hooking our fingers. Then he sank back on the pillows and gazed at me. Brenda had slipped out of the room. We were alone and together for the first time in over a dozen years.

All those things I had always planned to ask Kelby if I ever saw him again evaporated like soap bubbles. Nothing like that mattered anymore. I just stood at his bedside holding his hand and he lay looking at me. Finally, "The girls are okay," I said. Kelby nodded, shut his eyes, and was soon asleep.

I stayed for two days and nights. We never said more than this. But we knew we were forgiven, both of us, for whatever it was. I slept in a small guest room on a hard studio bed. A rack of crystal and silver glass beads hung in the window. They looked like a waterfall, a Perseides shower. And before I fell asleep each night, I explored my memories of falling asleep in so many different and significant places, the Badin apartment, the Greensboro house, my place in Lake Waccamaw with the soft lap of water outside.

Now somewhere outside was the Pacific Ocean, a whole new ocean, and I'd crossed a continent to get here, flying over those tourist landmarks, the Mississippi River, the Grand Canyon, and I never saw them and so they didn't mean a thing.

And I thought of the men and women who had so fascinated and exasperated me, Franklin and Joan, Sebastian and Ginger, Rory. And most of all Kelby. We made some kind of a baroque family. And California was a peculiar family arrangement: Brenda in her room, me in the guest room, Kelby in his death room.

Then I flew home. I could not stay through Kelby's dying. He did not want me to. I took a bus back to the terminal in Burbank. I told Brenda I would be okay. I didn't want her to leave Kelby just to take me to the plane. Somebody should stay there, stay with him. And so we parted for good, Kelby and I.

I flew straight across the continent, straight back to those old times and those old memories. To those old names and lists written in fresh blue ink. To my girls, my parents, Badin and Lake Waccamaw. To what Kelby and I had been part of. It seemed a benediction.

Nobody knows why they do a thing.

THE NIGHT BEFORE THE twirling competition, I was sick as a dog, gagging over the toilet. Nothing came up. I was empty and dry, as withered as Madine Ponds. My eyes twitched and my knees stiffened. The only healthy part of me was my crooked finger.

Joan Gentry had starched and ironed the red shorts and the navy blue halter. She wanted to curl my bobbed hair. "Look." She moistened a finger. "We can do spit curls. They'd look wonderful. Let me do it, Titania."

But I held firm. For the first time in thirteen years, I actually said, "No, I won't, ma'am," and got away with it. The ease of it surprised me. Joan seemed to recognize something and to appreciate the significance of it. She backed off. Including the lipstick. "Use a bright red," Joan had suggested, "it'll show up better from the stage."

"There won't be a stage," I said. "It's in the American Legion Ballpark. People will be up in the bleachers."

"All the more reason." Joan held out the red lipstick.

"No." Red shorts and navy blue halter and a bare tanned midriff had to be enough to satisfy Joan Gentry this time. Nothing, and I meant nothing, was going to take people's attention away from the fire. The big surprise. Who was going to be looking at red lipstick when that was going on?

Those people in Albemarle, I realized, were going to be shocked at the big blaze I made. They were going to wonder where I got the gas ration stamps to burn like that. Is that what they do with their ration books out in Badin? Give 'em to a kid to burn up? Jesus. I'm going to report this to the Office of Price Administration. That's got to be against the law. There's a war going on.

I shuddered, what if I drop it again and it burns up right there in front of everybody? I didn't want any bright red lipstick. Or any spit curls. I didn't want anything to make me stand out other than my fantastic and hard-earned skill.

For old time's sake, I decided to give Carol Jean Spence one more chance. I called her up and generously invited her to go to Albemarle for the competition.

"My mother will pay your way on the bus." I tried to make it as appealing as possible. "And we will get a hamburger at Harmanco's when it's over. Sonny's going. Don't you want to go, too?"

"I have to keep Pam that afternoon," said Carol Jean.

"Oh." I listened for any disappointment in her voice. "I'm sorry. Are you sure, Carol Jean? Maybe somebody else could keep Pam?"

"Ti, I hope you win. I'll keep my fingers crossed, okay? Bye." Carol Jean hung up. She had other things to do. Pam was more important than twirling competitions.

The generous feeling faded off. I suffered only a little. "Bye, Carol Jean," I agreed into the empty phone. We both had other things to do. Ever since that ugly grass skirt back in March.

I took the eighty-one dollars out of my red drawstring bag and separated the change from the bills. "I'll keep the change. Walter Vanhoy deserves to lose the change."

I repaid Franklin the dollar and a half, all in Walter Vanhoy's coins, stacking them up across the adjustment table. The seventy-eight in bills, I sealed in an envelope from the box of poodle stationery I got for Christmas.

I looked up Vanhoys in the Badin listings of the phone book, *Wanda, Willie, Wooster*. No Walter Vanhoy. I flipped to the Albemarle listings. There he was, *Walter P. Vanhoy*, an address on Commonwealth Avenue, a street I didn't recognize, nothing around

Uncle Morton's neighborhood, nothing close to the American Legion Ballpark.

I addressed the poodle envelope, scrawling my script sideways to disguise it. What about my fingerprints? I held up the little gold pen with the poodle on top, wiped it off, then wiped off the envelope, too.

He'll just be damned glad to get back his whole seventy-eight dollars. I stuck on the stamp and took it to the post office.

"There." I felt honest again, watching the poodles slip through the mail slot. "I got through that okay." All that was left was the twirling.

20

The morning of the competition, Franklin was arranging his health pamphlets in their wire racks, getting ready for his Saturday chiropractic. I fingered them. They were as strident and colorful as Reverend Percy's tracts. People clutched at their shoulders or their lower backs while big jagged arrows and stars shot out indicating excruciating pain.

SHOULDER PAIN? PINCHED NERVE? shouted some. RUPTURED DISC? EPILEPSY? FEMALE TROUBLE? asked others. KEEP THAT HEALTHY HAPPY FEELING they all promised. TURN THE PAGE!

I wished my life could be adjusted so easily.

"What do you want, Ti Baby?" Franklin straightened the pamphlets, smoothing out corners. Next he straightened the big wall chart showing the five segments of lumbar spinal degeneration. I admired the firm, efficient sweep of his hands. Dr. Gentry, Boston Red Sox, could rub miseries right out of you and exorcise agonies with just a shove of his palm. I liked that.

"I don't know." I lifted my shoulders and sighed. I stared at the colored drawings of backbones falling to pieces. The drawings started with a backbone labeled NEAR NORMAL and stopped with a pile of disgusting debris labeled RUINED. The fine print at the bottom of Franklin's chart reminded his patients: *Care Given For Relief Of Symptoms Only. Not For Correction.*

"I don't feel good," I admitted. I lifted my shoulders again. A sharp little pain crawled between them and forked like lightning.

"Nervous? Tense, aren't you?" Franklin sounded like his health pamphlets. He gazed at me a moment, then smiled. "Come over here, sugar." He pointed at the adjustment table.

I climbed up, stretched out on my stomach. Franklin Gentry confidently rubbed my shoulders, the back of my neck. He could fix it. I shut my eyes, yielding to his round motions, round and round, then a firm shove. He spread his left palm over my spine, clasped his wrist with his right hand and pressed hard.

Franklin knows his business, I approved, basking in the pressure, the skill. "That feels good."

"You're going to be okay." He pounded lightly up and down my backbone. "Don't dwell on it, Ti Baby. Just go over there and get up and knock their damned eyes out. I mean it."

I soaked up Dr. Gentry's adjustment. I knew why those people came in there every Saturday and let him knock them around. He did a good job. Uncle Morton was wrong. Franklin was the best.

I wanted to lie there and let him rub out every agony, shove every nagging misery from my body and my brain. I didn't care if I ever got over to Albemarle and twirled fire.

"You remember that time Uncle Morton had an inner growing toenail?" I smirked.

"He wouldn't let me touch it," remembered Franklin. He drummed his fingers along my shoulder blades. "I said, 'Let me adjust your old toe, Morton.' And he said, 'I'd as soon put it through the wringer. Don't touch me.'"

I sighed, feeling relief flood my tight muscles. "And you said, 'Well, if you want to keep on hurting, then goddammit, hurt.'"

"Don't say goddammit, Ti Baby," Franklin grinned. He pushed his right hand with his left, pushing me into a warm safe place, innocent and healthy and honest.

"Uncle Morton was wrong, Daddy." Then I added, "I wish I could play baseball, Daddy. I wish I could give adjustments."

My impulse, genuine and wide open and goofy as a saint's, was to make up to Franklin right then for things. For Renee Ames and the earrings and for him staying in a boardinghouse out on Highway 740. For Joan Gentry smacking him in the face. And for a lot more than that. I didn't care what he had done to cause me all those nights of being wrapped in a crocheted afghan and dragged around by Joan to spy on him through apartment windows. I didn't resent anymore the mean hard little baseballs he had deliberately thrown and hurt my hand with. I loved Franklin Gentry right then. I wanted him to know it. I opened my eyes and flashed him my two dimples.

"I mean it, Daddy. I wish I could give adjustments like you, and play baseball."

He laughed. "No you don't, Ti Baby. You don't want to play baseball. And if you ever start to give adjustments, it'll break my back in two."

He gave me a hand off the table. "You go twirl your baton, Ti Baby. Go show those jerks over in Albemarle." He winked in his familiar silly way, the dark moustache quivering.

JOAN AND I CAUGHT the bus to Albemarle. The driver pushed open the door with his big handle attached to the steering wheel and I was shocked to see who he was. Hootchie, the red and black snakes coiling over his arms, their green forked tongues like bright threads in his arm hairs. Hootchie in a bus company's khaki uniform and visored khaki hat and dark glasses. *Hootchie! I wanted you on the chain gang! On the great and mighty Congo, Hootchie! You let me down!*

He punched the tickets Joan handed him, pulled the door shut and steered the big bus around the zebra-striped Dead Man in front of the Carolina Aluminum gatehouse and the Olympia Cafe. *Walter Vanhoy, I wondered, did you get the mail yet? Are you counting your seventy-eight dollars and looking at that poodle envelope with the Badin, North Carolina, postmark?*

Hootchie accelerated toward Albemarle.

I took a seat, stunned, three rows behind Hootchie. I watched his arms driving the bus, looked at his rough face in the rearview mirror. Every so often, he yelled at people in the back, "Sit down! I ain't responsible if you stand up. Sit down!"

Somehow he looked like a wizened old José Iturbi. It was terrible.

Joan primped me all the way to Albemarle, smoothing my hair, jerking at my shorts and halter, with no more concern for my dignity than if I were a doll.

I began to get sick again. Things jumped in my stomach. I smelled the exhaust every time Hootchie-José slowed to take on passengers. The passengers smelled like sweat and baby oil and farts. I hoped I'd throw up right there, gushing over three rows to splatter and foul Hootchie-José's uniform.

I clenched the old chrome-plated baton. It wouldn't twirl to glory with me. I couldn't stand for Sebastian to punch holes in it. I was taking it to Albemarle as a decoy, part of our plan to fool Joan and the others. I kissed its rubber bulb and apologized.

The stiff red shorts chafed my legs and the halter straps dug into my shoulders. I ran a thumb over the faint flaps of my breasts. This midriff, ma'am, I wanted to warn Joan, better not bare anything besides my good tan. It better not slide up and show everybody in the American Legion Ballpark that I don't have any real titties.

I gritted my teeth and sat still, watching Hootchie-José drive, letting Joan primp me. I fastened my mind on Sebastian and Ginger and Erskine "Sonny" Kelly. They all promised to be there when I got there. It was their job to bring the fire, the clever wooden baton, its clever black asbestos soaked in Old Sabby's special mix of kerosene and gasoline, the clever metal tube with the screw cap, the matches, all to me in Albemarle.

Things jumped inside my stomach, clogged my lungs, dried up all my blood, and cut off both my hands. I barely noticed when Hootchie-José pulled the bus into the station in Albemarle, cut the ignition, pushed open the door and hollered, "We're in Albemarle, folks. Next bus back to Badin in a half-hour."

He got out and unlocked the cargo hatch, began throwing out people's suitcases. Joan and I went inside the waiting room to look for Uncle Morton and Aunt Della.

"Here we are!" Both of them waved on the other side of the ticket booth. Everybody kissed and hugged. Della turned me around, inspecting the red shorts and navy halter. She clicked her tongue over the cropped hair, then pronounced, "Well, actually, you know her hair looks better this way. She looks good. Looks real cute, Joan."

Joan, accepting the credit, smiled. "Well, it was time we cut it off. She was getting too old for those pigtails." Then she added graciously, "We sure appreciate you two coming down here to meet us and take us to the ballpark." She glanced at me. "Titania thinks she's going to win this thing."

"Well, I hope she does." Uncle Morton hugged me again. "This old baton stuff. She's been slinging that thing around long enough. It's about time it paid off. Ain't that right, girl?"

It seemed everybody agreed everything had been going on long enough and that it was about time for something to happen: my hair to get cut off, my twirling to win a prize, something, something. I nodded and gave Uncle Morton both dimples. I wondered if he noticed old Hootchie-José driving the bus. I was tempted to point

277

Hootchie-José out, remind Uncle Morton of the time we watched him deliberately fart in front of the Badin Methodist Church.

But Uncle Morton rushed us into the black Ford and straight to the American Legion Ballpark. There were a million people already there. City policemen directed Uncle Morton to the parking lot. We got out and Della and Joan both primped me some more. We walked to the entrance together and Della and Joan both kissed me again. Uncle Morton patted my head. "Good luck, girl."

I went through the crowd and found the place reserved for the contestants. I gave the lady in charge my entry slip with Joan Gentry's signature and took a seat among a teeming glut of girls. I saw at once they were serious. In the worst way. They meant to win.

I saw nobody with fire. I saw a big shiny hoop and that bothered me. A short kid in red satin bloomers twirled it. Her tight red coat had frogs and epaulets. Somebody, no doubt her mother, had painted two red dots on either cheek. She smiled winningly with cute red lips as she practiced twirling the big hoop, but she didn't have any dimples.

I had to beat that hoop.

We sat on hard benches, hard as Badin Methodist Church pews, the same kind of hard benches the ballplayers sat on. I turned around, twisting to see if Sebastian and Ginger and Sonny Kelly were anywhere around yet. I spotted Joan and Della and Uncle Morton sitting high in the bleachers. I waved, but they didn't see me yet. I turned back and fixed my whole attention on the dingy tips of my old baton, turning it slowly around and around. I concentrated hard. I sweated in the shorts and halter.

The short kid got up and did her routine with the hoop. She looked good twirling it, the hoop so big and she so small and satiny red. She did a few cute tap shuffles, turned a flip, grabbed her hoop and jumped through it for a finale.

The crowd clapped with delight. I watched the judges at their table noting such things, I imagined, as poise, personality, show-manship. Those kinds of things I'd read about in Joan's magazines.

Why don't you give a prize for a big grown girl playing a baby piece? For people stealing eighty-one dollars out of Walter Vanhoy's black billfold and then sending seventy-eight of it back? Why don't you give a prize for living with Joan and Franklin? Don't you know there's a war going on?

Oh, God, I said, staring at the baton, just let me beat that hoop. Just let me throw the baton and catch it this time. Listen to what I said. I can't stand this kind of thing. This kind of thing kills me.

More kids performed. Some dropped their batons. Others stumbled and slid down on one knee, embarrassed and about to cry. I was glad when they made mistakes. I loved it when they fell and got back up grass-stained and humiliated.

You get two minutes to do it in, Sister!

I twisted around again. It was getting close to my turn. And there, as we'd planned it, as I wanted it to happen, was Old Sabby strolling leisurely along inside the ballpark fence with the gear. And there was Erskine "Sonny" Kelly carrying the tube. And there strolling behind them was Ginger, freckled and friendly, wearing shorts and a halter-top herself, baring her own midriff, showing everybody in the place her curly exotic armpits.

I sucked in and bit my lip. Then I grinned and waved wildly to make them notice where I was on the bench. It was my turn.

"Novelty Baton," staticked the public address system and a line of kids stood up. I slipped from the bench. Sebastian and Sonny met me just short of third base. Sebastian took out the wooden baton and wiped it off carefully, shook it briskly, and wiped again.

"Now, Sister," he warned, "goddamn your ass, if you catch fire, I didn't have anything to do with it."

"Yes, yes, you did, Sebastian." I smiled at him. "And all these people out here, and my mother and Uncle Morton and Aunt Della, too, are all going to see it right now. I've got witnesses."

"Win it, Ti," cheered Sonny. He had the cap to the tube in one hand, the tube leaning against his jeans.

Ginger smiled. She held up crossed fingers. "You'll do it, Titania," she promised. "You'll win."

Sebastian struck the match.

I felt the crowd murmur, stunned with surprise and fear and then admiration for my holy fire. The whole American Legion Ballpark hushed up, poised with me on the brink of something significant barreling down hard. The judges' mouths, I guessed, dropped open.

I paced out down the baseline and posed on home plate, smiling, *You ought to be here, Franklin Gentry!* And with a rapid, repeating-rifle precision, with the strength of a mean little baseball, I twirled fire.

Turn it, turn it, don't stop, keep going. Huge circles burned in the clear blue. I didn't need the dark of night anymore, no Number 9 fairway. This fire baton showed up good and it didn't miss. Through high fast Figure 8's, spectacular Pinwheels, the baton whistled and flamed like a red dart. I imagined the Hollywood Bowl Orchestra played stirringly behind me in the backfield "Sabre Dance," stinging like a thousand bees, a thousand maddened gypsy fiddlers, all in love with me.

Risking everything, I finished with a breathtaking aerial pitch. The fire baton whistled up, turned like a fiery blade, zoomed straight back down and I caught it.

A big smile for the judges, both my dimples deep enough to lose a thumb in, I paced back to third base, *turn it, turn it, don't stop, keep going.* I gave the baton to Old Sabby, who dropped it in the tube, and Sonny Kelly screwed on the cap.

They exhaled with relief. Ginger applauded. I was panting. "Did you see, Sebastian? Was I good? Did I do okay?" I clamored. "Tell me I am the best one out here in this whole ballpark."

"Good, Sister. You did damn good. You knocked their eyes out."
And he began gathering the gear, turning to take Ginger's arm and
leave.

"Wait." I pulled at them both. "You're not going?" I trotted
behind. "Ginger, make him stay."

Sebastian stopped and looked down at me. His eyes were blue
and sort of vacant in the hot brutal August light. I saw for certain
that he didn't spend a whole lot of his time thinking about me or
worrying about what I thought. He patted my head like Uncle
Morton. "We got to go, Sister. We can't stick around. It's okay."

"But," I refused to turn loose, "I haven't won yet. I want you to
stick around until I win."

He waved me off and took Ginger's hand. "Ginger?" I begged
one more time. "Ginger, make him stay."

Ginger bent and wrapped her arms around me and hugged tight.
I saw into the cleft of her breasts. Freckled, smooth, promising.
"Look, Titania." Ginger reached up to pat my sweaty hair and I saw
again the curly tufts of hair sprawl from Ginger's armpits. "Look, it's
done now. This is what we came for. To see you twirl. We know
you're going to win. We don't have to stick around any longer to see.
Okay?"

And she gave me a cheery little shake loose. It was over.

They moved on. At the exit, they paused and Old Sabby yelled
back, "Hey, Sister! You're the best in the whole damn ballpark and
don't you forget it, you hear?"

The ground that had already split between me and Sebastian
McSherry broke in two. I stalked off toward the bench.

"I'm staying, Ti." Sonny Kelly grinned, dogging me. "I'm still
here and I'm staying until they put that crown on your head."

"I don't care." I sat down hard on the bench.

The other contestants glared at me. "That's not fair!" hissed
one. "Using fire. You're a cheater!" She shoved at me.

"Drop dead." I shoved back.

I reached around under the bench for the old baton and pulled it close, cradling it like some worn-out and used-up baby. "I did it, sugar," I told the baton. "I showed the jerks."

I sat and watched the rest of the competition, but I didn't care anymore whether I won. Sonny Kelly teased me, brought me cherry Coca-Cola in a paper cone of smashed ice, a Cherry Smash, he called it. "You're gonna get a big crown, Ti," he bragged, "you'll look like the Statue of Liberty."

"Shut up, Sonny." I slurped the Cherry Smash. "I hate you and you know it."

I felt spent, as exhausted as Joan Gentry sounded when she gave out one of her long dramatic sighs. I felt, I imagined, the way Sebastian and Ginger felt after they'd done it to each other all night on the other side of my wall.

I just sat. The hot smell of summer coming to an end blew over the American Legion Ballpark, the smell of heavy, bruised and ripened life, too heavy and too bruised and too ripe to hang around much longer. The smell of too damn much.

Nobody knows why they do a thing, Sister.

Then the thing was over. The judges stood up from their table and, after conferring excitedly for a few more seconds, began to announce the winners. The cute kid with the hoop won the grand prize. She would lead the military marching band at Fort Bragg.

"Aw, shit," lamented Sonny Kelly. "You didn't get it, Ti, after all we went through."

"Shut up."

I watched the kid take her prize. She gave a little curtsy to the crowd, blew kisses through the hoop. One of the judges stepped to the microphone and announced a special prize, a Best of Show prize. When I heard him struggle to pronounce the name, I knew I had won.

"Tanya?" he faltered. "Tee-toonya?"

"Titania! Titania!" I yelled and jumped up, shoving the girl who had called me a cheater right off the bench.

I stood straight-shouldered. I showed off my good tan and flexed my fingers still smelling of fire and Old Sabby. The August sky was clear over the ballpark. My mother stood applauding in the bleachers, my Uncle Morton whistled and cheered. My Aunt Della, I knew, bragged to everybody around her, "That's my little niece from out at Badin."

"Where that aluminum mill is," Uncle Morton would interrupt.

Della could continue, "Her daddy used to play big league right here in this same ballpark."

I flexed my fingers. I threw a hard honest gaze all over Sonny and smiled brazenly. "When I get through with this," I promised him, "I'm going to come back over here and kiss you on your mouth, Erskine."

Then like the powerful woman I was, I, Titania Anne Gentry, walked out in a sure and regular gait to claim my prize.

AND THIS IS WHAT I would like for my girls to know about me. I did not win the big prize for twirling fire. But I did win the Best of Show. That was enough. Twirling fire batons, in the bigger scheme, is a trivial thing. There is no real talent involved, no beauty. But there is determination. You have to want the thing bad enough.

I was thirteen years old in Badin, North Carolina, an aluminum-smelting town, at the end of the Second World War. I was not the child my parents wanted, no big-league baseball player, no player of baby grand pianos, and definitely no healer of bones, no exquisite movie star.

I did not twirl the baton anymore after that summer. Carol Jean and Erskine and I went to high school and did the usual things and drifted apart in different directions. Sebastian McSherry sold the apartment in Badin. He moved his old daddy and Ginger to Charlotte. Ginger sent me a few Christmas cards with grinning healthy babies covered in freckles. Then I never heard from them again.

I went to The Woman's College of the University of North Carolina at Greensboro to major in journalism. I married Kelby and we lived in Greensboro with two little girls, Sarah Anne and Hannah Joan. Then he left us for reasons best known to himself and to me. My parents stayed in Badin and aged a great deal more gracefully than I'd ever imagined they would. I was proud of them for that.

I moved Sarah and Hannah and myself to Columbus County, to stark white sand and cypress trees, dark water and Spanish moss. And I liked myself and what I was doing fairly well until they stuck that pink Post-it on my head, *A Born Loser.*

I am amazed that, after all these years, I still want to prove people wrong about me. The people now being my own children, who never scoffed at or criticized me, never tried to keep my hair in French braids long past the time when I was turning into a grown woman, and who never tried to turn me into something I was not, playing a borrowed York piano.

In any case, I abandoned the blue ledger and stuffed it back in the bureau under those oversized gray T-shirts. Shirts I had also gotten at Wal-Mart, actually BVDs, with a polo neck and a breast pocket. I love those shirts. They wrap me up completely and make me feel so cozy and anonymous, so safe.

Unlike the ledger. All I'd written there were names: *Old Sabby, Sonny Kelly, Joan and Franklin. Kelby.* I pressed the pen, glistening with blue ink, over and over each letter. I connected the curves and curls of the names and sniffed the ink and that was enough, I concluded, for me. The ledger opened itself in front of me, threatening and invasive, all those blank pages where anything could happen, conjuring up vivid memories. A place where I could get devoured.

The big gray shirts just wrap me and comfort me. Shirts that I can wrinkle up and throw in the wash and pull back out later, warm and fragrant, from the dryer. The names, too, are safe enough. The names glow, packed full of power like emblems and relics and totems. They will hold the past safe enough for me until I am ready to tell my girls. And I have decided I do want to tell them, really tell them, and have them listen to those names, rather than sit and read through a ledger from Wal-Mart. I want Sarah and Hannah right there in the flesh, their warm skin and health, eyes and smiles, breath and heart-beat, everything that makes them my girls—listening.

Somehow, I know, the sound of my voice will do it better.

Melissa Miller

T he author of fourteen books, including stories, poems, and novels, HEATHER ROSS MILLER is a member of an extended writing family that includes her father, an uncle, and two aunts and their husbands. Miller grew up in North Carolina listening to people tell stories and ponder motives. Miller's late husband, Clyde Miller, was a park ranger and forester; they lived for many years in various North Carolina state parks. A recipient of the North Carolina Award for Literature, she is the Thomas H. Broadus, Jr., Professor of English at Washington and Lee University in Lexington, Virginia. She has two grown children, Melissa Miller and Kirk Miller.